Ashari

Song of the Rising Dragon

C. M. Karys

Literary Wanderlust | Denver, Colorado

Published in the United States by Literary Wanderlust LLC, Denver, Colorado. www.LiteraryWanderlust.com

ISBN print: 978-1-956615-42-5
ISBN digital: 978-1-956615-43-2

Chapter Header Illustration: Carmen Di Mauro
@carmen.dmdesign

Map: Aleksandra Dimoska - Acedimski

Cover Design: Gabriella Bujdoso

Printed in the United States of America

Content Warning

This book contains references to torture (brief scenes and descriptions), death of a loved one (brief mentions), blood, gore and death, and explicit sexual content.

Dedication

To Kiche, the best writing cave pup.
The writing cave is a little colder without you, but you'll always
be alive in these pages and all those to come.
We miss you, and we love you.

HAVANYA
EATHELIN
THE SIREN COVES
MERANIA
THROUGH BLOOD
AND FIRE
THE BURNING
SEA
ILAH

FROSTHEAD HALL
DAGANVER
TEIRAK'S MAW
VOLARIA
MAKKAN
THE'ILAH
THE HALL OF KINGS
HEARTSTAR
THE ARTERY
TYRRA
LUR
ADARA
EMBERNEST
ARA

1

Derron

Derron Argarys was loyal, and he was a traitor.

Standing on the forecastle deck of a Meranian ship, Derron watched as the Embernest's outline loomed ever closer. The golden castle perched on white cliffs towered over the city. His home. Over a month ago, he'd left to chase after a girl the whole of Ilahara thought dead for fourteen years. Instead, he'd found a young woman who challenged and fought him at every turn. A woman he should have killed but didn't.

Asharaya Myrassar.

The last survivor of the Dragon-Blessed dynasty brought down by his mother, Aerella Argarys, with the Coup of Fire. As a girl, Asharaya had been princess of Ilahara and sister to Derron's best friend. Now, her survival jeopardized his family's position as rulers. Queen Aerella had entrusted Derron to find and end her, to put his past entanglement with the Myrassar behind him and prove his unwavering loyalty to his family. *An*

Argarys blade earned us the throne. An Argarys blade will keep it. Gods knew he'd tried.

Gods knew he'd failed. Multiple times.

And when Asharaya had the chance to kill him, she'd spared him instead.

Footsteps thudded on the wood behind him. Derron acknowledged the approaching man with a subtle turn of the head. General Nahar mirrored Derron's posture, clasping his hands behind his back and staring at the docks. The sea breeze brushed through his black hair like a lover's caress. Even outside water, Raxan Nahar couldn't be mistaken for anything other than a merman. "It won't be long now," said Raxan. "Your mother won't be pleased."

Derron kept his features blank to mask his stomach's churning.

The general's blue eyes paled against the backdrop of the cloudy sky. "If you ask me, your plan to capture Asharaya in Merania was a tad overdramatic. Pretending Mykal Todrak and Arkael were guests on your ship, luring the Myrassar girl into the castle by dropping hints into the city, ambushing them as they escaped—"

"I don't remember you chiming in with ideas," Derron cut in, a muscle feathering in his jaw.

"It was almost as if you were hoping she'd get away." Derron whipped his head to the black-haired fae, who chuckled. "Worry not, I won't tell the queen."

"There's nothing to tell. Asharaya bested me."

General Nahar smiled impertinently as the crew maneuvered the ship into the harbor. "Ah, there's no doubt about that." He then addressed a woman on his crew. "Bring up the prisoner."

A stone dropped in Derron's chest, but the general was looking at him again, likely waiting for a reaction. "I'd be careful how I use my words if I were you. You might be the golden boy in Merania, but out of your fishbowl you're only a soldier."

Raxan's smile wavered but didn't fade. "My family has been faithful to the Argarys ever since Queen Aerella ascended the throne."

"Remember that loyalty when you choose to give breath to your words, or the next time you question mine I'll embed one sword in your forehead and shove the other down your throat."

Iron clinked as four guards brought up the prisoner from belowdecks. Two men held the chains while the others guarded his front and back, and for good reason. Despite the regular doses of renike to weaken his magic and the wounds that hadn't completely healed, Arkael thrashed against his captors. He yanked one forward with a forceful pull on his chains, headbutting the man in the face. The guard went sprawling, but another in the rear smacked a spear to the back of Arkael's head and put an end to his rebellion. Arkael fell on his knees, throwing out his chained hands to arrest his fall.

Beside Derron, Raxan clicked his tongue as he followed the prince across the deck. "I never understood what Mykal saw in that half-breed prick."

A guard pulled on Arkael's hair at the prince's approach, forcing his head up. His blue eyes blazed with a hatred so at odds with the brimming hope Derron had glimpsed in Merania. Arkael had believed Derron chose to side with them against the Nahar for his sake. Because even though they'd been raised miles apart and within two rival families, blood was blood and they were brothers.

Half brothers.

Derron refused to acknowledge the pang in his chest and stared down at Arkael and all those details that set them apart. The freckles. The full lips. The rounded ears. Arkael wasn't an Argarys. Yet a week's worth of grime coated his Argarys silver-blond hair, and that chiseled jaw held up disdainfully resembled what Derron saw in the mirror every day. The longer Derron looked, the more he recognized Cassia in the drawn lines of Arkael's frown. This was why Derron hadn't visited him in the brig. Not that he would've been welcome, but branding Arkael as a rebel and a traitor to the Crown was easier when he wasn't faced with the evidence of their shared blood.

The Meranians hadn't bothered giving Arkael clean clothes. His battle-ruined leathers bore the wear and stench of seven days of travel and imprisonment. At least his wounds were cleaned and treated. The one requiring the most attention was the hole in his shoulder where the arrow had pierced him and sent him tumbling off the dragon's back, separating him from Todrak, Asharaya, and her human sister, Solana.

There had been another moment where Arkael had been helpless on a ship's deck. That time, Derron saved him from a siren's claws. He'd held out his hand to help his brother stand.

If he did the same now, Arkael would likely spit on it.

Derron flicked his gaze to the guard fisting Arkael's chin-length hair. "Let him stand." When the guard made to pull him up by the hair, Derron added, "Civilly. We're not animals."

The guard cut a glance at Raxan, who nodded. Arkael grunted as he was forced to his feet but didn't fight back. His eyes remained fixed on Derron, devoid of warmth. Even when they'd been nothing more than strangers, and Derron had only been the Argarys prince, Arkael hadn't been this cold. Now it was as if his Do'strath's Ice frosted his gaze.

The veins of Arkael's neck bulged, his breathing heavy. Derron looked at the wound on his right shoulder. "Does it hurt?"

"Don't pretend to care."

"There's no point dying out of pride."

"No. I'll only die in an Adarian prison."

Someone called out that the ship had made safe anchor, shattering the brothers' standoff. "See that the prisoner is securely restrained before disembarking," Derron instructed the guards, though his eyes didn't stray from Arkael until the guards gave their unanimous assent. He turned away, ignoring the sour taste in his mouth.

Half brother.
Enemy.

The sea breeze sinking beneath the fur collar of his cloak chilled Derron to his bones. When he'd left Ilahara, Adara had barely begun to show the first signs of winter. Now the season had swept into the southern lands. Derron stepped off the ramp and inhaled the brine and scents of wine, beer, and damp clinging to the piers. The unmistakable sweet smell of cinnamon and something fresh like lemon wafted from the city. It was nearly noon, and someone nearby was preparing lunch. Derron's stomach growled in response.

Though the docks were as busy as ever, men and women wearing Argarys blue and silver kept people away. In the cleared space surrounded by a retinue of guards stood Semal Leneris, the queen's general and closest adviser and the man who'd played a bigger role in raising Derron than his own father.

"I should've brought food," Semal signed. He'd lost his hearing fighting in the Coup. The dragon that shattered his eardrums also shredded the left half of his face. Where others might have been ashamed of the disfigurement, Semal trimmed the sides of his white hair short so there was no hiding his scars or the left eye where the green of the iris had bled through.

Derron met his mentor's smile with one of his own. "That's strangely forgetful of you," he signed.

"I figured you would've bitten off General Nahar's head by now."

Derron grimaced. "And eat him? I'm not that bloodthirsty."

Semal's shoulders shook with laughter, and the two men embraced, heedless of formalities. In that moment, Semal wasn't the general greeting the prince, but a friend and a father welcoming a young man home.

When they pulled apart, Semal patted Derron's shoulders.

"I missed you, too," Derron said. "I hope it's been boring here."

Semal's hesitation was answer enough. Derron wasn't surprised. It would have been too easy if the seer's prophecy hadn't stirred trouble. With the dragon's return, it was likely the whole of Ilahara knew about Asharaya.

The guards dragged Arkael off the ship. Semal's gaze lingered on him before returning to Derron.

"Yes, he's Vaemor's son." Derron knew that wasn't what Semal was inquiring. He and the queen had been debriefed through the water networks, but Derron wasn't sure he could look his mentor in the eye and tell him he wasn't unaffected by this situation with his brother.

Semal's expression softened, as if he could read Derron's heart despite the words he wasn't saying, but he didn't insist. Instead, he slipped back into the role of the general as Raxan Nahar approached. After exchanging brief pleasantries during which Derron acted as translator, Semal invited everyone to follow him to the carriages that would take them to the castle.

Home.

2

Shara

Daganver's forest was a fairy-tale landscape. White carpeted every surface and pine-scented air blew from the mountains into dense clusters of trees. The path was rarely silent. In the early morning hours, the happy twittering of birds filled the quiet, replaced during the day by barks and growls and the haunting howling of the wind. It was enchanting and brutal in the way only a land ruled by near-endless winter could be, but Asharaya Myrassar's wonderment was short-lived.

Shara feared there was no end to the forest. The meager rations of winterberries did little to quiet her stomach's rumbling, but hunger she could tolerate. The cold less so.

A flurry of snow was their constant companion and it clung to Shara's skin in a glacial vise, turning her fighting leathers frigid as she sat huddled against a tree. A breath plumed before her, a pale wisp in the midday gloom. Beside her, her sister, Solana, shivered, her teeth chattering loud enough to wake the dead. "We need to get into a town."

"It's t-t-oo dang-g-erous," Solana stuttered.

"You won't make it to Frosthead Hall this way."

If Daganver's frigid temperatures were harsh for Shara, who could at least find comfort in her Fire, they were even more so for Solana's human body, especially since all she wore was the white dress the Meranians had put on her. When they traveled, Shara let Solana ride Deimok as much as she was able, but even so her sister's brown skin had taken on a blue tone and her nose was redder than a berry. It only made the black circles beneath her brown eyes stand out more. Hunger, grief, cold...how much could a body endure without breaking?

"Fuck this." Shara got to her feet, the cold greedily clinging to her where the snow had dampened her breeches, and stomped over to the nearest bush. She snapped off a branch, and then another, piling them against her chest.

"What are you d-doing?" Solana asked.

"I'm making a fire."

"You can't." Solana coughed. "Mykal and Deimok will be b-back soon. The smoke—"

"You need heat, Lana." The Dragon only knew how long it would take Deimok to return from his hunt. What harm would a small fire do? "I'm not letting you freeze to death."

Once she had a satisfactory heap, Shara returned to Solana and set her narrow branches together in a pile. Heat pooled in her extended hand, spreading fast with little effort. Not too long ago, this feat would have been impossible, if not catastrophic, but her training was paying off and Deimok's nearness gave her magic direction. The red and golden threads branching through her staved off the cold. The warmth intensified, and Shara nipped her lip in concentration as a flame formed in her palm. *Just a flame. No more than a flame.* With a small tilt of her hand, the flame bounced onto the branches, and a small fire flickered to life. She couldn't help her pleased grin as she faced Solana.

"Mykal's going to bite your head off for t-this." Solana lips curled in a small smile as she leaned closer to the flames and held out her shaking hands to savor the warmth. That look of contentedness alone was worth the earful she was bound to receive from Mykal Todrak, heir of Daganver and bane of her existence, once he returned with their meager lunch of winterberries.

Shara huddled closer to Solana, locking their arms together as she rested her head on her sister's shoulder. She would have killed for a cushion, even if it was old, worn, and infested with lice. For a bed and the chance to lie down, she might have done far worse. "Are you ready to talk about it?"

Solana hadn't cried for Xoro after the first days, but the sadness clinging to her in the week since the pirate captain lost his life seemed never-ending. Her sister sighed, sounding weary. "No," she whispered, resting her head against Shara's. "I'll be fine, I promise. You have more important things to worry about."

Shara was about to reply when a shout had her attention snapping to the trees.

"There's a fire!"

Shara jumped to her feet. Solana followed suit and helped her kick snow onto the flames, their eyes fixed on the tree line as running footsteps came closer. The hairs on the back of Shara's neck stood on end. "We need to leave before—"

"Over there!"

Dragon, Maiden, and all five fucking gods. In perfect synchronicity, Shara and Solana armed themselves with daggers as four men bounded into the camp. They didn't sport the Argarys silver flame sigil on their plain leather jerkins, but their greedy expressions marked them as unfriendly.

"Kill the human." The man who was likely the leader of the group jerked his chin Shara's way. "It's her the queen wants."

The men spread out to surround them, and Shara and Solana lunged. Shara ducked to avoid the wide swing of an opponent's sword and cut into his unprotected calf. As she rolled aside to avoid a second opponent, Solana occupied the spot Shara vacated. She sliced her assailant's throat and twisted with the momentum to plunge her blade into the man Shara wounded. When he dropped his sword, Shara collected it and drove it into his stomach. Warm blood coated her hands, and the man's bowels cascaded to the ground in a bloody heap. Apprehension shifted into a forbidden thrill. The adrenaline of the fight brought back a vigor Shara hadn't felt in days. She had a lot to learn when it came to leading, but fighting came as naturally to her as breathing. Perhaps this was exactly what she needed to take the edge off the failures of the past days.

Back to back, the sisters faced off against the remaining two opponents.

"Surrender now, Asharaya," the leader said. He sported a bloody cut to his cheek, courtesy of Solana. "You and your friends stand no chance against the queen."

He made to attack but instead fell forward into the snow. Blue frost raced up his legs, the thinnest vein of red trapped within the ice. A slow smile bloomed on Shara's lips as Mykal stepped into the camp, holding the hem of his shirt close to his chest with one hand and keeping the other extended toward the man on the ground. One glance at the still smoking remains of their improvised campfire and his lips thinned. Shimmering veins of arctic blue spread in his honey-brown eyes as he fixed a glare on Shara. The bright color's contrast was even more mesmerizing against his snow-speckled dark brown skin. "Really?"

Bounding footsteps had Shara spinning around to the last man, who was running back toward the trees.

"Craven," the leader shouted after him, but the runaway made it only a few feet before a growl shook the forest, so loud it silenced the man's terrified screams.

Deimok's teeth clamped around the man's middle, lifting him off the ground. With a violent shake of the dragon's head, the lower half of the man's body flew across the clearing, raining blood onto the snow, while the other half dropped with a heavy thud.

The leader bent over, and as he heaved the remnants of his last meal, Shara yanked back his head and cut his throat.

"Nice catch," Shara praised Deimok, who chirped in satisfaction as he neared her. The dragon's amusement was a stark contrast to Mykal's clouded expression. "I'm sorry, Myk."

"What in the Dragon's name were you thinking?"

"We were freezing, and I didn't think there was a patrol nearby." Shara didn't dare put the blame solely on Solana, though Mykal seemed to understand the cause of her concern. He looked at Solana, who'd wrapped herself in one of the dead men's cloaks and was pilfering their pouches for coin.

Mykal sighed. "You're lucky it was bounty hunters."

"We're lucky Deimok's magic throws off tracking spells, or who knows how many times we would have been tracked by now with your shit sitting in Frosthead Hall."

Mykal handed Shara some berries, and then did the same with Solana. "Aerella must be sending more men up north. I spotted another patrol a couple miles from here."

"She's expecting us," Shara surmised. "She knows this is where I'll find more support, and that you won't abandon your family."

After barely escaping Merania with their lives, they'd flown Deimok to Daganver, but approaching a territory watched for association with the last Myrassar wasn't easy. Once Deimok neared the shores of Ilahara's northernmost region, they found soldiers waiting with a volley of arrows to take down the dragon. It was all Shara and her friends could do to dive into the forest and find shelter in the thick cover of trees. Coming here of all places had been a risk, but they needed allies to stand a chance against Aerella. With the Todrak's connections in Daganver, this was the best place to start. Shara was a stranger to Ilahara's politics, but Mykal's father, Lord Darrok, had been her parents' devoted friend and ally. If anyone could help her understand who to trust, it would be him. But first they needed to free Frosthead Hall from Aerella's influence.

Easier said than done.

"How much longer until we reach Frosthead Hall?" Shara inquired.

"Three days," Mykal replied. "Maybe four."

Despite Mykal's sure-footedness, Deimok's lumbering gait forced them to travel slowly and increased the chances of running into patrols, which seemed to multiply as days passed. Fear of discovery was ever-present. Shara's blades were always within reach, the cold touch of steel grounding even though wariness sat heavy on her chest. The images plaguing her made her yearn for her lost sketchbook: the arrow striking Kael from Deimok's back, Mykal's hand reaching for his Do'strath as they left him behind, the surprised flash in Derron Argarys's eyes when Shara spared his life. Shara hated herself for hesitating when fate dealt her the opportunity for a killing blow. Nothing would have changed, but Derron's death would have been a just punishment for the torment her friends now endured and for those they'd lost along the way.

At night Derron haunted her in different ways. At times, he was a child pretending to be a knight in the Embernest gardens. At others, he was closer to the man who'd offered her flowers in a dream than the one who'd betrayed her. She could picture him vividly, lying in a bed in a ship's hull, kept awake by regrets. But this wasn't one of Shara's novels, where behind every villain was a tormented soul waiting for someone to offer them redemption. This was reality, where people changed and deceived to serve their own agendas. Derron was no different, no matter how much she'd secretly longed for him to be the friend from her past.

"If I never see snow again for the rest of my life, it'll be too soon," Shara mumbled.

Deimok's approval rumbled down the soulbond. The feel of

her dragon's emotions alongside her own had yet to yield its novelty. The embodiment of Fire he may be, but he disliked the cold more intensely than his rider.

"At least the snow is covering our tracks," Solana reasoned. "And now we have cloaks."

Shara didn't miss Mykal's bashful look as he accepted a cloak from Solana. He'd been acting this way ever since they'd decided to temporarily set aside the plan to track her lost brother. Mykal had tried, but without Kael he hadn't found a trail—or so he said. The look he'd given Shara suggested another grim alternative, one he hadn't had the heart to share with Solana. If the boy had died, there would be no trail to find.

Shara wrapped herself in her cloak, and then braced herself to face Mykal. "We need to stop in the closest town." She raised her voice when Mykal made to protest. "Winterberries won't sustain us forever. We need provisions, warmer clothes to deal with this blasted cold, and insight on what we're up against in Daganver." Snow danced around Mykal's frame, as if desperate to linger in his presence. The forest was Daganver's beating heart, and Mykal would someday rule over this territory as Head. The land recognized him, but Mykal seemed impervious to his homeland's fussing. Shara hoped that he'd fight her, despite the valid points she'd raised. The young man she'd met in Havanya would have, but that man had been held together by his Do'strath's steadfast presence. With Kael gone, a fundamental part of Mykal was gone, too. He'd spoken more words now than he had in the past week.

"If we manage to stay alive for a few more hours, we might be able to stop in Glacemir," Mykal yielded. "But we'll need glamours, and we'll have to steer clear of windows and any other reflective surface as much as possible."

"It does not sound like reliable magic," Solana commented.

"It isn't. Glamours can only be crafted by high fae, and the concentration required to master them is too taxing for most to bother learning. Those who do learn use them for vanity. It's hardly a criminal's best asset."

"We won't stay in town long," Shara said. "Only long enough to get what we need."

"Then let's get going." Mykal turned his back on them without another word. He retreated into the trees, and Shara's heart sank.

Give him time, Asharaya. Deimok's Drakasi echoed down the soulbond as he nudged her fingers in reassurance. *Being separated from one's Dragaelan is a terrible hardship to endure. Distance weakens the bond. None knows it more than you and I.*

Shara stroked his scales as they followed after Mykal. *Do you think Kael is alive?* Even thinking the words felt like tempting fate.

We would know if he was not, her dragon replied after a moment of somber silence.

The words did little to reassure Shara.

Death could be a mercy if one's life was in the wrong hands.

3

Derron

A prison wagon waited behind the blue and silver carriage that would take them to the Embernest, the guards ready to follow either on foot or on horseback. Walking to his ride, Derron couldn't help glancing back. Arkael was hauled into the wagon and locked behind the iron bars. A crawling sensation started at the base of his stomach, but Derron squashed it down when he found Semal staring at him, waiting.

Though Raxan tried to engage in friendly conversation, the ride to the Embernest was mostly silent. Derron was too distracted by the city to care about what the Meranian general had to say. He hadn't realized how strongly he'd missed the narrow streets, the buildings colored in varying shades of red, peach, yellow, and cream, the scents of citrus fruits from the orchards, the spices the Adarians favored in their cooking. The people. Neighbors talked from windows while others moved into an alcove or pressed against the wall to make way for carriages. Children ran sideways and climbed over feet rather than wait, their little packs bouncing on their backs. Judging by the hour, they were returning home from school in time for lunch.

The weight of Semal's assessment was reminiscent of the times he'd oversee Derron's training and watch for any flaw in his form. Derron had long since outgrown the instinct to squirm under the general's scrutiny, but keeping his eyes fixed on the window was no easy feat in light of his recent failures and tangled feelings.

Time moved both too slow and too fast. Derron couldn't tell if he was relieved or not when the carriage crossed the bridge to the Embernest's gates. The guards stationed there saluted the general and their prince with a hand to their hearts and a deferential nod, the words "my prince" and "Your Highness" whispered as the carriage passed through the gates.

Inside, the path veered progressively uphill through a series of elevated levels and three different archways serving as checkpoints. Rynar Myrassar had chosen to build the castle atop the cliff so that the Dragon-Blessed may live in the sky with their dragons. The cliff was also a natural defense against sieges. This had proven true for centuries, and with time the Myrassar had eased into thinking they were invincible. Perhaps that was why Gailen Myrassar hadn't seen Derron's mother's attack coming.

At the last archway, the prison wagon veered left toward the prison tower. Derron peeked out the window as Arkael was driven away. When he sat back, Semal gave him a look, as if knowing exactly what went on in Derron's head.

That made one of them, at least.

Heat radiated through Derron's chest at the sight of the familiar golden balustrades and the fragrance of roses coming from the royal g

ardens. Despite the anxious knot twisting his insides and the tension accompanying him since Merania, he was happy to be home.

Following Semal out of the carriage, Raxan Nahar fell into step beside Derron, peering up at the grandiose marble and gold structure. "I'd forgotten how magnificent the Embernest was."

"It's quite impressive," Derron agreed. He stood there a moment longer as Raxan walked ahead. The sun shone through the thinning layer of clouds, radiating light onto the walls and turning them the color of burnt gold. Like the Myrassar eyes.

Her eyes.

Derron shook his head and raced to catch up. Guards held open the double doors, giving him a full view of an amused Meranian prick and an equally diverted Semal. Derron paused his apology upon glimpsing the nobles lining both sides of the blue and silver hall. He'd hoped his would be a quiet homecoming. High fae bowed as he passed, some keeping their stares resolutely on their feet while others spied him coquettishly through their lashes. Derron scanned the crowds for his twin, but Cassia wasn't among them.

Derron squashed his disappointment and followed Semal. The higher up they went, the quieter the halls became. Nobles spent most of their time in the lower levels, where they loitered in the dozens of open sitting areas, the library, or the gardens. The castle's higher levels held the living quarters. Unless one was a guest staying at the Embernest, access to these levels was on an invitation-only basis.

Semal entered the queen's receiving room first, giving Derron and Raxan some quality time to spend in silence outside the hall. With only a door separating him from his mother, Derron couldn't help his heart's panicked thumping. He was moments away from facing her monumental disappointment. His back stung with the memory of the last time Queen Aerella had been displeased. Derron's hands turned clammy as he remembered the heat, the pain, his blood, his screams.

Raxan leaned closer to the door. "I can't hear anything."

Derron blinked and he was out of the dungeons, back into the queen's illuminated halls. Breathing deep, he faced the Meranian general and exhaled. "Of course you can't. They're using sign language."

The opening door spared Raxan the effort of finding an appropriate comeback. Semal looked first to Raxan, then to Derron, and nodded.

The queen was ready to see them.

Derron hesitated only a moment before entering the room. He didn't linger on his surroundings—not the white walls or the familiar blue drapes, or the divan where he and Cassia had spent hours watching and learning. Queen Aerella stood from her seat behind the desk. Silver locked on silver as her gaze met Derron's. In her silver and lilac dress, with her hair pulled back at the sides and cascading down her back, Aerella Argarys resembled every bit the queen she'd fought to become rather than a concerned mother. Yet there was the subtle hint of relief behind her stern facade, which was more than Derron expected. Aerella had never been one for hugs and kisses, always doling out her affection in small doses even before the Coup of Fire made her a queen.

Raxan bowed. "Your Majesty. Memory doesn't do your beauty justice."

Derron bent his head as well, a fist to his heart.

"General Nahar. I'd say it's a delight to see you, but circumstances dictate otherwise."

There it was. Derron lifted his gaze slowly, sensing his mother's attention. "I've failed you."

Aerella's lips thinned, but she gestured to her right, encompassing the desk. It was then Derron noticed the man in the brown robes. "Allow me to introduce Maenar Errigen, the Embernest's new maenar."

The maenari were scholars who devoted their lives to research and counsel. They trained and lived in Lur, the city of knowledge where the great Library of Lur resided and where a council chose who among the scholars would best serve the noble houses. Maenar Elvik had been the Embernest's previous maenar. He'd looked old, which was a testament to how many years, kings, and queens he'd seen pass. The man standing behind the desk looked barely older than the queen, his brown hair a messy mop that grazed the tips of his pointed ears.

Maenar Errigen acknowledged them with a respectful bow. "Your Highness, it's a pleasure to finally make your acquaintance. I hear you're a man devoted to the arts. I shall be happy to assist you in any way."

"Thank you, maenar."

"Leave us," the queen ordered. "I'd like to speak to my son and the general alone."

Though Semal was also present, only Maenar Errigen bowed and left. Aerella and Semal were a unit. What one knew, so did the other. The queen's dismissals could include her children, but not Semal, something those used to dealing with her knew well.

"I see we're not taking chances," Raxan said several moments after the door clicked shut. "I guess after the stunt Elvik pulled, one can't be too careful." Maenar Elvik had betrayed his post out of love for the Myrassar he'd served for centuries. His message to the Todrak with the seer's prophecy foretelling Asharaya's return to Ilahara had set off the chain of events that had them standing in this room now, discussing Derron's biggest mistake.

Aerella sat back in her armchair, Semal half sitting beside her on the desk. With the queen's silent permission, Raxan lounged on one of the armchairs across from her. Derron unstrapped his swords with blue jay pommels from his back and set them aside before making himself comfortable—or as comfortable as he could be. His eyes went to the silver flame sigil hung on the wall behind the queen. His family's emblem.

Aerella slowly folded her fingers around the armrests. "There's been no sign of Asharaya or her dragon since they were last seen by our archers in Daganver. Same goes for their allies. It's as if they've vanished into thin air."

"Tracking spells don't seem to work," Semal explained, with Derron filling Raxan in. "We suspect the dragon is rebuking them."

"One would think a dragon would be easy to spot," Raxan mused. "And Mykal? I find it unlikely that a Todrak could move through the North without anyone recognizing him."

"Either the Daganverans are aiding him or they're very resourceful, both options which I'm unwilling to exclude. I've sent another garrison to the North and promised a generous reward to whoever delivers Asharaya and her traitor friends to me. Let's see how well she fares against the hunters." Aerella's smile was deceptively docile as she addressed the Meranian general. "I hope the Crown can count on Eathelin's support in rooting out the rebels."

"You can count on my cousin's forces to patrol the northern coast. If they fly anywhere near the water, we'll find them."

"I want all your efforts on this endeavor, General. Convince the sirens to expand their hunting grounds, if you must. I want them trapped like the rats they are."

"We'll do our best, Your Majesty."

Aerella nodded, not in thanks but close. Gratitude was for unexpected acts of kindness, not when one's service was a given fact. "You and your men are welcome to stay at the Embernest for as long as you need to prepare for your journey back to Merania."

"We require two days at most." Likely sensing his audience with the queen was over, Raxan stood and bowed. "There's a new guest in your dungeons, Your Majesty. Consider him a gift." With a smirk in Derron's direction, General Nahar took his leave.

Seconds stretched into minutes as the silence grew charged.

"Was Vaemor's half-breed bastard the reason you hesitated in Havanya, or was it Asharaya?" the queen finally asked.

Neither, Derron wanted to confess. *Both*. He did his best to remain the picture of calm, though inside he was anything but. This close to Queen Aerella's unblinking stare, he could almost smell the stench of smoke and burning flesh. That and the anticipation of the lashes had been worse than the pain itself, for which he'd built a high tolerance thanks to Semal's rigid training.

"The woman I found in Havanya was no damsel." Derron addressed Semal because it was easier to speak to him and remain in control. "Asharaya was fostered and trained by a sect of assassins with unusual powers. I've never fought anything like it."

"You mentioned something of the sort when you last communicated with us," Semal signed. "But what is it exactly she can do?"

"Besides wielding Fire like all Myrassar, she can access shadows. I don't know how the humans have this power, but she learned to walk through them and appear in another spot in the blink of an eye." The powers also had a toll. When Asharaya's human sister, Solana, dragged the *No One* through darkness, the woman nearly spilled her lifeblood to perform such a feat. For whatever reason, he kept this information tucked away. "Asharaya had strong allies among the humans and among our own kind."

"It doesn't justify what you've done," Aerella snapped. "Which is nothing."

The words ricocheted in Derron's emptying mind. Saying he'd tried wouldn't make a difference. The result was that he'd failed.

"It's not Derron's fault, Aerella. We chose stealth and discretion over brute force. It was a gamble, and we lost. Derron was alone and faced with difficult odds," Semal interceded.

Aerella leaned back in her chair and grabbed her chin, eyes fixed on nothing. "Perhaps having Vaemor's spawn could work to our advantage. I remember he followed the young Todrak here for Eileen's sixteenth birthday. They must be close." Derron held his tongue about the extent of Arkael and Todrak's relationship. If his mother knew they were Do'strath, she wouldn't hesitate in killing Arkael for having practiced a ritual exclusive to the Dragon Faith, banned with the fall of the Myrassar reign.

"And if it doesn't?"

"Then we'll get rid of the Todrak once and for all."

"This will lead to war, Mother."

"They chose war the moment they set out to find the last Myrassar. And your inaction has led to this." Queen Aerella grabbed a parchment from her desk and thrust it at her son. Derron fumbled with the paper without removing his gaze from his mother.

The parchment bore the red-painted outline of a dragon's profile. Flames erupted from the beast's open maw, and its wings were folded back, ready to attack. To take flight.

"Our soldiers have been pulling these off Adara's walls for the past four days. Don't speak to me about starting a war. War is on our doorstep. If your allegiance is to your family, you'll do your duty and help us eradicate these Dragon fanatics before dissent spreads like a disease. You know many artists in the city. Figure out who's behind this and all shall be forgiven."

Derron nodded. "Yes, Your Majesty."

Queen Aerella stared at her son a moment longer and then said, "You may go."

Derron grabbed his swords as he stood and bowed. Semal smiled reassuringly. Overall, the meeting had gone well. Derron was still in one piece and there hadn't been a lick of flame in sight.

Standing outside the queen's study, Derron strapped his swords onto his back and released a small sigh.

"Derron."

He spun, a grin splitting his face. Eileen Todrak raced to him, dark curls sticking out of her braid. Derron met her halfway, and Eileen's arms flew around his neck as he lifted her off her feet. She made a sound halfway between laughter and crying. Derron set her down and took hold of her hands as they slid down along his chest, as if she wanted to make sure he was whole. Her brown eyes glistened. "I'm so happy you're home." Her voice trembled with emotion.

"It's good to see you." Now that the initial rush of happiness was ebbing, Derron couldn't help comparing Mykal Todrak to his friend. Eileen had been only four when the Argarys took her as their ward, an unwitting victim of politics and power plays. Growing up together, Derron and his twin found it increasingly more difficult to remember Eileen wasn't family. After spending over two weeks in the presence of another Todrak, Derron found it impossible to ignore.

Though Eileen's umber skin was a shade darker than her brother's, they shared the same remarkable brown eyes, as if honey had melted within their core. Eileen's eyes also sparked blue whenever she accessed her Ice, though the color had never looked as intense as Mykal's. Perhaps his magic was stronger because of the Soul Binding that bound his soul to Arkael's and combined their magic. That the Meranians hadn't witnessed their powers had been dumb luck.

Eileen shook her head, as if still unable to believe he stood there. "There's so much I need to tell you. Cassia..."

Derron's pulse jumped in his throat. "What happened to Cassia?"

4

Mykal

When Mykal Todrak found Asharaya Myrassar on the Human Continent, he'd imagined a grandiose homecoming with dragons singing, people cheering, and his Do'strath as ever by his side. Three weeks later, that version of himself felt like a fool. Reality was far from the hero's welcome he'd envisioned. None sang his praises as they awaited his triumphant return, his family was hostage in their own home, the only dragon within reach hid in the forest, and his Do'strath was a prisoner in his worst enemy's hands.

Kael was gone.

Not a second went by that Mykal wasn't aware of that loss. Every instinct roared to track Kael, despite that the smallest use of magic caused a pang in his chest. For Kael, Mykal would take that risk, and if Frostbite tried to stop him, he'd endure it. But alongside the wild beast calling for bloodshed, a steadfast voice reminded him Asharaya Myrassar was too precious to risk and

Daganver must be freed if they were to surround their rightful queen with allies. *It's your duty, Myk. You're the heir of Daganver.*

So he marched on, forcing every weighed-down step away from the one he'd sworn never to abandon. The feeble feeling of Kael's magic through the soulbond reassured Mykal that he lived, but that certainty meant little when Kael could already be in Aerella's hands. He couldn't access his Do'strath's thoughts or feelings, and trying to reach the other end of the bond was like grasping water. A useless attempt that left Mykal's knees quaking.

"We're here," Mykal announced.

Shara raced forward to catch up with him past the cover of trees. Jagged granite rocks and snow-tipped pines emerged from the trail leading to the town below. Red and brown slanted roofs covered stone buildings and horses dragged wooden carriages through the white streets. Among the civilians, the glint of steel revealed the presence of armed patrols.

"Welcome to Glacemir," Mykal deadpanned. "Remember, we won't be able to hold the glamours for long and they're not infallible. Keep your hood up, and don't draw attention to yourself. We get in, get what we need, and we get out."

"I am coming with you." Solana slid down Deimok's back, shooting the dragon a look that was halfway between wonderment and caution. Mykal couldn't blame her. He'd spent his whole life praying for dragons to return to Ilahara, and even he struggled to believe the creature was real and that he wouldn't incinerate them if the fancy struck. "I am human. No one will spare me a second glance."

"They may be looking for a fae man and woman with a human."

"Then we split up once we get past the gates," Shara proposed.

Mykal agreed with a nod. His black hair lightened to brown, the wavy strands morphing into tight curls, and his eyes turned a navy shade speckled with darker flecks. Kael's eyes.

"Stay hidden," Shara told Deimok.

Glamours in place, the trio descended the cliff, sticking to the cover of tall pine trees lining the natural path. Once the patrol they'd spotted turned away, they slipped into town behind a group lugging a cart filled with lumber. No walls kept the forest at bay. Pine trees often invaded the spaces between stone houses and filled the air with freshness. Shara and Solana were silent wraiths following his lead. They hid their curiosity well, but Mykal recognized Solana's poised assessment and Shara's scrutinizing look, so similar to her dragon's that it made him want to smile and shiver simultaneously. Their eyes skimmed the wide streets—a far cry from those of the Human Continent—and traveled along the stone structures.

"The heir is quite handsome."

Mykal furrowed his brow, confused by Shara's praise until he spotted his face plastered on the stone wall, and his skin crawled. How many times had he scowled at similar posters? Now he was a criminal in his own homeland.

"The queen's offering a handsome reward to whoever finds him and the last Myrassar," Shara read in a whisper. "I wonder if the Nahar will send over her portrait as well. Word has it Asharaya is magnificent. I'd like to see for myself."

A soft smile touched the women's lips. Mykal's attention snagged on Shara's unfamiliar features. Hazel replaced the gold in her eyes, and her amber skin lacked the golden undertones reminiscent of Queen Jaemys, making it a lighter shade of brown than Solana's. The small changes did little to alter her beauty, but the glamour's deception left a bitter taste on Mykal's tongue. That he'd stooped as low as to don one was only further proof of how significantly events had derailed from his original plans.

"What if the guards are wearing glamours, too?" Solana asked in Ilahein as they entered a less crowded street. A forge's sizzle and the music of hammer striking anvil played at a distance.

"Low fae only have basic healing magic," Mykal explained. "Only the high fae have elemental magic, and the nobles you'll find in the army are second sons with high-ranking roles. I doubt they'd lower themselves to patrolling the streets in a small town like this."

"Wouldn't it be wiser to have more magic wielders in the army?" Shara pondered aloud.

"Perhaps, but a month ago Ilahara was at peace. The queen had no reason to add more magic wielders to her forces." How much longer would that way of thinking hold? Mykal shuddered to think what the queen might have unleashed on Daganver's capital. The patrols they'd come across so far would likely multiply tenfold closer to Frosthead Hall, not to mention the forces the queen's few northern allies would devote to the cause.

They followed some woodcutters to the town square. Shops lined the perimeter, and at its center three round, snow-covered steps circled a stone well. "Lana and I will look for some clothes while you get provisions," Shara said. "Let's meet back here in an hour, and keep your ears open for any gossip. The more information we get, the better."

"Here." Solana slipped a pouch in Mykal's hand, the coins within jingling. It hadn't looked so full when she pilfered it off the dead bounty hunters.

"How much coin were those hunters carrying?" he asked.

"Not enough, which is why I had to get more."

Mykal's eyes would have fallen from their sockets if he widened them any further. "Did you..." He checked his tone, lowering his voice to a whisper. "When did you steal those?"

"Does it matter?"

Guilt burned its way through Mykal like an acid wave. Did Solana's sleight of hand affect a single man? A family? Children? Daganver's people had suffered enough since the Coup of Fire, and they would likely know more pain before this war was over. The young woman who'd nearly bled herself dry to save a ship full of men couldn't be so callous.

Solana brushed past, and Mykal could do nothing but stare after her in befuddlement. Shara gave his forearm a gentle squeeze. "We won't survive this war by playing fair."

Of course the fae princess and assassin would defend the human assassin and thief. A week ago he would have voiced the retort, enflamed by the need to see a wrong fixed, and Kael would have sent a wave of soothing heat down the soulbond to calm him. Now that too faded in the void left behind by Kael's absence. Nothing lasted, and nothing made a difference.

"Don't get into trouble," Mykal said, putting an end to the matter.

Once he was alone, Mykal focused his attention back on the square. A ramshackle inn was wedged between a wheeler's shop and a carpenter. The name on the wooden sign was hard to read, but Mykal made out the faded outline of a green bear above the worn letters. The same bear that decorated his family's banners. His heart squeezed, and his feet carried him to the inn. It was as good a place as any to acquire warm food for the road.

Four tables occupied the compact space—three small ones by the windows and a longer one for eight people, likely reserved for feasts or gatherings. At the far end of the chamber, a counter served as both bar and reception, and a rickety staircase led to rooms for travelers. The only other person there was a boy seated on one of the tall stools, who shot to his feet at the sight of Mykal and raced to a room in the back. The kitchen, if the smell of vegetable broth wafting in from the open doorway was any indication.

The inn's simplicity was no surprise. Apart from the costs necessary to maintain their activity, Daganveran business owners were required to pay a quarter of their yearly incomes to the Crown, not to mention the import and export taxes for trade with other regions. As Head, his father shouldered most of the latter fees, especially when it came to importing fruits and vegetables from Tyrra. Mykal loved Daganver's constant flurries and yearlong chill, but agriculture was hard to sustain with their frigid temperatures, and their people needed to eat.

A woman emerged from the kitchen with the child sticking close to her skirts. Her pinned-up hair revealed the tip of pointed ears through frizzy curls and drew attention to the taut skin across her collarbones. "Good evening," she greeted. "Would you like a bowl of mutton stew?"

"Something easier to take on the road would be better," he said, his voice raucous. Kael was the one gifted in making small talk. People melted when faced with his kindness and easy charm. "I'm traveling from Tyrra to collect my wife. We have a few days of travel ahead of us."

"Oh." The woman's forced smile did little to hide her suspicion. Maybe he should have come up with a better excuse. "Where are you headed?"

"Daganver."

"You're going to the capital?"

"Her family lives near Frosthead Hall." Mykal swallowed a lump in his throat. "It'll be the first time they meet our youngest."

The woman's brow smoothened, and she brushed her son's close-cropped curls. Dragon, he felt like scum lying this way, preying on her motherhood to gain her trust and sympathy. *You're lying to protect her, Myk*, Kael would say. *If she knew the truth, you'd be putting her in danger.*

"I wish your travel to the North had more favorable timing. These are hard times to be sure."

"Because of Ash—" The child's loud shushing cut Mykal's question short. His tawny-brown fingers tightened around his mother's skirt.

"Don't say her name," the boy whispered. "The bad men will be angry if you do."

As if summoned, two men in Argarys livery entered the inn and took a seat at one of the empty tables. Mykal adjusted his hood a little closer to his face.

"It's all right, Tobya." The innkeeper's voice lowered as she addressed Mykal again. "If she and the young Todrak are truly back, they haven't come around these parts."

Was Mykal imagining her disappointment?

"They're likely headed straight for the capital, like the rest of the high fae," she continued.

"The high fae were summoned to Frosthead Hall?" Daganver was too vast a territory to have all the nobles reunited in one place. It never happened without good reason. "Why?"

"Don't you know?" The woman's silence settled like a stone on Mykal's chest. She looked at the guards and then leaned closer, giving voice to Mykal's worst fears. "Lord Darrok was arrested. He's been taken to Adara to face trial with the queen."

5

Cassia

Words withered and died on the page.

Cassia Argarys released a frustrated sigh and reread the paragraph, but the lines blurred and her mind drifted off again. She wondered how Derron could spend hours poring over tomes and parchments in Lur. All she wanted was to clear her mind, but all she found within the library's white and gilded walls was the solace of silence.

The library wasn't a room Cassia frequented often. She preferred the smell of roses and the whisper of trees. The problem was most courtiers enjoyed that as well. Seeing as she could swallow only so much of the court's gossip at a time, the room that better fit her brother became her refuge. The massive space was split into thirty different halls, and the same golden swirls framing the shelves decorated the balconies accessible through the large marble staircase at each end of the room.

For the umpteenth time, Cassia pretended not to notice how

the librarian glanced her way beneath the rim of her glasses. Not only was it rare to see the princess here, but this was her first time outside of her rooms in a week. Cassia's only company had been Eileen, though she often pretended to sleep while her friend was in the room.

The library door groaned open. With no interest in investigating who'd come in, Cassia nestled into the plush nook. If she was lucky, no one would bother her.

The librarian gasped.

"I'd like to be alone with my sister, please."

Cassia cast the book aside at that voice, inhaling hard enough for her throat to ache. She'd longed for this moment, imagined it a thousand times, yet words failed her now that her brother was right there, clean and unharmed as if he'd never left. "Derron."

Silver eyes mirroring her own twinkled with a slew of emotions. "Hello, sister."

Cassia jumped to her feet and raced into Derron's open arms. He kissed her head and hugged her close, and she drew in her first real breath in days. With Derron home, a little piece of her soul returned as well.

"How long have you been back?" she asked.

"A few hours."

"Is it true Arkael returned with you?"

"That makes it sound as if he had a choice." Derron's smile was grim. "He's being held in the dungeons. I imagine Mother will interrogate him soon."

Cassia looked past her brother's shoulders to be sure the librarian didn't lurk behind the shelf. When she was confident they were alone, she clutched the back of Derron's shirt. "Don't go see him. I don't want to know what happened between the two of you while you were away. It doesn't matter. If Mother thinks you care for him, it'll turn ugly for both of you."

Cassia pressed her ear against her brother's chest and counted his heartbeats, as she used to do when they were young and she dreamed of the room. Dreams of the mysterious cavernous space had been recurring this past week. With time she'd learned to live with the frustration and sense of impotence they brought, but now the room felt almost peaceful, and sometimes she preferred staying there to what she would find once she awoke.

Ten steady heartbeats passed before Derron's voice rumbled in her ear. "How are you feeling? Eileen said you had a Burning and that you were in bed for a week."

Cassia stilled. "What else did she say?"

"She told me everything. The arranged marriage with High Keeper Baramun, Korban. What Mother did—"

Cassia twisted out of Derron's embrace. She couldn't stand to look at his sad eyes, to look inside herself, afraid of the emptiness she would find. "Korban was human. A distraction."

"You loved him."

"My marriage to Baramun is important for our family." Cassia paused to stop the quaver in her voice. "The Heads of Makkan aided our mother's coup in exchange for my hand in marriage to their brother."

"And his rise to high keeper. The Farwynd already got enough from the Argarys. They don't need you."

"They want a crown."

"How could you be so impassive about this? You've always disliked the high keeper, yet you speak of marrying him as if it's nothing." He spread his arms out to encompass the room. "You're in the library."

"And?"

"And you're not okay." Derron stepped toward her. "Mother killed your lover, Cassia."

She'd done more than that. Queen Aerella had tortured Korban with Fire.

"I know why you pretend everything is fine."

The queen had carved a neat little message in Korban's flesh and then she'd left him for Cassia to find.

Derron took her hands and brushed his thumbs over her knuckles. "But this is me. You don't have to hide or shut me out. You're allowed to feel."

Show your power, hide your heart.

"Don't antagonize Mother about this. I almost lost you to the Todrak. I won't lose you to her."

Derron opened his mouth as if to protest, but he stayed his tongue as the librarian appeared. Both twins turned to her simultaneously, startling the woman. "A note just came in, my prince. Your presence is required in the throne room."

"Tell them I'm tired or that I've lost my mind and I'm strutting around naked."

Despite herself, Cassia bit the inside of her cheek to hold back the beginning of a laugh. It was very much like Derron to spew nonsense when he tried to avoid the unavoidable. The librarian blinked repeatedly. "I'm afraid the servant didn't wait for a reply," she mumbled. "As in no reply was expected. Surely you understand I'm in no position to argue."

"It's best we go." Cassia locked her arm with Derron's—to support him, but also to remind herself he was truly there, back from a mission that had kept them apart far too long.

Together, the twins walked down the Embernest's white halls and headed for the throne room. Two silver-armored guards stood by the wide-open doors. Like the rest of the castle, the room was white, but once the walls had been the softest amber and covered in frescoes. Derron's mouth always hung wide no matter how many times he saw the throne room. Jaemys Myrassar had been a lover of art, and so was he.

Now, her brother looked rather pale as he stared ahead at the empty dais. The throne was made entirely of copper except for the red velvet seat. The handles resembled the open maws of roaring dragons, but the folded wings sculpted onto the back were its most impressive feature. When the queen sat on the throne, it seemed like they belonged to her, making her seem more imposing. More dangerous. Cassia scoffed at the irony.

Despite her mother's efforts to rid Ilahara of dragons, she hadn't let go of the copper throne and the power it held.

Sometimes, Cassia couldn't help but wonder what it would be like to have those wings. To fly.

Courtiers huddled in groups. The topics of conversation varied from the new shipment of silks to the coming winter and the latest gossip, which happened to be Cassia. The nobles had nothing but fake smiles and false niceties for their princess, but once she left, they went back to whispering about how she'd nearly burned down an entire hall after finding her human lover dead in her bed. A man's death was reason to speculate, and that of a human, one to mock. Either way, Cassia had turned into the court's favorite laughingstock.

Korban deserved better.

Curious stares trained on Derron and Cassia as they walked down the aisle leading to the throne, where their mother was bound to appear. Buzzing whispers filled the hall, following the prince who'd failed to vanquish the last Myrassar and the princess who mourned a human. Chin high, Cassia bottled up her sorrow and reined in her rage. They'd all get what was coming to them.

The side door on the dais sighed open, and the queen strode out, resplendent in a silver and lilac dress. The men bowed at their waist and the women curtsied low. This time their silence held, as if the queen's mere presence snuffed out all sound. Cassia's eyes went to the train of her mother's dress. She blinked and saw it sweeping across a stone floor weeping with Korban's blood. She blinked again and her mother sat upon the throne. Semal stood beside her, and Vaemor took a seat by her side on a smaller and much simpler throne.

The twins bowed before the queen and waited for her subtle nod to join her on the dais. Derron stood between Cassia and Semal, his posture deceptively casual.

"My Queen." Markos Raemis stepped forward and bowed again. A stark line divided his dark hair in two neat rows. "Are the rumors true? Did you arrest who they say you did?"

"Don't fear the name, Lord Markos. The man in question surely doesn't fear you." The queen's silver eyes swept the hall as she addressed the crowd. "The rumors are true. Darrok Todrak is being taken to the Embernest dungeons as we speak. An envoy from Makkan has overseen his arrest and transportation to ensure the speed and safety of his imprisonment."

Cassia felt the slightest twinge of grief for Eileen. Lord Darrok was her father, and the weeks following the seer's prophecy hadn't been easy on her friend. As a Todrak, Eileen's every move was watched by the court and her allegiance questioned. Cassia herself hadn't understood the northern girl's obstinate fretting over strangers she barely knew. It wasn't until her own mother plotted against her that Cassia learned the lines between love, hate, and indifference were difficult to untangle.

Derron's face turned ashen. "You arrested Daganver's Head?"

A placid smile stretched across the queen's lips, revealing her irritation. Derron shouldn't have questioned her, even more so in public. She ignored him and reestablished control by speaking over the crowd's worried whispering. "The proof of Lord Darrok's treachery was irrefutable. His son was seen aiding Asharaya Myrassar in Eathelin." The courtiers followed the line of her gaze to a dark-haired man with sea-colored eyes. Derron bristled imperceptibly.

"What the queen says is true." The man stepped forward, his lips curved into a perpetual smirk. He wore a pin fashioned into a mermaid's tail emerging from the water. This had to be Raxan Nahar, Andren Nahar's cousin and general, who accompanied Derron home. The general stopped in front of the dais and bowed before turning his distracting eyes in Cassia's direction.

No, not hers. Derron's.

Derron swallowed. "Yes, Darrok Todrak sent his son to find Asharaya and return her home."

"I'd hardly call Ilahara her home." Though she hid behind her fan, Cassia needn't have bothered looking to recognize Lady Maree Louvas's annoyingly shrill voice. She batted her long lashes as Derron acknowledged her with a look. "She's been gone for so long. And the Argarys are our fair rulers." Lady Maree bent her head deferentially at the queen.

Cassia was going to gag.

Though she had a point.

"Semantics." Derron barely hid his fraying patience. Cassia frowned. "What I'm trying to say is that perhaps we haven't exhausted all our options. Do we really want to dive headfirst into a conflict when there could be a more reasonable road to peace?" Some of the high fae nodded and whispered. It seemed the court agreed.

Judging by the subtle feathering of muscles in their mother's jaw, Queen Aerella noticed as well. "The Crown will consider every route before coming to a decision. Ultimately, it will depend on Darrok Todrak and his son. I'm a forgiving ruler." Cassia sensed the deception in the queen's sweet but firm tone. "If they cooperate, I shall be lenient."

The queen stood and the nobles bowed. Cassia forced her eyes resolutely ahead as her mother passed by. The queen paused, and a part of Cassia longed for her to show some remorse for what she'd done. But the queen continued in her stride and didn't deign her daughter of a glance.

The Fire stirring in Cassia found no peace.

Derron guided her out of the throne room, toward the gardens. Cassia's chest heaved with the weight of the pressure building inside her.

"What was that?" she asked pointedly. "It almost seemed as if you were trying to defend the Todrak. Not even Eileen dared utter a word about her family once their scheming was unmasked. By none other than you, might I add."

"I'm only trying to avoid a war, Cassia."

"Is that why Asharaya still lives? Two swords and the ability to manipulate minds and she still defeated you."

A muscle ticked in Derron's jaw. "Asharaya has been training her entire life. We were wrong to assume she'd be easy to kill."

Cassia uncurled her fingers from their fisted position. If an hour ago she'd been happy, now she couldn't help the sour taste at the back of her throat. Derron had one job: remove the Myrassar threat.

He hadn't.

Derron promised he'd be there when she needed him most.

He wasn't.

Korban died and Cassia had been alone with her Fire and grief, surrounded by people who considered her pain either an inconvenience or a new piece of gossip. A noose tightened around her neck with every day she was betrothed to Baramun, and by killing Korban the queen demonstrated she wouldn't hesitate to take everything from Cassia if she made things difficult again.

Cassia would marry and be miserable, and still she risked losing all she had because of Asharaya Myrassar. "Was Asharaya too good, or were you too soft?"

Derron tensed. "What's that supposed to mean?"

"Despite your promise to me, you saw her and thought of Elon." Though Cassia hadn't shouted, the words were hard. Derron bunched his brows but said nothing. "As if sparing her life will make any difference. Elon's dead. He's been dead for fourteen years and you're still sucking up to him."

"He was my friend."

"You still can't let him go."

"I tried to kill Asharaya. For you."

"If you really wanted to do it, you would have." Cassia stepped closer, jabbing her finger in Derron's chest. Her brother's eyes bored down on her, but she didn't let herself acknowledge the hurt in them. "The Derron Argarys I know never fails."

Derron jerked away from her touch, and after a moment that dragged on forever, sighed. "I'm tired. I'll see you later." He didn't sound angry, but Cassia sensed her bitterness had cut deep.

Derron left her standing in the desolate hallway. Alone. The divide between them echoed with a name that stirred the Fire in Cassia's veins, lighting up the dark, empty hole in her chest.

Asharaya Myrassar.

6

Shara

After days in the forest, being back in a town and surrounded by people had Shara buzzing with energy. In the quiet moments of their trek, she'd mastered glamours to the best of her ability, and she welcomed the chance to be someone new for a few hours. Glamours were no different from the roles she'd played as a vrah. Where before she relied on silks and cosmetics, with magic she could warp not just the color but the texture and length of her hair and change her skin tone, her eye color, her bone structure. Minor changes were easy. The challenge was altering larger areas while balancing magic's toll on her physical strength.

Despite the glamour, Shara could do little to stop the pang of fear each time they crossed an armed patrol in Glacemir's busy streets. In a world where high fae could hide behind magic, the guards would look for other things—a dragon, a slip of magic, a word uttered to a stranger in an unfamiliar accent.

Shara and Solana witnessed suspects being forced in front of windows, where reflections would reveal the true face behind a glamour. As far as the guards knew, Shara could have disguised herself as any one of the low fae commoners.

"We're not safe here," Solana whispered. They'd already purchased a clean set of clothes. The shopkeeper hadn't asked, but Shara had blabbered about a husband and his infinite pickiness when it came to his clothing to avoid the risk of raising suspicions. There was little that could bring women together faster than solidarity over obnoxious men, and the shopkeeper had taken to sharing some of her husband's quirks in return. Solana now carried most of their bags—a bitter pill Shara struggled to swallow, but one that was necessary to keep a low profile. Daganver may have been kinder to humans than most Ilahein territories, but even here a fae woman aiding her human help would stand out.

The dusting of snow on the ground created a fine contrast with the dark gray stones of the buildings flanking either side of the street. Winter clematis climbed along the walls, framing doors and windows. Its creamy bell-shaped buds emanated a welcoming citrus scent, and the colorful shades of wool dresses and heavy cloaks were splashes of color in the winter monotone. Most people they encountered were low fae, but some had humans following them who made every effort to become invisible. Mykal said that humans here enjoyed more liberties than on the rest of the continent, and yet this meek existence was still far from the life they could have had in Havanya and the freedom Shara herself had enjoyed for fourteen long years. A part of her felt guilty, as if she had somehow stolen that liberty from them. Not that she could have done anything about it back then. Though her sister remained mostly quiet, Shara didn't miss the hitch in her breath whenever Solana spotted a human. No doubt she was searching for gray eyes among the men—an arduous feat, given how common the color was among Havanians.

"Our friend would have found him if he'd been in Daganver," Shara whispered when she noticed a woman squinting their way, likely because Solana had been staring a little too hard at the human carrying her bags. She didn't dare speak Mykal's name aloud. "He's too old to be your brother."

Solana exhaled deeply, nodding once.

They turned the first corner to avoid further attention from the fae woman. Across the street, Shara spotted an art supplies shop—or rather, the mahogany easel in the shop's display that seemed to be calling her name. Solana hissed a "my lady" that Shara ignored as she all but floated to the window. As a vrah, she didn't have much free time to dedicate to painting. Favoring black and white sketches had been a forced decision, a way to keep her artistic passion alive in between training and appointed jobs, but it didn't stop her from dreaming in colors. Beside the easel was a selection of mortars, pestles, brushes, and a set of charcoals and sticks of mineral pigments. Shara's attention snagged on the blue. It was a rich shade, the color of the sea kissed by the midday sun and the darker flecks in Derron Argarys's eyes. Shara had been close enough to plunge a dagger into his chest, yet she hadn't noticed them until Merania. They'd gleamed like sapphires trapped beneath liquid silver when she'd touched the old burns on his back.

I don't see why you should concern yourself with my scars.
We were friends once.

"We cannot linger in front of the window."

Solana's urgent tone snapped Shara out of her reverie. She stepped away from the window as if she'd been caught stealing, a flush of heat rising to her cheeks. It was her body's favorite reaction to intrusive thoughts of the Argarys prince. "Sorry."

Solana's expression softened. "You miss your sketchbook." Shara had lost it on the *No One*, years of memories gone in a blink. She didn't even know what had happened to the ship after Xoro's death—or its crew for that matter. "We have some coin left if you want a new one." Solana peered through the window.

"I see some by the—"

A scream boomed from somewhere down the street. The ground shook beneath Shara's feet, and suddenly people swarmed the alley, rushing in their direction.

"What's happening?" Solana asked as Shara found the hilt of her dagger beneath the cloak.

The crowd swallowed them in its flow, and though the sisters tried to grasp each other, the current of bodies tore them apart. Shara shouted her sister's name, trying to squeeze her way through. Whenever she evaded one person, three more blocked her path and knocked her back. Shara's foot slipped, and she caught onto those around her to stay standing. She had no choice but to follow along or be trampled.

"Where are we going?" Her voice was a kitten's meow compared to the chaos around her. The Daganveran's thick accent and the large number of voices made it hard to decipher more than a few words. The ones she grasped only worsened her fear.

Soldiers. Myrassar. Prisoner.

Had Mykal been captured?

The crowd gathered into a packed square. Shara could note nothing of it—not its buildings or its shops. Her legs turned leaden once she spotted the wooden platform erected at its center, where two soldiers held a woman in chains and another brandished a broadsword. The stench of urine tainted the air, overpowering the pines and snow. Someone near her muttered a prayer to the Five Gods. Shara stared at the blood staining the wooden platform.

"Mercy," a woman cried.

The man with the broadsword looked down impassively at the woman before addressing the prisoner. "Sanda Talard, you stand accused of affiliation with the terrorist movement led by Asharaya Myrassar." A fourth man stepped forward, holding an aged wooden bucket and a brush stained with crimson paint. "My men caught you painting red dragons in the night. Do you deny it?"

The woman lifted her chin but said nothing. Shara squeezed her way forward. If it had been night, she would have sliced her arm open to access the Maiden's shadows and materialize onto the stage. Instead, daylight forced her to this slow progression, clawing for space.

"The Myrassar sympathizers have poisoned your mind with lies, but the queen is merciful." The guard raised his voice on that last part, the words spoken to the crowd. "Admit to your crimes and reveal the names of your accomplices. The queen will grant you mercy. You'll serve your penance with the maenari in Lur. No harm will come to you. This, the queen vows. Refuse, and you'll be found guilty of treason and sentenced to instant execution."

Someone gasped. Others murmured to their neighbors or prayed to their useless gods. The woman on the stairs wailed her sorrow, but none moved.

"Make your choice, Sanda Talard."

Sanda spat at the soldier's feet, fixing her gaze forward. Shara could have sworn she was looking right at her. "Asharaya is coming, and the dragons will sing again when Aerella burns."

"Get her on her knees."

"Let me through." Shara rammed her shoulder into the man standing in her way. His arm wound around her waist and Shara spun, extracting her dagger. The man caught her wrist as she pressed the blade to his stomach, as if he'd expected the reaction. As if he knew the way she fought. The glamour altering his features flickered. *Myk.*

Relief at seeing her friend unharmed was short-lived. The screech of a blade cutting through air had Shara whirling to the platform. Every sound seemed covered by a layer of cotton—the woman crying Sanda's name, the witnesses' shocked shouts, the protests rising when it was too late. Fire rushed to Shara's palms. She lifted her hands, but Mykal forced them back to her sides.

Shara screamed as the sword descended on Sanda's neck.

7

Kael

Kael woke with a start, trading one darkness for another. The Argarys soldiers had dragged him into the Embernest dungeons and thrown him into a windowless room. Sconces placed at even intervals in the hallway served as the only illumination in this otherwise forgotten shithole, but they didn't give off much light when the hatch in the door was closed. Kael had no way of telling night from day, and he couldn't count on his meals to track the time—or on his body's needs to eat or sleep—while cooped up in the dark, rendered useless by renike and inactivity.

In moments of clarity, Kael tried to piece together what he knew of his prison. The soldiers had forced him out of the wagon at one of the castle's outermost towers. East or west, he couldn't tell, not with the wagon's continued jostling and the acidic panic clawing up his throat thinking of what Aerella Argarys might do to him. He'd been forced up a small flight of stone stairs and through an arched iron door, then on to stairs leading down into darkness that swallowed him whole, a space where footsteps echoed against high ceilings and cavernous walls. He'd tried counting the doors but continuously forgot the number he'd reached. By the time they thrust him into the cell, he'd lost count for the fifth time. At least the space was adequately clean. Kael couldn't hear the pitter-patter of rats' paws. Had the dungeons been cleaned, or were the creatures too afraid to venture into these halls?

Kael had received two meals and was hungry often. It was safe to assume they fed him only once a day. If that was true, it had been two days since their arrival in Adara. Two days since he'd experienced the smell of spices, sweat, and manure through the rickety prison wagon. The southern heat plastered the clothes to his skin. Kael would have blamed the wound in his shoulder festering and giving him a fever, but it was clean. Despite the winter winds blowing southward, Adara would never know the cold of Daganver. Of home.

He'd had no visitors outside of the occasional guard bringing his meal or injecting him with renike. Kael assumed the option of serving the drug with his food was off the plate lest he refused to eat long enough to regain some power. No sign of the queen, or her general. Not the prince, or his sister—their sister. Not his father, Vaemor Argarys. Did they deem him of so little consequence—a lowly half-breed who would die in their dungeons soon enough—or was this delay its own kind of torture?

Alone in the dark, Kael couldn't stop his wayward thoughts from spiraling. In Merania, Andren Nahar alluded to the Todrak being kept under surveillance. His mother and the other human servants might be in danger. Without Kael to protect her, who was to say what his mother endured at the hands of enemy fae? If his mind wasn't stuck northward, it went to that cursed day in Merania. When Kael closed his eyes, he heard his Do'strath screaming his name, his outstretched hand always a breadth too far. And Kael would fall, and fall, and fall.

Mykal.

Pain shot up Kael's shoulder whenever he jerked awake. His

body ached, and fear and worry gnawed at his insides, yet nothing hurt or scared him more than the void in his heart. The place where his Do'strath had once been was empty, the thread tying them together whisper thin. The biggest torture was reaching out to Mykal and receiving no response. While Kael maintained a healthy dose of optimism that his friends had successfully fled Merania, horrible images flashed before his eyes when he least expected them—Deimok shot from the sky, Solana shattering on impact, Asharaya captured.

Mykal dead.

Those invasive thoughts froze Kael's blood, like the echo of Frostbite he often felt through the bond. The only thing keeping him sane was the absence of his friends' names on his captors' lips and that meager thread assuring him that, though far away, Mykal was alive. As long as that invisible line between them held, Kael would endure.

Groaning metal echoed through the dungeons. Kael braced himself for another scuffle that would end with him drugged. Footsteps resounded through the cavernous halls—more than Kael had heard since he arrived. He shuffled closer to the door and tried estimating how many people there were. The fog in his mind made it difficult to focus. The sounds grew more distant, and soon another cell creaked open. Had someone else been captured, or had Kael never been alone to begin with?

Please, don't let it be my friends. Don't let it be Mykal.

Kael pressed his ear against the door. If words were being exchanged, he couldn't hear them. Strange, seeing how the slightest sound carried through the hall. How big were these dungeons?

Footsteps had Kael's eyes snap open. He'd fallen asleep again and he wasn't sure how long he'd been out. Wasn't he just at the door? There were two sets of footfalls. When they got closer, he scrambled back against the wall in time for a guard to open the door. Kael vaguely recognized one of his captors. She and her comrade grabbed Kael and hauled him to his feet.

"I can walk myself," Kael snapped, though his legs felt like lead with every step. How much were they drugging him?

The guards dragged him to a different hall. Kael counted three, all lined with empty cells, which wasn't strange. In bigger cities like Adara, the city guard—who had their own quarters—apprehended common criminals. To land in the castle's dungeons meant either the offense was great or the prisoner was high profile. It was likely that the Embernest dungeons hadn't been full since the Uprisings.

They went down the third hall where the doors were spaced further apart. Kael assumed the cells were larger, probably to host important prisoners, not a king's half-human bastard. *Or maybe these are all torture chambers and you're going to die.* "Where are you taking me?" Kael asked, the words coming out slower than he'd intended.

As if in answer, one of the doors opened. Kael planted his feet on the ground, dreading that approaching door and the possibility of what awaited him inside. But for all his struggling, the guards were stronger. They shoved him forward without losing their grip.

The room was indeed bigger than his cell, but it also held more people. Kael counted another five guards before his muscles locked up and his heart plummeted into his shoes.

Sitting in a wooden wheelchair was the man who'd been both a lord and a father to Kael. The man who'd given a servant's son the opportunity to train and study alongside his heir, who'd led him and Mykal to the Stone Altar on the day of their Soul Binding.

The Head of Daganver. Mykal's father.

Even confined in the Embernest dungeons, Darrok Todrak looked every bit the lord. Thick black braids crowned his stoic face, so similar to the one Kael loved, albeit darker and with sharper edges. Lord Darrok wasn't dressed in his usual midnight blue tunic and dark pants but in a dove gray outfit made of lighter material. Even his chair wasn't the familiar one

Kael knew was a masterpiece made by Daganver's best woodcarvers and smithies. The designs carved in the wood told the story of Izhan, the only Ice dragon Ilahara had ever known.

This chair was plain. Kael couldn't define the heat spiking up his spine to the base of his neck. Seeing Lord Darrok stripped of his clothes, his wheelchair, his home would have his palms burning if he had control of his Fire.

The two men stared at one another. Lord and soldier, mentor and disciple. Mykal's father and Do'strath locked in the same hell, removed from the people they loved. With the Head of Daganver in Adara, who sat in Frosthead Hall? What had become of Kael's mother? Of Lady Alissa and Luna?

Lord Darrok tightened his hands around the wheelchair's armrests, his chest expanding. Had he not been staring, Kael wouldn't have noticed. He wished he could voice the answers to the questions behind the Head's gaze. *I'm okay. Mykal isn't with me. He's safe, or at least I hope so. Asharaya is with him.*

A contented, feminine sigh had Kael's head whipping to the left. "I adore reunions."

Aerella Argarys sat on a chair on the left side of the room, positioned as if she and Lord Darrok were having a polite conversation before Kael's arrival. Semal Leneris stood by her side, his one good eye fixed on Kael, who swallowed the lump in his throat and fought the urge to squirm under the general's scrutiny.

Kael had only seen the queen the one time he'd traveled with Mykal and Lady Alissa to the capital for Eileen's sixteenth birthday. Time had chiseled away some of the queen's striking beauty from his memory. He scanned the queen's silver eyes and hair, the shape of her lips and the length of the fingers curled around her chin. There was so much of Derron in his mother's face—or so much of his mother in Derron's. Perhaps if Kael had remembered the queen more clearly, he wouldn't have fallen for Derron's act so easily. If only he'd listened to Mykal.

Several heartbeats passed as the queen contemplated Kael,

perhaps recognizing her husband in some of his features.

Aerella faced Lord Darrok, her mouth stretching in a smile. "Now, Darrok. I dangle your daughter before you and you don't bat an eye, but when I bring in the half-breed you go soft on me." The queen leaned back in her seat, folding her fingers around the armrests. "Alissa doesn't share your penchant for martyrdom. She loves her children, and her one desire is to reunite her family. You, however, are more interested in those of others. Vaemor's bastard, Jaemys's daughter..." At the mention of the late Myrassar queen, Lord Darrok closed his eyes, if only for a moment. This seemed to please Aerella, like a cat toying with a mouse.

The lies this woman spun.

"Lord Darrok loves his children," Kael barked before he could leash his temper. If his Do'strath had been here, it would have been Mykal lashing out and Kael urging him to silence.

"Does he?" Aerella crooned.

Certainly more than you. In Havanya, Kael had spared Derron's life by convincing Mykal the prince would be a valuable bartering tool for Lord Darrok to use against Aerella. Derron, however, had been sure Kael's plan would fail. *The queen won't accept his terms, not even for me. She always has Cassia.* "You have no right to question his honor or his love."

"And you have no right to speak to your queen," said one of the guards holding him.

Aerella raised a conciliatory hand. "Such devotion."

Fire shot from her palm and barreled toward Kael. He closed his eyes instinctively, anticipating the pain. Without his power, he couldn't control the flames. He'd die consumed by the queen's Fire.

Kael felt its kiss, but not the burn. He opened his eyes slowly, sucking in a breath as a spearheaded flame hovered an inch from his nose. One wrong move, one shove from the guards, and he'd fall face first into it.

Aerella's hand was still up, but her attention was on Lord

Darrok, who'd leaned forward in his chair as if to launch himself in front of Kael, broken spine and all. "You can keep your silence, Darrok. Your actions and those of the people closest to you speak for themselves."

"I'll never hand over the North," Lord Darrok said with deathly calm, in spite of the ironclad grip on his chair's armrests. "Not even to my daughter. I'm not my wife. I've no illusion that you haven't twisted Eileen to be your puppet."

"Pity."

The flaming spearhead dropped lower and pressed into the wound on Kael's right shoulder. Kael smothered a scream, hissing though his clenched teeth. The smell of burned fiber and flesh filled the room. His limbs shook with the effort to control the pain. The flame was burrowing into the wound, scorching as it dug deeper.

"Does this boy deserve to die for your pride?" Aerella asked, pausing. "Does your son?"

The Fire receded and Kael slumped forward. The guards didn't bother holding him upright and let his knees crash to the floor. Kael looked up, chest heaving. "Mykal..." he croaked. *Not Mykal. Please, not my Do'strath.*

"Your traitor son is trapped, Darrok. It won't be long before I find him. Once I burn through your half-breed pet, I'll move on to him, and then to your darling daughter. What was her name? Luana? Liana? Luna, that's the one." Aerella stood from her seat and gripped the wheelchair's backrest, glaring down at Lord Darrok. The queen wasn't using any magic, and the Head was undoubtedly dosed with renike, yet witnessing their locked gazes was like watching a battle of Fire and Ice. "I will burn every pine and stone, every valley and mountain and village, everything and everyone you ever loved, until you break."

"You'll never tame the North."

"Would you really watch it suffer to prove a point?" At the lord's answering silence, Aerella straightened. "Admit to your treason and concede Daganver to Eileen. Repent, and Daganver shall know peace. Your son shall live." She eyed Kael, still kneeling on the floor. "I'll even throw in the mutt to sweeten the deal."

Aerella's steps clicked on the stone floor as she moved past Kael. General Leneris cast a look at Lord Darrok before following her out, their small retinue of guards in tow. Kael had only the time to exchange one last, desperate glance with the Head of Daganver before the guards dragged him out, not even allowing him to find his feet. He gasped against the barking pain in his shoulder as he struggled to stand.

Only now did Kael notice the circles beneath the lord's eyes and the sweat beading on his brow, as if his resolve were cracking now that the queen was out of sight. Lord Darrok held out his hand, the beginning of Kael's name on his lips. Would Lord Darrok break to save Kael? To spare Mykal the pain of losing his Do'strath? *No, that cannot happen. Mykal would die. My mother would die. Daganver would die.*

Kael had been trained to be a warrior, yet he couldn't ignore the bitterness in his mouth, or the way the muscles of his lower regions clamped. He was afraid. In pain. Alone. Yet for the man holding out his hand, for the mother who'd loved him despite the horror of his conception, for his home and his friends, Kael would endure.

For Mykal, Kael would endure.

"Through blood and fire," he whispered. The Dragon's Oath, the vow he'd made to Mykal when they became Do'strath. Kael wasn't sure the guards heard him, but Lord Darrok had, and he nodded grimly.

Kael felt a little less lonely.

8

Derron

Derron pored over three different portraits by candlelight. He rubbed his tired eyes, the sleepless night finally catching up to him. Beside him lay the latest dragon banner he'd swiped off the city walls. It had been two days since his return, and hundreds of drawings sprouted up in the capital, as if his arrival and failure to capture Asharaya made the rebels braver. The portraits were drawn by different hands. Derron reached out to several contacts, but only one had answered—Liam, for whom Derron had twice posed in the nude. They'd stumbled into bed once on a drunken night, but Derron never repeated the experience. Now Liam coyly suggested they do another portrait, and maybe Derron would accept, if only to glean anything from the artist gossip mill.

He told himself the city's unrest wasn't his fault. The rebels would have risen regardless of the outcome of his mission. Asharaya's survival had given hope to those who hated his mother. That he'd failed to kill her was of little consequence. Still, if she'd been dead, perhaps there wouldn't be this many dissonant voices. And to think fate had dealt him several opportunities to be done with her. The rooftop at the Vrah's Keep, when he'd chosen to spare her while she was unconscious. On the *No One*, when he'd slipped into her nightmare to stop her from burning down the entire ship. The blasted sirens.

His eyes drooped closed, and he was in the Embernest gardens, sitting under a large tree. The smell of roses almost lulled him into a dreamless sleep, but he sat upright at the start of distant dragonsong. He remembered his bed, the papers, the candle that would begin dropping wax soon. This was a dream.

The last time he'd been here was with Asharaya. She'd been in the throes of a Burning, and her fever would have set the ship ablaze with everyone on it. He'd used the feeble dregs of his Song to plunge into her mind and rip her from her nightmares. Sensing movement, Derron shot to his feet, hands reaching for his swords and coming away empty. Asharaya stood in front of him with a stunned expression that undoubtedly mirrored his own. She wore her familiar black leathers, her long hair loose over her shoulders. Twilight lit her golden eyes as everything they'd been and could've been lay between them. Did she regret not killing him, or did she long for the man he could have been? Had she lost a night's sleep wondering about the taste of his mouth? Gods knew he'd thought of hers, for some unfathomable reason. Perhaps to feed his growing self-loathing.

"Stop haunting my thoughts."

As quickly as she'd appeared, she vanished.

You saved her. It shows you have a heart. Elon's voice seemed so real that Derron almost expected to find his friend in the flesh, but the brutal reality of his death followed him in dreams, too.

"Perhaps that was a mistake," Derron said to himself, yet the bitter pang of regret never came.

Has it come to the point that your happiness hinges upon the last of my family dying? I know the answer. The question is, do you?

While Derron wasn't sure he was ready to answer that question, other answers were easier to attain.

The maenar's office was in one of the Embernest's eastern towers. In the week he'd been here, Maenar Errigen had transformed the once tidy space that had belonged to Maenar Elvik. Books were open or stacked on every available surface, sometimes on the floor. Vials sizzled and bubbled on a side desk with an array of plants and powders scattered around, while junk littered the main desk. Still the young maenar—or so he appeared compared to Maenar Elvik—moved about the space with purpose, as if seeing order in his chaos. In that, he and the prince were alike.

Maenar Errigen looked up from one of the potions, the tips of his hair singed and his nose blackened by the smoke rising from a dark liquid. "I apologize for the wait, Your Highness. This potion cannot be left unattended."

"There's no need." Derron eyed the purplish-green concoction with suspicion. "Is it some kind of explosive?"

The maenar's face brimmed with ecstatic energy. "Indeed."

"Is it wise to brew it here?"

"In its current state it would only burn my desk, but combined with fire... Best not light any candles."

"Why do it then?"

"For Ilahara. Knowledge is the highest power, a fact of which the queen is well aware."

Derron eyed the many potions and herbs littering the room. "She's been keeping you busy."

"It's my duty to serve, my prince."

Derron walked around a pile of books to put distance between himself and the flammable liquid. He pulled a tome from a shelf and leafed through it as the maenar resumed his work. Though he scanned the page, Derron sensed Errigen's inquisitive gaze. He let the silence grow before snapping the book shut. "Something's been nagging at me. I was wondering if you could help."

Maenar Errigen made himself taller, beaming. "Of course, my prince."

"The queen suspects the Crown's attempts to locate Asharaya Myrassar and Mykal Todrak are thwarted by the dragon. Is it true?"

Errigen almost skipped to his desk, as if he'd been waiting for the opportunity to share his knowledge, his explosive brew forgotten. Derron glanced at the bubbling potion, a bead of sweat forming on his brow. "The dragon's acting as a buffer—a shield, if you may. Tracking spells can easily be repelled by a strong enough magic source. And what could be stronger than magic given flesh?"

Derron paced in front of the desk. "And is that the only way? I remember wards surrounding Lur that make tracking impossible."

"Those are ancient enchantments, Your Highness. None have been able to recreate them." The maenar licked his lips, an excited gleam in his eyes. "But the maenari have been making huge leaps in this field of study, one of which concerns a mineral taken from the embers of the Burning Sea."

As Errigen droned on, Derron wondered if Asharaya was aware she was making his mother's forces run in circles. Deep down, he knew the answer, and for some inexplicable reason a smile ghosted his lips.

"Sounds dangerous," Derron said. "And costly." The Burning Sea was molten lava. Only the most skilled maenari could perform the incantations to protect a ship against burning, and so the number of vessels able to withstand the voyage and the crews willing to venture there were few.

"There's also renike. Recent studies show it makes magic

inaccessible to wielders, but it also makes wielders inaccessible to magic."

"Does my mother know about this?"

"She's been informed, but it's unlikely Asharaya and her accomplices have access to the herb while on the run."

A prickling sensation started beneath Derron's skin, the excitement of learning something new mixed with the dangerous thrill of having stumbled upon information his mother hadn't shared with him. He leaned over the desk, drawing Errigen's attention. His magic swept out like an invisible wave over the maenar's mind, cresting over his thirst for knowledge and his desire to please. Derron seized it, lacing his next words with the Song's influence. "The queen won't hear about this conversation."

The light dimmed from Maenar Errigen's eyes. "It'll be our secret."

Satisfied, Derron cast one last look at the potion. "You might want to stop that thing from incinerating your desk."

9

Shara

Shara hardly remembered how they'd gotten out of Glacemir. The drop of the executioner's blade had cut the fight right out of her, and she stood paralyzed, staring at the head rolling across the wooden platform and the red lake pooling around it, streaming from the stump of Sanda's neck. Distantly, she remembered Mykal's arms locking around her middle. He'd dragged her away from the riotous crowd, and sometime later Solana had found them—or maybe they'd found Solana. She wasn't sure.

When they were safely back in the forest, Mykal informed them of Lord Darrok's arrest. Another blow that landed twice as hard after her failure to help Sanda. The lord's fate loomed over them like a dark cloud. Mykal hardly uttered a word after that, and the trek through the forest the following day in the direction of Frosthead Hall was a quiet one. Shara couldn't help but feel responsible. Her return was meant to repair Mykal's family, not break it further. How was she to help an entire continent if she couldn't even keep one man's family safe?

She welcomed the oblivion of sleep once they made camp for the night. The rumble of Deimok's snores and the chill against her shoulder from Mykal's body were far away as she drifted off.

In her dreams, she stood in a room with minimal furniture and a small bookcase. Art was stacked on the floor and covered the walls, like a mosaic occupying every inch of space. The different styles suggested they belonged to more than one artist and hadn't been chosen with a theme in mind, only with the desire to collect. Shara could have easily imagined a room like this being her own, if only she'd had the opportunity to hoard so many treasures.

From the door leading to the adjacent room, Shara gleaned the hulking shape of a black pianoforte. Her brother, Elon, had owned one just like it with beautiful golden keys, though the one in her memory was bigger. Perhaps because she'd only been a child and barely tall enough to sit on the bench without climbing onto it first. Curious, she edged closer to the open door. Candlelight flickered against the piano's polished surface and bathed the room in a romantic amber hue. When she crossed the threshold, she realized two things at once.

The room wasn't a music room, but a bedroom.

The bedroom belonged to Derron Argarys.

Shara reached for a blade only to discover she was unarmed. Despite her loud curse, the Argarys prince remained unperturbed by her presence, as if he couldn't see her. *Of course he can't see you. This is a dream. None of it is real.*

Derron lay sprawled on a large bed littered with parchments, propped up on his elbow as he rifled through a stack. Artwork, if the colored stains seeping onto the back of the pages were anything to go by. He somehow looked even cleaner than the last time she'd seen him in Merania, as if he'd shed the final lingering bits of travel and imprisonment. Silver-blond hair grazed his collarbone, which was left annoyingly exposed by the deep neckline of his nightshirt. A perfect mark for her blade, if only she had one.

He rubbed his eyes, drawing Shara's attention to the deep black circles beneath them. Perhaps he wasn't as polished as he'd first appeared. Maybe there had been some truth to her dreams of his sleepless nights. *Don't feel sorry for him. He doesn't deserve it.*

Derron's eyes drooped closed, and suddenly the scene warped. Her head spun, though her feet remained firmly planted on...grass. The smell of roses filled the air, and dragonsong played sweetly in the distance. These were the Embernest gardens as she'd seen them in the dream Derron created on the *No One.*

And indeed, there he was, shooting to his feet beneath the shade of a tree. Derron reached for his swords, and just as she had before, he came away empty. She might have snorted, if only his silver eyes weren't trained on her. Wide. Haunted. Tortured.

"Stop haunting my thoughts."

Shara woke with a start, pulling down the cloak's clasp that had burrowed in her throat, stealing her air. Her backbone throbbed, and snow fell in a slow rhythm outside the circle of Deimok's magic.

"What were you dreaming?" The sudden sound of Mykal's voice almost made her gasp. She flushed, twisting to find him toying with a loose thread of his cape, his hair falling forward to shadow his haunted eyes.

"The Embernest," Shara replied once her heartbeat slowed. No point torturing him by mentioning Derron. "Did I wake you?"

"Can't sleep," Mykal said. "I was thinking of how I'd tell Luna her father's dead. If I ever see her again, that is."

"He's not dead, Myk."

"You weren't there after the Uprisings. You didn't see the

bodies strung on the battlements." Mykal leaned back against Deimok. "She's going to make an example of him."

"I'm sorry." She wished she could give him more. All his loved ones were in Argarys hands, and whatever they did in Daganver could affect Kael and Lord Darrok. Even if she flew Deimok to Adara—as she had planned to do what seemed like a lifetime ago, before she had friends counting on her and a dragon to protect—they'd both die before making it to the Embernest's gates. "We'll find a way to fix this."

"How did you do it?" Mykal asked, his voice tremulous. "How did you survive all those years without Deimok?"

Shara squeezed Mykal's fingers. "I found other reasons to go on. But in my heart I never stopped hoping we'd find our way back to each other. That he wasn't really gone."

Mykal quieted once more, but his head fell gently onto Shara's shoulder, and his fingers finally curled around hers.

10

Kael

Kael thrashed against the guards' hold. Some clarity returned with his rage, but it wasn't enough. The renike kept his body sluggish, and his captors were stronger. They all but carried him out of his cell kicking and screaming.

Blood pumped to Kael's brain as they dragged him down the dungeon's dark halls. His vision blurred, and his stomach lurched with the meager food he'd been given what felt like an eternity ago. This didn't seem the way to Lord Darrok's cell, but between the drug and the fear threatening to override his senses, he didn't trust what he saw or remembered.

They stopped by a large iron door. The female guard released him to grab a ring of keys from her belt. That she'd let go of Kael and had her back to him was a testament to his weakness. Once the door opened, Kael planted his feet and willed his limbs to turn heavier. One vigorous pull from the guard holding him almost dislodged his arm and propelled him into the room.

Panic seized Kael's chest.

Except for a long iron table at its center with built-in manacles at all four corners, the room was empty. The smell of soap clung to the space, and yet dark spots stained the walls and floor, as if no amount of water could wash away the evidence of what transpired here. It certainly hadn't removed the stench of blood. Kael's gaze flicked about the windowless room, as if a door would materialize into the wall if he searched hard enough. His eyes landed on the drain near the table, where the stains were darkest.

Pressure released in his lower belly, staining the front of his breeches. Kael's ears burned with shame as the stench of piss rose to his nose, and undoubtedly to that of the guards.

His mind jumped out of his body, away from the guards removing his shirt and then shackling him to the table. He was powerless to stop it. The shock of cold from the metal table was almost a surprise.

A pair of footsteps came from outside. Humorless laughter burst out of him when Queen Aerella and General Leneris darkened the doorstep, though in truth he wanted to scream. While the general looked at him with indifference, a subtle glint lit the queen's silver eyes. Was she enjoying his helplessness? Did she hate him—the idea of him—that much? Kael tugged against his restraints. The proof of his soulbond was laid bare to the queen, etched on his skin in a pale scar where the minister had pierced his heart. Would she recognize it?

"Leave us," the queen ordered. The guards filed out without a word or a look in his direction.

Kael flinched at the sound of the iron door closing behind them.

Silence stretched for a minute, an hour, a day. Kael's heart pumped rapidly, so loud the queen could likely hear it. Did his desperation and the stench of piss give her pleasure?

I'm going to die.

The queen's heels clicked on the stone floor as she approached the table. "There are two ways we can go about this." She stared down at him, her silver-blonde hair falling over one shoulder. "Either you tell me where to find Asharaya Myrassar and Mykal Todrak, or General Leneris will carve the answers out of your milky skin."

Tremors racked Kael's arms and legs, but he clenched his jaw to avoid even the slightest hitch in his breath. More than the torture, he feared the idea of betraying his Do'strath.

"Be smart, Arkael. A young man like you has much to give and take from life. Would you gamble it all on a man who left you behind?"

Kael didn't rise to the bait. He'd been the one to plead with Mykal to go, to beg Shara to fly away and leave him to his fate lest they all lose. He'd do it again in a heartbeat. Better him here than any of his friends. Better him than Mykal, Solana. "I'm already dead either way," Kael said, his voice surprisingly steady.

The glint in the queen's eyes vanished. The general came closer, pulling a thin knife from his belt. He grabbed one of Kael's fingers, angling the blade beneath his nail.

Kael released a whimper.

Don't look, Kael, Mykal whispered, while Solana said, *It's only blood*.

"This would have been less unpleasant if you hadn't been Vaemor's son."

The blade sank into his flesh.

11

Derron

Derron sat at his piano, fingers dropping over the keys one at a time. Whatever song meant to burst from his imagination remained cooped up somewhere between his throat and his chest, like a persistent pang. Sometimes the music flowed freely. At other times, he felt the need to create, but thinking up the notes was like pulling out one's own teeth. He was too distracted, his thoughts bouncing between his conversation with the maenar the day before and his unfruitful research on the artists—and Asharaya.

Sighing, Derron shut the lid of his piano and leaned over it, dragging both hands across his face and through his hair. Music sheets lay scattered across his unmade bed. The servants had come in twice already, but he'd sent them away. The mess in his room was a fitting metaphor for the chaos in his mind.

The queen had gone to the dungeons yesterday. During dinner—the only time he wasn't allowed to dine in his chambers—his mother's placid smile and his father's distant gaze tied Derron's stomach in knots. It didn't take a seer to understand Aerella had visited Arkael, and that their conversation wasn't pleasant.

If Cassia was perturbed by what their brother endured, she didn't show it. Then again, Cassia had warned Derron to stay away from Arkael to avoid complications. She had a point. Aerella was merciless when people displeased her, even her own children. Derron bore the scars on his back, and Cassia on her heart. Yet a small voice inside him whispered to put a stop to it. To help Arkael. The voice of an old friend, though it didn't belong to Elon. It held the musicality of a foreign accent, and it stung as efficiently as one of her daggers.

I saw scars, Derron, not ashes.

Asharaya would confront Aerella and damn the consequences. She was brave and selfless, despite the tough front she presented. A true Myrassar. Derron could picture her as she prompted him to fight, to be the hero she remembered and not the villain born from bloodshed.

A knock on his bedroom door startled him from his thoughts. Eileen leaned against it, black curls unbound and falling over her shoulders. She held a plate with a cinnamon pastry, smoke still rising from it and sweetening the air. "I spared the servant the trouble of having to deal with your brooding."

Derron smiled. "And so the burden falls on you."

"It's difficult work, but someone has to do it." She sauntered to the piano, holding out the plate. Heat singed Derron's ears at Eileen's wistful smile. Those and the stolen stares had become more frequent since his mother decided they should marry. Eileen seemed happy with the arrangement. Derron wasn't as enthusiastic, and not for any fault of Eileen's. She was kind, gentle, and beautiful. Anyone in his place would count down the days to her Bleeding so they could wed, but Derron couldn't shake his brotherly affection. Maybe with time he could teach himself to love her as Eileen longed for him to.

Derron plucked the plate from her grasp and set it on the piano. As he took a bite, Eileen cast a disapproving look around the room. "I'll clean it later," he said, wolfing down the last of the pastry.

"You're aware there are servants to do those things for you?"

Derron huffed and stood, pacing into his living room. Unlike his bedroom, this area was relatively clean aside from his research. He'd spent the past days going through the artwork, journals, and sheets littering the area. Derron wasn't too keen on ratting out the rebel artists, but the curiosity to find them goaded him on. So far, he hadn't had much luck.

Eileen followed him and sat on the divan. Her white dress against the blue and silver dominating the room made it appear as if she belonged. As if she were already an Argarys. "Did you and Cassia fight?"

"She's not happy I let Asharaya get away."

"You were unlucky. Asharaya had help while you only had a handful of guards."

Had it truly been misfortune, or had he secretly hoped his mission would fail?

Eileen watched him with no small amount of concern.

"You never asked me about him," Derron said.

"About who?"

"Mykal."

Eileen hugged her middle. "And have you tell me he never once spoke of me? That he hasn't spared a single thought for me?"

"That's not true." Derron sat beside her. "Todrak hoped to use me to barter your freedom."

Surprise rounded Eileen's eyes. "He did?"

"He didn't like it when I alluded we were friends."

Eileen's face softened with a smile, though it didn't reach her eyes. "My father would have used you to barter for Asharaya's throne. He doesn't care about me."

"You're his daughter. Of course he cares." Though Derron remembered having a similar conversation about his mother with Arkael. "I'm sure if he had the chance—"

"But he did." The words shocked Derron into silence. "My father didn't say a word when I saw him. He hardly looked at me." Her voice shuddered at the end, but she didn't cry. Eileen might have been raised a southerner, but she had the northern pride.

"When did this happen?"

"The day after his arrival and the day after that, too, after which I asked your mother not to see him."

"And she allowed it?"

Eileen nodded.

"Why didn't you tell me?" At Eileen's apologetic smile, understanding dawned on him. "My mother ordered this?"

"Perhaps she thought you would speak against it."

"The only thing I would speak against is her using you as her pawn." When Eileen didn't answer, Derron scoffed. "Which is exactly what she's doing. We can't control the North. It's too big, too wild."

"I'm a Todrak."

"You've always lived as an Argarys." Derron cursed himself for his callousness the moment the words left his mouth.

Eileen stood so they were eye to eye. "Yes, I lived as an Argarys. And gods willing, one day soon I'll be one." She took his hands tenderly. "Please understand that it wasn't the queen's orders that stayed our tongues."

"Cassia knew this, too? And she's speaking to you?"

"Not much. She's been avoiding everyone, but she would speak to you if you weren't so adamant about avoiding everybody. You even missed Raxan Nahar's departure." Derron couldn't help his eye roll, but Eileen drew back his attention. "We were trying to protect you. Your mother's testing you. After you failed to bring in Asharaya, your every movement is watched, Derron. And gods know you're prone to doing stupid things for love."

"I don't love your father."

"No, but you love Ilahara. You love its people, even those who don't love you." Her voice softened as she said, "And I like to believe you love me, too."

Derron squeezed her hands and then released them, pacing the room. His mind churned with the possible outcomes of his mother's actions. The Daganverans would see Eileen as an outsider. The better option would be to insert another Northern house in Frosthead Hall permanently, but it would take time before Daganver accepted the new rule. Time and bloodshed. The Todrak earned the love and loyalty of their people by being fair and brave. With a move like that, the Argarys would always be villains in their eyes.

"We have to fix this." Derron scrambled to the bookcase, pulling out the crumpled dragon poster. "The first step is figuring out who's pasting these all over Adara. If we put a stop to the dissenters, we may appease my mother and have some leverage in negotiating with her."

"Negotiating my father's release?"

"To pursue a more sensible course of action. Your brother doesn't like me, but he can be reasoned with, and the people know him. We could find an agreement."

"You know that's not going to be enough. Asharaya's still out there. Your mother wants her, and my father won't stop supporting her even when threatened. You know my brother better than I do. Tell me, would he give up Asharaya?"

Maybe for Arkael. Derron's hands shook imperceptibly as he folded the parchment and pocketed it. Ilahara had seen enough bloodshed with the Coup of Fire and the Uprisings fourteen years ago. Derron couldn't let that happen again, not when he was in a position to change things. Queen Aerella wouldn't stop until she had Asharaya, but he would start crossing those bridges when he came to them.

"Will you help me?" he asked.

Eileen sighed. "Do you know where to start?"

"I need to visit an old friend."

12

Cassia

Eyes closed, Cassia listened to the darkness breathing. A river trickled nearby, the sound seeming to echo from somewhere above her, and the rocky wall at her back scraped the skin left exposed by her nightgown. Not a creature scurried, not a bird sang. The room was as empty and lonely as she was. Cassia almost thought she'd imagined it, but there it was again, the purposeful intake of breath and the steady release.

Cassia opened her eyes. She could make out a vast space and an arched ceiling, but nothing more. The ground beneath her was rough and pebbled, slightly damp. When she was young, she'd named the place of her nightmares a room, but in time she realized it was more a dungeon, a cave, or the buried wing of a castle. *Room* was too limiting a word, but it was how she knew this place and the visions that somehow turned from nightmares to dreams.

Who's there? The useless organ in her chest thumped

against her ribcage.

No answer came. The only things in the room had always been the dark and her restless need to get out. That was why she enjoyed being here lately. The dark was the only witness to her tears, her screams, her silence. It knew the depth of her hopelessness and the dangerous slope of her thoughts. A part of her longed for companionship. Another wanted to render the world to cinders so everyone saw her pain, ugly as it was.

Cassia scoffed as she stood, cleaning off her gown. *I suppose I've achieved true loneliness since I'm talking to myself.*

You've never been alone, Cassia, the darkness whispered, a soft rumble sneaking into her bones.

Cassia scanned the dark space in front of her, heart beating so loud she was certain the sound was bouncing off the walls. Though she was curious to follow the sound to its source, fear held her back. She had no way of telling who or what the mysterious voice belonged to—if it was real at all. *Who's there?*

You wouldn't believe me if I told you, the darkness replied. *Who I am isn't as important as why you're here. I thought this cycle of self-pity would end with your brother's return. Why are you still moping?*

Moping? If she weren't convinced she was alone and losing her mind, she would have hurled a shoe at whoever was speaking. Or better yet, her Fire. The maenar had prescribed absolute rest from her power, but the rules didn't apply to dreams, did they? *Since you're so sure of yourself, what would you do in my place?*

I would burn everyone who wronged me, but I'm no princess.

A princess is no match for a queen.

I've never known you to be a quitter, Cassia Argarys. Something in the darkness shifted. A glimmer of bronze, there one moment and gone the next. *You're an ember simmering among ashes, waiting for the wind to help her ignite. The gods have given you plenty of wind lately. It's you who chooses to let the ember dim.*

From where I'm standing, I don't have many options.

Then stand somewhere else.

Cassia squinted, searching for another glimpse of whatever had moved within the shadows. She glimpsed a shape, something large and unmoving that could have been part of the cave wall. Yet her heart beat a little faster as she debated moving closer. *Are you real?*

The darkness chuckled, the rumble warming her to her bones. *Time to go, Little Ember.*

The covers pooled on Cassia's lap. It had been ten days—or was it more?—since Korban's death, and every night she'd dreamed of the room. The darkness had never spoken until today, and for the first time she'd felt closer to the person she'd been when her life was near perfect. That spark of exhilaration was fading now that she was awake. Cassia was tempted to lie down again and hide beneath her covers. She longed for the days when her biggest problem was missing Derron, and Korban would emerge from the tapestry in her room with a clever smirk and smiling gray eyes.

Cassia often relived that dreadful night, retracing her steps and singling out her mistakes. One had been answering her father's fake summons. If she hadn't gone to Vaemor, Korban wouldn't have been abducted from her rooms. Another had been to let Korban pull her aside and kiss her in the empty hallway so close to the queen's chambers.

But Cassia's biggest mistake could be traced further back, when she let a human into her bed. Foolish of her to believe she could keep and dispose of a lover like one did a dress, as if a person didn't have the looks and charm to thwart her plans. By either her mother's hands or that of time, Cassia and Korban were bound to end in tragedy.

Finding her slippers, Cassia donned a robe and padded into

her living room. Though the furnishings were nearly identical to her old rooms, everything was flipped now that she was situated in an opposite hall. A tray with steaming tea and salmon sandwiches waited on the side table. Her stomach growled at the sight. Since Korban's death, she'd been receiving the same breakfast every morning, always warm. Cassia mistook it for her mother's idea of an apology until she noticed a folded note with the letter *K*. She and Korban had been the Embernest's worst kept secret among the servants, and this kindness came from them. After all, it was the maids who cleaned her room and changed her sheets. And yet, they'd kept their secret. Perhaps they'd been Korban's friends. Shame singed Cassia's cheeks. She knew so little of Korban. Some things he'd been unwilling to share, others she'd never asked.

Two letters sat beside her tea today, the envelopes too elaborate to be mistaken as a servant's message. The first bore the Ilah on the wax seal. Cassia ripped through it, skimming through the contents. High Keeper Baramun invited her to the temple from where he'd take her on a small tour of the countryside to speed her recovery. The queen, of course, gave her blessing.

Cassia threw the letter onto the tray with a huff, and her eyes landed on the other envelope. Her chest panged. The copper mask sigil stamped onto the seal meant this letter came from Heartstar. From the Vynatis.

Using a letter opener from her desk, Cassia made sure she didn't rip through the parchment inside. Once it was out, she smoothened the folds before reading the letter's contents. Her belly clamped with a mix of dread and anticipation. She couldn't be certain the letter came from Johan—it could have been his mother, Imiri, who'd always been kind to Cassia. Then again, neither she nor her son had contacted Cassia since she'd broken things off with Johan to follow her mother's wishes.

Her heart gave an involuntary spasm when she recognized the neat scrawl on the page, a scrawl seen dozens of times on letters hidden in a drawer.

Should you need a place to escape, Tyrra's doors will always be open to you.

Johan

There was a black spot on the creamy parchment, as if he'd hesitated before signing and forgot to lift his quill. It mustn't have been easy to reach out after she'd broken his heart, yet he'd done so anyway, all because she was hurting. The realization should have sent her spiraling—if Johan had learned about Korban, then word had traveled as far as Tyrra—and yet she was too taken with reading the words again and again. She could almost picture Johan pacing his room, running his hands through his hair as he thought of what to say. As he pushed aside his pride to offer her comfort.

Gods, she missed him.

Someone cleared their throat, and Cassia clutched the letter to her chest, spinning to face the intruder. A maid stood on the threshold of her receiving room. "Is there anything I can help you with, princess?"

Cassia folded Johan's letter and hid it within her palm. She didn't want anyone seeing or taking it. "Fetch me a dress of your choosing. I'm to meet the high keeper."

The keeper's voice echoed through the half-empty temple. Low fae dressed in simple garb sat scattered throughout the pews along with high fae in finer clothes. Cassia stood hidden behind one of the tall marble columns. The faithful gobbled up the drivel about the gods being just to those of unwavering faith and loyalty, but the gods were nothing but a story invented by people like her mother and Baramun to keep the flock in check.

The rebels might have been Myrassar sympathizers, but at least they worshipped something people had seen, heard, and touched. Something that could kill.

Three people kneeled in prayer in front of the small altar,

where a wooden carving of the Ilah was impressed into the wall. Cassia stepped lightly to not disturb their prayer. A door opened on the left, revealing Queen Aerella and two men. One was Baramun. Her betrothed was as imposing as ever, tall and broad, his golden hair swept away from his face. Surprisingly, he wore only two rings. His black stare was enough to stop the air in her throat.

The queen noticed Cassia. Hands folded in front and heels clinking softly with every step, she walked to her daughter while Baramun spoke with the third man. He was dressed in finery, with a silver and green sash looped over one shoulder. "That's Markos Raemis."

"He's made a considerable donation to the temple," Aerella said.

"I'm assuming he wants something in return."

"I've appointed him as the new captain of the city guard. He has useful connections, and he's a pragmatic problem solver." The queen glanced at the altar, her brow creasing. "When you're queen, there's no room for regret." Cassia had a feeling her mother wasn't talking about Markos Raemis. She wanted to walk away, but she was drawn to the queen's unexpected honesty. As if sensing her daughter had chosen to listen, the queen's shoulders lifted a little higher. "Everything I've done, my sweet, I've done for the Argarys. For you and Derron."

Cassia hated the sting in her eye. Hated how, even now, her heart swelled at the love underlying her mother's tone when she called her "my sweet." She also hated her wavering voice as she said, "I will never forgive you."

"But one day you'll understand."

With a final glance at the altar, Aerella walked away. It was a kindness—Cassia would have despised herself if she'd let her tears fall in front of the woman who'd provoked them.

She sensed the high keeper's approach before his deep voice grated in her ears. "I'm happy to see you're doing better."

"Is this the moment you tell me the gods would be most

pleased to see us wed tomorrow?"

Baramun smiled, though the tic in his jaw betrayed his true feelings. "I was suggesting five days from now, so that my beloved may fully recover from her illness."

Cassia wished she had claws, so she could rake them across his face. He spoke of the Burning as if he and her mother hadn't sent her over the edge. "I still feel quite frail," she lied. "I'm here because Maenar Errigen insisted it would do me good."

Baramun gave her his arm and led her to the temple doors. They trekked down the carved-in staircase. Cassia was forced to walk next to the cliff's wall, when she usually preferred to stay close to the edge. The overhang went to the sea, almost inviting Cassia to jump. If only it would turn to flight.

A carriage as opulent as one of Baramun's ruby rings waited for them at the foot of the stairs. He helped her climb inside and followed after her. Cassia observed the familiar landscape, her spirits withering at the sight of the yellowing lavender fields.

"My brothers grow tired of waiting." Cassia flinched at the sudden sound of Baramun's voice. "They've already put much on the line, especially when they arrested Darrok Todrak."

"Do the Heads of Makkan need to be rewarded every time they serve their queen?"

"The Farwynd's loyalty is unquestionable. The Vynatis, on the other hand, remain suspiciously quiet. Tyrra also shares a border with Daganver. Shouldn't they be aiding to uphold the queen's justice?"

Cassia ground her teeth, refusing to break the stare-off with her husband-to-be. Her past relationship with the Vynatis was no secret, and Cassia was tired of Baramun and her mother using her feelings as weapons against her. Perhaps Johan's letter folded within the hidden pocket of her gown made her bolder, or the darkness's pep talk reawakened a part of her that refused to stay silent. "Your brothers will have their wedding soon enough. What's a few more weeks compared to fourteen years?"

"Does the maenar think it'll take you that long to be at full strength?"

"The stress of a wedding celebration could make me relapse."

The high keeper grinned, dark eyes lowering to Cassia's lips. "Marriage holds little value to shifters. Perhaps we should skip directly to our mating." Cassia simmered, tempted to show her teeth. Baramun chuckled, as if he knew. "I'll enjoy being your husband. I hope in time you'll see the benefits of this arrangement."

"From where I stand, you're the only one gaining."

"You'll be the most powerful woman in Ilahara, second only to the queen."

That's what her mother wanted her to believe. The truth was she'd continue to be a pawn, with no real power outside the one meted out to her from her mother and future husband. "I'll be your shadow, you mean."

Cassia turned to the dying fields. Bent beneath the sun's rays and withering in the brisk air, they looked like her. For days she'd felt helpless, crushed beneath events that had slipped out of her control. But Cassia wasn't rooted to the ground. She could lift her head, if she dared.

All she needed was the courage to stand somewhere else.

13

Shara

The wooden stick made deep grooves into the snow dusting the forest ground. Every line was a battle, the dirt and rocks beneath hindering Shara's work. She missed the fluid stroke of a brush or the gentle scratch of charcoal on smooth parchment, but she'd take any outlet to free her mind. Two days had passed since Glacemir and her throat was still raw from her screams. There were times when she'd see Lord Darrok—or the idea she had of him—in Sanda's stead on the executioner's block and Aerella Argarys swinging the sword.

"Shara?"

Shara blinked and looked up as Mykal extended a strip of dried jerky. She imagined his haunted expression was a perfect mirror of her own. With a shaky smile, she accepted the jerky but the image of Lord Darrok's head rolling across the wooden platform silenced the bite of hunger.

Eat, Asharaya. Deimok's exhaustion merged with her own.

Today had been particularly tiring, with more miles covered to avoid the multiplying patrols they'd encountered along the way. It was as if a dark cloud had tagged along since Glacemir.

Settling deeper against Deimok's flank, she took a tentative bite. Without being able to build a fire, Deimok was their best option to keep warm, albeit not the most comfortable one.

Beside her, Solana massaged the soles of her feet. "Are we close to Daganver?"

Mykal sat across from them, biting into his jerky. "We'll be there in a day, I reckon."

"What is our plan?"

"I'll reach out to my father's allies. With their men and resources, we can put together a force to lay siege on Frosthead Hall. Once we win it back, we can negotiate for a prisoner exchange."

Shara stabbed her stick into the snow. "You think Aerella would release the Head of Daganver for any prisoner?"

"Maybe not my father, but she might agree to Kael. He has no value to her so long as she doesn't know about the soulbond." His voice shook. "She won't kill my father unless she has a solid grip on the North. If she'd wanted him dead, she would have done it already."

"If we take back Frosthead Hall, she'll kill your father in retaliation and to weaken your position." Mykal bent his head against his knees, but Shara pressed on, smoke curling around her fingers. "Your father's allies will be under surveillance. The bitch put bounties on our heads. The patrols get harder to avoid every day. She knows we're coming, Myk. We won't make it three steps into Daganver without being cornered like pigs for the slaughter. I wouldn't be surprised if she sent an army already."

Mykal hit his head against the tree trunk. "Do you have a better idea? This was your plan, too, before Glacemir."

"No," Shara admitted. *Not yet.* "But we need a better plan. I'm not letting anyone else die for me."

"My father would want us to do everything in our power to free Frosthead Hall. He'd never allow the North to fall, even at the cost of his life." Mykal's breath shuddered. "It's not easy for me either, Shara, but this is war. We won't get anywhere without allies, and to get them we need to be ready to make sacrifices. We can't save everyone."

Shara thrust the stick back into the snow and stood. Her dragon's hulking form shadowed the ground, and his heat enveloped her like armor. "I'm going to check for patrols. Keep your eyes open."

"Shara, wait," Mykal called after her.

She stalked away from their clearing and into thicker vegetation, Deimok faithfully at her heels. The more her chest tightened, the more Shara quickened her pace, devouring the path with long strides. Past the snow-tipped pines, lilac clouds rolled in a rose-gold sky as the sun progressively lowered toward the horizon. Shara lifted her head, heedless of the cold flakes. If only she could soar toward them. She longed for the sky, for the freedom she'd known all too briefly before shackling herself and her dragon to the ground.

Deimok nudged his snout into Shara's abdomen, demanding attention. Her fingers skimmed the rough scales over his lips, mere inches away from his sharp teeth. *I don't know if I can do what Mykal is asking of me, Deimok,* Shara confessed in a whisper. To do so felt like ripping open her chest.

That woman's death has touched you deeply.

No stranger has ever died for me. Shara was well-versed in death and loss, and yet it was the first time she mourned a stranger and feared for someone she hardly remembered. *What compels someone to sacrifice their life for a person they've never met?*

You are Asharaya Myrassar. Be it with a brush or a sword, people will fight for the change you represent.

How do they know I won't be as horrible as Aerella?

They do not. But they hope, and that is enough. Though you may not see it now, I know their faith is well placed. In time, so will you.

Shara stretched her arms across Deimok's chest, drawing in his earthy scent. The dragon's pleased purr echoed loudly in her ear. He curled his neck around her in an embrace, cocooning her in his warmth. *Go hunt. You're insufferable on an empty stomach.*

Deimok nudged her playfully. *Return to the camp.*

Shara waited until Deimok's silhouette was no longer visible before leaving the tree's shade. She needed time alone, and the crisp winter air offered a welcome distraction. Through the soulbond, she sensed her dragon as he prepared for the hunt. It was an unusual time for deer, but he'd no doubt find something to satisfy his appetite. The dragon's eagerness warred with the tight knots in Shara's stomach. Her hand drifted to her mother's necklace and her father's obsidian ring hidden beneath her blouse.

I won't go far, she promised Deimok before erecting a wall around her mind, leaving only a sliver so both would know the other was safe.

A white hare peeked from behind a mound of snow, its long ears flicking before it hopped out of its cover. Shara felt more kinship to the spooked little animal than she did with her confident dragon. Sanda's death was a crude reminder that Ilahara was more than its forests, valleys, and rivers. It was the people who hated her, and those who awaited her.

Asharaya is coming, and the dragons will sing again when Aerella burns.

But what came next? Did the rebels truly believe she'd make a difference and somehow lure the dragons back to Ilahara? Would they continue to believe it once they met her, or would they use her for all she was worth and then discard her the way Aerella had done with the Myrassar?

The Argarys queen plagued her mind almost as much as her son. There had to be a reason for all this bloodshed. For all

Aerella had taken from her—her family, her dragon, the sweet boy she'd considered a friend—Shara's need for revenge was as strong now as it had been the day she'd left Havanya. Vengeance was her drive, but what drove Aerella Argarys? What had Shara's family done to warrant Aerella's hatred?

The hare stopped abruptly and jerked its head from side to side, alert. Shara's fingers curled around her dagger's hilt and her breaths evened out, slow where her heart quickened with adrenaline. The forest was alive with sound—a creek murmuring in the distance, an owl hooting within the cover of trees, a bird twittering a song as it returned to its nest, the snapping of wood.

Shara wandered farther than she'd intended, but it was a straight line back to the camp. Despite the steady downfall of snow covering her tracks, she could easily find her way.

The hare dashed, and Shara eased a dagger from its holster. Knees bent and blade angled before her abdomen, she snaked her way around tree trunks. The darkening evening light played to her advantage. The Maiden's shadows called to her, a whisper in her blood growing stronger as night fell. Having her goddess's gifts within reach emboldened her in the unfamiliar surroundings.

It wasn't long before Shara found the intruder. She slipped behind a tree, crouching low. Judging from the breadth of the cloaked figure's shoulders, it was a man. The nearest town was Daganver's homonymous capital, a full day away if one kept a steady pace on foot. There didn't seem to be anyone else, but the stranger looked around as if expecting company.

Shara flattened to the trunk, her heart hammering against the blade pressed to her chest.

Asharaya, what are you doing?

14

Derron

The afternoon sun began its descent over the narrow Adarian streets, and Derron was moments away from removing his coat. Beside him, arm entwined with his, Eileen looked as composed among the crowd as she did in the castle halls. Her cloak's hood sat neatly atop her black curls, protecting her ears from the chill. Eileen browsed the open stalls lining the streets, reserving a sweet smile or a pleasant comment for everyone who tried to grab their attention—an act the vendors and passersby did animatedly at the first glimpse of Derron's silver-blond hair.

Derron couldn't help a frustrated sigh when she stopped to smell some apricots. He knew what to expect when he went into the city without a proper disguise and was used to the obeisance that came along with his title. Yet a new tension in the crowd made him eager to keep moving. While Eileen seemed oblivious to the change, Derron noticed the usual smiles were a tad too wide and the screams for his attention a little too loud. Those who tried blending into the crowd or the alcoves didn't avoid his detection. No matter Derron's actions, he couldn't outrun the shadow of his family name. He would always either be the prince or the usurper. Always an Argarys, never Derron.

When Eileen bought four apricots, the stall's owner kissed Derron's hand as if he'd been the one purchasing her wares. "Something's off today," Derron commented, as he and Eileen walked away. He didn't have a name for the uncomfortable pinpricks underneath his skin, as if something were crawling inside him and trying to push out.

"You're the prince." Eileen munched on an apricot, and then continued, "You should have worn your hood up if you didn't want to be recognized."

"The guards give us away."

Eileen pinched her lips, and Derron regretted his words. The guards were meant to protect him but also to watch Eileen. Her tail wasn't as discreet outside the castle walls.

"I'm sorry. Maybe I'm impatient to get this over with. We have a mission."

"You have a mission. I'm tagging along to see if your plan works."

"What happened to your optimism?"

Eileen gave him a one-shouldered shrug. "Things were difficult while you were gone. The accusations against my family were severe. I tried to help, and for what? There was no love in Lord Darrok's eyes."

"Your father's in a difficult position. Besides, he's not your entire family."

"I only saw my mother once. I hardly know Mykal, and Luna was born after I left. What's the point of caring if I'll always be a stranger?"

Derron swallowed past the knot in his throat. If only his Song could erase the sorrow from Eileen's eyes, but nothing could change the heart, not even magic. "Love is complicated,

Eileen. You can't fight it or explain it."

"Yet my father would deem me a monster if he knew you're my family, too. Perhaps that's why he hates me."

Derron threaded his fingers through hers and squeezed her hand gently. "We are family." *You're like a sister, and that's why I can't love you as you wish I did.* The words were on the tip of his tongue, but he bit them back. Eileen didn't need another reason to be sad.

Adara was the biggest city in the south, thus giving its name to the entire region. Because it had been the home of the Dragon-Blessed for centuries, the Adarians had named the city's sections with dragon parts. The district closest to the castle was Dragon's Womb. Then came Heart and later Wings, the center and the outskirts of the capital. Although the buildings were the same vibrant shades of pink, yellow, and red, everything else gradually changed farther from the castle. The clothes became less refined, the stalls shabbier. In Heart, voices drowned out one another in the streets, the buildings pressed closer together, and neighbors hung their laundry on shared lines crossing opposite windows. The hustle of Dragon's Womb was an orderly chaos in comparison.

Anrea's workshop was nestled in a rose-colored building at a crossroads at the very center of Heart, with no markers besides the murals painted onto the wall. The images had no coherent logic. Lavenders and daisies, roses, birds in flight, flames high enough to devour the building, the shadows of mighty wings that could only belong to a dragon. There were other workshops throughout the city, but Anrea's was the place artists of every kind gathered.

Derron had first found the workshop during the citywide celebrations in honor of the queen's birthday. Anrea and other artists displayed some of their works for the occasion, and a musician played the harp as the queen passed in her silver carriage. Aerella Argarys hadn't deigned them a glance, but Derron's heart soared on the harp's notes and his soul wandered through the paintings. He visited often after that, losing countless hours to magic that went beyond the powers granted by the Ilah. Sometimes he evaded his armed escort in favor of anonymity while walking the city streets. Not that it mattered. With or without guards, everyone knew who he was, and though most artists tried winning the prince's favor by showering him with adulation, they'd made him feel like one of their own.

Eileen squeezed Derron's arm, reminding him of a spooked deer. "I don't like how these people are looking at us," she whispered.

While some tried approaching for a greeting, most gave them a wide berth. Others froze before the Argarys colors or cast suspicious glares their way. "A cold Heart."

"Could you be serious?"

"I'm not joking," Derron said. "This is what I meant earlier."

"Maybe we should head back and return to this folly of a mission with more guards."

"More than we already have?"

A grand space welcomed them inside the workshop, littered with easels, stools, long tables, and a wide array of art supplies. Several clay vases were set in a corner to dry while their sculptor worked on another piece. Two men and a woman sat on a divan, one of the men scribbling in his notebook while his companions chattered over him. Derron vaguely recognized the woman, but she looked away the moment their gazes met. At the end of the room, sitting on plush pillows, others smoked from their pipes. The fragrant lavender and rosemary oils placed in all corners overpowered the stench of tobacco.

Eileen's hood fell from her raven-dark hair as she tilted her head to examine the paintings, her mouth forming an "O." Derron led her to one of the two adjoining rooms. The one they entered benefited from a coexistence of art mediums, but it was the music room. It held four pianos, five cellos, a dozen violins, two harps, and a wall of stringed instruments ordered by size for anyone who didn't bring their own.

"So, this is where you run off to play sometimes?" Eileen said, marveling. Derron neared the closest piano while she observed everything as if imagining the place teeming with people. "How do you get anything done with everyone playing and painting around you?"

Derron glided his fingers over the keyboard, emitting a gentle sound. "The energy is inspiring."

"Hello, stranger."

Anrea walked out of a back room, untying her apron and flinging it onto one of the empty easels. He knew he'd find her at this hour—it had been the whole point of coming so late into the day—and yet seeing her sent a jolt of surprise down his spine. White dust stained her tawny skin and golden-brown curls. Not even the tips of her ears, visible through hair cropped on the sides, were spared. "Your Highness. To what do I owe the pleasure?"

"Couldn't it be that I missed you?"

Anrea scrunched her lips, casting Eileen a glance. "You wouldn't have company if you did."

Derron couldn't help the twinge of red on his ears, which Eileen noticed with a narrow-eyed glare. He hadn't mentioned that he'd also chased other forms of pleasure here, Anrea being one of them. Derron squashed the need to explain himself and skewered Anrea with silent reproach. The woman bit down on her growing grin.

"Your dogs outside my shop are scaring potential customers."

"So, you sell the art?" Eileen asked. Her voice was light, and Derron couldn't tell if he'd imagined the slight edge to her tone.

Anrea arched a brow and studied Eileen with a quick, cursory sweep of her amber eyes. "We have to live somehow."

"You never minded my dogs before," Derron said. *What changed now? Are you hiding dragon banners? Are you sheltering the rebel artists? Are you one of them?* "I wrote to you."

"The queen raised taxes three times this year, twice in the past month and a half." Derron couldn't hide his surprise fast enough. "You didn't know?"

"I've been away."

Anrea edged closer to whisper, "Will it be war with the northerners?"

"I'm trying to fix it."

"By coming to my workshop?"

Beside him, Eileen's silence spoke volumes.

"Derron, the people are worried—rightfully so. Now it's our coin. How long will it be until our children are drafted into the army, used as fodder for the high fae's petty squabbles?"

"It won't come to that," Derron assured her. "Eileen, could you wait outside?"

Eileen looked ready to protest, but the tight set of Derron's jaw held her tongue. With a final hesitant glance from Derron to Anrea, she nodded and joined the guards outside.

"Took you long enough to send her away." Though Anrea's words were teasing, her tone was far from it.

"I had a feeling you were about to say something foolish."

"You mean speak the truth?"

Derron ground his teeth, unable to refute her claim. If any one of the guards waiting outside was listening to the conversation, his every action could damn Derron in his mother's eyes, especially in the wake of his failure in Havanya.

"These are strange times, Derron." Anrea gestured for him to follow with a nudge of her head. "Friends look at each other with suspicion. People are afraid to speak their minds, but they whisper things to exorcise the fear."

"You can trust me."

"I know I can. For now." Anrea brushed her fingers along one of the more abstract paintings on the walls, black and red smudges on a white background. Shapes that had no sense.

"A choice was made long ago," Anrea said. Derron finally

understood. The smaller figure was a man, and the big one, tinged with red stripes, a dragon. Derron recalled telling that exact story in a Havanian marketplace to a girl he knew and dreaded was Asharaya Myrassar.

The mighty Teirak bowing before Garon Myrassar. The first Dragon-Blessed.

Derron's ears whistled with his blood's building pressure. Queen Aerella destroyed any trace of the dragons from Adara except at the Library of Lur. Or so she thought. If Anrea were discovered harboring such a piece—worse, if she was the creator—she'd be arrested for treason. How many images like these were there? How many Adarians held on to the Dragon in secret?

Anrea's gaze held new weight, as if she were waiting for her dangerous secret to ignite a reaction. Derron grabbed her elbow and pulled her close enough that their exchange would appear intimate to wandering eyes. "Do you know anything about the dragon banners?"

"If I knew, I wouldn't tell a soul."

"Then why show me this?"

"In honor of what we shared, and what this place meant to you." *Meant.* Anrea stepped away, and something told Derron this would be the last time he'd see her.

"Are you afraid of me?"

"Of you. For you. Who knows what the days will bring? A new song is rising."

Anrea walked back the way she came, and Derron stood alone in front of a painted dragon, waiting for the stab of pain from the knowledge he'd lost something that made him happy.

It never came.

Because you're already broken. Perhaps it was because he was staring at the dragon, but the voice belonged to neither his twin nor his dead friend. It was hers. Asharaya. *You can't tell the fresh wounds and the old ones apart anymore.*

Derron turned his back on the portrait, on the art, and the

workshop, and joined Eileen outside. Every step Derron took from the workshop was a step distancing him from a chapter of his life. Pressure built behind his eyes, a steady sting. Perhaps he wasn't as broken as he'd feared.

"Did she say anything?" Eileen inquired.

Derron shook his head, though he wasn't sure. It wasn't in the things Anrea had said, but more in what she'd done. She'd taken a risk showing him that painting. Would she risk herself further by riddling Adara with dragon posters?

A crowd formed in the middle of the street, blocking the passage for carriages and pedestrians alike.

"Where is the city guard when you need them?" One of the guards grumbled, pushing away a man getting too close to Derron.

"We should find another way back," Derron said.

"Oh, gods." Eileen pulled him closer, almost shoving him into the people in front of them. "Derron, look."

Someone noticed his silver-blond hair, and the news of the prince's presence rippled among the crowd. The people parted, granting Derron an easy view of the wall. His gratitude fled into the soles of his boots along with his stomach.

Dozens of red dragons were pinned to the wall.

15

Shara

Deimok's presence flooded past Shara's lowered shields, laced with an intense aftertaste of blood. Her dragon had found his dinner after all.

There's someone in the woods, she whispered down the bond, momentarily forgetting none but her dragon could hear.

Deimok's concern flared, so sudden that Shara felt dizzy with its intensity. *Why have you not returned to the camp?*

I think it's a man. Shara waited a moment before peeking over the side of the trunk. *Looks like he's waiting for someone.*

All the more reason to return to the camp.

What if he's one of the rebels? Sanda's executioners alluded to accomplices. Maybe this person was one of them.

Asharaya, do not engage.

A horse neighed and the earth vibrated beneath Shara's feet with the thunder of hooves. The cloaked figure tripped over the tree's roots in his haste to step away. He hadn't fully regained his balance before skirting in the opposite direction, looking like the hare that had alerted Shara of his existence. Only this time, the predators were here.

Shara flattened against the tree at the first glimpse of horses—large, broad-chested beasts that made up for what they lacked in speed with brute force and endurance. The three guards mounting them sported the silver and blue livery of the Argarys, all of them armed. Metal sang as swords left their sheaths. A crossbow's dull thud echoed over the whinny of horses, followed by the whistle of a loosed bolt cutting through air.

Shara peered around the tree, muscles taut as the patrol rode past. Had the cloaked figure been slower, the shot would have found its mark in flesh instead of wood. His luck wouldn't hold for long. The horses were surer on their feet and better equipped to give chase in the snow. Still, the stranger ran, fueled by either fear or determination. His reckless impulse to survive was admirable.

Shara bolted to her feet. The wise course of action would be to run back to camp while the patrol's attention was elsewhere. With a little luck, the snow would hide her tracks.

And the stranger would die.

A memory of Rami's shit-eating grin squeezed her heart in a vise. *The enemy of my enemy is my friend*, he'd told her once. If this stranger ran from the Argarys, what were the chances he wasn't connected to the rebel network rising in Daganver? She could let him die and never know, or she could act now to save this stranger's life and maybe find some answers.

Shara thrust up her mental shields, silencing her dragon's roars. She could feel him raging on the other end of the bond, throwing the full weight of his consciousness into her defenses. For as long as she could, Shara wouldn't let him. She was no longer in Glacemir, shackled into inaction by Mykal's frozen grip. This time, she would do things her way.

Shara sprinted from her cover. One of the horses had almost

caught up to the rebel. She slashed into her palm without breaking pace. Blood poured from the gash, dripping into the snow. The shadows absorbed it ravenously and came alive at the dark song held within each drop. They yawned open at her approach, plunging Shara into a world of depthless shapes and silence where she was incorporeal and as weightless as a leaf on water.

A twisting tangle of shadows came into view. Swift as a viper, she lunged for them and barreled back into the night. Her ears popped with the sudden flood of sounds—panting breaths, pounding hooves, shouts, and the snap of reins. Shara pulled free a second dagger from her sheath as she dropped from a pine's branches and landed on a horse's back. Pain flared at impact, burning between her thighs and up her spine. The horse reared up on its hind legs, and its rider—the guard with the crossbow—squeezed her legs around the saddle, feet digging into the stirrups.

The woman's surprise ended in a gurgle. Shara slashed both daggers across the guard's neck. Blood spurted, its heat bathing Shara's fingers. She dropped the dagger in her right hand and yanked the loaded crossbow from the guard's fingers. Her hands came away red with blood.

Shara pushed the lifeless body off the horse and took over. Despite years spent off the saddle, muscle memory kicked in. Her feet slipped into the stirrups and she eased forward, angled over the horse's center of gravity to accommodate its motion. Every muscle in her core and hips engaged in keeping her balanced while she handled her weapons.

She had only a few seconds to take aim at the rider chasing the rebel, a challenge, given the moving horse and the weight of the weapon causing a burning in her wrist.

The rebel stumbled into the snow, rolling to avoid being trampled.

The guard's sword arced down.

Shara pressed the trigger and the bolt fired with a satisfying *whoosh.*

The rider screamed, but Shara didn't see where her bolt struck. The second guard's horse was level with hers and its rider slashed for her head. The blade missed her by a breadth.

Shara shifted her grip on the crossbow and sat upright with the horse's motion, bellowing as she pummeled the weapon into the guard's face.

The attack was messy and unbalanced. She fell off the side, her left shoulder absorbing the worst of the impact with a loud pop. Stars danced in Shara's vision. She yowled, but adrenaline kept her moving. The guard had fallen off her horse. Blood coated the right side of her face and dripped copiously in the snow. Had she been human, the injury might have killed her. Instead, the guard crawled across the bloodied snow toward her sword at the same time Shara rolled to her feet and lunged. She snatched her dagger and was upon the guard as her hand closed around the blade's pommel.

With a growl, the woman tried one last, desperate swipe for Shara, but there was little strength behind the attack. The crossbow's blow hadn't killed her but made her movements sluggish. Shara evaded the sword with ease and plunged her dagger into the woman's chest. The woman's hold on the blade immediately slackened as blood bubbled from her lips.

The blade disappeared within the woman's chest, but Shara pushed it deeper. She'd underestimated a fae's endurance to stabbing once. *A little deeper and you would have ended me,* Derron had taunted her from the Keep's rooftop. She wouldn't make that mistake again.

Only when the woman's chest stilled and not even the whisper of a heartbeat echoed beneath Shara's hands did she lean back. Pain flared in her shoulder, and shivers racked her body even as she burned up. With shaking fingers, Shara eased the fabric of her shirt over her shoulder. Purple bruising surrounded the bulge of her dislodged bone. Even the brush of wind made her whimper. She grabbed her left wrist and squeezed her eyes as she stretched her arm straight and forward. "Dragon, Maiden and all five fucking gods," she cursed. Any more of this and she'd drop dead where she kneeled.

Shara squeezed her wrist and pulled.

Her scream was louder than her shoulder's pop. Shara cradled her arm to her chest. Hopefully fae healing would take care of the pain quickly. Until then, she gathered a handful of snow and pressed it to her shoulder to help with the swelling and hurt. As she made to stand, thunder drew her eyes skyward.

Dark wings stretched against the navy blue sky. Shara bolted to her feet as Deimok screeched. Branches clung to his body where he'd torn through trees. He might as well have drawn an arrow to point out their location.

When the dragon identified her, his screech was less anguished and more relieved. Shara winced at the snapping branches succumbing to Deimok's mighty build.

Are you trying to get us killed? Shara asked the dragon as they stalked toward one another. She wished she could be angry with him—and perhaps she was—but to see Deimok airborne, even for a few stolen moments, lifted a weight from her heart. A dragon was meant for the sky, not the confines of a forest and long treks on land.

Deimok chirped as Shara brushed his face, the touch an apology and a reassurance. He sniffed at her injured shoulder. *I'm all right.*

Movement at Shara's back caught Deimok's attention. His nostrils flared, crimson eyes brimming with rage. Shara spun as her dragon roared. She nearly laughed at the unfolding scene. The horses were long gone, but the guard who'd been chasing after the rebel was dead in the snow, lying beside his cowering assassin.

The rebel was a man after all. She couldn't make out much of his features beneath the hood, but the sharp, pointed chin didn't lie. "It's you," the man said, in a voice rough but pleasant.

Shara caressed Deimok's neck. She doubted she looked very regal, bloodied up and dirty as she was, but she stood straighter. She hadn't felt more like herself in a while. "I have questions, and you're going to answer them."

16

Derron

After ripping a banner from the wall, Derron ordered the rest of the parchments removed and tasked two guards with organizing a patrol for the city guard. Any other dragon banners were to be taken down. If they were lucky, the damage would be under control by the time news reached the queen.

Eileen looked upon everyone with suspicion. "How did no one notice? There's no way anyone could hang all those banners without witnesses. Are the people afraid of the rebels or do they agree with them?" Both options were valid, although with the queen raising taxes and the low fae's worry over war, the rebels garnered sympathy with each dragon they painted.

Once they returned to the Embernest, Derron sought the queen in her quarters without success. Queen Aerella was sequestered in the council room with her general and some of her closest advisers, and the guards were under orders to deny everyone, including the prince. Derron pretended the rebuff didn't sting but holding the guards' stare had been difficult. As the crown prince, Derron's place was by the queen's side. That she was keeping him away was further proof that whatever trust she'd placed in him was broken. It didn't matter that Derron had battled his conscience for the Argarys legacy and almost died multiple times for that same purpose.

He'd found a brother only to disappoint him. He'd met the ghost of his dead friend in an assassin's fierce eyes, only to betray his memory. Yet Derron's failures would always weigh more than his sacrifices.

Hours later, when the sky turned a sad shade of dark blue, Semal found Derron in the library. He looked tired, his short hair mussed as if he'd been running his hands through it. "Your mother wishes to see you," he signed.

"She has a funny way of showing it."

The general squeezed the prince's shoulder, and Derron shut the book he'd been reading. "Fine."

Derron's hand stopped a breadth from his mother's door at the sound of voices, one belonging to the queen, the other to Vaemor. "The renike may render his thoughts unreliable."

"We'll diminish tonight's dose, if it'll ease your mind. Just get it done." Venom coated the queen's voice. "If your dirty half-breed is soulbound to Darrok's son, I want to know."

The words shocked Derron enough that his fist struck the door of its own volition. The two quieted, and Queen Aerella allowed him inside. While she sat on the divan, Vaemor stood in the corner as unmovable as a statue. With his long hair bound back, his face looked sharper in the candlelight. Seeing his parents together during informal occasions was uncommon, unless they were conspiring. Somehow, Aerella suspected Arkael was bound to Todrak, but she couldn't mean for Vaemor to use his abilities on him. Being the king's son, Arkael was immune to the Song.

Darrok Todrak wasn't. The lord's memories would confirm the queen's suspicions.

The queen wasted no time with pleasantries, and Derron forced himself to appear calm. "One of our spies sent word through the water network." It meant the news came from a merfolk under Vaemor's thumb and in Grandmother Catlana's pocket. "A dragon was spotted not far from Daganver."

Asharaya's name clamored in Derron's emptying mind. "When?"

"We received the news moments ago. I've already issued an order to put the beast down. Let's see how well Asharaya fares without her pet."

"I'm surprised it's been able to hide this long," Vaemor commented.

"The beast is resourceful, I'll give it that, but once we put it back in the grave it crawled out of, Asharaya will be as good as defeated. She has no allies, no armies, no resources."

Memories of conversations with Elon blended with the hours spent poring over tomes in the Library of Lur. *Dragons are the Ilah made flesh. They can glamour themselves better than any fae.* Though his mind formed the words, Derron didn't release them. Surely, as Gailen Myrassar's closest adviser, his mother knew the dragon's ability. Yet, her irritation was evident when she spoke of its evasiveness. Derron should share his knowledge in case he was the only one privy to it.

Then again, the queen hadn't asked for his counsel.

Derron would never forget the dragon's ferocious attack to defend Asharaya in Merania. That he'd flown now could only mean he'd sensed danger. That *she* was in danger.

"Did they see anyone else?"

Derron didn't waver despite the tightness in his throat that had nothing to do with the subtle narrowing of his mother's brows.

"Only the dragon." She folded her hands in her lap and tilted her head to the closest armchair, inviting Derron to sit. Conscious that his mother watched his steps, Derron approached the chair warily. "We mustn't allow our enemies to gain ground, which is why we must act fast. I wished to give Eileen more time, but if we wait for her Bleeding, it could take another five to seven years."

If Derron swallowed ice, his intestines wouldn't be half as numb as they were now. "You're not suggesting I marry Eileen before she bleeds."

"It's not a suggestion. You'll wed a fortnight after Cassia."

"A reasonable time," Vaemor agreed. "Derron's wedding won't obscure the grand celebration the Farwynd desire."

"We'll ask Baramun to feed the people some nonsense. Let him say the gods appeared to him in a dream and allowed the early union of two kindred souls." Derron hardly heard the rest of his mother's words over the roaring in his ears. "Peasants and nobles alike guzzle that sort of drivel like wine."

"Mother." His voice came out oddly smooth. "The people will see through this sham. It'll look like I'm staking my claim on Daganver."

"And?"

"First, you imprison its Head in our dungeons, and now this? War will be inevitable no matter what offer we bring to the table."

"The Todrak conspired against us. There's nothing to negotiate. Daganver deserves every lick of flame I'll rain down on them."

"Lord Darrok won't concede the North to Eileen. He won't even look at her." Derron banished the image of Eileen's crestfallen face and gripped onto the sheer desperation of veering his country away from bloodshed.

"If he won't see reason on his own, I'll make him see it." The words she didn't say hung between them. His mother had never hidden her dislike of the Song, but to ensure their survival—to protect her rule—she'd use any weapon at her disposal. "Eileen's a Todrak, and once you're wed she'll be an Argarys."

"Mykal Todrak is the heir. He's still alive."

"For now."

"You expect me to kill my betrothed's family and then marry her?" A mirthless laugh tumbled out, catching Derron by surprise. The only sound he'd expected was a scream stuck somewhere between frustration and panic. "Mother, please. There's still time to stop this madness from unfolding. A way for peace."

"You said so yourself, Son," Vaemor said. "Peace is a fickle illusion not even our Song could conjure."

Derron shook his head, leaning farther out from the chair. "Cut the taxes. The Adarians are weary, and your subjects from the other territories won't look kindly to you if their Heads enforce your taxes. The rebels would have a harder time plastering those dragons all over the city if the people were on your side. Broker a peace with Daganver. Tell Lord Darrok you'll let bygones be bygones if he abdicates in favor of his son. Exile him to another territory, if you must. Makkan, or Merania."

Queen Aerella fisted her gown, her knuckles bone white. "Consider your next words carefully."

Derron was past caution. If there was anything he dreaded more than the threat of his mother's Fire, it was the idea of looking at his reflection one day and finding a man who'd followed his fear instead of his heart. Gods knew he'd already damned himself enough. "Darrok Todrak might listen to you if you swear to offer Asharaya a truce."

Silence had never been quite this loud.

"Asharaya hates us, but she hates the idea of innocents dying more. She'd accept a meeting." If only to drive a dagger through his mother's heart, Asharaya would agree to anything. Derron was sure of it. "Fuck it, if not a truce, then a duel. You against her."

The queen's answer dropped like a stone in a long, dark well. "No."

"Then her against me."

"No."

Derron shot to his feet. "You want Ilahara to bleed?"

The queen followed suit. "I've taught you to be strong, yet I look at you and see a mewling kitten, not a lion. Truce, compromises. These people would see us dead the moment we bare our throats to them. Ilahara will bleed three times over before I surrender to your ridiculous notions of honor and peace."

Show your power, hide your heart.

Derron had hoped his mother's love for their country would outweigh her pride. A fool's hope.

"What do you know of the half-breed?"

"I told you everything I know." Derron couldn't show his surprise at the queen's sudden question. Catching people off guard was one of her favorite ways to reveal liars in her midst.

"I hope so, Derron. For your sake." The queen eased back in her seat but remained as vigilant as a viper. "The next time you disappoint me will be your last."

A knock on the door interrupted the strained exchange between mother and son. The king answered, and a guard opened the door. "Your Majesty. My king, my prince. The princess has returned."

"Baramun takes liberties," Vaemor said. "She's been gone the entire day."

Derron skin crawled. "You allowed Cassia to be alone with him?"

"She'll be his wife soon enough," Aerella said.

"Propriety isn't what concerns me. How many times is she going to have to tell you that man disgusts her before you listen?"

"Cassia will do what she must for this family. Will you?"

Derron all but slammed the door on his way out. What did war have to do with his family's welfare? And marrying Eileen...though it would be an advantageous match, Derron had no desire to be lord of the North, and even less to take advantage of Eileen's feelings in the name of politics. She'd see her love crowned by marriage, not how miserable Derron would make her in the long run.

His feet carried him to Cassia's old chambers out of habit. He realized his mistake when he spotted the charred spots on the wall, yet Cassia was there, standing at the end of the hall staring at the ruin she'd unleashed. "Hey," he said gently.

"Hey."

A moment stretched into eternity as the twins stared at one another. A chasm Derron hadn't been aware of slowly knitted itself. He was tempted to reach out and take his sister's hands, but he held back. Derron had seen Cassia happy, scared, and angry, but never hurt. Not like this.

"Did you murder the high keeper?" Derron flinched once the words were out. Standing on the site of Korban's demise, his had been a poor choice of words.

Cassia's smile was razor-sharp. "He lives." She gestured to her neck, where a large necklace with far too many rubies rested against her collarbone. "I think he's trying to woo me. He wore only two rings today."

"As if jewels could impress you."

"Immense adoration does wonders for my ego." The words didn't deliver the levity they were meant to. Cassia surveyed him from top to bottom. "You look like shit."

"It's been a day."

"Let me guess. Mother told you you'll marry Eileen."

Surprise hit him like a punch to the stomach. "You knew?"

"It was only a matter of time. She doesn't show it, but she's desperate." Cassia shook her head, a small "V" creasing the space between her brows. For a moment, Derron saw Arkael instead of their sister. "Eileen is kind, smart, beautiful, and she's smitten with you. She's the key to the biggest territory in Ilahara. There's literally no fault in her, yet the moment someone mentions marriage you seal shut like a clam."

"That's not a very flattering analogy."

Cassia stepped close enough they almost shared breath.

"Did you hesitate because you care for her?"

Air rushed out of him. She'd named no names, but he perceived she wasn't talking about Eileen. Derron could have protested and denied, he could have laughed away her accusation. He wanted to do those things, but the words stuck in his throat.

Cassia turned away with the confidence of someone who'd won a duel. "Careful with your heart, brother. These days it's easy to lose."

17

Mykal

Myk, go after her.

Instead of listening to his Do'strath's disembodied voice, Mykal threw his head back and muttered a prayer to the Dragon. He'd never been good with words. Not because he lacked them, but because his mind and his tongue didn't always communicate, and there was no predicting the damage that disconnect could generate. *Because you're honest*, Kael would say. Mykal blamed it on the bone-deep exhaustion that had taken permanent residence inside him. The longer it did, the more detached he felt from anything but his own loneliness. He should have been proud of Shara—proud that his queen could mourn a stranger's death and refuse to gamble with people's lives. Not too long ago, he would have done the same.

But not too long ago, he'd had Kael. Without him, Mykal was a husk—empty, hollow, and rotting inside. Basic needs like breathing, drinking, or eating were reflexes. He no longer found enjoyment in scents that once brought him comfort or in the sugar-sweet taste of berries that used to be his guilty pleasure. All he could think was that Kael was gone, alone in a godsforsaken dungeon in Adara, and that Mykal wasn't with him. How could he guide Asharaya to victory in this state? Was this the Dragon's way of teaching him humility for the glory and fame he'd desired?

I've learned my lesson. Now give him back.

If only it were that simple. Deities were quick to punish and slow to reward. He feared that even one more day of this torture would twist him into something Kael would despise.

"Shouldn't you go after her?" Mykal asked Solana, who sat against a tree. He should have spoken Havanian for her benefit, but his dexterity with the human language hadn't improved in the brief time spent on the Human Continent and aboard the *No One.*

Solana munched on the last of her berries. "It is best to give Shara room to brood on her own. The dragon is with her. She will be all right." She pulled a small knife from her boot. The number of blades hidden on her person increased each time they ran into hunters or patrols. "Do not worry for Shara, lordling. My sister is not one for quitting. Once she makes a promise, she does not go back on her word, and she does not stop until she succeeds."

"Lordling?" Mykal lifted a brow.

"You were calling me 'Selena' until not long ago."

Mykal harrumphed and Solana gave him a small smile in return.

"Shara will see this war through," she said, solemn. "Of that, you can be certain."

Mykal propped his elbow onto his knee, snowflakes dusting the back of his hand. Across from him, Solana raised her hood and tucked the cloak tighter around her slim frame. Only the tip of her nose, the plump shape of her lips, and the round curve of her chin remained visible. Her hands emerged from the cloak's folds—reddened despite the gloves she wore most of the day. She nicked her thumb and drew a straight, bloody line from her bottom lip to the dimple in her chin. Solana performed this same ritual every night for the past week, and like every time before, not a single shadow stirred.

Mykal had seen this woman mastering darkness in broad daylight and ripping apart the fabric of the world at the risk of her own life. Even with his limited knowledge of the human goddess's magic, he knew something wasn't right.

"Why do you do that?" he asked when he could no longer rein in his curiosity.

"I am praying."

"For?"

Solana didn't reply.

She's praying for Captain Xoro, Myk. Kael would have known how to comfort Solana, but Mykal lacked his Do'strath's tact. He knew only how to be suspicious of others until he wasn't. Once again, Mykal shuddered at his own selfishness. Kael's loss was terrible, but at least he lived. Mykal couldn't fathom the desolation in Solana's heart. All this time traveling together and he hadn't offered a single word of condolences for the No One's captain.

"I'm sorry," Mykal blurted out, the barest hint of heat warming the tip of his ears. "About Xoro."

Solana's quiet assessment could strip a man bare. He fought the urge to cower until her throat bobbed and she dipped her chin in acknowledgment.

The tension in Mykal's shoulders slowly eased, and then the dragon roared, and it returned tenfold.

Mykal jumped to his feet. Deimok was a shadow reflected against the dawn as he took off flying.

"Has he gone mad?" Solana asked. "He will give away our position."

The dragon's call rang in Mykal's ears. That high-pitched note sounded desperate, and it resonated to the weakened, numb thread of magic stitched into Mykal's soul.

"Shara's in trouble."

By the time they reached the general location of Deimok's landing, Mykal's legs ached. He didn't dare imagine the agony plaguing Solana's body, but the assassin hid her fatigue well. Mykal nearly gagged on the reek of blood contaminating the fresh breeze of his homeland.

"You were right," Solana panted. "We should not have left her alone."

They followed Deimok's roar a short way deeper into the forest and found the dragon's hulking form among the pines. His protective stance meant Shara was alive if not unharmed.

"I have questions, and you're going to answer them."

Solana launched her dagger with deathly precision.

Three imprecations rose at once—Mykal's in Ilahein, Shara's in Havanian, and that of the man lying in blood-drenched snow, Solana's dagger now pinning his cloak to the nearest trunk.

Mykal took in the slaughter as he stepped into the clearing. There were three corpses: A man with a crossbow bolt in his back, a woman with a ruined face and a chest wound still leaking blood, and another woman not too far behind. All wore Argarys colors.

As Solana sauntered over to the man, Mykal's eyes raked over Shara's figure. Apart from the purple bruising on her shoulder, she seemed unharmed. Judging by the blood on her, she must have been the one to fight off the guards.

"What happened?" he asked, as Shara adjusted her shirt.

"Nothing I couldn't handle."

The man grunted as Solana forcibly yanked back his hood, tugging his thick hair in the process. Slick strands of ebony toppled over his forehead, shadowing sharp, gray eyes so light they were only a few shades darker than the snow. The color was even more striking against his tawny-brown skin. He didn't have Raxan's overwhelming beauty or the classical perfection of the Argarys, but the sharp lines of his young face held a roguish allure. Mykal was instantly distrustful.

"I'm not a threat," the man addressed Solana with a raking voice.

"I would not expect you to admit it if you were."

Shara placed a hand on her sister's shoulder. Mykal could have sworn the fae held his breath when her golden Myrassar eyes leveled on him. "You're one of the rebels, aren't you?"

The man gave a stiff nod. "My name is Jaero."

"I'm Sh—Asharaya. And this is Solana and Mykal."

Jaero acknowledged Mykal with a look. "I know who you are."

Shara pulled free the dagger pinning Jaero to the tree and handed it back to Solana. The assassin leisurely stroked the blade instead of putting it back in its sheath. Jaero must have recognized the gesture for the silent threat it was. He stood, never removing his attention from Solana's hands. Mykal almost chuckled.

"Who were you waiting for before you were attacked?" Shara asked.

"You, Your Majesty."

"Titles aren't necessary."

Mykal snatched Shara's elbow and forced her back a step. "How did you know she'd be in that forest? Have you been following us?" Though he doubted anyone would have made it past Deimok's detection.

"Not in the way you think." Jaero glanced at him, but it was to Shara he looked when he replied. "Ares saw her."

"Who the hell is Ares?" Mykal prodded.

"A friend," Jaero said. "A seer."

"Another who believes this nonsense," Solana muttered in Havanian.

"Another who doesn't."

Mykal's jaw slackened at Jaero's perfect Havanian. Most fae didn't speak the language of their human servants, and those who did only learned the basics. Even Mykal, who'd made an effort to learn for Kael's sake, was nowhere close to mastering the language. And here was this fae speaking it as if it were his mother tongue.

Must you always be this suspicious? Kael's ghost asked.

Must you always be so trusting?

Shara's discomfort bled through to her tone. "It's not the most absurd thing we've heard. You wouldn't even know I'm alive if it hadn't been seen."

"That seer had been spinning prophecies for Aerella for years," Mykal rebuked. "Her powers were verified."

"I have proof in my cloak."

Warning bells sounded in Mykal's ears, but Shara nodded and Jaero produced a white sheet of parchment from his cloak. Shara unfolded it, revealing the red outline of a dragon's profile. She wasn't fast enough to mask her surprise. "What's this?"

"The Rising's symbol. Myrassar sympathizers are painting it all over Ilahara," Jaero explained. He rotated his index finger. "Flip it."

Shara did, slowly. The disorganized script had an arrogant feel to it. *A new song is rising in the cold, among the trees. Find it at the Veins closest to the Ice's heart.*

"This is gibberish," Mykal said.

Solana sheathed her dagger with stunned slowness. "It is a code."

"Asharaya Dragonsong is in the northern forest. Find her at the Veins closest to Frosthead Hall," Jaero translated.

"What are the Veins?" Shara asked.

"It's easier if I show you."

18

Kael

Kael's vision blurred behind a thin film of tears. He'd been questioned again. This time, the general had taken his time breaking the bones of his hand one by one. The littlest finger and the ring finger of his left hand bent at odd angles, and his thumbnail was partially ripped off. Kael had barely been conscious by that point. Even the queen's incessant questions had begun to run together. One sentence, however, rang through his mind. The one she'd said again before she left.

This would have been less unpleasant if you hadn't been Vaemor's son.

Rationally, Kael knew the queen meant she would have used her husband's gift to compel the answers out of him if Kael hadn't been immune to the Song, but he wondered if she wasn't being vicious out of spite. Without magic to heal him, Kael had to set his bones on his own. He'd done it for his nose, arm, and fingers. If only he could do something about his knee, bruised ribs, or swollen lip.

Gently, Kael touched his broken fingers and hissed through clenched teeth. A tear dripped from his lashes, leaving a searing path down his bloodstained cheek. Besides the pain, Kael also had to live with his stench and the progressive worsening of his cell's state. The guards were giving him no water to wash himself, and his chamber pot remained dirty more times than not. He was treated no better than a pig for slaughter.

Kael took quick, short breaths, and then swallowed.

Come on. Mykal's voice came to him like the light at the end of the Siren Coves. Kael's imagination filled the gaps in their dwindling bond. *You've been through worse.*

For a moment, Kael believed Mykal truly spoke to his mind. "Like?" he rasped.

My mother's lectures. He imagined Mykal's grin. *The sirens were nasty, too.*

Kael released a wet sound halfway between a sob and a laugh.

Then he set his bones straight.

He couldn't help the whimper escaping his lips, as he couldn't help the cries when he was with the queen and the general. The questions were always the same. *Where is Mykal Todrak? Where would he hide? What would Mykal do? Who's supporting your cause?*

How do I find Asharaya?

Kael would sooner die than reveal anything to Aerella Argarys, but he feared his body would betray him in favor of the primordial instinct to survive. His only relief was that he truly didn't know Mykal's whereabouts or what he and the women would do. Still, the risk he might accidentally doom his friends was a nightmare worse than the torture itself.

He imagined the gentle touch of nimble, calloused fingers across his forehead, wiping away the fevered beads of sweat from his skin. The smell of ginger lilies and vanilla surfaced from his memory to replace those of his filth. *You'll never break*, Solana said in Havanian, his mother's language. *You're stronger than them.*

"Lana." Her name was a rasp on his parched lips. He could almost see her, long raven hair falling over one shoulder, and brown eyes that remained sweet despite a life made of blood and sacrifice. Kael leaned closer to her parted lips, her soft breath like air to his tired lungs.

A beautiful ghost come to take his pain away.

The cavernous halls echoed the sound of approaching footsteps. Kael scrambled deeper into his cell. His chamber pot's stench was almost unbearable, yet it wasn't the reason for the fresh tears in his eyes. It couldn't be the general already. Kael needed more time.

Too soon too soon too soon.

The steps stopped right outside the door. Kael held his breath, bruised ribs aching. Whoever was on the other side had paused, and somehow that worried Kael more. There was no telltale sound of keys turning in a lock. Instead, the panel in the rectangular hatch in the door opened to reveal bright silver eyes.

"You." Kael's surprise was too great for his loathing to register in his tone.

Derron took in the sorry state of the cell and of Kael himself. The prince's face was unreadable, with neither the hint of the queen's disdain nor a trace of the guilt Kael longed to see, if only for the pleasure of denying him absolution.

Kael didn't question how Derron was here. He was the prince. "Took you long enough to come and gloat."

"I know there are other people you'd rather see," Derron began.

"Not really." Seeing his friends now meant their capture and a fate worse than his. He rose to his feet, wincing. Silver met blue as the brothers locked gazes through the hatch separating them, immobilized by the curiosity and distrust that had been a constant in their every interaction. "Did you find them?"

"No. But a dragon was spotted several hours ago."

Kael's throat burned with his panicked intake of breath, the feeling quickly accompanied by suspicion. He'd trusted Derron once, and then he'd shown how wretched his heart was and ambushed Kael and his friends. Kael limped forward and tried looking past Derron, though it was difficult to tell if the prince was alone. "What are you doing?" At Derron's frown, Kael pressed on. "If you're trying to break me, it won't work."

Derron slipped a rolled piece of parchment through the hatch. Kael's fingers throbbed as he took it. A dragon's long taloned wing winked up at him as he unrolled the parchment, followed by a mighty head and its powerful body. "What's this?" Kael asked.

"A cry for help."

Kael looked from the painting to the prince, arching a brow.

"You were right. I couldn't do anything during the Coup, but I can now." Derron gestured for Kael to return the painting, and then let two small pouches slip into the cell.

Kael caught them out of instinct, looking at the brown leather bags dubiously. One smelled like rosemary.

"One is for the swelling, the other for the pain. Chew them together," Derron explained. He then slipped a loaf of bread through the hatch. It was still warm, and the freshly baked aroma set Kael's empty stomach to grumbling. "I couldn't hide a larger one."

"How do you know these will work?"

"The queen is onto you and Todrak. Don't give her any more reasons to look deeper. Give her something, Arkael. It's the only way to protect him."

There it was, the ulterior motive behind the unexpected kindness. "I'll never betray Mykal."

Derron was grim. "You might not have a choice."

19

Shara

As they followed Jaero across blood-streaked snow, Shara retrieved her daggers and Mykal busied himself looking askance at Jaero's back. Her friend's guarded attitude sharpened her own unease at the seer's message. Growing up in Havanya had hardened her against those who claimed to see the future in cards and stars, but Ilahein seers were different. She couldn't deny the truthfulness of their visions, though the idea of her future moving along a charted path was unnerving. If Ares was privy to it, how many others were? Sight was a rare gift, but if Aerella got her hands on another seer, she'd be harder to outsmart.

Thoughts of the queen came hand in hand with those of her son. Shara hadn't dreamed of Derron again after seeing him in the Embernest gardens—a dream she'd forcefully cast from her mind. She'd made no mention of it to anyone but Deimok in the privacy of their shared bond, and they'd both agreed dreams were just that—dreams. Alarming the others when they had so much on their plate seemed pointless, but her mind would circle back to it when she least expected it. The surprise on Derron's face, as if she were a ghost. She itched for her sketchbook, if only to capture that look on paper and remove it from her mind for good.

Jaero led them to an old hollow tree, its large roots half buried in snow. A small dirk glinted in his hand. Deimok hissed, Shara and Solana's blades found their palms in a perfect duet, and Mykal summoned Ice daggers before anyone could blink.

"I wouldn't go against a dragon armed with a knife," Jaero said.

"What do you need it for?" Shara countered.

"To carve a mark on this tree. Unless you'd rather wait for the next patrol." An emotion she couldn't name gleamed in Jaero's eyes, there one moment and gone the next. "So long as we have a common enemy, Asharaya, you've no reason to doubt me."

Shara didn't know if she could trust him, but he hadn't given her a reason not to. She pocketed her knife, gesturing for Solana to do the same. "Go on, then."

The wood peeled off beneath Jaero's knife with little difficulty, like a soft layer of skin. The engraving looked like a cross. Each end consisted of three lines curling in on themselves, the longest in the middle, and the others stemming from its center. They reminded Shara of gusts of wind.

She almost missed the brief blink of sapphire light emanating from the symbol when surprise bounced down the soulbond. *What is it, Deimok?*

Mykal gasped. "The Star of Izhan."

Mykal approached the trunk. He placed his hand against it, and the sapphire light returned in a blaze, glowing steadily instead of disappearing. His wonderstruck expression ignited Shara's curiosity. "Izhan?"

"She was the only Ice dragon in recorded history. In some

accounts predating Garon Myrassar's truce with Teirak, Izhan willed the trees to open so Daganver's fae could hide from the dragons. She transformed into an Ice barrier to shield Daganver from her brethren's flames, and when the dragons left, all that remained of Izhan was this symbol traced in the snow. According to some folktales, our yearlong flurries are lingering fragments of her shield still falling apart to this day."

"Once traced, the trees allow us entry for a short time." As he explained, Jaero lifted his leg into the hollow space, and then flashed Shara a handsome grin.

For a moment, she was reminded of Rami. The two men looked nothing alike. Jaero's features were sharper, and he looked a few years younger. His eyes were a striking gray, not the soft green she'd never be able to replicate in sketches, and his hair lacked the rebellious curls she'd loved to touch. The headstrong attitude, however, and that damned grin were the same.

"Welcome to the Veins, Your Majesty."

A crisp breeze followed them into the Veins, echoing like a ghost's haunting song in the many tunnels beckoning from either side. Gnarled roots dug into the tall dirt walls in silver and sapphire blue gradients, their tantalizing glow illuminating their path.

"Why do they look like that?" Solana asked, her voice softened by awe.

"It's the Ilah's magic," Mykal explained in a reverent whisper.

"You mean the giant tree in the middle of Ilahara?"

Her sister's blunt honesty held little regard for the fae's worship of the tree whose essence gifted their land and blood with magic. Mykal grumbled something about humans and their lack of respect.

Shara tried counting the openings they passed, but the

numbers jumbled in her head. Memories of Merania's intersecting hallways distracted her—the feeling of freedom within their grasp before a Meranian spear blocked her path, Andren Nahar's shark-like smile, the rhythmic clenching of Derron's fists and those silver eyes that gave away nothing and everything.

"How far do the Veins go?" Shara asked Jaero, if only to stay rooted to the present. The roots' glow reflected in the rebel's pale eyes, as unreadable as a sky promising rain without shedding a single drop. How he could orient himself so confidently within the tunnels was a mystery. The openings all looked the same to Shara, with few elements to use as markers.

"There's a vast network beneath Daganver and parts of Tyrra. It'll take time to expand farther, especially closer to Adara."

"Are you actually digging these passages?"

"The first openings we found were like this one, large but disconnected. Tyrrans helped us unite them. Fossorial shifters have more practical uses than predators."

"Are you a meerkat, then?"

The corner of Jaero's lip tipped up. "Until recently, the Veins were mostly used to export food from Tyrra and weaponry and furs from Daganver without going through border clearance. Now we also use them to avoid perimeters around the bigger cities when we're on the move. Most won't let anyone in or out unless they're searched and checked for glamours."

"You must have benefactors if you're able to maintain all that."

"We do."

"Who's funding you in Tyrra?" Surely not the Head, Imiri Vynatis. She'd been one of Jaemys's closest friends, and yet she'd turned her back on the Myrassar to support Aerella's coup in the Uprisings.

"They prefer to stay anonymous, but our contacts are

trustworthy or we wouldn't be having this conversation."

Shara tamped down her suspicion as they stopped at an opening on her right. The glowing roots revealed narrow stairs packed with dirt and rocks that spiraled upward, suggesting the shape of the large, white trunk housing them. "Where do these lead?"

"A friend's home."

Solana harrumphed. "Who grows a tree in their house?"

Mykal shoved Jaero ahead, nearly making the rebel trip over the first step. "After you, pretty boy," he said, and then turned to Shara and Solana. "Stay behind me."

A strong current smelling heavily of sage leaves blew against Shara as she climbed the stairs. Her hair whipped against her face and limited her visibility. She fought to keep up with the others, a growl working its way up her throat. If Ilahara had decided to reject her, it should have done so before she started this dragon-damned climb.

Slamming her hands hard on either side of the tree's walls to steady herself, Shara finally found the final step. The sage was strongest here, tickling her nose like too heavy cologne. As if in mocking, the current eased the moment she reached Mykal's side. His eyebrows shot up in silent inquiry and Shara almost throttled him for looking unruffled. *Damn the northern weather and its obsession with Mykal Todrak.*

"Not a word," Shara warned through gritted teeth.

A flash of sapphire alerted them that Jaero completed his spell, and a rectangular cavity replaced the once-smooth wood. Beyond it was a blur of emerald green and gold, the colors distorting as if one was looking through water.

Mykal craned his head like a confused hound. "Seems a bit colorful to be Daganver."

Warmth radiated from the magical barrier, the sage strong enough to taste. As Shara pushed her hand through, a tickling sensation skipped along her arm. The feeling of vertigo lasted all but a second, the crossing as simple as walking over a door's threshold. The tree jutted from a patch of green at the center of a glossy, wood-paneled floor, its trunk bisecting and twisting toward the ceiling in elegant, pale spires. Moss green and gilded russet-brown leaves hung precariously from spindly branches, some occasionally floating to the ground.

"Definitely too colorful," Mykal mumbled.

Jaero stepped in after him, followed by Solana.

"How can a tree survive without sunlight?" her sister wondered aloud. "There are no windows."

"As most things do in Ilahara," said Jaero. "With magic."

An archway led to an adjacent room, where pillow seats surrounded a low table and a fire burned in a small hearth, likely meant for cooking and boiling water for tea. Portraits occupied an entire wall, fitting together like a puzzle. Some created whimsical scenes with broad strokes, while others were complex portraits of naked bodies or minimalist compositions with lines and bursts of color. Shara recognized an element of the Ilahein regions in each one—the white of Daganver's snow, a man's naked back with an arm stretched on one side and a feathered wing on the other, wolf eyes on a woman's face, and a golden castle on a cliff etched against waterfalls.

While her friends sat on the cushions and Jaero busied himself at the hearth, Shara walked closer to the wall, staring transfixed at her former home.

Looking at the portrait summoned the memory of the waterfall's spray against her skin as she and Deimok flew over the water. Following the castle's watercolor lines, she found her room's window, where she'd sing along with the dragons at sundown. She couldn't see the garden in the artwork, but she knew where it would be, with its fragrant lilacs and bright red and white roses. Once, she would have remembered practicing her stances behind Deimok's wing, but now she saw herself in a red dress that hugged her curves like a second skin, with a handsome prince leaning against a tree, the sunshine gilding his silver hair. Her throat bobbed as she swallowed and looked away.

"Where's your friend?" Mykal asked.

"On a mission in Tyrra. I don't expect they'll return soon." The teakettle whistled, and Jaero removed it from the fire. He'd prepared a tea tray while Shara's back was turned, and he now carried it over to the low table.

"Is that vanilla?" Shara didn't miss the eagerness in Solana's tone. She accepted the cup Jaero offered and moaned at the first sip of the pale blend. Mykal refused the cup with a nose curl. Shara wasn't a fan of tea herself.

Silence stretched between them, broken only by their slurping. Not all of it was unpleasant. The initial tension between Mykal, Solana, and Jaero dissipated enough for them to sit cordially together, and Shara was happy to allow her sister a few moments of tranquility. In Havanya, they'd often spend their afternoons in the Keep's parlor, Shara sketching and Solana sipping her vanilla tea. The normalcy was a welcome distraction, but soon Shara's mind wandered back to the rebels and the Embernest portrait at her back.

She joined the others at the small table, taking a seat by Mykal's side. "How many rebels are in Daganver?"

Judging by Jaero's expression, he enjoyed the vanilla tea as much as Solana. "I don't know the numbers. I haven't been in Daganver long."

"Where were you before?"

"Makkan."

"Are you a shifter?" Mykal asked.

Jaero shook his head, setting down his half-empty cup and staring into it as if it held the secrets of the universe. Like in the forest, he was quick to steel himself. Shara couldn't help but notice that though he was forthcoming with information on the rebels, he was less so when it came to his friends and his personal life. She couldn't blame him. Asharaya Dragonsong she may be, but they were still strangers. She'd have pegged him a fool if he'd lavished her with blind trust.

Mykal must have come to the same conclusion for his expression softened. "In Daganver we don't judge people by the magic in their veins, but by their character. I'm glad you chose to come here."

Jaero's grateful smile was brief and didn't reach his eyes. "The resistance has been building in Daganver long before news of Asharaya's survival spread. I know we're many, but we don't gather often. Communications usually happen through coded messages left in the Veins or in trusted hot spots."

"And you also get reports from other regions?" Mykal asked, the hint of fearful hope in his voice unmistakable.

"I have no news of your father's welfare, my lord, nor that of your friend."

Solana's hand found Mykal's across the table. Shara closed her eyes against the sting of emotion before she asked, "What do you know of the lords gathering in Daganver?"

"Lady Alissa has been consulting with representatives of the high fae families for the past two days, but it's likely that whatever decision is being made comes from Aerella, especially given how often the Hawicks and Yronwoods are seen at Frosthead Hall."

Mykal scoffed, and Shara asked, "Friends of yours?"

"Hardly."

"Lady Alissa will be addressing the people tomorrow," Jaero continued. "Everything the Rising has built in these months hangs in the balance. Every rebel looks to the North. If Aerella squashes Daganver, it won't be easy to keep the dragonsong alive. We can't afford to lose it."

"That makes things simple, then," Shara said. "We'll be at the gathering tomorrow, and we'll see what words Aerella has put into Lady Alissa's mouth."

Mykal nodded in agreement. "It'll give us an opportunity to feel out the high fae."

"Sounds like a plan."

Jaero sipped on the last of his tea. "I suppose it does,

Asharaya Dragonsong."

Hours later, Shara swiped at her tired eyes, careful to avoid the paint staining the back of her hand. Exhaustion weighed heavy on her lids, but she couldn't rest. Her work wasn't finished.

Shara had asked Jaero for painting supplies and a quiet place to check up on Deimok in the forest. Hunters had converged where the dragon was last spotted not long after Shara entered the Veins, and Deimok had to hide to avoid their detection—until he lost his patience. Shara felt full of the meal the dragon had made of his pursuers.

Jaero had led her into a study as extravagant as the rest of the house. Its most peculiar decoration was the shelf overflowing with trinkets and amulets. Either Jaero's friend was a collector of oddities, or they were a shaman of sorts.

As she worked, Shara filled Deimok in on everything she'd learned from Jaero and mentioned the Embernest portrait. The conversation eased into memories, not only of their adventures together but also of the rest of the family. Sneaking into the secret passages with Elon, Uncle Daemian's surprise visits and the gifts he'd bring from every new corner of Ilahara, flying beneath the waterfall with her father, the Myrassar dragons singing around them or diving along. Memory summoned memory, grief and melancholy mixing as easily as the colors on her canvas. As a child, she'd resented the life of the princess. She'd been too young to understand the privileges and comforts that came with it, instead feeling caged by the expectations and rules. All she'd wanted was to fight in epic battles like the dragon riders of old, but now that she was neck deep in a war, her fantasies failed to meet reality. She'd had a good life, and she wished she hadn't taken a moment of it for granted.

Why did she kill them, Deimok?

Must there be a reason?

Shara hadn't believed so. Knowing why her family died

wouldn't bring them back, and ignoring the reasons made it easier to go on. At least, until the fae stormed back into her life and her former friend tried to kill her. Revenge had seemed the only answer to years of grief, but with every passing day one question burned hotter in the back of her mind, as invasive as a siren's song—Why?

A familiar feeling filled the crevices that sadness had left in her soul. Shara burned with it, the heat of rage so strong its smoky taste coated her tongue and warmed the back of her throat. Her past was riddled with death, and if she wasn't careful Sanda's would be but the first of many to define her future. Shara couldn't let that happen. She owed it to her family, to Maenar Elvik, to Sanda, and to the nameless rebels who'd met the same end not to grow hard-hearted. She owed it to herself to put an end to the bloodshed quickly and with as few casualties as possible.

She was a Dragon, after all. A living flame. She wasn't made to sit idle and wait.

The door opened and Jaero peeked inside. "Are you still…" His mouth hung open at the sight of the parchments lining every available inch of the floor. Red paint gleamed, and hundreds of dragons held their maws open in silent screams— both a threat, and a promise.

"How quickly can we deliver messages through these?" she asked.

Jaero blinked through his stupor. "A few hours. If we give them to the right people."

"Do you know the right people?"

"I don't understand what it is you're asking of me."

"Mykal wants to build an army of soldiers, but we won't be able to do that while Aerella keeps the North crushed beneath her boot. We need to free Frosthead Hall, and we need to do it now, not in weeks or months. That's too much time for Aerella to solidify her position and hurt innocents. I won't have more people dying for me." She gestured to the paintings on the ground. "I'm not fighting this war for the high fae of Ilahara. I'm fighting for the people, and it's the people we must look to for help."

"Gods be good." Jaero looked over his shoulder and stepped inside, closing the door behind him. "Are you thinking of attacking tomorrow?"

"For it to work, we need as many people fighting as we can. I need a secure network that won't be intercepted by Aerella's forces. We can't allow the news to spread. The plan needs to be contained if we're to keep an advantage."

The idea had seemed less frightening when it only existed in her head. No one in their right mind would launch the first battle of this war with only a dragon and the hope that low fae would rally to help. The price to pay if she made a mistake was not one to take lightly. She could lose everything—Deimok and her friends, not to mention what Kael would endure as punishment for her actions. Yet Aerella wouldn't expect her to make such a move. She'd stolen King Gailen's crown by knowing the way he thought and acted. Maybe Shara needed to be unpredictable. "I know it sounds crazy," she said. "But I need you to trust me. The only way I can make this work is if you help me."

Jaero glanced down at the dragon banners, his expression unreadable. "Lord Mykal won't agree to this. If your plan fails—and if we walk out of it with our lives—Frosthead Hall will be lost for good."

"Which is why I'm telling you and not him." Shara clutched the ring at her throat, the gold warming against her skin. She liked to imagine it was her father's way of telling her she wasn't making a monumental mistake, and that gave her voice a little more authority when she said, "Can you help me or not?"

Jaero nodded.

"Then help me gather these. We have work to do."

20

Cassia

The day following their outing, Cassia found a new note from High Keeper Baramun. Ruby earrings winked at her from the envelope, sitting alongside a note that read *I enjoyed our time together*. Cassia fit the earrings into the palm of her hand. Light reflected off their single stone. They were less opulent than the necklace he'd gifted her but no less marvelous.

Eileen chose that moment to arrive, let in by the page who'd delivered the gift. "Those look beautiful," she said, with no small amount of hesitancy. Her friend seemed to walk on eggshells around Cassia ever since Korban's death.

"A gift from Baramun." Cassia dismissed the boy and walked back to her bedroom, knowing Eileen would follow. She opened a box on her vanity and dropped the earrings beside Baramun's necklace. "I might keep them. There's no point throwing away perfectly fine jewels."

She headed to the bed, where a dress had been prepared by

her maid before Cassia dismissed her.

"Does this mean you're accepting the marriage?" Eileen asked.

Cassia slipped into her dress and turned in a silent request for help with the strings. She waited for Eileen to approach before she whispered, "I want to rekindle my relationship with Johan."

Eileen tugged the strings a little too tightly, stealing the princess's air from her lungs. "You what?"

"Keep your voice down." Cassia walked back to her vanity, where she pulled Johan's letter out from one of the drawers. "I received a letter from him yesterday. He's offering me sanctuary."

"Your mother will never agree."

"I'll deal with my mother." Cassia hid the letter within the hidden pocket of her gown and grasped Eileen's hands. "Alone I don't have the means to go against them." She didn't dare utter her mother's and the high keeper's names, lest she summon their wrath. "But with Johan, I might stand a chance."

"You can't fight her, Cassia."

"Watch me."

Fear shone through Eileen's brown eyes, yet a smile hesitantly stretched across her lips. She turned their joined hands until she was the one holding Cassia. "For a moment there I worried I'd never see you again."

Cassia pulled Eileen in for a hug, eyes stinging as she inhaled Eileen's sweet scent. "My only regret is that I won't be able to bring you with me."

"Don't worry about me."

Cassia leaned back, holding Eileen's chin so that their gazes met. "Do what you must to survive while we're divided. I won't abandon you, I promise."

Eileen's lips trembled, and she blinked back tears. "Would you like to come to the gardens with me? It's been a while since we spent time together."

There would be nobles in the garden. Their compliments would turn to sneers, their smiles into mocking laughs. Cassia balled her clammy hands into fists and willed the anxiety away. If she avoided the court, she'd only stoke the gossip. Cassia Argarys wouldn't fear those pigeons. They would fear her. Besides, if she played her cards right, this would be one of her last moments with Eileen.

Winter had come to Cassia's favorite place. Most of the flowers withered, and the grass was yellow-green instead of summer's vibrant green. Yet the white roses grew stronger and more beautiful than ever, their fragrance giving life to her dying garden. Cassia ignored a group of courtiers who'd said hello and sat on the bench beside one of the rose bushes, stroking the candid petals with a single finger. Johan's note burned in her pocket. She couldn't bring herself to leave it behind.

Eileen's sudden surprise made Cassia turn. Queen Aerella walked toward them, dressed in a rose gown that sweetened her features. The polite smile she reserved for the few courtiers strolling about was deceptively docile. She stopped by their bench, the smile wavering. "Hello, ladies."

"You look lovely today, my queen," Eileen said.

"Soon you'll call me mother." Eileen beamed, and the queen added, "Could you leave us? I wish to speak to my daughter."

Cassia grasped her friend's arm as she stood. She stared into her eyes as if to memorize every shade of brown in them, their gentleness, before their silent goodbye came to an end.

Aerella sat in the spot vacated by Eileen, and for a moment that stretched on forever she did nothing but glance around the garden at the white roses. Something almost feral awoke within Cassia. Besides his letters, these roses were the keepers of her memories of Johan. Of when she'd been happiest.

"You and Baramun spent a lot of time together," the queen said.

"The majority of it was spent waiting for the servants to fix a wheel."

"Still, that's quite a lot of time. Did you talk?"

"If you're hoping I've suddenly fallen madly in love, you'll be sorely disappointed." No amount of jewels was going to change her mind about this sham of a marriage. Cassia had left the man she loved because she was convinced she'd have to marry someone from Adara, only to find out she'd be marrying a man from another territory. Just not the one she wanted. Yet Eileen would marry the man of her dreams because of politics. If only her mother had made an agreement with Tyrra and not Makkan.

The queen sighed. "When my parents arranged the marriage with your father, I wasn't happy," she confessed. "Vaemor was a cousin I barely knew, and I disliked the idea of being tied to a man who could use his Song on me. But we did our duty, and it wasn't always unpleasant. Baramun may be conceited, but he's not as bad as you believe him to be."

"He looks at me as if I'm a prized mare ready for the mount."

"He lusts for you. There's power in that."

Cassia crossed her arms and looked away.

"You can either succumb to your fate or own it. Baramun desires power, and he desires you. Make him want you more, and soon you'll hold the strings of one of the most powerful men in Ilahara."

Cassia gazed back to the white roses, the memories tied to them bolstering her courage. The only time she'd been truly happy was in Tyrra. Johan's home. Now, he could hold the key to her future, if she was brave. If she stood somewhere else. "Something Baramun said yesterday got me thinking. Tyrra has been quiet. It could be a problem."

"Imiri Vynatis likes to sit on the sidelines licking her paws while others battle it out. She did the same fourteen years ago, despite Daemian Myrassar warming her sheets."

"Gailen's brother?" Cassia remembered a man with a sharp

face, dark, shoulder-length hair, and a devilish grin who whispered in the king's ear. He was a favorite at court, a dozen courtiers always fluttering around him whenever he deigned to show. "I can convince Lady Imiri we're the winning side."

"You want me to send you to Tyrra?" Aerella shook her head. "The Farwynd know of your history with Johan. They won't look favorably on you visiting while you remain unwed, and we need the Farwynd to hold Daganver."

"Would you rather let Tyrra continue their trade with Daganver? The Tyrran crops make up most of the food those people put on their table. Would you rather Tyrra side with Asharaya to spite you?"

"They wouldn't dare."

"You denied them a princess. I think Imiri is pissed." *I'm pissed.*

Her mother's smile was almost sad. "Seeing Johan again will make what you have to do harder."

"If only you'd doled out the same motherly advice with Korban instead of burning it into his flesh." The atmosphere between mother and daughter grew tense. In any other moment, Cassia would have taken that as her cue to leave, but now wasn't the time to act childishly.

She had to go to Tyrra. There had been a time when she thought she'd spend the rest of her days there, married to the future Head, ruling the territory by his side and giving him worthy heirs. Receiving Johan's letter opened a door in her heart and let in a sliver of light. She'd given up on him once to adhere to her mother's plans, and all she'd gotten from it was heartbreak. If seeing Johan again was her last chance to grasp a shred of happiness, she had to take it.

"Let me go to Tyrra, for our family." *And for myself.* "Let me talk to Imiri." *Let me see Johan.* "And..." The words stuck in her throat. "And once I return, I'll marry Baramun on that same day, if I must."

"Marry Baramun now, and then go to Tyrra."

"If I go there as Cassia Farwynd, Imiri will refuse whatever terms I bring." Would Johan even want to see her then? "Dangle me as a potential prize."

Her mother seemed to consider Cassia's words. Cassia had no doubt she could see right through her, but removing the Vynatis from Asharaya's potential allies was as important as keeping the Farwynd happy.

"I'm happy to see you putting our family's needs before your desires and your past, my sweet." *Unlike your brother* was what she didn't say. Cassia's heartbeat jumped in her throat as the queen brushed back a lock of hair from her face—a gentle touch that could turn merciless if Cassia wasn't careful. "Like a true Argarys. You'll leave for Tyrra first thing tomorrow. I want Imiri Vynatis on her knees."

For the rest of the day, Cassia oversaw the preparations for her imminent travel, though her mind was already drifting to Tyrra. Would Johan be happy to see her, or would he regret writing to her once she materialized on his doorstep like a ghost from the past? The bond they'd shared had been special, but Cassia had hurt him, and it led to two years of silence on both of their parts. Still, that he'd sent that letter meant he hadn't forgotten her, as she hadn't forgotten him.

Once her rooms were empty of bustling servants and her bags prepared, Cassia readied for bed. Yet something tugged in her chest, urging her out of her room. An invisible string leading her straight to her brother.

Cassia knocked softly on Derron's door, and footsteps shuffled inside. Derron opened the door, the cut of his shirt revealing some of his toned chest, his hair mostly flung to the right. Candlelight shone behind him in an otherwise dark room. "The sconces are there for a reason."

He stepped aside to let her pass. "I don't need them."

It was one of those days, then. Sometimes, Derron would act

as if he feared nothing. Other times, the memories of their mother's fiery lashing would drive him away from light or fire. "What's bothering you?"

Derron walked to his small couch, where dozens of parchments lay scattered. Cassia recognized the red dragon from the rebel posters and lifted one for closer inspection. "How many of these did you take?"

"Call it morbid curiosity."

Cassia let the parchment fall back onto the coffee table. "I'm going to Tyrra, and I don't want to leave things awkward between us."

"You're leaving?" A beat of silence passed between them, and when Derron spoke again, his voice was as gentle as his eyes. "Do you want to go?"

"I do."

Derron nodded in understanding. "Try to stay anonymous. It isn't safe to be an Argarys so far from home these days." He gave her a small smile. "I feel like we haven't had enough time together."

"It's my fault." Cassia swallowed. "You're the last person I wish to hurt, Derron. This thing inside me...it's vicious. It grows angry and I lash out. I want everyone to hurt, but not you. I'm sorry."

Derron stood and pulled his sister in for a hug. She burrowed her face in his shoulder, savoring his strength, his love. This was what she'd wanted, and she'd pushed him away at every turn because it was better to inflict pain than feel it. What a wretched thing she was.

Cassia leaned back to look him in the face. Her instinct was to tell him the whole truth, as she had with Eileen, but if Eileen would stand aside and let Cassia fight her battle, Derron would be more difficult to convince. She couldn't trust that he would let her do this alone, and she didn't want to land him in more trouble. What she could trust was that when they saw each other again, he'd understand. "I'm going to miss you."

Derron cupped Cassia's face in his hands and brushed her cheeks, as if wiping away invisible tears. "She'll pay for what she did. For hurting you." He remained quiet for a moment as he searched her eyes. "Maybe we should leave."

Cassia arched her brow, the ghost of a laugh on her lips. "And go where?"

"I don't know, but I discovered how we can evade tracking spells. Mother and Father wouldn't be able to find us. You'd be free of this terrible family."

The warmth in Cassia's chest retreated. "You mean I'd spend the rest of my life in hiding."

"Only until this is a safe place for you again."

Cassia remained frozen. In the silence, Derron's expectant expression turned confused. She was suddenly aware of his hands around her elbows and the space separating them. "You're not even asking about the tracking spell."

"What would I do while I wait for our mother to die?" Cassia tore free of his embrace, squaring her shoulders, and Derron blinked, looking stunned. "Would you have me playing the part of the meek and obedient peasant girl? Maybe a nice low fae will love and shelter me and I'll be oh-so-happy. Or better yet, another human—that way I can live my forbidden love fantasies again. I was a fool once, I can be a fool again, right?

"You might be okay with hiding away in some stinking hole to play your music for the rest of your days, but that's not me. I'm Princess Cassia Argarys. People snicker now, but they'll learn to fear me."

"And in the meanwhile, you'll marry Baramun like our mother decreed?"

"I'd rather be miserable and powerful than an inconsolable nobody." Cassia was aware she'd ruined everything again. She'd hurt him—again. "Your heart is in the right place," she said softly. "But I wouldn't give this up for anything in the world." *Not even you.*

Shame warmed her cheeks at the sorrow in her brother's

eyes. "Everything I did for this family, I did for you."

The words found their mark. Cassia held her stomach, as if she could stop the pain blooming there from spreading. She walked out the door, though the invisible string tying her to Derron told her to turn back, to fix what she'd broken. *No, not broken. Never broken.* "Try not to get yourself killed while I'm gone."

The crumpling of paper followed her out.

21

Mykal

Rain and snow dropped in tandem from a gloomy sky, each drop a stab wound in the white piles at the side of the road. If Mykal pulled out his heart, he expected it would be as punctured as the snow. He'd sailed to the Human Continent and back with Daganver like a beacon, and now that he was home, a cold wind howled inside him. The roads lined with small shops were the same, as were the cobbled roads and the trees stretching from the surrounding forest to invade the sidewalks, but this wasn't his Daganver. It was the city of his nightmares, where his face stared back at him from wanted posters and guards in Argarys silver and blue perched like vultures outside shops and at crossroads, glowering at his people.

Two guards forced a vial of liquid—most likely renike—down a young woman's throat, while another rifled through the bags she'd dropped. The resigned expressions of the witnesses suggested it wasn't the first time they attended a similar show of force. Had Kael been there, Mykal would have sought his Do'strath's comfort. Instead, he looked to Shara. Her stillness reminded him of her dragon before a hunt. As if sensing his stare, she faced him, fire burning behind her glamoured brown eyes. In moments like these, it was impossible to question why the dragons had chosen her family over all others. It made Mykal want to channel his desperation into anger and fight, if only to make her proud.

A stone archway led into the heart of the city. Beneath it, Mykal had wondered for the first time if Kael's mouth was as warm as the rest of him. He couldn't bear to look at the stones as they walked beneath it, afraid his eyes would trick him into seeing Kael's dimpled smile. He spotted the blacksmith where they'd forged their first swords, and the tailor where Kael commissioned a gown for his mother's birthday. On the sidewalk was the lamppost Mykal frosted in a fit of jealousy after Kael exchanged a coy glance with a village girl. Every road, shop, and tree was connected to the countless memories they shared.

Towering over it all, past the village's slanted brown roofs, were the towers of Frosthead Hall.

It was all he could do to keep walking without sprinting to the gates. The Todrak's deep blue banners flapped wildly, warping the shape of the growling bear at their center. If the display was meant to mock the people into believing nothing had changed, the military presence was a grim reminder that war was on Daganver's doorstep. As Shara predicted, soldiers swarmed the city. There must have been four times the number of men they'd seen in Glacemir—not just infantry, but cavalry too. On the battlements, archers positioned themselves between each square opening. Surrounded as they were, the smallest misstep could spell their doom.

"I have an errand to run before the meeting," Jaero said.

"What errand?" Suspicion slithered unwelcome into

Mykal's gut. "Were you given a task by the ghosts who kept you scurrying about all night?"

Shara pushed him along and exchanged a long stare with Jaero, nearly making Mykal gag. *Why is everyone so quick to trust a pretty face?* "We'll meet you at the gates."

Once they reached the fortress, they blended into the crowd a few messy rows short of the closed iron gates. Icicles of varying sizes framed them on either side. At their center, Kalran Todrak bowed as Garon Myrassar proclaimed him Head of Daganver and Teirak watched the exchange with imperious indifference. Despite pressure from Adara, his father never changed the engraving.

Mykal's breaths echoed like bells in his ears. He imagined Luna and Kael engaged in a duel in the courtyard and summoned his sister's laughter, the pitter-patter of working servants, and the gentle creak of his father's wheelchair as he moved about the fortress grounds. Moments of everyday happiness, despite the shadow of Rendal's death and Eileen's forced move to Adara.

The fantasy vanished at the first groan of ancient hinges. Mykal's right hand opened and closed, as if to find the comforting grip of Kael's hand. The cloak's string about his neck tightened. All he wanted was to tear it away.

Alissa Todrak stepped out with Luna pressed to her side. Two guards flanked her while two more guarded her back. None belonged to the Todrak personal guard. Representatives of Daganver's nobility streamed out after them, including Aerella's northern lapdogs: his uncle, Kevvan Hawick, and Jacke Yronwood.

But it was to his mother his attention turned.

If Darrok Todrak was a centuries-old oak, stoic even within the worst storms, Alissa was the sapling bending beneath the pressure of a strong wind. Despite Mykal's desire to resemble his father, he'd taken more from his mother's side: the brown skin, the slender bridge of his nose, the slight wave of his thick hair. He'd never forget her wails when they deposited Rendal's body at her feet—Rendal, a brother who was less than a person and more a specter whose boots he had to fill—and her pleading when Aerella's men tore Eileen from her arms. *I'll take her to Adara as a companion for my Cassia.*

She'll pay for your every misstep is what she meant. Even Mykal had recognized the implicit threat. He heard those words when his mother prayed to the small shrine dedicated to Borethes in the fortress's crypts, when she paled at the sight of Luna with a sword, when she begged him not to search for the last Myrassar. Her spirit seemed fragile compared to the solidity of his father's ideals, but Mykal couldn't fault her for thinking and acting with a mother's ferocious heart.

The words were all he could hear now.

Lady Alissa held her youngest in a vise and Luna huddled close to her mother's skirts, looking more afraid than Mykal had ever seen her. Had they been threatened? Hurt? Mykal reached for his Ice, but pain speared his chest in warning. He shuddered, and Shara caught his hand. Her thumb traced over his skin, each stroke deliberate. A pattern.

Not yet, she traced.

"Friends." Lady Alissa's voice echoed in the sullen quiet of those gathered. Not a whisper rose to break the tense spell. Even the rain had stopped beating down. "Rumors have run rampant in the past weeks, but I've called you here so you may carry the truth to your homes and your workplaces. It's true— Asharaya Myrassar lives, and she's now in Ilahara. Though it pains me to admit it, my son Mykal is with her. But the gods are just, and they stand by our queen so she may protect us and vanquish this threat."

"If the gods were just, they'd put an end to this sad display." Mykal recognized his father's blacksmith.

His wife by his side shushed him. "Please, Martok, don't cause a scene."

"Lord Darrok believed in the Myrassar. Daganver thrived

under their rule. They were good to us," a woman protested. "Now I can hardly feed my children."

Many among the high fae showed their agreement with loud whispers and subtle nods. In Mykal's peripheral vision, soldiers intervened to quiet the commotion.

"The Myrassar were liars," Alissa rebuked, pressing Luna harder to her body. "Queen Aerella freed us from their manipulation and their monsters. Have you forgotten what they did to our ancestors?"

"Perhaps it's you who's forgotten."

Mykal's head whipped to Shara as curious murmurs lifted from the quiet crowd. The northerners were boisterous people by nature, but none—not even the high fae—dared contradict Alissa's words so brazenly.

None but the woman standing by his side.

She's brave, Kael's ghost acknowledged with no shortage of pride.

Even idiots can be brave. Why bring attention to herself?

Would you have stayed quiet while your family's name was dragged through the dirt? Kael's ghost asked. *You, who couldn't keep your mouth shut when a human lied about the origin of measly pearls?*

The guards inched closer, ordering the crowd to let them through. Instead of dispersing, the people compacted around Shara like shields of flesh and bone. A shy spark of pride ignited beneath Mykal's heart. He didn't know if his people understood who they protected, but it proved the fight hadn't been beaten out of them yet.

From the gates, Alissa's stare pinched his skin like thousands of needles. Her lips thinned and her hold on Luna's shoulder tightened. "I beg your pardon?"

"They haven't forgotten what the dragons did when your ancestors invaded their land, nor have they forgotten who put an end to the killings, who the dragons chose to rule alongside them. You did."

Shara lowered her hood with calculated slowness, and Mykal's heart dropped with it as she revealed her true face. Those around her released a collective gasp at the unmistakable shimmer of her amber skin and the glow of her golden eyes. Her name became a whisper through the crowd, echoed by voices young and old. A prayer and a war chant.

Blood rushed loud and fast in Mykal's ears. As the people pushed back the guards attempting to force their way through, he sought out his mother. He wanted to save his family and free his home, but not like this. Not without a proper plan.

We're all going to die.

The guards formed a circle around a horrified Lady Alissa and Luna.

"Seize them," his uncle bellowed.

Thunder boomed overhead, each echo louder than the one before. The ground vibrated, and the small rocks beside Mykal's boots bounced erratically. A storm couldn't do that, but something far more dangerous could. Something Shara could control mind to mind, heart to heart. Every hair on Mykal's body stood on end.

"Vatrazae."

The dragon roared at his soulbound's command.

Shouts lifted as Deimok plummeted like a falling meteor, his massive body cutting through the clouds he'd used as cover. Shara's outburst, the dragon's arrival—it all happened too fast to be a coincidence. When had she put together this reckless plan?

Someone knocked Mykal to the ground as Deimok dove over the crowd. Dragonfire washed over the Argarys soldiers who hadn't found cover. Mykal's ears whistled, smoke and dust clouding his vision. Even out of focus, the flailing flames couldn't be mistaken as anything but people. Most were Argarys soldiers, but some were Daganverans who hadn't scurried away in time.

When had his people become collateral damage?

When had Kael become disposable?

Solana coughed and lifted her gaze from Mykal's chest to look him in the face. Soot stained her brown cheeks. "Are you all right?"

"Did you know what she was planning?"

He didn't give her the time to respond. Not for the first time, Shara had conspired behind his back. Why did he keep expecting better from an assassin? He pushed Solana to the side and stumbled to his feet.

I should've jumped after you. Mykal gripped the soulbond's threadbare string. *I should've never left you behind.*

Deimok's bloodlust fed the people's. Daganverans turned on any Argarys soldier within reach. Many had weapons and used them with blind violence, while the rest used their hands to tackle the enemy. The screams were bloodcurdling, but not as much as the sounds of tearing flesh.

The dragon dove lower, forcing people to scatter and clear a path between him and his soulbound. Shara latched onto his extended wing and climbed onto his back. Together, dragon and rider gained altitude, their forms reduced to little more than shadows through the thick black clouds of smoke rising from the carnage.

Anger couldn't ebb the wonder at the sight of them together. Shara fit between Deimok's shoulders as if his body were molded to hers, naturally leaning in to accommodate his movements and favor his speed. Two souls merged in perfect synchronicity, no longer separate but one.

A blur circled Deimok and Shara, so swift Mykal could have missed it if he hadn't been staring. Two more followed in quick succession before an eagle's war cry clashed with the dragon's screech.

"Makkani," someone shouted.

Fire bathed the sky in red light. Mykal took an involuntary step forward. Though the birds of prey were no match for Deimok's gargantuan size, they were about as long as his neck—

at least three times the size of any large bird. They seemed to be born of the wind itself and propelled by its currents. Brown-speckled wings stretched high behind them as they charged. Deimok hovered in a vertical position, the furious beats of his wings in tune with the irritated flick of his tail. He blew fire at the Makkani, but the shifters separated and avoided the flames. Talons out, one attacked Deimok's face. The dragon snapped his teeth at the eagle's feet in answer.

Deimok's distraction at the Makkani gave its companions the perfect opening. Together, they aimed at opposite sides of Deimok's neck. The dragon discouraged the first with flames, but the other sank its talons in his scales.

Deimok writhed and screamed as the eagle ripped off a strip of flesh. Blood rained down, spattering people and snow alike. The eagles were relentless. Deimok was larger, but the shifters were faster and more agile. They circled him like hungry dogs to keep him from flying off, all the while avoiding his fangs and fire. Whenever they found an opening, more blood poured from Deimok's neck, from his flanks. The dragon swiveled to the best of his ability, offering himself to the attacks to protect the woman on his back.

"We have to help them," Solana cried.

Drops of blood splattered Mykal's cheeks. His fingers flexed, the ache in his chest building. *Too far.* Without Kael, he lacked the strength to spear his magic to such heights.

Above him, a glowing flame whipped the fabric of the sky, smaller than Deimok's but no less lethal. It chased one of the shifters as Deimok's teeth closed around another's talons. The eagle released a pained screech as the dragon dragged it down and then bit into its middle, shredding skin and bones. He dropped the carcass, another following in a rain of burning ashes.

With a cry that rang like a war declaration, the remaining shifter charged the dragon. Dragonfire lit Deimok's parted maw. Flames burst forth, and the shifter ducked the fiery jet, circling beneath the dragon's belly. The dragon dove to give chase, but the eagle emerged on Deimok's left and thrust forward.

Toward Shara.

Fae and shifter collided in a jumble of limbs and feathers. The eagle's golden-brown wings came forward as if to embrace her. Shara's blade winked as she slashed at the shifter's middle, but gravity yanked her down, and the tip only grazed the eagle's abdomen.

Then she was falling.

Like an arrow shot from a bow, Deimok chased after her. The shifter sprang up, and its claws sank into the dragon's face.

Deimok roared and thrashed his head, glistening blood painting his black scales red. Still, the shifter held fast. Shara screamed Deimok's name. She clawed at the air as if she could shred the sky and grip it to slow her fall.

Her cries were for Deimok, as if her bones shattering on impact with the ground didn't matter while her dragon was in danger. And damn him, Mykal wanted to throttle her for what she'd done, but watching her plummet from the sky tore something inside him.

Mykal ground his teeth. Blue frosted his fingers as he exhaled in quick bursts. Channeling every fragment of energy he could muster, he thrust his hands toward the sky and let free his Ice.

A thousand whips lacerated his insides. Mykal howled, tears clouding his vision. He didn't need his eyes to direct his magic, only instinct. His Ice—so ordinarily blue, with barely a vein of red in its core—latched onto the falling snow and climbed up, lengthening, thickening.

Cold copper clung to his upper lip and wedged into his mouth as his wall grew, racing against Shara's increasing speed. Mykal's ribcage compressed, squeezed. He was aware of every bone, their cold impressions like brands against his skin. The cold stretched to his muscles, his blood.

Mykal's knees buckled.

Arms wound around his torso, slim but surprisingly strong. Beneath the smoke and blood, he caught a whiff of vanilla.

Mykal's Ice wall almost grazed Shara's side as they met in the air. Without missing a beat, she stabbed the wall as she fumbled with the weapons at her belt and produced a second dagger. Mykal bent forward.

"A little longer," Solana urged in a whisper.

Sparks leaped where Shara's blade skidded against the Ice. With a challenging cry, she twisted toward the wall and embedded the second dagger into it. All the while, her eyes remained pinned to the sky where the dragon and the eagle battled on.

A shot of sapphire joined Mykal's. Buckling against Solana, he followed the Ice to its source—Lady Daenna Quinston. More high fae stepped forward, and more sapphire spires joined theirs, feeding Mykal's wall.

It's okay, Myk. They have her.

Mykal's arms dropped heavily. Only Solana's body kept him up. As the magic died out, the invisible hand that punched through his chest yanked back, and Mykal gasped as cold replaced it.

His magic flowed inward, crawling through his blood. Ice coated his lungs and wrapped chains of iron around his ribcage. A stabbing pain pierced his chest, and his eyes widened as the world tilted, showing a dull sky made duller by smoke. Fear loosened his bladder, but Mykal couldn't even feel that humiliating warmth. *Kael...*

It's all right, Myk.

It was a deception Mykal conjured to exorcise the pain, as was the voice in his head. Each panicked beat of Mykal's heart came slower than the last, and every beat hurt more than the one before.

The Ice kept him prisoner until he felt nothing at all.

22

Shara

Shara's vision flickered between the red blood and the sapphire blue of the Ice wall. The right side of her face pounded, her eye burned and pain flared from her ribs and back where talons as sharp as swords had torn apart flesh. No, not her flesh. Deimok's. Her strained muscles shook as she hung suspended from Mykal's wall. Telling apart her pain from Deimok's was an arduous task when the lines between dragon and rider were this blurred, like colors blended on a palette by an inexperienced hand. Only her rage stood out from the tangle, a string of vibrant red feeding energy into her tired and aching limbs. She yanked a dagger from the ice. No matter what it took, she'd reach the Makkani, and she'd draw out its death as long as possible.

Below, Solana called Shara's name. Shara blinked around another wave of blood and looked down. Sapphire Ice spires fed the wall keeping her up. Her battle-hardened edges softened at the sight. Without the Ice wall, she'd be one of the shattered corpses in the snow. Whether or not this camaraderie survived the test of time, she was glad the Daganveran high fae had come to her aid—to Mykal's aid. The name sent a shock of awareness through her, and she noticed the empty spot where the brightest Ice spire should have been.

In its stead, she found Mykal crumpled in the snow with his head in Solana's lap.

Do you wonder how much energy he used to erect that wall as quickly as he did? She hated how her mind had taken to conjuring Derron's voice whenever self-deprecation surfaced. Hated how she couldn't wring it from her skull and strangle it. *He's probably dead because of you.*

Shara let go of the daggers and fell the rest of the way down, bending her knees to soften her landing. She ran to Mykal and Solana. Her sister's fingers on Mykal's neck trembled. "I can't feel his pulse."

"It's the Frostbite." Shara had never seen it in action, but there was no other name for the blue tinge of his skin and the brine spreading across his body. The Frostbite was the mirror of the Burning, which had kept her bedridden for a week after she burned Rami. Mykal said his episodes started after the Soul Binding and were caused by the addition of Kael's power, but now she wondered if Kael's distance wasn't what upset Mykal's magic in the first place.

Shara made quick work of removing Mykal's leather vest and his shirt. Brine outlined his lithe muscles, clinging to his skin like a greedy lover. Beneath the layer of frost, Shara made out a scar over his heart.

"What are you doing?" Solana asked, as Shara let her cloak fall to the snow.

"We need to warm him. The heat will travel faster through skin." She undressed, modesty be damned. Cold nipped at her bare flesh as she sat astride Mykal and pulled him in an embrace.

Solana draped the cloak around them. "What in the Maiden's name have you done, Shara?"

"I'm sorry I didn't tell you. There was no time."

"But you had time to talk to Jaero about it? That's why he suddenly had this errand to run and why so many people were armed. They knew about the attack."

Jaero had helped her encode the call to arms in a message behind each dragon banner. *A new song rises in the cold to free the bear from the pale flame. Join the song at the Ice's Heart.* They'd spent the night skirting patrols and dispatching banners to inns run by rebel sympathizers, hiding them in nooks within the Veins dedicated to the transport of correspondence, rousing shopkeepers from their rest and tasking them with spreading the message come morning. Embracing the stealth of her vrah routine, Shara had felt much more confident in that part of the plan, for once finding a perfect synchronicity between the assassin and the princess sides of herself. However, she hadn't really believed her plan would work, or that so many would answer her call. Not until she revealed herself and the Daganverans fought at her side.

"Mykal wouldn't have agreed to it. There wasn't time to fight him."

"Of course he wouldn't." Solana widened her arms, looking more exasperated than Shara had ever seen her. "This reckless idea endangered his people, and you know who will pay for this."

"His people are fighting with us," Shara snapped back. "And do you think I've forgotten Kael?"

"I'm hoping you'll prove me wrong."

Shara focused on her Fire rather than the sting of Solana's words. Her magic warmed at her attention, and she gently guided its heat to her skin. "Come on, Myk," she whispered. The scent of pines and snow lifted from his skin. "You can't die on me." She placed a hand over his heart. "Don't you want to know the next part of my daring plan?"

As the Ice melted around her hand, a small, fragile beat pulsed against her palm.

The sound of Deimok's fire had her look up. He dove headfirst into the jet of flames, and while the fire left him unscathed, an unforgiving flare replaced the eagle still clinging to his face.

Deimok.

I am all right, Dragaelan. A lie to keep her calm, as if she couldn't feel his exhaustion and the unrelenting pain of his injuries. Everything was decidedly not all right, and his slow and uncoordinated landing was proof of it.

Across the clearing, Jaero made his way to her. The fae flanking him left to aid in the dying fight. Soot stained the rebel's cheeks, making the fevered light in his pale eyes shine with even more intensity. "What news do you bring?" Shara asked.

"The fighting has spread to the streets. Soldiers are being chased out of the city with every means." They were being slaughtered, is what he meant. Shara couldn't summon an ounce of pity. "Your plan worked, Asharaya. Frosthead Hall is yours, as is the city."

"And the ship?"

"It'll be ready come nightfall."

Shara squeezed Mykal a little tighter as a spasm went through him. "I want any high fae in Aerella's pocket brought to the dungeons and the rest guarded until I can speak to them."

"Consider it done."

"One more thing, Jaero." Shara stopped him before he could leave. "Kill the ravens."

23

Kael

Silence, and with it the unbearable wait that was both curse and relief. Lord Darrok's shouts had long since faded, but they still rang in Kael's ears. It was the first time Kael heard Lord Darrok since that time in the lord's cell. Not knowing what had been done to him was its own form of torture. The screaming hadn't lasted long, but the quiet made Kael fear for the worst.

The general would come for him next.

The distant groaning of the dungeon's main gate had Kael perk up his ears in the door's direction. Loud footsteps followed, new leather squeaking with every move. These sounds surprised Kael, who hadn't been able to notice things this clearly in a while. A key turned in the lock and the door swung open, revealing the female guard with the strong hold.

Kael's throat clogged at the syringe full of fetid renike she produced. Every time he tried and failed to stop his injection, but for the first time since his imprisonment his limbs were stronger and his focus sharper. Perhaps the Dragon was finally smiling on him today. "There'll be no need for that." A sinuous voice came from the open door. The guard's posture slackened as Kael went rigid. Vaemor Argarys held out his hand. "Give that to me." His voice held the unmistakable texture of the Song. The guard's resolve didn't crumble—it simply became nonexistent as she handed the syringe to the king. "Leave us."

Kael shook with barely repressed rage. This was the closest he'd ever been to the wretched man who'd fathered him. The one time Kael had traveled to Adara, he'd barely seen his father. As if the king couldn't be bothered to lay his silver gaze upon the bastard he'd forced into this world.

"Does my sorry state bring you joy?" Kael ground out through clenched teeth.

Vaemor stepped farther into the room, his focus remaining on Kael rather than on taking in his surroundings. Kael observed him in turn, and the two stared at each other long and hard, Kael brimming with hate and the king revealing nothing. His silver eyes bordered on glacial, colder and sharper than Derron's smooth gaze. No love, no sympathy or curiosity. "You're a fool."

Kael's muscles tensed. "You don't know me."

"I know plenty."

Kael flashed his teeth, no better than a rabid wolf. Acid pumped through his veins and corroded his stomach. He wanted to scream, to punch, to maim, but he remained seated, his fists digging into the cot.

"It's in your best interest to cooperate, Arkael." Kael's chest squeezed in a vise hearing his name on this man's lips. "Aerella's patience is wearing thin."

Kael stared at his father with all the loathing he carried in his heart, as vast as his mother's unconditional love. Vaemor didn't blink or flinch, nor did he show any emotion. It was as if the king were a marble statue given life.

"Would Elsa want you to die for pride or glory?"

Kael's heart stumbled in his chest.

"You look a lot like her. She was exceptionally beautiful for a human. I wish you had her ginger hair."

"Stop talking."

"Would you rather talk about Mykal Todrak, then?" Vaemor crooned. "Your Do'strath?"

Hurling a battle cry, Kael wound his hands around the king's throat. For once, surprise flashed across Vaemor's face. Rage and panic tinged Kael's vision red and granted him newfound strength. If Vaemor knew about the bond, then so did the queen. Kael was a dead man, but he'd be damned if he left this world without taking Vaemor Argarys with him. His fingers curled around his sire's neck, pressing half-moon scars into his skin.

Something jabbed Kael's shoulder. Pain flared, but he didn't let go. He squeezed harder, watching his sire's veins bulge and turn purple, drinking in the panic flooding his cold eyes.

Gravity beckoned, and Kael's legs folded beneath him. He grasped onto Vaemor's tunic to stop his fall, but he went down like a wilted flower. Vaemor's chest heaved as he drew in precious air, a few strands of his hair in disarray, the white of his eyes drowning out the pupil. The king pulled out the syringe he'd plunged into Kael's shoulder. For a moment, he stood frozen. Then he brought the needle to his finger, collecting a droplet of the liquid and bringing it to his lips. "I see."

Recomposing himself, Vaemor left Kael on the floor and strode to the door. "I haven't told Aerella, but touch me again, and I may change my mind."

24

Mykal

Mykal felt like he hadn't left his bed in days—or at least, he thought it was his bed. The gray stones and the wooden dragon on the bedside table were familiar. The dragon had been a gift from Rendal. For a time Mykal clutched it every time he sat by the open window, waiting for the dragons to return. No drapes obscured the view of the forest, per Mykal's request. He savored the pine-kissed breeze and the view of the sun grazing the trees that greeted him every morning. The same view spread out beyond his window now, though the sun no longer touched the trees but rose higher than their crowns. Higher than Mykal was used to.

It was definitely his room, and he'd slept in.

Unlike Kael, who welcomed any opportunity to linger in bed, Mykal always woke at first light. He must have been truly exhausted, though he couldn't recall why. Nor did he care to. His Do'strath stared down at him with a smile dimpling his cheek and stars glittering in his dark blue eyes. Mykal wanted to pull Kael into bed to feel that dimple beneath his tongue and muss up the perfect cloud of his moonlit hair. He'd take his time doing it, collecting the taste of smoky wood and citrus from Kael's skin and getting drunk on every sound he could elicit.

"I missed you," Mykal murmured. The smile left Kael's plump lips, making Mykal instantly alert. "What is it, Kael?"

Mykal made to sit up but couldn't. Despite his efforts, his body was trapped. The more he struggled, the more exhaustion sunk into his bones and the weight dragged him down.

An odd weight gained pressure beneath the numbness of Mykal's left side. He followed the feeling, aches giving shape and substance to what had been dormant for…how long had it been?

"I don't want him to die." The familiar voice put some order to the scrambled puzzle of Mykal's consciousness. He wasn't sleeping in just any bed but in his own, in his room at Frosthead Hall. Shara and Deimok had chased away the Argarys men with Dragonfire. He'd had Frostbite. Kael.

What happened to Kael?

The hand wrapped around his was smaller than the one he missed, but no less dear. The faint calluses on the small pads of her fingers were barely formed secrets hardening her skin, and he loved every one of them.

"He will not die, kotin." Mykal tried to draw together his brows at Solana's unfamiliar word, but he didn't think his muscles responded. He hardly felt Luna's breaths fanning against his cheek. "You heard your maenar. He will wake soon."

"Kotin?" he croaked. The syllables grated against his parched throat, the effort to push them out almost too exhausting to repeat.

"He talked," gasped Luna. The sudden loss of her head's weight on his shoulder sent an uncomfortable spasm through

Mykal's arm.

His eyelids twitched as he pried them open. Light fractured around two indiscernible shapes bleeding into one another until black curls filled most of his vision.

"You're alive!" Luna's shriek pierced his eardrums and exploded in his temple. Mykal didn't have time to wince before his little sister tackled him. "If you die again, I'll kill you."

Mykal would have laughed if his heart weren't breaking. He hated to be the cause of Luna's tears. With some difficulty, he wound an arm around her shoulders, embracing her as tightly as he could. There had been times during the voyage to Havanya and back when he'd stopped hoping he'd ever get to do it again. "It's not ladylike to murder your siblings. Mother won't be pleased."

Luna sniffled and drew back. A tear remained nestled between the bow of her full lips. "And who would tell her? You'd be dead, and Kael would never."

Luna's lips clamped together with a tremor, and a lump formed in his throat as he drew her in for another fierce hug. Friend, lover, soulbound—Mykal didn't have the right word to fully encompass everything Kael meant to him, but children weren't encumbered by the complexities of adult feelings. Kael had been a constant presence by Mykal's side long before Luna was born. He was her playmate, the one she could rely on to teach her how to hold a sword without breaking her trust. Luna loved him as much as she did Mykal. He wasn't a brother by blood, but by choice. Suddenly, Kael's absence became all the more harrowing. Even a nightmare in which he couldn't speak to his Do'strath or touch him was better than the reality of not having Kael at all.

"Let me have a look at him now, my lady."

Luna made room for Maenar Jannas, the maenar who'd served Frosthead Hall for as long as Mykal could remember. His appearance had hardly changed over the years. A dark, wispy beard framed the man's round face in patches and made him appear more mature than the thirty or so years he showed. Beards weren't common on fae faces, and Mykal always wondered how long it had taken the maenar to grow his a few inches longer than his chin.

"How long was I down?" Mykal asked, as the maenar rolled down the quilt to expose his bare chest. His brown skin was smooth and devoid of frost. Mykal sighed, relieved.

"Several hours. You missed a lot of action. Shara has been busy," Solana replied, leaning against the bedside table. Without the travel-worn clothes and the dirt clinging to her skin, she hardly looked like the wraith he'd come to know. Had her hair always been so straight and lustrous?

"You suffered a nasty Frostbite, my lord," Maenar Jannas explained, prodding Mykal's ribs and then his chest. Mykal winced, and the man's lips puckered thoughtfully. "It's a good thing Asharaya was there."

"One could argue my son's life wouldn't have been in danger to begin with had she not."

Mykal's head whipped to the side fast enough to blacken his vision. That his mother had chosen a seat to the side wasn't a surprise. Once, she might have sat on his mattress, nestling his hands between her own. Not anymore. Not since losing Rendal and Eileen.

Mykal's blood chilled. "If Father heard you…"

"Would there be consequences? I wish that had ever been enough to stop him."

Mykal sank deeper into his pillows, wishing the soft fabric would suck him in and save him from this conversation. His mother was like a sponge, silently soaking up anger until she leaked from every pore. "Father has always done what he believed was right for this family and our people."

"Your father has always done what was right for the Myrassar. He would've rolled over like a loyal dog for Gailen and thrown himself into the Burning Sea if Jaemys asked. They're dead and buried, yet nothing has changed."

Mykal shook his head. "The dragons chose the Myrassar."

"Yes, the dragons chose. We'll all be pleased for it when Aerella delivers us your father's head in a box alongside Eileen's and Arkael's."

Mykal flinched, his hand snaking to the scar of the Soul Binding on his heart. The bond arched at his summons like an old cat seeking affection, so delicate Mykal feared snapping it with a thought. So long as he could feel it, no matter how worn down it was, it meant Kael was alive. Mykal had to hold on to that. He couldn't stand the alternative. "What happened while I was away?"

"What was to be expected. You weren't gone a week before Aerella's soldiers arrived, with a leave signed by the queen herself for Kevvan and Lord Yronwood to take charge of Frosthead Hall in all but title. Your absence didn't go unnoticed."

Luna latched onto Mykal's hand. "They asked about you and Kael all the time."

"Did they hurt you?" Mykal asked. When she shook her head, breathing came a little easier, and he lifted her hand to his lips to kiss her knuckles. "You were brave, little sister."

"Aerella couldn't have Darrok arrested without risking an uprising," Alissa continued. "She needed solid proof of our treason, facts none could deny, and the Myrassar girl handed them over when her dragon destroyed the Nahar's palace." She stood, her calm at odds with her scathing words. "I know you share your father's vision, Mykal," she said, nearing the bed. "I know you resent me for complying with Aerella's demands, but I was alone. I needed to protect Luna."

"I've never resented you, Mother." Despite the sting in his eyes, his voice was steady, if tired. "I'm going to fix this, I promise."

Lady Alissa brushed Mykal's chin, the touch so brief it was over before Mykal's surprise abated. "Think with your own head, Myk. Not the Myrassar girl's." Alissa held out her hand for Luna, who reluctantly slipped to her mother's side. "She has her mother's beauty and her father's restless spirit. Many will stop at nothing to have her, and she will stop at nothing to get what she wants. It's in her blood."

The maenar followed them to the door, and as it clicked shut, Mykal sagged into the pillows, letting the cotton muffle Solana's slithering. The wraith paced at the foot of his bed, looking like she might actually assassinate his mother. He almost smiled.

Solana whirled on Mykal instead. "Shara can be impulsive, but she is not the monster that wretched woman makes her out to be."

"That wretched woman is my mother."

"Mothers can say bullshit." Solana crossed her arms over her small chest. "You know she is wrong, do you not?"

Mykal's lips pressed into a fine line. Shara wasn't a monster, but she was determined and capable of deception. "She should've told us."

Solana sighed. "I know."

"We could have coveted alliances, built our army one day at a time."

"That would have taken months. Perhaps years."

"And what will it matter to have conquered Frosthead Hall in minutes when we have no hold on the rest of the region? As things are, I have no power over the North. No power to save my father or Kael."

Had that been the meaning of his nightmare? Had Kael come to say goodbye? Had Shara's actions sealed his fate?

The mattress dipped under a new weight, startling Mykal back to the present. Heat flushed to the tip of his ears as Solana settled the quilt over her legs. He wasn't a stranger to sharing his bed, but something about Solana's boldness made him feel self-conscious. He was naked, for Dragon's sake. "What are you doing?" he squeaked.

Solana grabbed his chin and forced him to look at her.

"Kael will not die."

"You don't know that."

"I do." Mykal frowned at her surety. "The Maiden has taken enough from us all. I will not let her take more."

"No one has the power to defy the gods, Solana," he whispered, though if anyone could, it would be her. She'd imposed her will on her goddess once before. *And she hasn't summoned a shadow since.* It was impossible, but her vehemence made him want to defy reason and hope. Her eyes were more black than brown, fringed by long lashes that brushed her cheeks when she blinked. Like a doe, but with bones of steel beneath the delicate beauty and gentle temperament.

A line of pink bloomed over the ridge of her nose. "We must trust that we will see Kael again."

Before he could reply, Solana leaned forward. Mykal held his breath, her face lingering close to his. Then she rested her head on his shoulder, and his hand found hers. Neither clung to the other, yet mere touch brought with it a tentative comfort. Mykal relaxed, leaning his head atop Solana's.

"What did you call Luna?" he asked after a while.

"Kotin." The lilt in Solana's voice gave away her smile. "It means kitten."

He snorted. "Of course, it does."

And though his heart ached, he managed a smile of his own.

25

Shara

With her eyes closed, Shara could pretend she was in Havanya, twisting a dagger's tip against her finger as she sat in the Keep's crypt. Drops fell slowly from a leak, the ping like a wind chime against the ice dusting the floors and spiderwebbed across the cavernous walls. In her mind's eye, the drops were red, and they fell from the Maiden's marmoreal finger. She'd felt small before the towering statue, unnerved by the choir of souls echoing in the stairwell, but the memory calmed some of her tension, replacing the unknown with something familiar. She missed her life in Havanya. Once, she'd missed Ilahara in the same way. Fate had a shit sense of humor.

With the barest pressure, the dagger drew a bead of blood. The shadows stirred like hounds on the game's trail. Feet shuffled across the slick floor, and quicker breaths than Shara's interrupted the choir's tempo in her mind. Her caged companions likely expected a Myrassar to feed them to her dragon or burn them on a pyre lit by her own Fire, so she'd decided to surprise them.

Judging by the fear weighing the air, her show was effective.

"It's been a long day, gentlemen." Shara opened her eyes, shedding Havanya's memory. Kevvan Hawick and Jacke Yronwood pressed against the cell's far wall, staring at the shadows crawling to Shara across the floor. "Believe me, I've no pleasure keeping you in this cell."

"Have you come to torture us?" Jacke Yronwood asked. Despite the haughtiness of his tone, his throat bobbed at the hint of Shara's grin.

"If I wanted you to sing for me, you'd be singing," Shara crooned. "I'm here to talk."

The lord slinked away from the wall and approached the bars. Jacke Yronwood was handsome in the way all fae were. Firelight streaked his ebony skin with gold and accentuated the deep hollows of his cheeks. His tall, lithe frame lacked toned muscle, giving him the look of the sophisticated lord. Shara could easily imagine him twiddling his thumbs behind a desk, fostering his greed while others dirtied their hands following his orders. His fingers closed around the bars as his eyes roamed her body. "Your mother nurtured friendships lying on her back. You'd do well to learn from her."

Shara kept her expression blank, but she couldn't help the tightening hold on the dagger. She'd developed thick skin against lewd comments. Greed and lust were a human's most common vices, and the fae's too, it seemed. The insinuation against her mother, on the other hand, found its mark. It wasn't the claim itself but the calculated way Jacke used it to defile her mother's reputation. She knew Jaemys Myrassar as a mother, not a queen. Shara had been too young to know her as anything else.

Focus, Rami's voice whispered. *Don't let this asshole rile you.*

"Did you give Aerella the same advice?" Shara eased off the wall, and the lords' shadows backed away at her approach, groveling in submission. "We'll see how effective your bedroom conversations are when she receives my proposition."

Jacke blinked. "You're offering an exchange?"

She wasn't, though like Mykal, Daganver's high fae had suggested it during their meeting. But Jacke and Kevvan didn't know it, and she could let their hope stew a while before ripping it away. Perhaps that would convince them to share whatever information they had on Aerella.

Shara let the silence stretch long enough for fear to flicker on their faces. "Aerella left you in charge of the North, and you lost it." Her dagger dragged along the prison bars until she stood face to face with Jacke. It was her turn to leer while her dagger scratched up the side of the bar. "I'm not against spreading my legs, Jacke Yronwood. I'm against wasting my time."

"What will you do with us?" Kevvan Hawick's voice reminded her of a deeper, lower version of Mykal's. The similarities stretched to the black wavy hair and the shape of their eyes, traits the lord shared with his sister, Lady Alissa.

"The silent one speaks."

"What will you do with us?" the lord repeated.

"I haven't decided, but I'll soon be needing space in these dungeons. For your sake, I hope I'll find a use for you by the time I return."

"And when will that be?"

Shara let them see her sly smile and the shadows stretched thin across the floor. "Soon."

A tenuous calm pervaded the courtyard. The bloodied snow from the morning's battle had been shoveled away and replaced by a pristine moonlit layer. Immediately after she'd ordered the ravens killed, battered and dirty men—whom she later discovered were the Todrak personal guard, newly freed from the dungeons—filled the courtyard. Two had approached her to pry Mykal's unconscious body from her arms.

"Where are you taking him?" she'd asked, posing resistance.

"Lord Mykal needs to see the maenar, Your Majesty."

The title successfully mollified her grip, and that was the last she'd seen of Mykal and Solana, who'd followed their friend with nary a glance in Shara's direction.

Shara occupied her time by aiding the wounded and gathering the dead, both in the courtyard and out in the streets. As the adrenaline from the fight ebbed, her mind became foggy, the sleepless night making itself felt. People greeted her with varying degrees of wonder, some ogling from a distance, others weeping as if she were a war hero returned home at last, grabbing her dirty and bloody hands to kiss them as she passed them by.

"It's Jaemys."

"She looks just like her mother."

Bodies piled up with no end. Those belonging to civilians were loaded onto carts and brought to Frosthead Hall to burn on a pyre fueled by Shara's Fire—her thanks for having answered her call before the Dragon claimed their eternal souls.

By the time she met with Daganver's high fae, only anxiety kept her upright. The lords lavished her with praise, promised her armies and funds to aid in the war effort. None failed to offer their condolences for her family or share their personal memories of her father's humor and her mother's beauty and grace.

"You look so much like her" they all said. Who meant it with affection and who saw her as a prize to be won? Mykal would know, but she hadn't received news about him since the guards took him to the maenar.

Once Shara and the lords came to an agreement on how the lords would aid the Rising's efforts to free their cities, she'd raced to the courtyard and vomited into the snow. The meeting itself had gone well, but she couldn't help feeling under scrutiny. It would've been easier with Deimok by her side, but her dragon hid in the forest, his mental shields high in a clear sign he wished to be alone. The soulbond throbbed with the echo of his pain, but he was safe. Only that made honoring his need for privacy bearable.

Deimok was wounded, Mykal had Frostbite, and Solana was upset, yet all Shara could do was stay out of their way.

Now, the dead had long since become ashes, but dark cinders danced in the dim light, tangling with the snow weeping from the sky. The cold nipped at Shara's face and blew through her blouse. A rip stretched over her belly, courtesy of the eagle's claws. Blood and dirt stained the rest. She hadn't even had the time to clean up in the aftermath of the battle. She reached for the kernel of flame at her core, reveling in the heat spreading through her body.

"You did well today." Shara lifted her gaze to Jaero, who must have spotted her coming out of the fortress. With his bloodstained clothes and the evening light turning the pale orbs of his eyes into a luminescent pearl gray, he looked like the sort of rogue mothers dreaded and their children loved. "You didn't pull out your dagger once. I'm impressed."

The teasing scrape of his voice elicited Shara's first real smile of the day. "You look like a pirate."

"I've always liked the sea. I could enlist on a ship when the war is over." As sly and resourceful as he was, Shara had no doubt he'd fare well as an outlaw, shattering hearts in every port.

"I suggest surviving the war before fantasizing about what comes next."

"Having something to look forward to is motivating. Surely you must fantasize."

Shara's smile faltered, and she looked away. "We had the element of surprise today. Next time will be different. The lords have agreed to supply weapons to the Rising, but whoever wishes to join the war effort needs training or we won't get far in the field."

"You could train them." Jaero's proposition struck her like a bludgeon. "You know your way around weapons, and you give people hope, Asharaya. You saw how many answered your call today. I don't think there's anything your supporters wouldn't do for you."

"I can't. I made a promise, and if this Asharaya Dragonsong thing is going to work, I need the people to know me as more than just a Myrassar. I want them to know I honor my promises."

Jaero's knowing smile was nothing short of dazzling. "Ares was right."

"About?"

"You." His low baritone heightened Shara's awareness of him. He seemed like he wanted to step closer or touch her. Though he did neither, his gaze anchored hers, solemn and intense. "You've seen the worst Ilahara has to offer, and still you care about its people. You weren't raised like those that came before you. You don't see the world the way most Ilahein do. That is why you'll change things, and why the people will follow you, not your name."

His opinion of her warmed her and made her bashful at once. "None of what happened today would've been possible without your help."

"I would do it again in a heartbeat." Jaero took her hand and lifted it to his lips. It might have been a mockery of the obeisance Shara had been shown all day, but it felt different coming from him, especially when his pale eyes remained fixed on her with that odd intensity. His were the rough and calloused hands of someone used to manual labor. What did he do when he wasn't serving the Rising? "Safe travels, Asharaya Dragonsong."

"You never told me why you fight," Shara called after him. Jaero stilled. "Will you ever share your story with me?"

"Someday."

Not long after Jaero left, Shara followed the soulbond to the back of the fortress. Deimok lay in a nest of blackened bones, neck stretched and eyes shut as the torches illuminated the red sheen in his black scales. Snow dissolved before touching his body, a small but significant sign her dragon was feeling better. Relief almost had her falling to her knees.

Keep this up and you'll set yourself on fire, she whispered.

Deimok glanced in her direction, a wet sheen in his left eye while the right remained swollen shut beneath three nasty gashes. He snorted, defiant. *A dragon does not burn.*

Shara refused to acknowledge the stench of charred bones as she climbed into the nest. Beneath the dried blood, the new wounds healed, leaving only the scars from his first death and the gashes around his eye. Apart from the occasional twitch of his tail, Deimok remained immobile during her perusal. Even his wings—which he usually kept stretched and relaxed—were stiff against his side.

You're still in pain. The skin beneath the scales was red and raw, though magic had cleared away the infection. She barely brushed his face before Deimok flinched with a warning hiss. The panicked echo of his heartbeat triggered hers into a faster rhythm. *Why haven't these healed?*

The dragon dragged his head against the bones, turning away from Shara.

Don't hide from me. Shara circled to Deimok's left and sat beside his head. His hot breath draped over her like a warm blanket. She neared her hand to his nose, and after a moment's hesitation, Deimok pressed it to her palm. With small rubs, Shara glided up to the space between his nostrils. *Don't be ashamed of your scars.*

Magic cannot heal what was damaged beyond repair, Deimok's rumble was heavy with exhaustion. Shara forced her hand to continue moving in reassuring strokes over her dragon's snout. *I will need time to adjust.* A pause, and a long exhale. *And to fly.*

A tear rolled down her cheek. *I'm tired of you getting hurt because of me.*

There is nothing I would not endure for you. Nothing I would not give.

Shara cradled his face between her hands. *You've given enough.* She pressed her forehead to his snout. *I can't change my plans. It's too risky.*

The Todrak boy...

He can't do it alone.

Deimok released a panicked huff. *Then I will come.*

It'll be more dangerous for me if I'm worried about you getting killed. I need you to take care of yourself for once. This war is far from over. There will be more battles. Deimok made to rear his head back, but Shara held fast and he eased his face back to her with a mournful chirp. She cried with him, absorbing his earthy scent and the power emanating from him even at his weakest. *There is nowhere I could go that you wouldn't be with me.*

"Your Majesty?"

The woman repeated the title several times before Shara realized she was being hailed. Light age marks stretched from the corners of the human woman's eyes, the kind that crinkled when one laughed. Streaks of silver gleamed in her ginger hair. Shara's heart squeezed. Perhaps it was the signs of time worn so proudly on her rotund body, familiar to Shara after years spent among humans and yet so rare among the fae.

"I'm sorry to interrupt. Lord Mykal wants to see you in the Head's study."

"Myk's awake?" Shara blurted, and then cleared her throat. "I don't know the way."

An understanding smile formed on the woman's full lips, but her eyes remained sad. "Follow me."

After a parting stroke on the horns framing Deimok's face and a whispered goodbye down the soulbond, Shara followed the woman back to the fortress. The gray stone and dim illumination gave the interior a cavernous feeling. The lack of runners was likely to favor Lord Darrok's wheelchair, but no other embellishments adorned the space. No frills flaunted the family's wealth and status; no portraits hung on the walls, though at closer inspection Shara noticed stains left from long ago frames.

"What's your name?" she asked the human, if only to quiet the wind's howling echo in the large hallway.

"Elsa."

"How long have you been in Ilahara?" *Do you miss Havanya, too?*

"My whole life. My parents were children when they were sold to the fae."

Shara swallowed hard, her next question a whisper. "Are you happy here?"

"Lord Darrok was—is good to us." She shivered, as if the mistake had raked nails down the column of her spine. "I've known no other life, and if mine had been different, I wouldn't have my son."

"You have a son?"

Elsa stopped before a door and faced Shara, something fierce stealing over her kindly features. "He's Lord Mykal's Do'strath."

Shara wondered how she hadn't seen it sooner. The similarities were hard to miss. They had the same dark blue eyes, the same light freckles spread across their cheeks, the same lips—the bottom one fuller than the upper. Her mouth opened and closed. What could she say to Kael's mother when she was the reason her son was in danger?

Elsa cleared her throat and smoothed out her gown. "This is the study."

Only the unintelligible murmuring from the other side of the door kept her company once Elsa was gone. Shara placed her hand on the doorknob, giving herself a moment to calm down. Her fingers shook around the iron knob, and the exhaustion she'd been warding off all day rushed her all at once. *You've reached the final act, Shara. Pull yourself together.*

The murmuring stopped as she entered the Head's study. The open windows let in a chilling breeze carrying the lingering smell of burned flesh, which mingled with the heavy tang of a room gone unused for too long. Shara resisted the urge to curl her nose. "You summoned me, my lord?" she teased, as if irony could shield her from Mykal's voiceless accusations.

Solana straightened with a feline's slow grace, her ankles crossed as she leaned against a large, oak desk. Beside her, Mykal was more slumped than reclined in his chair placed on the visitor's side of the desk. The lord's side was empty.

Shara shut the door, the quiet click enough to make her flinch. Like the rest of the fortress, the furnishings in the study were minimal, which drew the eye to the bookshelf's old tomes and the empty top shelves. "It's good to see you on your feet."

Mykal's jaw twitched. "Is that all you have to say?"

"You're welcome for saving your life."

"I'm not in the mood for games."

"Neither am I." Shara sauntered to the bookshelf. The worn, leather-bound manuscripts were far from the sort of books she loved. History tomes, royal genealogies, philosophical and medical treatises, and books on warfare were only some of the topics. Her fingers skimmed the delicate spines and the titles impressed upon them in gold filigree. One on the history of Ilahara had Maenar Elvik's name. Shara hadn't known the maenar was a writer.

She hadn't known a great many things.

"Funny you should say that, seeing how you went behind my back to set up this foolhardy siege. You put my people in danger, Shara, and my family. Everything is a game to you, including my Do'strath's life."

"By all means, prattle on about how careless I've been." Shara tapped the shelf with the tip of her finger. "I guess none of us will be boarding my ship."

"What ship?" Solana asked at the same time Mykal groaned, "What in damnation are you talking about?"

"While your mother was giving her lovely speech about how terrible my family was, Jaero secured us passage on a merchant schooner. It's a fast ship with a small crew, ideal for swift travel."

Mykal twisted in the chair, finally facing her. "A merchant schooner?"

"Winter is rolling in fast. The lords and ladies of Adara will appreciate Daganver's famed fur coats."

"Adara?" Solana gripped the back of Mykal's chair, slipping into Havanian. "Shara, you can't go after Aerella on your own."

"Aerella isn't our objective." Shara leaned over the desk, her hands bracing the edges with a firm grip. "Kael and Lord Darrok are. There are tunnels beneath the Embernest. Only my family and few others knew of their existence."

"You haven't been to the Embernest in fourteen years," Solana said.

"I could never forget it." Shara had known it to be true when she'd seen the painting in the rebel's home.

"You want to sneak into the Embernest?" asked Mykal. "Are you mad?"

"What if Aerella knows about these passages and they're guarded?" Solana added.

"Then we'll use the shadows when we can, and steel when we can't."

Mykal ran a hand over his face. "It's never going to work. News of what happened here will spread."

"It will," Shara agreed. "But we'll be faster. I had the ravens killed, and the Rising will do their best to keep the news from leaving the confines of the region. Word will get out eventually, but with the schooner we'll be in Adara in five days, maybe six. It'll be enough to get into the Embernest before Aerella is alerted."

"The city isn't secure—"

"Already taken care of." Shara interrupted. "Now that we've cut off the snake's head, the high fae and the Rising will work together to free the rest of the region. Jaero will coordinate the Rising while we're gone."

"You've thought of everything." The emotions fleeting across Mykal's face were too fast to read.

"I told you I'd find another way."

Mykal shook his head, but Shara smiled at the hesitant glimmer of hope in his glistening eyes. He wouldn't meet her gaze—she didn't expect him to forgive her quickly for acting on her own—but he wasn't screaming, and that was a start. "When does the ship set sail?"

"An hour, give or take."

"I must speak to my mother. I'll meet you in the foyer."

As soon as the door shut behind Mykal, Solana circled the table. Her sister's arms wound around her, and Shara relaxed. Their temples touched as Solana rested her chin on Shara's shoulder. "Do you really think it'll work?"

The fire in the hearth crackled loudly, nearly devouring Shara's whispered reply.

"I hope so."

26

Kael

Kael tasted copper and acid. Limbs shaking on the metal table, he couldn't help his flinch when General Leneris stepped away. His hands were covered in Kael's blood and his blade dripped with it. More stained the table and streamed into the drain.

The queen advanced from her chosen corner, arms crossed around her middle and gown dragging in his blood. "Most would have broken by now."

Kael shrunk back as much as the manacles would allow at the queen's approach. From his angle, she looked as terrible and lovely as a goddess. She extended her hand, and he shut his eyes, the pain in his cut cheek flaring. Her touch was gentle, barely skimming his fresh scar. "What a pretty face." Her thumb grazed his lower lip. "You take this from your mother, I presume. She must have been quite the beauty."

Kael's nostrils flared. "Don't you dare harm her."

The queen chuckled, dragging her fingers over the ridge of Kael's nose. "I have no interest in her." She caressed the bruised skin under his eyes. "These are hers, too." The queen moved her hand to his hair, curling her fingers through the dirty strands. "What if I told you I could make the pain disappear?"

Kael hated how his ears perked up. How his body sang with relief.

"The scars will fade, and this will be a distant memory. You could have a place at this court. Enjoy luxuries a man like you could only dream of." All the while, her fingers threaded his hair. "You're wasted on Darrok Todrak, and I doubt Lady Alissa would know what to do with you."

Kael jerked his head from the queen's touch, understanding her vile implication. "I'm no pet," he croaked, voice raw.

The queen straightened, her smile falling as she lowered her gaze to the scar above his heart. Had Vaemor gone back on his promise of keeping the truth from the queen? Kael had no reason to trust his sire, but he doubted he'd be alive if the queen knew he'd performed a ritual exclusive to the Dragon Faith. "Yet you're happy to die as the Todrak's dog."

Kael fought the instinct to turn away and met the queen's gaze with a new wave of courage. *I'm alive and unbroken and I love you, Myk.*

Aerella lifted her hand. Fire danced around her fingers. "Perhaps you lack a permanent reminder of who you truly belong to."

She brought a single, searing finger down on his abdomen. Kael jolted, veins swelling in his neck from the effort of holding back a scream. But the queen lingered, and fighting was futile.

Later, in the dark of his cell, Kael sat on the hard floor, shivering with aftershocks. He lifted his shirt with a trembling hand, fingers tracing the marks left by the queen. He followed the shape until it formed a letter.

A, like Argarys.

Kael tried to summon Mykal's voice again so his Do'strath

could remind him that his blood didn't define who he was. That he was good and worthy of love. That they belonged together, no matter how silver his hair. But as hard as he tried, his mind returned to the imprint on his flesh. He traced the lines first with the pads of his fingers, then with his broken nails, until he drew blood and he heard the queen's voice. *Perhaps you lack a permanent reminder of who you truly belong to.*

"I'm alive," he recited in a broken whisper. "And I love you, Myk."

The dungeons echoed with Kael's crying.

27

Derron

Sunlight filtered through the open curtains of the queen's study. Derron squinted against the light, craving his room's semi-darkness or the perpetual gloom that had blanketed Adara for the last four days. Lately, Derron lay awake half the night, too consumed by his search for the artists behind the dragon banners. He'd found several leads that took him nowhere, and none of his old contacts were answering his letters or accepting offers to meet. Word of his search had spread through the artist circles, and people he'd considered friends now feared him.

The scratch of the quill against parchment jerked his attention back to the queen's elegant loops. Late in the morning, a servant had delivered a note from his mother. However, she had yet to utter a single word. Writing missives while someone waited was one of her favorite ploys to put the other person on edge.

Had she figured out he'd tampered with Kael's renike?

Derron stretched in his seat, casting a long glance at his mother's letter. He made out the name "Xanver" before his mother caught him peeking. "You're writing to Makkan." No point denying he'd gleaned the name of one of the two Makkani Heads.

"Your father has been having trouble contacting our man in Daganver," she explained. "I want someone to look into it."

"Can't you send a raven to Frosthead Hall?"

"As long as I give the Farwynd what they want, they're my eyes and wings. I'll trust those over any letter."

Derron tightened his fingers around the armrests. Cassia might have chosen to accept her fate and marry Baramun, but that didn't mean he had to like it. "You called for me," he said flatly.

The queen signed the letter. "Any leads on the artist?"

"Not yet."

"Not even from that pretty artist you liked to fuck a few years ago?"

Derron couldn't stop his eyes from widening. He'd been wrong in assuming he had ownership of his secrets. What did his mother know about Anrea? "She's clean."

"No leathers today. Will you be joining us at the temple?"

The sudden change of subject was like a whiplash. "I promised Eileen I'd accompany her." *It would do well for the future king to show his face now and then*, she'd said, the corner of her lips tilted in a coy smile. They weren't married, yet Eileen already acted like the doting wife. All the while Derron dreamed of a woman he'd do best to cast out of his mind.

These days he was torn between craving the sweet oblivion of sleep and wishing he could avoid it altogether. Every time he closed his eyes, Asharaya was there to haunt him. Sometimes he'd see her as if he were standing there with her, the constant northern flurries surrounding her, her dragon—wounded like he hadn't been in Merania—ever by her side. In those instances, she wouldn't see him, and he'd let himself linger, perversely clinging onto the bittersweet taste of regret and longing that would forever tie him to the Myrassar. Other times, she would appear in the Embernest gardens like that very first dream they'd shared, and her eyes would land on him, golden and fierce. He only allowed those dreams to last a few moments before he banished her from his mind, though her scolding glare remained with him like a brand on his flesh long after he woke.

"Semal says you skipped your routine training this morning." The queen's tone suggested the general wasn't pleased.

"I overslept."

"I do hope whatever you're up to at night won't break our poor Eileen's heart." Queen Aerella sealed the letter with wax and pressed her flaming sigil upon it. "I'll see you at the temple."

Eileen opened her door upon his first knock, as if she'd been waiting behind it. She wore her hair swept up at the side with a silver comb and a mint green dress that complemented his dove gray suit. One could suspect she had the servants spying on him if he weren't alone in his room.

Eileen appraised him, her smile bright. "No leathers, and no swords."

"Unless you want me to challenge Baramun to a duel."

Eileen scrunched her nose. "Like shifters?"

"The rest of us fae used to engage in such practices until not too long ago."

Eileen placed her hand in the crook of his offered arm. "It's been a few centuries, Derron."

"Careful how you speak, Lady Eileen," Derron whispered mockingly. "Some people here still remember those days."

Eileen sobered, triggering Derron's concern. "What is it?"

"I was thinking about Cassia. Perhaps I should have accompanied her to Tyrra. I'm worried about her, Derron. I worry I haven't done enough."

Derron's chest squeezed at the mention of his sister.

"That makes two of us," he confessed. "Though I doubt my mother would have let you go far with tension so high with Daganver. You're more valuable than ever."

Eileen clenched her jaw and said nothing.

The carriage ride to the temple was pleasant, but if it lightened the weight off Derron's chest, the high keeper's sermon aggravated it once more. Cooped up in the pew with Eileen on one side and Semal on the other, Derron was forced to listen to Baramun drone on about the heresy that had struck Adara. Dragon heretics were sprouting like weeds, but the gods would remember the good people of unwavering faith. Eileen scrunched her brows in either concentration or concern, while Derron focused on the spirals in the columns to pass the time. He didn't bother holding back his sigh of relief once it was over, earning a pinch on the arm from Eileen. "And you wonder why I hardly attend."

"Someone could hear you," she scolded. "Semal took it with more grace than you did."

"I'm surprised he's here." Semal was beside the queen and king, who were speaking with Baramun by the doors. "He usually hates these more than I do."

"Unsurprising why you're like this, then."

They reached the group as Lord Markos, the newly appointed captain of the city guard, strode through the temple doors. Sweat pearled the man's brown forehead, as if he'd run up the stairs. "Everything's ready, my queen."

Chatter, footsteps, and groaning benches echoed behind them as the other attendees prepared to leave. The queen nodded and followed Lord Markos out.

Derron and Eileen trekked down the carved-in staircase side by side, the ward from the North next to the cliff's wall and the prince close to the edge. The sea reminded him of Cassia. Despite the words exchanged the night before she'd left for

Tyrra four days ago, he missed her.

The queen stopped before she reached the bottom, forcing those behind her to pause. A large crowd waited at the foot of the stairs. Derron recognized the gray and blue uniforms of the city guard lined up nearby. The air grew charged with something akin to dread. These people didn't find themselves here by chance.

Queen Aerella had no need to demand her people's attention. The crowd grew silent of its own accord. "I want you to carry this message to every corner of the city and beyond," declared the queen. Chills crawled up Derron's spine. His mother had a way of speaking as if she were looking everyone in the eye, including those standing behind her. "A group of heretics continues to vandalize our city. They call it provocation. I call it treason." Hushed murmurs traveled through the crowd. "I've given the culprits more than enough time to repent, but the high keeper and I are in agreement. Pinning dragon symbols to our walls is a slight to both Crown and Faith. This kind of behavior can no longer be ignored or go unpunished.

"You have until sundown to reveal the traitors. Do so, and you shall be rewarded beyond your wildest imaginings. Fail, and you will meet their same fate. Their crime is your own."

Derron found Semal, whose eye was already trained on him. His mother had asked him about leads that same morning, but this must have been planned in advance. The city guard had known exactly where to gather the people, and the chosen location wasn't casual. The queen had appointed herself as the avenging goddess.

The quiet bled fear.

"Make haste," she said. "The clock's ticking."

28

Derron

Royal and city guards staved off the panicked crowd and cleared the royal family's path to their carriages. Too many voices blended together. Like a fish in a bowl, Derron's perception warped, his mind sluggish, moving both too fast and too slow.

A separate carriage awaited him and Eileen. They were expected to return to the castle together and maintain the happy appearance of two young people in love, as if the queen hadn't just threatened her people. Derron aimed for his parents' carriage instead. One guard tried to stop him, while three more invited Eileen to enter the carriage. Derron shoved the guard aside and caught up to Semal, blocking the carriage's opening so that his parents couldn't get out and the general couldn't get in. "What are you planning?" he demanded.

"This is neither the time nor the place," Vaemor replied in the queen's stead. "Get to your carriage before the mob closes in."

Derron pointed an accusatory finger at his mother. "She unleashed the mob."

Semal yanked Derron away with a sound akin to a snarl. The force sent Derron careening into two guards, who each grasped an arm to keep him from throwing himself at the general. "You're just going to let this happen?"

"I told her it was best you didn't know."

Derron shook with rage. "Ilahara is on the brink of civil war. Don't you want to see it at peace?"

Semal stepped closer, teeth bared. "You cannot achieve peace without sacrifice."

"Whose sacrifice?" The two men stared at each other, the moment pregnant with shock and hurt. Semal would think him young and inexperienced, but Derron was unwilling to stand by and let his mother's plan unfold. Whatever it was, it couldn't be good.

The prince shrugged off the guards' hold and returned to his carriage. Eileen watched him through the window. Around them rang the desperate pleas of the people, the words jumbled together in a way Derron could hardly understand. He entered the carriage like a wolf would a cage.

As the carriage rolled forward, Eileen grabbed both his hands. "For a moment I didn't know if I had to fear the crowd, the guards, or Semal. What were you thinking?"

"I need to stop whatever she's planning."

"How?"

"I don't know."

A mob crowded the narrow streets and surrounded their carriage. Cries of "My prince" and "It's the prince" rose from the crowd. They reached for the carriage only to be kicked back by the guards on horseback, but it didn't deter them from begging for an audience with their prince. Derron's knuckles turned white with how tightly he clenched his hands. A woman's agonized cry shattered his self-control and had him knocking on the carriage ceiling. The driver didn't stop, and he banged harder.

Eileen grabbed his wrist. "What are you doing?"

Derron addressed the guard outside his window. "Let me out."

"Your Highness, the crowd's too close. It's dangerous."

Derron looked to the streets, steeling his resolve by shutting out the voices. When he looked back to the guard, his single command was laced with magic. "Move."

The guard didn't object now, his gaze vacant as the carriage rattled to a halt.

Eileen lunged for the handle to keep Derron inside. "The crowd's going to eat you alive."

"I'll use my Song to keep them away if I have to, but I need to figure out how to stop my mother."

"The only thing that would make her happy is seeing some rebels lined up for execution. Do you have any names? Do you want to give her people to kill?" The silence that followed was his answer. "I thought so."

"I have to try."

Eileen worried her lower lip. "You won't be able to control all these fae."

"I'll be careful."

"No, we'll be careful. I'm coming with you."

"Absolutely not." Derron turned on the seat to face her. "You'll go to the Embernest and lock yourself in your room until I return."

"You'll have to compel me to go back without you."

Derron clenched his jaw. "I could."

"But you won't." Eileen jerked her chin toward the carriage door. "We do this together or not at all."

"I don't want you to get hurt."

"And I don't want the problematic prince to disappear mysteriously." If anyone else heard Eileen alluding to the queen's schemes, it would put her in a difficult position. But she had a point. If anything happened to Derron now, it would be easy to pin on the mob. Frost coated Eileen's fingers, but her eyes remained a warm brown. "Let's go."

Derron used his Song to command the crowd and the guards to stand down. His temples pounded almost immediately from the strain. These were all low fae. Their mental barriers were protected by a thin layer of magic, making them harder to cross than a human's. It was like ramming his shoulder into a door rather than striding into an open room.

Eileen took one of the horses from the guards. "We'll be safer on horseback," she explained, as she climbed up. Derron mounted behind her and grabbed the reins. Eileen tensed as his arms came around her before leaning against his chest.

Derron spurred the horse forward. Despite their stupor, the people jumped aside to let them through. He looked back only once to ensure that no one had been hurt, but he'd never make it deeper into the city if he stopped out of guilt. The queen had given them until sundown. With winter coming, daylight hours were shrinking. Sundown was only two hours away, three at most.

The city guard stormed into houses and arrested people in the streets. Crowds gathered around the guards, voices climbing over one another in a tangle of names and accusations. The suspects kicked and protested, most shouting their innocence. They all had the clean faces of low fae of modest means and hardly seemed like the rebel type. Then again, if there were a physical mark denoting a rebel, they wouldn't be hard to find.

Children cried as their parents were dragged out of their homes. Hurried promises to spouses or older children were made as the guards yanked the supposed rebels from their loved ones. Fear tinged the chaotic streets. Some fought, others ran. Neighbor turned on neighbor in hopes of appeasing their bloodthirsty queen.

The shadows moved too fast and Derron too slow. With

every inch gained, he wondered if this madness would quell the queen's vengeance. Was her goal to paint the rebels as the villains? If they wouldn't surrender themselves for the good of the city, then they weren't worth protecting.

Anrea's workshop was a beacon of color and hope. Derron dismounted his horse in one fluid movement and ducked through the frantic crowd to cross the street. Nobody spared him or Eileen a glance. Derron pounded on the workshop's door, screaming at Anrea to open. A part of him hoped she'd be smart and keep it locked.

When no answer came, Eileen turned the door handle.

It opened.

"Sometimes the easy solution is the right one." She walked into the studio with a smug smile, Derron filing in after her. "What are you hoping to find?"

Anrea was the only, although shaky, link he had to the rebels. Even though it sickened him, he'd rather pry a name from her than see his mother's mysterious plans for Adara unfold.

Anrea was nowhere to be found.

The workshop was deserted, and judging by the cold seeping through the walls, the smell of closed spaces, and the subtle layer of dust collected on the surfaces, it must have been so for at least a few days. Every easel and instrument remained in its place, phantoms of a life full of color and music.

Eileen shivered behind Derron, her eyes darting from one corner of the ceiling to the next. "It almost feels haunted."

Memories flashed before Derron's eyes as he took in the empty space. Sweat beading on tawny skin in a bed too small and much too crowded. Dust from Anrea's hair that burrowed under his nails three days later no matter how many times he'd tried washing it off. The feeling that was neither friendship nor love, but somewhere in between, a dream had while being wide awake.

Derron walked to the piano. A note sat on the keyboard.

Curious, he picked it up.

You're a shit singer, but you're a wonderful musician. Don't let them ruin you.

There were no names, but he knew Anrea left it for him. He could have used his Song to learn her secrets—should have done so to obey his queen's orders—but he hadn't. Anrea had given him a space where he could be less than a prince and somehow more than what he was.

His gratitude might have condemned the whole of Adara.

Derron scrunched the note in his fist and threw it aside. "This was a bad idea."

"You've had worse," Eileen teased in a clear attempt to lighten the mood. "What do we do now?"

"It's best I get you back to the Embernest and try to figure out what's going on from there."

Derron kept Eileen tucked close as they exited the workshop. The sun was setting. Time was running out. People ran up and down the street as if they could outrun the queen's eye and the city guard. Derron took the brunt of their jostling and shoves, shielding Eileen with his body. She clutched his suit as if he were a lifeline. "Derron, the horse." He almost didn't hear her through the commotion.

The post where they'd tied the horse was empty. "Five fucking gods," Derron muttered. Wading through Adara's streets was a difficult feat on a good day, but now it would be near impossible to reach the castle.

Men and women in the city guard's gray and blue uniforms marched down the street. A fae couple sped past Derron and Eileen, shoulders scrunched as if trying to make themselves smaller to avoid attention. The armed guards stopped not three doors down from Anrea's shop and kicked in the door. Children screamed as the guards stormed inside.

"What are they going to do with all these people they're arresting?" Eileen asked in a tremulous voice. Derron wished he had an answer that would appease his inner turmoil, her horror, and the people's fear, but they both knew the truth—the queen might use some to make an example. The slightest shadow on their conduct could lead to their doom. The city's prisons would overflow with innocents, and the castle's dungeons would as well.

His mother already held one known rebel in her custody. One she had no use for but that would send a message.

"Arkael," he breathed.

Eileen grabbed onto his wrist, as if that could stop him from unraveling.

The city guard filed out of the home, this time with no prisoners. Derron absentmindedly watched them go, but his mind was locked in a dark dungeon cell. His head pulsed to the panicked rhythm of his blood, and his limbs tingled with dread. He had no right to feel this way. The moment Arkael had been arrested in Merania, his life had been forfeit. There was no changing his fate, only prolonging the inevitable. Yet now that Arkael's life hung on a thread, Derron felt weighed down by doom and held together by stubborn resolve. He couldn't let his brother die.

"He's still alive," Eileen reassured him. "She'd make it a spectacle to break Mykal."

A spark in his peripheral vision stopped Derron from answering. It came from the house the city guard had searched.

A flash of orange and red blazed through the air, followed by a deafening explosion. The wall tore open as Derron grabbed Eileen. The impact sent them flying into the nearest alley. They hit the ground, Derron landing on top of Eileen. Debris rained down upon his back. Heat singed the air. Tall flames climbed over buildings and devoured them, bathing everything in orange and red. Smoke obscured the twilight sky.

Eileen held out her hands and released her power with a loud grunt. An Ice shield formed around them as a wave of fire licked past. Melted ice dripped onto Derron's hair and down his nose, falling upon Eileen's umber cheeks.

Someone ran into the alley, fire climbing up their body. Derron curled tighter against Eileen. The person tripped over their own feet, flailing on the floor, desperately trying to douse the flames. Maintaining the wall around them, Eileen sobbed and hid her face in Derron's neck. He shut his eyes hard until black and red stars blinked behind his closed lids. That didn't stop the screams, or the sickly stench of burning flesh.

The heat receded. Eileen's arms dropped to the ground, her magic fading. Fire crackled around them, but it no longer washed over the street in a devastating wave. Derron rolled over and retched onto the cobblestones. The scars on his back pulsed in a sick reminder. His skin had gone clammy. He couldn't think, couldn't breathe.

You're not in the dungeons, his subconscious fought to save him, using words that could have belonged to either Cassia or Elon.

This is Aerella. She's doing this to the city. This time, it was Asharaya. *Move, Argarys, or I won't have the pleasure of killing you myself.*

The sun was cloaked behind a smoke-infested sky. His mother hadn't even waited until sundown to deliver her punishment.

Eileen called his name. Her hands came around his face, checking for injuries.

Derron coughed and groaned as he grabbed onto the wall to pull himself up. "Are you okay?"

Screams and wails rose from the streets. Men, women, children. Derron's eyes landed on Anrea's workshop, heart sinking as the flames engulfed the building. Fire spat as if cackling.

A burst of adrenaline rushed through him. The prince dashed into the streets. Someone called for help. Derron ran toward the voice, ignoring Eileen's warnings, and covered his face with his arm once he reached the burning building. A dead man lay face down on the ground, a soot-stained cape around his shoulders. Derron pulled the cloak with a grimace, throwing it over himself as he rammed into the door. The heat was unbearable, the fire too close. Derron's vision swam in and out of focus, threatening to black out.

"Stand back," Derron shouted against his own fear as he barreled into the door again. The wood gave way with a loud crack. Fire tunneled into the house. Veins of green twisted within its core. The color wanted to trigger a memory a step out of reach.

Two young girls ran out, followed by a man with a younger boy in his arms. Face covered in soot and tears, the man nearly dropped to his knees in gratitude. "Get to safety," Derron said. Not far away, Eileen produced an Ice slide to help a woman out of a window.

They rushed to where the cries were loudest, coughing against the smoke. Houses crumbled and shriveled, shops and stands turned to pillars of flames. The stench of burning flesh tinged the air. Bodies littered the streets, half burned and deformed, skin and hair peeling off, clothes turning to dust. The fire raged and devoured Heart with limitless hunger.

More explosions boomed in the heart of Adara. Fire barreled through streets and alleys in licks of wicked greens and oranges, destroying everything in its path. Eileen conjured another shield, but too slow. Fire singed the tips of Derron's hair and caught his borrowed cloak. He shrugged it off before flames could climb over his body.

Eileen lugged him in the direction of the Embernest. The castle shone bright in the smoldering horizon, unmovable as the city beneath it died. "Derron, we need to go," she cried.

"There are people who need our help."

"You won't help anyone if you're dead."

A loud crack resounded behind them. Wood groaned. Derron pushed Eileen and leaped from the building as it came crumbling down. Something heavy crushed him into the ground. Air rushed out of his lungs, and copper filled his mouth.

Eileen screamed.

Darkness curled around Derron's vision, and Maenar Errigen's words came back to him like an ill omen.

For Ilahara. Knowledge is the highest power.

29

Mykal

Mykal never understood the fascination so many had with sailing—not to mention the complete lack of hygiene that came with a seafaring life. As he stood on the schooner's deck, gripping the railing like his life depended on it, he wondered if on some instinctual level he'd always known he was incompatible with the sea. The constant rocking beneath his feet, the fear of falling onto his ass with every step, the indistinguishable mass he had to gobble down, and the constant nausea—no, Mykal didn't understand the appeal. But for once he was grateful to be on a ship, and he welcomed every bout of sickness. Without this schooner, he wouldn't be staring at the shimmering silhouette of the Embernest.

Five days at sea had gotten him closer to Kael than he'd been in a month.

Mykal called his Do'strath's name down the bond, which was no longer a threadbare string. His words flew along a spinning compass dial. He could sense Kael on the other side, caged between four walls while a storm denied Mykal entry. All he could do was keep reaching out, keep searching for a fissure in the wall until he found a way in. *I'm coming, Kael.*

At a distance, the veil shrouding the Embernest could be mistaken for fog, but the closer they sailed to shore, the more he recognized it for what it was: smoke. The air was heavy with the stench of fire. It dragged Mykal back to Daganver and the bodies consumed by Deimok's flames. A shudder racked his bones as his stomach clenched. What had happened ashore?

Solana joined him at the rail, filling his peripheral vision. A shadow tempting him to look away from the castle. Mykal resisted until he no longer could. His eyes trailed to the silent wraith and studied her rigid stance. She'd been on edge since they'd boarded the ship, too quiet even for her. The way she zeroed in on the coast, Mykal readied himself to catch her should she suddenly jump overboard and try to swim to shore. He wouldn't mind doing so himself, if he could manage to climb over the rail with his shaky legs. But while he wanted to run to Kael, Mykal feared Solana wanted to escape the ship—or rather the memories haunting her. Had she ever been on a ship that wasn't the *No One*?

Mykal angled his body so he could face Solana. "You could have stayed in Frosthead Hall," he said in careful Havanian. Scattered about the ship were the six men comprising the schooner's crew and their captain, who conversed with Shara at the helm. If speaking Havanian could give him and Solana privacy, he'd make the effort.

Solana's surprise lasted a moment before the hard grimace returned to her soft lips. "There's nothing for me in Frosthead Hall."

"You could have helped my mother."

"You mean I could've been her bodyguard while you were away. You'll forgive me if I'm not keen on the prospect of deferring to a fae like the rest of your human staff."

Mykal shifted on his feet, likely failing to hide his discomfort at the bite in her words. He'd always assumed humans in Daganver lived good lives because they were treated with respect, paid for their work, and could own their own homes instead of being crammed into servants' quarters in the bowels of the fortress. It was more than humans in other regions could strive for, and yet nothing compared to what the fae had. Nothing compared to what he'd seen in Havanya. The Human Continent was a land with no kings, where humans lived with the free pursuit of power, pleasure, and wealth. One could argue there was too much freedom, which explained the impressive number of murderers, liars, and thieves, but it was freedom nonetheless. Solana must have deemed the Daganveran benevolence a mocking illusion of rights, when the reality was humans were still one step below the fae and had no means to become their equals.

"I would not ask you to defer to anyone, least of all my kind."

Mykal didn't realize he'd stepped closer until Solana craned her head to meet his earnest gaze. The sea breeze played with the ebony strands falling loose from her braid, and the smell of her vanilla soap fluttered around him. Sweet and comforting, yet spicy enough to enrapture his senses. He followed the invisible trail to her throat. Beneath the skin-tight layer of her leathers, he imagined the scent would be strongest in the indent between neck and shoulder. He almost leaned in, imagining the hitch of her breath in the sighing waves. He cleared his throat and shuffled back a half step.

"Have you told Shara you can't conjure shadows?" he whispered in Ilahein, too rattled to remember the human words.

Solana smacked him hard behind the head. "Shut up."

Mykal massaged the aching spot but didn't back down. "You have to tell her."

"And give her something else to worry about?" she argued in Havanian, despite him having switched to Ilahein.

"We have to know each other's weaknesses if we want to get out of that castle alive."

"I used too much power, that's all. They'll come back."

Whether or not the shadows would return, Mykal understood the importance of hope when one was falling apart. He wouldn't take away Solana's, even if the desire to throttle her now replaced the impulse to bury his nose in her neck.

Shara's approaching footsteps cut their argument short. Mykal scooted farther away from Solana and cast away any lingering trace of her scent. Kael would have better luck dealing with these complicated women and their web of intricate secrets and lies. The longing for his Do'strath was a tangible thing, like a rope wound around his neck.

"The captain will drop anchor here," Shara said as she settled in the space between Solana and Mykal. "It'll be easier for us to reach shore undetected with a raft. The darkness and the cliffs will give us cover."

"Good," Solana said. After a moment, she whispered, "Are you all right?"

Mykal had been so focused on Kael that he'd nearly forgotten where they were sailing to and who stood beside him. This was Shara's first time in Adara in fourteen years. The last time she'd been in the Embernest's shadow, her family and dragon had been killed, and she'd boarded a ship to Havanya.

"It seems I can't be near Adara without something burning," Shara said after a moment of heavy silence.

Mykal studied Shara as she stood immobile, the slow rise and fall of her chest the only sign she breathed at all. He stared as if she were a complex portrait and he the observer trying to decipher the emotions behind every stroke. Beneath the calm exterior, a glimmer gave away the emotion in her golden eyes, mirrored by the ruby in the dragon ring around her neck.

King Gailen's ring, hanging by Queen Jaemys's necklace.

Shara grasped her dagger's hilt so tightly Mykal wondered if it would snap before they reached shore. He'd spent enough time with her to notice that nervous tell. The cold bite of steel eased her into an eerie battle calm that reminded him of a dragon's dangerous stillness. The quiet before the reckoning of a storm. He'd seen that look in Daganver, too.

"Promise me you'll stick to the plan," Mykal blurted. This was the closest he'd ever gotten to mending the broken shards of his family, a once-in-a-lifetime opportunity he couldn't squander. "No distractions, no surprises. We go in, get Kael, my father, and Eileen, and we get out." He placed his hand over Shara's hand gripping the dagger. The taut bones of her knuckles bit into his skin. "I wouldn't fault you for feeling like you should go after Aerella, but I'm begging you not to. Getting yourself killed won't bring back your family." *And it won't save mine.*

The raft's soft splash as it met the water filled the silence before Shara nodded. "We stick to the plan."

As Mykal followed her to the other side of the deck, he wondered if he'd imagined the hitch in her voice.

30

Shara

Shara's leathers stuck to her clammy skin as she, Mykal, and Solana rowed to land. *It's only sweat, not blood.* She'd hoped fourteen years away from the Embernest would have shielded her from the onslaught of memories, or that the white-and-golden castle would stir no reaction, and yet it hit her like a punch to the chest. It was as if she'd been dumped right back into the night of the Coup, and instead of sailing away from the death and destruction, Shara was rowing right into it.

Fire had chased Shara also in her nightmares. She hadn't slept long, too anxious over what awaited her come nightfall, but flashes of destruction and a panicked crowd swarming the streets haunted the little sleep she'd had. Derron had been right in the heart of the commotion. The sight of him there had terrified her into waking.

After half an hour, they reached the sliver of sandy shore at the foot of the Embernest's cliff. This close to the castle, one could hear the incessant beating of the waterfall at the castle's back. Water had memory, the scholars said. Perhaps that was why dragonsong and the mighty beat of wings seemed to echo around them.

Close to shore, they stepped into the water and pushed the raft the rest of the way, aided by the waves rushing to meet the shoreline. "Does this look familiar to you?" Mykal asked in a whisper once the raft was hidden from view.

It was all Shara could do to rein in the emotion threatening to choke her. The natural stone wall was as she remembered it, smooth in places and jagged in others. It concealed the beach unless one soared over it, as her father would do on the back of his golden dragon, Oruk, every day during his rounds. Each time she and Elon had been caught sneaking out was because Shara was too mesmerized by Oruk to look away. She could almost hear Elon snapping at her to hide while awe had rooted her to the spot.

Shara craned her head to the sky. Empty of dragons, yet veiled by smoke.

Mykal cleared his throat. "Shara?"

She swallowed back tears and didn't spare the cliff another glance as she walked along its border. "The passage is this way."

"How many passages are there?" The waterfall almost drowned out Mykal's voice.

"I'm not sure. They stretch beneath the entire castle and let out at different points in the city."

"Did your parents tell you about them?" Solana asked.

"They told my brother, but Elon wasn't good at keeping secrets."

They followed the cliff's half-moon outline to the back of the castle where the waterfall loomed. Smaller streams cascaded from the rocks directly below, carving paths into the stone. The water fell like a curtain of white mist, catching the glimmer of stars on its surface as it dropped into a large pool leading to the open sea. It was enchanting and intimidating, yet barren without the dragons soaring above it and playing among the numerous streams.

This close it was impossible to avoid the spray of water. By the time they reached the slope behind the largest waterfall, Shara's sodden clothes melded with her skin and water poured into her eyes. She set to work ripping and cutting away the tangled vines clinging to the rocks. Mykal and Solana followed her lead.

"There's nothing here, Shara," Mykal said.

"There has to be."

"There's nothing—" His words cut off in a yelp when his hand descended into empty space, upsetting his equilibrium on the slippery ground. He grasped the rock to stay upright as a cool draft kissed their skins.

Shara shuffled around him, careful of her footing. She stretched her hand into the hollow space, conjuring a flame to cast golden light against the cavernous walls. Mykal gaped like a fish out of water. She smirked, triumphant. "You were saying?"

Fire sprung from her hand and into the nearest sconce, illuminating the dusty webs hanging from the once-golden dragon wings. As they walked, the flames followed, fading from one sconce and appearing in another. Shara nicked her finger and smeared blood on the edge of her blade. The shadows danced along the walls to her blood's call, waiting to be summoned. If an ambush waited ahead, she'd know.

"We don't know where Kael is being held. You'll have to locate him through the bond." Shara's whisper echoed off the high ceilings. The only other sound accompanying their footsteps was the slow trickle of water and gentle, sporadic splashes.

"The connection isn't stable. I feel him on the other side, but I'm not sure he can hear me. It's like his mental shields are raised."

"Maybe it's not Kael's doing," Solana mused. "He might

have been drugged."

The Fire leaped into the next sconce, illuminating a new section of the tunnel. A gate stood at the end of it, the iron rusted over.

Shara bit back a curse. "I didn't remember any gates. They must be new."

"You said no one else knew about these fucking passages," Mykal snapped.

"That's not what I said." There it was again, that sharp edge to his voice that had been there since Daganver. "And in case you've forgotten, I haven't been here in fourteen years, Myk." What she didn't add was that Aerella had been one of her father's most trusted friends. Of course she'd know about the tunnels. Shara should have anticipated it, and yet she hadn't. Mykal's doubt in her was all the more vexing because of her disappointment in herself.

Solana pushed between them to take a closer look at the gate. "It is sealed shut."

"We could use the shadows to cross to the other side," Shara suggested.

"Save those for when we really need them." Mykal brushed past her, and despite fearing that any use of his magic would cause another Frostbite, Shara didn't dare stop him as he wrapped his hands around the rusted iron bars. Ice spread along them until the entire surface was coated with sapphire frost. One squeeze, and the Ice fractured within his hold. The gate collapsed to the ground with a sigh, no more than dust and crystals.

Relief washed over Shara when he remained standing and unharmed. "You're a showoff, but an effective one."

Mykal's eyes strayed to Solana for a moment before his hand flew over his heart. Shara rushed for him, but Solana was faster. "Are you all right?" she asked.

Mykal nodded, his eyes filling with tears. "I can hear him."

31

Kael

Kael was certain it had been four days since his wretched father's visit. Two since the queen branded him. The fog in his mind receded little by little, still there but not threatening to swallow his consciousness whole. With this newfound fragile and unexpected clarity, he calculated the passage of time by the temperature of his cell. Not the most accurate method, seeing as he was in the Embernest's lower levels, but the cliff itself served as the prison's walls, and the rocks were warmer at given moments and colder the next, depending on the sun's position.

Sounds of a commotion breached the dungeon's silence. The front gate groaned open. Cries. Shouts. People scuffled and pleaded innocence. There were too many voices and scents to make out. At least a dozen, though he couldn't be sure.

"On what charges are you arresting me?" The voice was feminine and angry, and it came right outside Kael's door. "Is idle gossip your only proof?"

A slap, and the woman whimpered. Kael jerked upright, instinct urging him to defend. The hatch in his door was closed, but he could open it from the inside. A kindness from whoever had engineered this dungeon so that the prisoners could call for their jailers.

If only Kael had a knife to stab one of them in the eye.

"Leave her alone," he warned, the rasp of his voice unrecognizable.

"We have a hero." Kael glimpsed blonde hair and startled blue eyes before the woman was thrown into the cell opposite his. "Someone needs their next fix."

Kael bared his teeth and spat in the guard's direction, his saliva smacking against the door. He slumped against the wall and slid onto the floor. The anger burned hot and fast. He was tired, hungry, the fog in his mind slowly slinking back. He stayed that way until nothing but the near-silent march of the guards making their rounds and the soft cries of his new cell mates filled the cavernous space. Sometimes he heard mention of Aerella, the temple, and a threat. Kael returned to the door. The hatch in the door opposite his was open. The woman paced in her cell. "What is this about the queen?" he asked.

"She threatened the entire city if the rebels weren't handed over. Feels like half the city's been arrested. The city guard can't hold everyone in their prisons, so they locked us here."

"Are you a rebel?"

The woman scoffed. "Wish I was one now."

An earsplitting explosion rent the air. The walls and floor shook with enough force to send Kael sprawling. To stop his fall, he grabbed at the wall's rough surface, his tender fingers screaming. It could have been an earthquake, but the earth didn't make that sound.

Raucous cries rose from the now-occupied cells. Men and women alike cried for their mothers or called out for their loved ones who were likely doing the same in the city. "The queen's vengeance!" someone screamed.

"Lord Darrok." A pang tugged Kael to the door. He rammed his shoulder into it, but though his skin and bone throbbed, the hinges remained intact.

The quaking settled within minutes. Prayers filled the halls. People asked the gods to keep their loved ones safe, to spare them from the queen's wrath. If the explosion had been strong enough to be felt in the dungeons, it was likely that the queen had set fire to an entire city block. How many survived?

Moved and rattled at the same time, Kael sent his silent request to the Dragon for his mother's safety, and that of his Do'strath, of Shara, Solana. *Please, protect them. Let them be safe.*

The walls grew colder with time's passing. The crying quieted into sniffles. The prayers stopped. Silence blanketed the halls. Whether they slept or not, the night would be long and restless.

Stomach grumbling, Kael sat on his cot, leaning against the wall. The stone's rough texture dug into his back, but he was too numb to move or care. He knew no one in Adara, therefore he had no one to mourn, but he wasn't a stranger to his fellow prisoners' plight. For days, he'd done nothing but cling to the desperate hope that the people he loved were safe, and then he'd descend into the deepest despair when the horrid alternative snuck its way into his mind and wouldn't let go.

Those feelings warred within him still. Kael massaged his chest against the invisible ache, cradling the warmth radiating there. The explosion had unsettled him. His thoughts dragged him to Daganver, to Mykal.

A frozen rose bloomed in his core, its roots webbing into his every nerve. Heat followed the icy path, a dull echo of his Fire surging in response to the cold presence growing inside him. Kael stood from the cot. The renike flowing through his blood kept his Fire dormant, but he knew that power. That Ice.

Myk?

The feeling vanished as soon as he dared think the name.

Kael clutched his shirt, heart pounding as if trying to reclaim that familiar feeling. He tried again, but to no avail.

Kael slumped back, grabbing and pulling fistfuls of hair. A tear beaded in his eye's corner. Had the illusion been the queen's doing? Had she finally found a way to use the soulbond to torment him?

A tug. A whisper of Ice trying to sneak past the fog in Kael's mind. Kael whimpered, his head falling against his knees. *Get out of my head*, he growled.

It's me, Kael.

Kael shot to his feet, biting his tongue to keep from calling out his Do'strath's name. Terror seized him. Mykal wasn't here—he couldn't be. Because if Mykal was in these dungeons, it meant Aerella had found him, that Daganver was lost and Asharaya dead.

You're not real, Kael whispered down the bond—a bond that no longer felt barren, but like a lifeline, a string connecting one soul to another.

Don't shut me out. Keep talking. I'm coming to get you.

Kael shook his head, choking on a sob. Of all the things Aerella had done, this was the cruelest. The soulbond was the most sacred thing in his life. He wasn't equipped to resist it, to fight against it. His body, his heart, his very soul fed on the illusion that Mykal was coming to save him. The bond was no longer a thin string but a rope, and then an iron chain.

Kael pressed his forehead to the door. Unwelcome cold seeped into his skin. The putrid odor of his cell clutched his throat. The physical aches, the repugnant feel of the renike flowing through his system, and the filth surrounding him were somehow grounding. This was his reality, not whatever the queen wanted him to believe. This Mykal wasn't real, and Kael was going to die here, alone in this cell, away from everyone he loved.

A grunt interrupted the rhythmic steps of the guard patrolling his corridor. Kael jolted up. The jingle of keys. A wooden hatch opening and closing. "Please, we're innocent!" a man cried. More hatches opened, rousing prisoners from their sleep. A sharp whisper called for silence. Something was familiar about that voice.

Kael paced away from the door. *Get out of my head.*

"Kael?"

Kael's heart leaped into his throat. He knew that voice better than his own. It spoke in his mind, echoed within his heartbeats, and filled the void inside him. For a moment he almost forgot this was an elaborate illusion. The temptation to call out grew stronger the more this imaginary Mykal searched for him within the cells.

The hatch in his door opened, golden eyes peeking through the bars. "He's here."

Running steps heralded a collision against his door. Blue frost spread across it.

"We have the keys." The voice sounded like Shara's. How had the queen replicated a voice she'd never heard? He held his ground far from the door.

The entire door froze over within moments and then crumbled to shimmering dust. Beyond it stood his friend. His other half. His soulbound.

Aerella's Mykal was exactly as Kael would have pictured him after weeks spent apart. Dark circles framed his lower lids, his cheeks stood in sharp relief, and his hair looked windswept and untamed. Despite the haggard appearance, he was as beautiful as ever in his dark leathers. But what stole Kael's breath was the hopeful look in his Do'strath's brown eyes, the shimmer of tears threatening to spill. The remnants of ice and wood fluttering about painted a magical picture, as if this were a dream.

Kael would have given anything for this to be real. "You win," he croaked. "You broke me."

"It's me." Mykal stepped forward, and Kael backed into the wall. Familiar eyes raked down Kael's body, assessing his sorry state. Anyone else would have softened with pity or shrunk back in disgust, but not Mykal—fake Mykal. The anger brimming through the brown was so real, Kael squeezed his eyes shut and shook his head.

"Please stop."

"We were born in the same year, exactly one month apart. I'm the eldest, though you're the one always cleaning up my messes."

"Please."

"We were raised together, schooled together, but we weren't always friends. You were too shy, and I was too much of a coward to take the first step. That's been a constant of our relationship."

"Stop."

"The first time we really spoke was when you found me crying in the stables. Rendal sent me to fetch his sword, but when I returned to the courtyard, he was gone. He'd run off with his friends. You sat next to me and told me he was a piece of shit. We were six years old. I stopped crying when you told me you'd train with me instead, and I think I started to fall in love with you then."

Kael opened his eyes, heart fluttering, but he stared at the wall ahead. *Not real not real not—*

"After Rendal died, you stayed with me the entire day and let me cry on your shoulder when no one was looking." Mykal cleared his throat, his next words tremulous. "When the queen took Eileen, you woke me up in the middle of the night. You'd saddled the horses so we could track down the carriage and bring her home. The day you asked me to be your Do'strath was the happiest day of my life."

Kael's gaze finally strayed to Mykal. He was a few steps away now, his hands raised where Kael could see them. "Our first kiss was on a ship in the middle of siren waters, but I've dreamed of giving you a thousand more. I know the exact number of breaths I've taken without you." Mykal held out his hand. *It's me,* he murmured down the bond. *I'm here, and I'm never leaving you again.*

Hope sparked in Kael's chest, feeble and dangerous. He slowly raised his dirty hands to Mykal's. The moment their fingers brushed, something stirred within him, like a dragon opening its eye. His Fire recognizing a friend.

"It's really you."

A tear slid down Mykal's cheek. "You really are slow to catch on, aren't you?"

Kael laughed, and then his laugh turned into a sob. The invisible cord holding him back snapped. He crashed into Mykal, whose arms enveloped him, and cried onto his shoulder. The scent of Daganver's forests clung to his Do'strath's skin, dissipating any lingering doubt. This was real. Mykal was real, and there in the flesh to save him.

Kael leaned away, tears still blurring his sight. Their lips crashed together, desperate, happy, hungry. His name was a reverent whisper on his Do'strath's lips in the brief moments between one kiss and another. "Forgive me," Mykal said.

"There's nothing to forgive." Before Mykal could protest, Kael claimed his mouth again. His Fire stirred, wanting to roar to life but held back by the renike's binds. Where his Fire was too weak, the core of Mykal's Ice living within him reawakened, bringing back some of his strength. Kael deepened the kiss, feeling alive with every sweep of his tongue. He tasted salt on his parched lips. "Don't cry." Kael's fingers trembled as they stroked Mykal's cheek. "Myk, it's not your fault."

"Maybe I'm just happy to see your stupid face," Mykal murmured against his lips. "I missed you so much."

"You're smothering him. Maybe wait until we're out of here to make him regret our daring rescue."

Kael still clung to Mykal as he acknowledged their friend. Shara stood on the threshold, the flame from a nearby sconce illuminating half of her face while the rest was bathed in shadow. Crimson stained her fingers and her blade, so at odds with the smile blooming on her lush lips.

Emotion welled in Kael's throat. "Thank you."

Shara came inside the cell and gave him a quick hug, made awkward by Mykal's refusal to move away. "Sorry it took so long."

"I took care of the other guard. Did you find—"

Air whooshed out of Kael as doe eyes met his. Though damp, not one of her luscious dark locks was out of its binding, and not a drop of blood marred her skin. Wreathed in darkness, she resembled a vengeful wraith, a beautiful goddess. Something swooped low in his belly as Kael remembered his hallucination. His vision hadn't done her justice. "Solana."

She ran to him, crashing into his side and squeezing his middle. Her sob vibrated against his neck. "Thank you," she was whispering in Havanian, and it took him a moment to realize she was addressing her goddess. Had she prayed for him while they'd been separated? For some reason, the thought intensified the warmth pooling in his belly.

Kael leaned his head against hers, inhaling vanilla and fresh rain from her silky hair. "I'm okay," he murmured in Havanian, even as tears streaked his cheeks. Using the human language added intimacy to the moment. Mykal pressed close to him on Kael's other side, and Kael raised their clasped hands first to his lips, then his heart. "I'm okay now."

Shara cleared her throat and the three disentangled. Kael's chest felt colder without Mykal's and Solana's hands against it. "I hate to interrupt, but since someone here forgot this was a covert mission, we don't have much time."

Kael struggled to rein in his smile when mock betrayal flashed on Mykal's face. It lasted a moment before he turned serious. "They have my father, Kael."

"I know. I've seen him."

They all perked up. "Would you be able to take us to him?" Shara asked.

Kael nodded. "I remember the way, but we should free the other prisoners, too."

"That's not a good idea," Solana said.

"They're innocent," Kael insisted. "Aerella arrested presumed rebels today and also blew up something in the city."

Shara tossed Solana the keys. "We'll find Lord Darrok. You free the other prisoners."

Mykal lifted his chin, a silent request for Kael to lead the way. His insides quivered with trepidation belonging to both him and Mykal. Now that they were together, Kael absorbed everything he could from the open channel between them, like parched earth soaking up rain. Mykal was reclaiming the space that belonged to him, the Do'strath bond yawning awake once more.

"I only saw your father once." Kael searched the hallways until he found a familiar one. He told himself his labored breath and wobbly legs were a consequence of their hurried pace and nothing more. "He seemed well." *Unbroken.* The word sped down the soulbond. "It should be one of these." The skin at the back of his neck prickled as he passed one of the doors, his body recalling the last time he'd been here. "This one."

Mykal blasted his power into the door.

Lord Darrok was on high alert when the door crumbled to dust, a look of utter bewilderment crossing his usually stoic face at the sight of his son. To Kael's relief, the lord appeared unharmed. "Have I gone mad?"

Mykal sprinted into the cell and fell to his knees. The lord's face crumpled with irrepressible emotion as he slowly returned Mykal's embrace. His hands hovered within an inch of his son's back, as if afraid to shatter an illusion. Only when his fingers stroked Mykal's hair did he finally grasp onto his son with vigor, a sob splintering his hard demeanor. "I have so much to tell you," Mykal croaked, leaning back to look his father in the face. "We took back Frosthead Hall."

"Alone?" Lord Darrok's surprise was a mirror to Kael's.

I'll explain later, Mykal promised down the soulbond.

"What of your mother and Luna?" Lord Darrok asked.

My mom? Kael shot down the bond, anxious.

"They're safe." Mykal said. *So is Elsa.* The lord seemed to deflate at the same time Kael did. *Safe.* When Shara and Kael stepped into the cell, the Head folded his arms onto his lap, though it looked more like gravity had pulled them down. His wide eyes shone through a veil of tears. "Jaemys."

The room succumbed to a heavy silence. Kael and Mykal exchanged a glance, and then looked to Shara, who remained closest to the cell's threshold.

"Asharaya." Lord Darrok cleared his throat. "You look just like your mother."

Shara visibly swallowed, her amber skin losing some of its luster. "There'll be time to reminisce later. Now we need to hurry."

Lord Darrok's mouth hung open as Kael approached, checking for any bindings on the chair. "What have they done to you?" Most of Kael's bruises were hidden beneath his raggy clothes, but there was no hiding the damage to his face.

Cheeks burning, Kael averted his eyes. It was no fault of his that he'd been captured and tortured, and yet he couldn't help feeling he'd failed his lord, his Do'strath, and even his mother, who'd been counting on him to return home. "It's okay now."

Mykal hurried behind the wheelchair, but Lord Darrok held on to the wheels. "I'd slow you down. Mykal, you're Daganver's future. I cannot risk you."

"I'm not leaving without you."

"It's an order." Lord Darrok's voice boomed in the cell. Years of obedience made Kael want to lower his head, but Mykal clenched his jaw.

"I'll carry you."

"I'll carry you and your son if I must." Shara's tone was light, but the way she gripped onto her blade betrayed her tension. The more time they wasted talking, the more chances they had of being caught.

Mykal pushed the wheelchair forward, and Lord Darrok no

longer protested.

"Were you in the city when that explosion went off?" Lord Darrok asked as they traversed the empty halls. Solana had mentioned she'd cleared out the rest of the guards. Since there were no bodies littering the floor, she must have hidden them in the cells to buy them some time in case new guards came in.

"We didn't come through the city," Mykal said.

"Whatever Aerella has done today is nothing she hasn't done before."

Shara's grip on her dagger turned iron tight.

Kael felt queasy as they ventured deeper into the dungeons. Solana had finished emptying the cells, and the silence reigning within the halls was almost unnatural.

The farther they walked, the emptier the dungeons, as if everyone had forgotten this part of the cave existed. The corridor stretched on forever, or maybe Kael's eagerness to be gone made every step closer to freedom seem to stretch on for miles. With eyes used to the dark, Kael spotted Solana's silhouette by an opening, which he assumed was the way his friends had sneaked into the castle.

Lord Darrok let out a small laugh. "I had no idea there was a secret tunnel giving into the dungeons."

"How long have I been gone?" Kael had barely given voice to the question, but it rang out in the cavernous hall. The heart-splitting pang in his chest came from Mykal.

His Do'strath met his stare. "Sixteen days."

Sixteen days.

Instead of taking the tunnel, Mykal and Shara stopped. Solana's expression betrayed a wariness she didn't voice. Kael looked from one to the other, tension building within him.

"Follow Solana," Shara said, as Mykal let go of his father's chair. "She'll lead you to safety."

Solana bent her head in acknowledgment to Lord Darrok, but no more than that. The lord returned the gesture and then gripped his chair's wheels, facing his son. "What about you?"

"There's one more Todrak we need to save."

"Eileen is lost" was Lord Darrok's sharp reply. "She's Aerella's puppet now." A pause, and then he asked, "Your mother put you up to this, didn't she?"

"Eileen's my sister. Your daughter."

"You wouldn't disagree if you'd spoken to her."

Is it true? Mykal spoke down the bond, the only place he'd allow the doubt to seep in.

I haven't seen her. Kael's instinct to protect Mykal and flee urged him to agree with Lord Darrok, but denying his Do'strath the chance to save his sister would mean betraying their bond. And going with him—even when every fiber of Kael's being begged him to—would only slow Mykal down and put him in more danger. *Do what you must, and then come back to me.*

Gratitude shone through Mykal's eyes, but his words were for Lord Darrok. "I won't abandon her."

"I'll keep him out of trouble," Shara promised.

Like that makes me feel better.

Mykal scoffed.

Shara looked between the Do'strath, eyes narrowing.

"It's not him I worry about," Solana said in Havanian. "The past is a dangerous enemy to face, sister."

"I won't lose myself."

Mykal placed his hand on Solana's shoulder. "I will not allow it." His Havanian was the surest Kael had ever heard it. Slipping back in Ilahein, he added, "I'll bring her back to you." Hearing those words, seeing his Do'strath's comforting gesture and Solana's trusting gaze, filled Kael with warmth. They'd grown closer in the time he'd been away.

Solana wrapped Shara in a hug, whispering something to her that even Kael couldn't hear. Then she addressed Kael and Lord Darrok. "Let me lead you through the dark."

"There's no one better suited for the task," Kael said. He turned to Mykal, his parting words sticking in his throat.

Mykal smiled. "I'll see you soon."

Shara pricked her finger and pulled Mykal into a shadow.

Lord Darrok jolted on his chair. "What happened?"

Kael turned the wheelchair into the tunnel's entrance. "I'll explain once we're safe."

32

Derron

Heart hammering, Derron opened his eyes. His instinct was to shoot upright, but pain speared through his head and limbs at the jerky movement. He winced and fell back onto something soft, shaking off a dream of fire, and later one of long, winding darkness. Asharaya appeared in the latter, illuminated by the light of her own conjured flame.

"He's awake." An umber hand came into focus and brushed the hair from his forehead. "How are you feeling?"

Derron was suddenly aware of every point in his body where magic was knitting his wounds. He was in his bed, Eileen at his side where his twin should have been. Cassia's absence felt like a severed limb. They'd never been apart as much as they had these past weeks, and he missed her more than ever.

"You gave us quite the scare, Son." Vaemor stood at the foot of the bed, his smile one of pure relief. Derron and his father weren't close, but he couldn't help the answering tilt of his lips.

He was glad to be alive.

Semal stood behind Aerella, who sat on the right side of Derron's bed. The general's expression was stern, as if blaming Derron for his injuries, while the queen didn't blink as she stared down at her son. "Eileen, leave us."

Eileen brushed her thumb against Derron's cheek, more hesitant than Derron had ever seen her. She still wore her soot-stained clothes. Had she sat by his bedside the entire time? Unbidden, the image of Asharaya from his dream—a beacon of light in a fathomless dark—flashed before his eyes. He blinked, and it was Eileen standing before him again. Derron experienced an irrational pang of disappointment, aggravating what seemed to be a constant state of guilt he felt toward Eileen. "I'll come back later," she promised.

No sooner had Eileen left than the queen inquired, "What were you doing out in the city?"

"Did you have your Fire wielders set off Maenar Errigen's mixture in the city?" Derron shot back, voice low and charged with unabashed horror.

"How do you know about that?"

Derron sat up too quickly. Air wheezed out of him at the abrupt movement. "How many did you hurt?"

"Two hundred thirty-six dead at the latest count." Vaemor side-eyed the queen. "Three times as many injured. The majority won't survive. Countless missing."

"How dare you judge me, of all people? You've done your share of misdeeds."

"Burning your own city isn't a misdeed, Mother. It's slaughter."

"It's justice. Those people aided the rebels who would see our family ruined and murdered. Some of them were likely part of the movement themselves. Either by action or association, they were traitors. I did what I had to."

"They were people—with a life, a family, a home. Hopes and dreams. A future." Derron's words were laced with despair and rage, the screams of his people still ringing in his ears. He shouted them, despite the burning in his throat, until an overwhelming feeling of helplessness drowned out everything else, leaving him hollow. "You took everything from them." He paused to stop the tremor in his voice. "Did you stop to consider why they'd rather help the rebels than obey you?"

"One cannot rule with a gentle heart."

Derron couldn't meet his mother's eyes.

Vaemor cleared his throat. "You should rest, Derron." Semal agreed with a nod.

"Go," the queen said, her tone clipped. "I want a moment alone with my son."

Derron didn't acknowledge Aerella's stare as the two men left. Much like his people, he was tired of the queen's ruthless games. Tired and ashamed. Fear of the queen and the desire to please his mother had made him do things he regretted. Derron was riddled with guilt for the Myrassar's fate, yet he often repeated to himself that he wasn't at fault. He'd been only eleven at the time of the Coup, but what excuse did he have now that he'd sailed to the Human Continent to end the last of them? How could he live with the knowledge that his actions had condemned his brother to torture and certain death?

"When will it end?" Derron asked his mother.

"When every last one of our enemies is dead."

33

Shara

Memories followed Shara into the dark. In the shadows' silence, innocents screamed, and dragons and warriors bellowed.

Wings booming.

Flames hissing.

Clear your mind. Stay in the present. Forget the past.

Shara pulled Mykal into the empty prison hall where they'd found Kael. Smoke permeated the air even here. How many had died in the city, victims of Aerella's paranoia? How many would blame Asharaya Myrassar for unleashing the queen's wrath or for not saving them when flames consumed their homes and loved ones?

"These shadows are almost worse than the ship," Mykal grumbled. The words lacked the bite of the past weeks. Seeing Kael returned color and light to Mykal's skin, and apparently some of his good mood. Shara was glad, but she couldn't suppress a twinge of envy now that she was the one separated from her soulbound. Deimok's presence was a dwindling flame barely holding onto the last fibers of a candle's wick. She could sense some of its heat but didn't dare near it for fear of blowing out its light. Leaving him behind was hard enough, but knowing he was hurt made it even more difficult. The sooner she returned to him, the better.

In their haste to flee, the prisoners had left cell doors ajar, but otherwise theirs had been a clean escape. Shara and Mykal quietly shut the doors as they passed, their footfalls and the squelching of their boots on the humid floor landing softly.

"Why is there no one in these rooms?"

Elon shushed her. "These aren't rooms. They're cells."

"I think Daddy fed all the bad men to the dragons."

Her memory faded with Elon's shudder, and the trinkets hanging by her neck grew warm against her skin. Shara wished she had something of her brother's. She remembered they looked alike, but did they really or did she just imagine him that way? Elon would be a man now. He should've had the chance to grow beneath the shadow of the Embernest and show these passages to a crush, perhaps stealing kisses between recitals of his ridiculously romantic verses. He deserved better than to die at eleven with a traitor's sword through his chest.

They walked in silence until they reached a stone wall with no openings. Mykal eyed it suspiciously but didn't protest when Shara walked up to it. With a shaky exhale, she pressed her fingers against the wall, the old stones warming beneath her touch. A vibration tickled her skin, like a cat giving in to a purr once it recognized a friendly hand.

That's right, you know me. Now let me through.

Shara summoned a lick of flame, which flowed red and bright into the crevices, spreading toward the ceiling and the muddy floor. Within seconds, veins of molten fire surrounded her hand. The stone beneath her palm pulsed like a beating heart, and Shara sighed, almost sagging against the wall at the magic's rush. Closing her eyes, she imagined Elon pressing his hand to the other side—not as the young boy he'd been, but as the man he would've become—a hand that was larger than hers, but with thin fingers and calluses born from quills, not swords.

A tear slid down her cheek as she applied the slightest pressure. The wall groaned and parted down the middle, the fire along the stones sliding into the new space to illuminate a dank and narrow passage. She'd known it would be empty, yet it didn't dull the spike of grief. Her family was dead. No matter how alive the stones felt, they were still nothing but a tomb for memories. A sob spilled from her lips, and she sucked in a breath before more tears followed.

Mykal's touch was as fresh as winter rain between her shoulder blades, a reminder that she wasn't alone. "Do you know where this passage leads?"

"Into the castle. Each tunnel leads to a different room. You'll have to use a tracking spell to locate Eileen." Their shared blood would be enough. "Can you do it?"

"I can."

Shara unclasped her necklace and slid her father's ring from the chain, offering it to Mykal. "If we get separated, remember what we discussed. You get everyone to Lur, and we'll meet there. You can track me with this."

"Hopefully it won't come to that." Mykal slid the ring onto his finger. "Do you still have my blood?"

Shara patted her pocket, where she'd tucked a small vial of Mykal's blood for tracking.

Mykal's hand clutched hers as they stepped inside. The passage closed behind them with a dull thud, and Shara jumped, her hold on Mykal's hand turning punishing.

Clear your mind. Stay in the present. Forget the past.

The passages had seemed larger and less confining to Shara as a child. Now, she had to duck to avoid the webs hanging from archways and dust gathering in the corners, and she could touch either side of the tunnel without stretching her arms fully.

The longer they followed Mykal's tracking spell, the more the walls seemed to close in on her.

"Talk to me," Mykal whispered, as they climbed up stairs jutting from the stone wall.

"I was in these passages the night of the Coup." *While Aerella's forces invaded my home.* "I'd sneaked into the library to read a book about Bhaessa Myrassar. Maenar Elvik left it on a table with a note warning me not to stay too long. I don't even know how he found out that I sneaked through the tunnels at night." *If I'd stayed in my room, I would've died like Elon and Mother.* Only her father had gone down fighting, felled by the woman who'd usurped his crown.

Now Shara was the invader, slinking in the belly of her ancestral home while somewhere above the usurper played her twisted games.

"Maenar Elvik must have loved you very much to do what he did, knowing the consequences," Mykal said. "I doubt he wanted a war. I think he wanted us to keep you safe, and for you not to be alone." He squeezed her fingers, and though tears fractured her vision, she lifted her eyes to his earnest ones. "You're both of those things, Shara. Not because you're my queen, but because you're my friend. Even if you drive me crazy."

The constricting hold on Shara's lungs loosened a fraction. "I'm sorry for not telling you what I was planning."

Mykal sighed. "We won't always see eye to eye, but we have to trust one another. If you keep trying to fight every battle on your own, you won't win this war."

Drafts indicated the presence of passageways at the end of the stairs. Shara released Mykal's hand, softening the hold on her dagger to adjust her grip. A flame lingered within easy reach beneath her palm.

Unlike the secret passage linking the castle and the dungeon tower, these openings weren't hidden by magic but chiseled into arches within the stone. Tapestries or portraits blocked some, while others connected to mechanisms in bookshelves or armoires. Shara clamped her teeth to stop their chattering. Muffled pitter-patter of feet or hushed conversations drifted from the rooms beyond—either high fae settling in for the night or servants cleaning out unused rooms. She braced herself for shouts, or ringing steel, or the crackle of flames consuming fabrics and flesh, but they never came.

Mykal abruptly stopped. The room on the other side of the archway was silent, but his nostrils flared. Shara tested the tapestry masking the passage, leaning close to peek into the room. The canvas was too thick to make out much, but there were shapes that might have been people—four, maybe—most likely huddled around a bed. She couldn't tell if anyone was in it. A large shape occupied most of the space. A table perhaps, or a pianoforte.

Shara's heart jolted twice in quick succession—once as she caught movement in the bed, and again as she remembered a younger version of herself lying belly down on a pianoforte that had seemed much too big at the time, chin tucked into the palms of her hands as a young Derron tested the keys.

"Play me a song."

The tip of Derron's ears turned pink and it made her giggle. "This is your brother's new piano. I shouldn't play it without his permission. Tell Elon to bring you along to my house, and I'll play for you."

"Elon never lets me come."

"If you want your song, you'll convince him."

She never had the chance.

A feminine voice inside the room said, "He's awake." Mykal took a quick step forward, as if he might throw himself through the tapestry. At Shara's inquisitive look, he nodded. The voice belonged to Eileen.

"You gave us quite the scare, Son."

"Vaemor Argarys," Mykal mouthed. The person Vaemor was speaking to had to be Derron. In her dream, she'd seen him shouldering his way through a mob in the burning streets. Was he hurt?

"Eileen, leave us."

Shara's entire body shook. She didn't need Mykal to tell her who that smooth, cold voice belonged to. Her whole being reacted to it. "Follow Eileen. I'll keep watch."

"Shara." Mykal grabbed her shoulder, and Shara shrugged out of his hold. "Come with me."

"This changes things," Shara bit out. It was a wonder she could keep her voice low. She could barely focus on Mykal's face through the film of tears veiling her vision. "Someone needs to keep an eye on them, and Eileen only knows one of us."

Mykal looked over his shoulder, visibly torn between following the tracking spell and staying with Shara. Her actions at Frosthead Hall compromised his trust in her, and his suspicion stung. "Remember what's at stake," Mykal pleaded. "If you reveal our position, we're all dead."

"No one is dying today." Shara pointed down the hallway with her chin. "Go. I'll meet you soon. If there's any trouble, remember the plan."

"And you remember what I told you. Don't do anything stupid."

When he was out of view, Shara twisted back to the tapestry and clutched the pendant around her neck. The weight felt wrong without her father's ring, yet she couldn't let go. Inside the room, Derron and Aerella argued animatedly about the explosion in the city. The numbers stoked the heat growing beneath her skin. Hundreds of innocents dead, countless more missing. If only Shara had arrived sooner, perhaps she could have saved some of them. Perhaps she could have found Aerella and ended her before she gave the order to sacrifice her own people on the altar of power.

To Shara's surprise, her outrage was mirrored in Derron's words. The passion and heartbreak in his voice were closer to the boy she'd known than the man who betrayed her in

Merania. Had he found some sense in the weeks they'd spent apart, or were strangers more worthy of his pity than a Myrassar and his half-breed brother? If Derron had been wounded in the city, then had her dream of him been real?

Aerella dismissed her husband, and two shadows neared what was likely the door. Shara edged closer to the tapestry. Without so many shapes huddled around the bed, the outline of Derron's body was clear.

"When will it end?"

"When every last one of our enemies is dead," the queen replied.

Shara's joints ached from her tight fists. In her mind's eye, Aerella wore the same silver gown that haunted Shara's nightmares, the same one she drew countless times dragging through blood. Her family's, Sanda's, that of the innocents she'd burned. So much blood soaked into that gown there likely wasn't a trace of silver left. It would be easy to step into the shadows, emerge behind the usurper queen, and slit her throat. The war would be over before it began. Her family would be avenged. She'd be free to make of her life whatever she desired without the constant fear of Aerella's shadow.

Don't do anything stupid.

Mykal's voice rooted her, despite every instinct screaming at her to attack. *Mykal, Solana, Kael*—their names became a litany, a prayer, and a reminder to do the right thing. If she attacked Aerella, would she be fast enough to murder her before Derron sounded the alarm? Shara couldn't be the reason why her friends were captured—or worse.

Shara's pulse drowned out the voices in the room. Her attention splintered between the present and a vision of her blade sinking into Aerella again and again. Only when the usurper's shadow shifted from the bed did Shara's muscles lock, her grip on the dagger shifting to give her a better hold. Every step she allowed Aerella to take brought her deeper into the safety of her stolen castle and the protection of the guards in her employ. Killing her would be that much harder.

Don't do anything stupid.

Derron turned toward the tapestry. Shara couldn't see his face, but she conjured the image of his silken hair brushing over his shoulder, the predatory gleam in his silver eyes. His gaze lingered, burrowing into Shara's chest like a knife.

"What is it?" the queen asked.

"Nothing."

Did he know she was there?

Now the queen looked at the tapestry. Shara bit her lip hard enough to draw blood, a scream building in her throat and her pulse quickening with every click of Aerella's heels. They echoed in Shara's ears like the ticking of a clock. She'd been too young to stop the Coup, too late to help Sanda, too distant to save the Adarian people from the flames, but now Aerella was here.

A draft hit Shara's back, as if to push her forward. Aerella was close enough that Shara could see the ivory hue of her skin, the silver locks framing her face dancing as the air breezed through them. "Interesting," Aerella said, taking another step forward.

Close enough that Shara could see the coldness in her silver eyes.

The scream she'd been holding back burst out with a vengeance. Shara's dagger slashed through the tapestry, and she tackled Aerella. She barely heard Derron's warning shout or Aerella's startled gasp as they crashed to the floor. She couldn't see the color of the usurper's gown—if it was silver like that night. The world narrowed to the weight of her blades, the hiss they made as they cut air, the wet squelch of Aerella's skin as Shara struck and struck and struck.

With a pained rasp, Aerella released a flame from her hand trapped between their bodies. The fire singed Shara's leather, and she leaped back with a hiss. Silver glinted in the queen's other hand. She slashed at Shara's hip with a belligerent roar.

Shara touched her side, her hand coming away red. The

wound burned, but not as much as the rage simmering through her. Not as much as her single-minded focus to see this villain dead. Dagger in hand, Aerella struggled to rise. Blood gushed from the cuts in her abdomen.

Shara grabbed the queen's hair and wrenched her head back. Raising the dagger to Aerella's throat, she bit out, "Tell me why you killed them."

"Jaemys…"

"You fucking bitch, tell me why! You owe me that."

An arm encircled Shara's middle, and a hand gripped her wrist. Shara bellowed like a trapped animal as she was wrenched away from the usurper, the door bursting open at the same time.

"You'll get yourself killed," Derron hissed in her ear as he pulled her away. As if her life meant anything to Shara in that moment. She struggled against him, and his legs buckled as if he were still too weak to sustain their combined weight. Yet he didn't let go.

Aerella bent in two, held up by one of her guards as the rest spilled into the room. "Seize her!"

A bell blared through the halls.

The alarm.

Myk…

Derron swayed and lost his footing, and Shara slipped free of his grip. Agony speared through her hip, her leg bending as she stumbled. The ruined tapestry was in front of her as the guards closed in on all sides. What had she done?

Terror seized her as she spun back to the room. Derron was sprawled on the floor, his wide eyes fixed on her as the guards seized her arms. Shara fought against them, letting her Fire's heat surge over her skin. The guards hissed, but their grip remained, relentless. She opened her fist, the blood staining her hand dripping onto the floor. *Maiden, please help me fix this.*

The shadows yawned open beneath her.

34

Mykal

Mykal leaned back against the stone wall, the chill seeping through his leathers. As Eileen chatted with a maid inside her room, he tried to steady his heartbeat. Her voice had changed since he'd last seen her, still gentle but clearly belonging to a grown woman. The silky tone she'd used with Argarys was a painful reminder of that.

Eileen kindly dismissed her maid. Mykal waited a few moments, tracking the patter of her slippers to ensure that she was alone in the room. Should he barge in, or call out first?

Like a damned idiot, his knuckle rapped the wooden paneling blocking his entry.

Eileen's steps halted. Tentatively, Mykal knocked again. Did his sister know about the passages or would she call for someone to identify the sound?

"Eileen?" he whisper-shouted. "It's me." Did she remember his voice enough to recognize him? Mykal cleared his throat.

"It's Myk."

Mykal didn't think Eileen heard, but then her steps resounded. A door clicked open. "Myk?" she squeaked.

The wooden paneling was still in place. "Ehm...what did you open?"

"My wardrobe." The shuffle of fabric accompanied her words. "Where are you hiding?"

"I'm in a passage. Try pushing the paneling."

A thud against the wood. Then another. The paneling gave way and he barely held his hands up in time to protect his face. Through the dresses, Eileen was the picture of shocked glee. An excited giggle burst from her lips and lit up her entire face along with Mykal's heart. He quickly eased the panel to the ground and launched himself into the wardrobe. Eileen's arms wrapped around him before he even made it into the room.

Tangled together, they stumbled inside, her body flush against his and his face buried in her fragrant curls. She was taller, her hair longer, and her dress accentuated a woman's body. A magnificent woman he hadn't had the opportunity to see grow. She was a stranger, and yet she wasn't. Those were his mother's eyes and his father's nose. His magic rushed through his body, as if recognizing kin. When she sobbed onto his chest, the years spent apart no longer mattered.

Was this the first time he hugged her? He must have done it countless times when they were children, and yet he couldn't remember. Their last encounter had been awkward with the guards' eyes fixed upon them and the queen's scrutiny. Mykal had counted the seconds until they left Adara and later loathed himself for all the things he hadn't said. This hug was a clean slate.

"We have to keep our voices down. There are guards in the hallway." Eileen looked up at him, chin resting on his chest. "How are you here?"

Mykal cupped her cheeks and wiped the tears with his thumb. "There's no time to explain. Kael and Father are waiting.

We need to go."

"Go?"

"Home." When Eileen didn't react, a sense of foreboding prodded him. "I'm taking you back to Daganver."

Eileen shoved away. "Y-you can't. The queen will never allow it."

"Would I be coming out of armoires if I had Aerella's blessing?" Mykal fought the urge to pull her close again, the need to protect her flaring up within him. He was used to feeling that way about Luna, but Eileen seemed fragile in a way their youngest sister never was. "Shara's waiting for us in the tunnels. By the time the queen finds out you're gone, it'll be too late."

"Shara?" Eileen pouted, and then gasped. "Asharaya is here? In the castle?" She peeked over his shoulders, toward the wardrobe. "Why isn't she with you?" The worry in her voice was tangible.

"She's safe, but not for long if we dally. Is there anything that might be of sentimental value to you? Anything Aerella might use to track you?"

"Myk, I'm not coming." Her stern expression was all their mother. "I have a life here. I can't take my things and leave."

"What life? You're a prisoner."

"It's not that simple," Eileen snapped. "I haven't been crying myself to sleep every night waiting to be rescued."

"No, you've been singing lullabies to Derron Argarys." At the mention of the prince, Eileen's face hardened. His father's disapproving face flashed before his eyes, opening a chasm between the siblings. Mykal desperately wanted to seal it shut. To stop Eileen from slipping away and destroying his dream of reuniting his broken family. If his father was right, if Eileen had really turned her back on them, it would destroy what was left of the Todrak. It would break his mother's heart beyond repair. "I heard you sighing over him earlier. Did that bastard tell you how he nearly got me killed in Merania? How he got Kael arrested and tortured?"

"He's your villain, Myk. Not mine."

"You're coming home with me."

"You're not listening." Eileen put another step between them, standing taller. "I love him. We're to be married."

"Over my dead body," Mykal snarled, his voice rising as anger turned his vision red.

He realized his mistake when Eileen's eyes zapped to the closed door. Mykal had only one dread-filled moment for his stomach to sink before the main door opened and the guards stormed the living room. "Lady Eileen, is everything all right?" a man asked.

Heart thundering, Mykal nudged Eileen so she'd answer.

"Yes," she stammered. "Everything is—"

A bell cut off the rest of her words. Shouts echoed from the hallways as the guards' footsteps receded in a rush. The words "queen" and "escaped" were all Mykal could make out over his blood's roaring.

Shara, what have you done?

"Get into the armoire," Mykal ordered, Ice covering his hands. "Now."

35

Derron

The guards startled at the shadows opening under Shara's feet, but they seemed to fuel her desire to escape. Fire sprang upon her wrists, and she elbowed her way out of their grasps. Her eyes found the queen's and then flicked to Derron's before she jumped into the opening she'd summoned with her blood.

"What magic is this?"

"She just vanished."

"Unnatural."

The queen rose to her feet, sweat pearling her brow as she shook off the offered hands of her men. "Don't just stand there. Search those tunnels. I want her found and brought to me alive so I can have the satisfaction of killing that little skank myself."

The guards followed the queen's orders in a flurry of movement. Semal and Vaemor entered in that moment, eyes wide with astonishment. While Semal rushed to the queen's side, Vaemor took in the room's state, his attention lingering on Derron as he grabbed onto the bed frame to lift himself onto the bed. Some wounds had reopened in his haste to stop Asharaya, and his legs shook with the effort of holding himself upright.

Asharaya. Here, in the Embernest. He thought he'd imagined her amber scent, and when she emerged from the tapestry, the sight had stunned him into momentary inaction. That she'd managed to come to Adara undetected was a testament to her resourcefulness and that of her allies. That she sneaked into the castle and used its secret passageways showed she had clung to more of her previous life as a Myrassar than she let on.

Gods, she'd almost killed his mother. Adrenaline and instinct had pushed him out of bed, yet there was another secret, horrifying feeling that had made him hesitate.

Relief.

"Vaemor, take a handful of guards and find out how Asharaya infiltrated the castle. Send word to the city guard. I want the city and ports searched for her allies. Semal, I want the castle surrounded. If the bitch is still on the grounds, I want her found."

She likely was. The shadows wouldn't allow her to travel long distances.

"You need to see the maenar," Vaemor said. Aerella leveled him with a glare that would have sent any other fae running.

"They entered through the dungeons," Semal signed. "The prisoners escaped."

Derron sucked in a breath that ricocheted through his aching chest. Arkael was free.

The queen snarled in frustration, flinging her arm into a stack of music sheets. "You," she shot at two guards. "Protect the prince."

Derron almost protested, but he stayed his tongue. He made a show of looking more worn out than he felt as the queen led a limping charge out of the room, her arm around Semal's shoulders and a trail of blood following in her wake. Only Vaemor turned to him, as if to verify he was unharmed.

Derron laid back against the pillows, waiting for everyone but the two guards to leave. When he was certain his parents and Semal were gone, he turned his attention to the guards. "Get out," he Sang.

The guards complied with vacant expressions.

Shooting out of bed, Derron flung a leather vest over his shirt and strapped his swords to his back. He climbed through the hole in the tapestry, ignoring the itch of his knitting wounds, and sped down the hall. Adrenaline added speed to his steps. From what he'd gleaned of the vrah's powers, Asharaya had likely used the shadows to escape through the tunnels, but she'd have to reemerge at some point. Only a handful of passageways led outside of the Embernest.

He hadn't gone far before the telltale signs of fighting pointed him in the right direction. Derron picked up his step, his injuries forgotten, hands itching for his swords. Ahead, at an intersection between hallways, a gaggle of guards fought an opponent who danced through the clang of steel. Her hair flowed behind her like a wisp of darkness, golden eyes blazing with determination.

Asharaya cut a line straight through her palm. Dark shapes slid against the floor and jumped along the walls to meet her stride. One spread like an ink stain on the ground, and she let herself fall in its black depths. She leaped out moments later, a few paces shy of the five guards. Asharaya unleashed her Fire, and the guards threw themselves against the walls to avoid the burst of flames.

"Shara!" he called out.

Asharaya spun, teeth bared as she shot a flame in his direction. Derron twisted aside, the flame so close he could smell wisps of smoke. Asharaya didn't linger to see if she'd incinerated him. Her steps barely sounded on the stone as she took off again. Derron gritted his teeth and dashed after her.

A streak of light cut across the hall. Asharaya pivoted for it, almost missing the guard blocking her path. She barely lifted her dagger in time to counter the deadly arch aimed at her stomach and wielded a second dagger. Blades crossed as she blocked the woman's new attack, metal screeching as they battled for the upper hand. Asharaya pushed the guard toward the narrow stairs leading to the lower levels. The woman grabbed the wall to arrest her fall. Quick as an adder, Asharaya sliced through the unprotected tendons of the woman's calf and came up behind her, thrusting her into Derron's path. He wasn't fast enough to avoid the impact. It took him a few moments to detangle himself from the guard and help her lean against a wall.

His chest heaved and his legs shook from exertion. Derron stopped to catch his breath before resuming his chase. By taking the stairs, Asharaya was headed toward the courtyard. The castle's perimeter was likely surrounded by now. There would be no escape.

He stopped short at the sight of the first guard face down on the stairs. Blood pooled on the stone, dripping over the edge and onto the next step with a macabre echo. Derron skirted the red puddle. Farther down there was another body, and another still. During his short respite, Asharaya had taken out a dozen guards, all dead or unconscious.

Derron finally glimpsed swaying branches against a sliver of night sky. The air stung his lungs, but he welcomed the chill as it chased away his lingering aches. He sprinted around the corner, the scent of roses wafting from the nearby gardens. Shara was running toward the gates, but Argarys soldiers surrounded her. One of them caught up to her and crashed the pommel of his sword against the back of her skull, sending her toppling forward with a wet rasp.

For the second time in what felt like the longest day of his life, Derron seemed to witness everything from behind a glass that warped his perception of time. Guards swarmed the first archway. Asharaya scrambled to stand, but hands caught her hair and yanked her to her feet. She writhed against her captors and screamed as a soul possessed. Her daggers were taken away. The belt at her waist hit the ground with a heavy thud.

And at the back, watching it all with greedy eyes, was Queen Aerella.

At her side, Semal took a bow and arrow from one of the archers and handed them to the queen. His mother snatched them without tearing her gaze from Asharaya, wincing almost imperceptibly as she lifted the bow, as she notched the arrow.

Asharaya searched the ground as she struggled to break free.

Call the shadows, he begged.

Despite the blood dripping from her hands and drenching her side, the darkness didn't stir.

Air rushed into Derron's throat at the same moment the queen loosed the arrow. He sprang forward, hand outstretched as if he could reverse time and bring the arrow back onto the bowstring, back into the quiver. The sharp end pierced Asharaya's center. She wheezed and fell forward, dipping her fingers into the blood spurting from the wound. Still, no shadow came to her aid.

Asharaya Myrassar was home at last, and she was dying. His mother seemed frozen, as if she could only breathe once Asharaya could not.

Asharaya is dying.

Suddenly he remembered her as a girl, torn skirts and dirty cheeks, with a stick in her hand as she copied his and Elon's fighting stances. Her little hand disappearing against a dragon's large snout. Her windswept hair and golden eyes glowing with joy as she slid down its enormous, scaled body. Those same eyes had looked away the first time he'd given her a rose.

And then he saw her in Havanya in that gossamer dress, the most arresting presence in a room of beautiful people. For a moment he'd wondered what might have happened if she'd chosen to wear such a dress were she still a princess and he her friend. He remembered the disappointment and relief when she hadn't recognized him, and later his lack of surprise when he'd discovered she'd learned her way around a blade after all.

Come and find me with that story.

He had, only to try to kill her. To prove his worth to a mother who only took and never gave.

At Semal's nod, a guard unsheathed his sword. The sound penetrated the ringing in Derron's ears. Instead of swinging the blade, the man offered it to the queen, who hobbled to him with a heavy limp. Her dress clung to her in the spots where blood drenched the fabric, but she hardly seemed to notice her wounds. Eyes fixed solely on her enemy, Queen Aerella grasped the blade. "You should have stayed dead, little one."

A trickle of blood reddened Asharaya's lips. With a defiant glare burning against her paling skin, she spat it into the queen's face.

Aerella's lip curled with distaste. "Just like your father."

The sword arched over her head.

"Stop." Derron staggered back with the amount of magic he poured into that single command. His Song zipped down invisible threads, claiming the minds of over two dozen fae. He sucked in a pained breath but held fast, his eyes measuring the distance between the sword and Asharaya's neck. "Don't touch her." He enunciated every word, his shoulders trembling with exertion, his wounds slowly tearing open again now that his magic was occupied elsewhere. "Put down your weapons."

Slowly, every unsheathed weapon either returned to its scabbard or dropped to the ground. But not the queen's. While the guards turned into living statues—their only movement the rise and fall of their chests—his mother shook with the effort to break free from his spell, knuckles white around the pommel, and silver eyes hauntingly transparent as they brimmed with betrayal. His scars throbbed beneath her scrutiny, reminding him why this could be a disastrous idea, but also giving him another reason to move forward.

Derron crouched beside Asharaya to inspect her injury. Her bloodstained shirt was burned in patches, the arrow embedded inches shy of her heart. Magic was keeping her alive, but for how long?

"Shara." His voice was barely a whisper.

"Don't..." Asharaya's fingers curled into the soil. "She'll...kill..."

"Stay with me." Derron strapped her belt around his waist, and then yanked the cloak off the nearest guard to wrap it around her. Asharaya winced as he hoisted her into his arms, blood trickling down her chin.

Semal's horrified expression and the queen's wrathful snarl landed like physical blows.

"This has to end," he said to his mother.

The queen twitched, fighting his compulsion. Derron trembled with the effort to keep her still. "You are no son of mine. I'll have you watch as I kill her, and then I will destroy you."

Derron swallowed past the lump in his throat. He couldn't help the twinge of sorrow. He hated the queen more than he loved her, but Aerella was still his mother.

"I hope you can forgive me," he said to Semal.

Derron's vision blurred the farther he walked away. His temples throbbed and perspiration dampened his forehead. Pain lanced his abdomen and ribs, and it was all he could do to hold onto Asharaya. It wouldn't be long until he lost control of the Song and the queen sent her guards to hunt him down.

Derron hurried to the stables. The stable hand grooming one of the horses took one look at the arrow protruding from the cloak, and his pleasant smile turned into unabashed horror. Derron enthralled him, rasping an order to have the fastest horse readied. By the time the boy was done, Derron tasted copper on his lips.

He helped Asharaya onto the horse and climbed up behind

her, draping his arms on either side of her as he held the reins. "Are you still awake?"

"Arrow."

"Not here."

"Why?" she rasped.

"I'm about to lose control." He guessed it wasn't what she meant, but that was a conversation for later. If there ever was one. "Thanks for Arkael."

"Myk..."

Asharaya's head lolled forward. Derron cursed and spurred the horse. A volley of arrows shot from the battlements the moment they were out of the stables. He ducked his head and bent forward to shield Asharaya. None of the arrows found its mark, but Derron urged the horse faster, his control dwindling. He prayed he had enough strength to use his Song to get out of the castle, and then he would have to find somewhere safe to help Asharaya heal.

Then he'd have to survive both the woman he was saving and the one he was escaping.

36

Shara

A fresh sea scent and the fragrance of roses and lavender kissed the balmy summer air. Dragons soared over the waterfall or dove toward the pool beneath. The sun shone through their wings' thin membranes and caught on their translucent scales. Shara nestled more comfortably in her window seat, sun-warmed sketchbook in her lap as she hummed along to the dragonsong. She'd already sketched the waterfall and most of the dragons, but she focused on the one basking alone in the water. It was the only detailed spot in the artwork, the line art defined and ready for coloring. The scales were mostly cobalt, darker where the water lapped against the dragon's body and with lighter silver highlights.

Like his eyes. A flush rose to her cheeks.

From inside the room, Elon snorted. Shara's eyes zapped to where he sat at the desk, bent over his journal as always. Dark waves toppled over his forehead as his quill scratched the parchment. "You're hopeless," he teased, laughter in his voice.

Shara pressed her lips together. "Are you writing Cassia another love letter you'll never give her?"

"Are you going to show Derron that artwork?"

Shara squeezed her fists, fighting not to punch Elon's grin off his youthful face. A tingle started in the back of her mind, one Shara swatted away as if it were a pesky fly.

"Derron has nothing to do with this," she snapped, defensive.

The smile on Elon's face sweetened, matching the tenderness of his golden eyes. "It's okay if you don't want to admit it, but I'm your big brother. You can't fool me."

Big brother. Shara looked down at her color-smeared fingers. A woman's fingers—long and calloused. The fly in the back of her mind landed, and it took her a moment too long to swat it away. Elon was her older brother, and yet she was older.

Two new dragons joined the song over the waterfall. One was as familiar as her own reflection. In her chest, his heart beat in tune with hers, strong and brave. Red highlights shone through his scales like fire over blackened coals. Even from afar, Deimok's eyes burned like the Burning Sea. Her heart squeezed inexplicably at the sight of him.

The other dragon—larger than Deimok and the others— circled the waterfall as he sang. Shara couldn't see Oruk's rider well, but the dragon's golden scales matched the dragon-shaped diadem circling his forehead. She leaned farther out the window to greet her father, a frantic anticipation building inside her with every steady flap of the dragon's wings.

Oruk lifted his head and flew higher. Her sketchbook forgotten, Shara scurried to her knees and grasped the windowsill to keep from falling. A bright flash of sunlight cut across her father's figure. Shara squinted—

🐚🐚

Darkness.

Shara felt her shiver as if from faraway. Reality barged back in flashes of sensation: hardness beneath her head, wetness against her forehead, bitterness on her tongue. The scent of the sea and a deep voice soothing her as she spasmed.

A cool hand touched her forehead, then the side of her neck. "The fever broke."

At first, he was only a shadow etched against the light, but slowly features came into focus. A long lock of hair shining silver with a stolen moonbeam's glow. Fair skin made golden by sun stretched against a handsome face. Full lips. A straight nose. Deep-set silver eyes speckled with cobalt.

Beautiful. Laughter slipped from his lips, and her pulse jumped against his fingers at the sound. Had she said it out loud?

"I hope you won't stab me for that."

Shit.

Shara jerked into a sitting position, recognition sharpening her focus. A starburst of pain flared at the center of her chest, but the burning in her hip was much worse, spreading up her side and down her leg.

"Careful." Derron's outstretched hand dropped at Shara's warning glare. She slowly lifted the unfamiliar brown hem of her shirt, whimpering as her fingers brushed her heated flesh. A bandage wrapped around her waist, a yellow-green stain growing at its center. The skin around it was red and swollen, with dark veins in stark relief. "You caught an infection, but magic should heal it soon."

Shara tugged at her neckline next. Another bandage wrapped her breasts and covered the arrow wound. The mere memory of it made her shiver, but even when she pressed the shirt back into place, looking away wasn't enough. She could still feel the throbbing behind her head, the guards' grip on her arms, the whizz of the arrow. In those moments, it was as if her Fire had receded altogether, and the shadows refused to come to her aid no matter how much she bled. Shara hadn't felt so helpless in years. She'd been certain she would die then, alone and surrounded by enemies.

She would have, if Derron hadn't saved her.

"You're lucky the arrow didn't pierce your heart," Derron said.

Three horses occupied the pens, and a lone rooster walked around, picking at the ground. No wonder Shara smelled like a haystack. "Where are we?"

"Just outside the city. I used my Song on the farmers to keep us hidden while you recovered, but I don't know how long the effects might last. I exerted too much power."

"I imagine you want me to thank you for saving my life?" Shara snapped. "I wouldn't have been in that castle in the first place if you hadn't betrayed us. You're the reason Xoro died and Kael was taken. One good deed doesn't erase all the rest."

"You think I don't know that?" Derron shot to his feet. For a moment she thought he was going to abandon her. Instead, he clenched his jaw and looked away but stayed at her side. "I did many things I regret, both to please and to protect people close to me, but I want to fix things."

"Then you should've let me kill her."

"You would've been killed."

Shara shook with rage. "People are being terrorized in their homes. Neighbors look at each other with fear and suspicion. Artists are being butchered for painting fucking dragons. Don't act like it doesn't affect you. I saw you in the city while she set her own people on fire."

"You were there?"

Shara bit the inside of her lip. Did he not know about the dreams? And if he didn't, would she be revealing a weakness by telling him? "Aerella is a plague, and the longer we allow her to live, the more pain she's going to spread. I'd gladly give my life to put an end to it."

"What drove you into that room was revenge, Shara."

Shara looked away, shame warming her cheeks. She

promised she wouldn't do anything stupid, and all it had taken was Aerella being within reach for her to break her word. Myk would be furious, and with good reason. "Don't call me that."

"Do you think your family would want to see you die?"

"That's rich coming from you. It was your family that killed mine. Your family that stole our home. You who wanted to kill me." She wanted to hurt him with the reminder, but it flayed her all the same, especially with her dream still so vivid. It was just like Elon to tease her over the simplest things, to see Shara's truths even when she tried to hide them. To see his sister and his best friend as enemies—to see them hurt each other as often as Derron and Shara did—would have crushed him.

"I thought I was protecting my family and sparing Ilahara another war."

"You unleashed the war when you came looking for me. You don't get to put the blame on me for fighting."

"No, it's not your fault." Derron crouched in front of her again. A red smear clung to his upper lip, as if he'd cleared a nosebleed with his sleeve. "You're right. If we want to heal Ilahara, we need to remove my mother from the throne."

"We?"

"You don't trust me, and that's fair, but I don't want Ilahara to bleed any more than you do. Those artists painting banners—I used to call them friends. The people you want to protect are my people, too. I can't bring back the dead, but I can stop more death from happening."

"And when your mother doles out her forgiveness?"

"I saved your life. She'll want my head mounted on a spike right beside yours."

Derron had a point, but logic couldn't bury the instinct to look out for herself. The last time she'd trusted Derron, his betrayal cost her and her friends dearly.

Perhaps her recklessness had cost them even more.

Had Mykal found Eileen? Had they reached Solana and the others? Had they gotten out safely, or had the schooner been detected?

A knot tightened Shara's insides, and she dug inside her pocket for the vial of Mykal's blood. Something sharp dug into her finger, and Shara hissed through her teeth as her heart dropped.

"What is it?" Derron asked.

Shara's throat was too tight to speak. She extracted the broken shards from her pocket, refusing to believe her eyes. Her thumb pushed around the pieces as if they'd magically reassemble and the blood would return to the vial. This couldn't be happening.

"I didn't know you had that in your pocket," Derron said. "Are you hurt?"

Shara cast aside the shards and pulled her pocket inside out. Derron muttered a curse at the red stain. He leaned closer to inspect it, and Shara pushed him away with a snarl. Maybe if she could squeeze some of the drops from the fabric, she'd be able to track Myk.

Derron caught her wrists and shook her. "Will you fucking talk to me?"

"It's not mine." Shara yanked free of his hold and grasped the fabric. "Can this be used to track?"

"It's dried. Blood needs to be fresh to be used for tracking spells."

Shara cussed, pulling at her hair.

"Did you need that to reunite with your friends?"

"I need to go back." Shara gritted her teeth as she stood. No sooner did she apply weight to her leg that it bent beneath her, and she would have toppled to the ground if Derron hadn't caught her. She panted as she battled the pain, but it didn't stop her from trying to free herself from Derron's confining hold. "I have to find them. They might be in danger." *Because of me.* Bile rose in Shara's throat.

"Going back will only put you in more danger," Derron reasoned. "You don't know they were taken. The best thing you can do now is heal and move forward with your plan. You must have had a rendezvous point in case this happened."

"Lur," Shara rasped, clutching his forearm. Wrong—it felt wrong to speak of leaving when Aerella might already have her hands on her friends. Her sister.

"Then I'll take you there."

"No." Shara stumbled over to the horses' stalls. She believed Derron was sincere in wanting to protect their people, but was that enough? If he were her childhood friend, yes, but Derron was and wasn't that boy. The man he'd grown into was a mystery wrapped in deceit and noble acts. If she found her friends in Lur, what would they think if she showed up with Derron Argarys?

A dappled gray mare curiously smelled Shara's hands, gifting her a momentary reprieve as she stroked the animal's long neck. After a few moments, Derron's hand joined hers. "You won't make it on your own, Shara. Let me help. We can go our separate ways once we reach Lur."

"Where will you go?"

"Cassia's in Tyrra. With Johan Vynatis." Derron leaned against the pen with a small eye roll. "She has her own reasons to hate our mother. As angry as she might be with me, she'll have my back. And Johan will have hers. Hopefully."

"The Vynatis are turncloaks. I wouldn't put my trust in them." *Or you.* What choice did she have? As much as stubbornness would have her move forward alone—or run back to the Embernest—she wouldn't get far. Having a guide to Lur would be less risky than stopping for directions. Her best chance was to trust that Derron wouldn't kill her, and that she'd be fully healed if he changed his mind. "If I agree to this, it doesn't mean I trust you."

"I know."

Shara straightened, her mind made. "To Lur, then?"

Derron nodded. "To Lur."

37

Mykal

Two days ago, Mykal was sure he'd achieved a rescue mission worthy of a song. With a human assassin and the last Myrassar in tow, he'd infiltrated the Embernest's womb and saved his Do'strath, his father, and his sister. Everything was perfect—until he'd left Shara behind.

As if she were some soldier and not his queen.

Mykal failed on every front. His father's disappointment when he'd emerged from the tunnels and Solana's fear-stricken eyes singed his lids every time he blinked. He wished he could make excuses—that they had to trust Shara, that she was the queen they chose, so they had to learn to follow her orders—but the truth was worse. Kael would have followed him if he went back into the belly of the beast, and Mykal couldn't risk losing him again. It was as simple as that.

The commotion in the castle spread quickly to the city and the port, but they waited until lingering became too dangerous and they'd lose their chance at sailing into open waters. Without Shara and the element of surprise, there was little he could do against Aerella's forces, and no way he could sneak in undetected. Kael needed time to recover. Daganver needed its Head. Mykal had his orders. No matter how much it went against his instincts, he had to hope Shara would find them in Lur.

The captain took them along Adara's eastern shore for a full day. Ports were too risky. They disembarked at a safe docking spot near the mountain passes and proceeded on foot to their destination. Hours later, sweat dripped from Mykal's hair and traced slow lines down his forehead. Whenever one reached his tear ducts, the sting made him want to rub his eyes raw. Instead, he welcomed the burn, as he did the aches in his joints and the weight on his back. The instinct to bend forward under his father's weight was there, but Mykal defied it. The only sign of strain he let show—the single one he couldn't control—was that constant dripping on his brow.

"There's a stream nearby. I smell it in the air." Lord Darrok said. "We can stop there so you can rest."

Mykal stumbled at his father's voice. It was more words than Lord Darrok had spoken in days, and the first time that he addressed Mykal directly since that night. His last words to him still echoed in Mykal's ears. *How could you lose her?* Disappointed. Ashamed. Mykal's voice hardened. "I'm fine."

"You need rest, Myk." Kael said, panting. "We all do."

It was Kael's admission, in the end, that bludgeoned through Mykal's stubborn refusal to yield.

Solana trekked ahead in search of the stream. She too had hardly spoken since that night, as if they'd gone back to the days after Xoro's death. Was it only fear for Shara tormenting her, or did she resent Mykal for leaving her sister to fend for herself? Mykal wouldn't blame her if she did, but damn he hated it. He and Solana finally had an understanding—not friendship, perhaps, but something close to it, and he'd ruined it.

Unlike the thick, dense forests of Daganver, Adara's terrain consisted mostly of open hills and valleys. One could walk for miles without coming across a single sapling, with no relief from the incessant sun. It was the ideal environment for dragons, who favored the warm climate and flying without hindrance.

The stream was in an open field, nestled between two hills and protected by the imposing mountain wall towering near its banks. The exhaustion he'd been warding off crashed down on him all at once. Mykal lumbered to the gurgling stream, dropping to his knees to ease his father off his back. Lord Darrok dragged himself beneath the meager shade of a thin tree. Without his father's weight, pain flared in Mykal's spine and his body shook with fatigue. Instead of standing, he fell forward on his palms, resting his forehead on the sun-warmed grass.

Hands stroked the space between his shoulders. Mykal recognized his Do'strath by touch—the weight of his fingers, their texture, the affection in every stroke. "I should be helping you," Kael whispered after a while, so low Mykal wondered if he hadn't meant to speak the words aloud.

Mykal shifted onto his knees to look at his Do'strath. The bruises were a little lighter today, the renike's effect slowly fading and allowing Kael's magic to heal his wounds. The physical ones, at least. Mykal was more worried about the ones hidden behind the raised walls of the soulbond. He wouldn't pressure Kael to speak of what happened to him in Aerella's dungeons, but he hoped his Do'strath wouldn't shut him out for long. "You already are," he said, catching Kael's hand as it slipped from his shoulders. He brushed his Do'strath's knuckles with his thumb, then raised them to his lips.

"I'm weak." Kael's clipped tone was heavy with contempt.

"You've been through hell, Kael. Give yourself a few days. I can handle it." He accepted the water flask Kael offered, and at the same time let his magic trickle down the soulbond, brushing

Kael's walls with a reassuring touch. Kael's jaw hardened.

"I'm slowing you down. Maybe you should leave me behind."

Mykal nearly choked on his water. "Where is this coming from?"

"We leave no one else behind," Lord Darrok said in an authoritative tone. Mykal tried to hide the sting of those words by keeping his attention on Kael. "Why don't you sit?"

Kael drew his hand away from Mykal and backed away. "Our tracks might stop at the Adarian port, but I have Vaemor's blood. He can find me."

"I'm sure the queen will find something in my room to track me as well," Eileen said in the sweet cadence one would use to calm a spooked animal. "In that, we're both liabilities."

"No one is a liability," Mykal snapped.

"My life will be a lot better once I drive a sword through Vaemor's heart." Kael ground his teeth as he regarded Eileen. "And I'll cut anyone who stands between me and the Argarys."

Without another word, Kael walked closer to the stream, where he exchanged a few quiet words with Solana. The wraith was talking then—just not with Mykal. She returned to the group with a flask of fresh water for Lord Darrok, and then dropped a damp rag on his lap. The knitting of his dark brow was the only sign of surprise his father showed. Anyone else would have helped him cool off, but not Solana. The wraith would die before she would serve a fae.

"She's spirited for a human," Lord Darrok said, as Solana joined Kael by the stream and the two walked off together.

"You have no idea," Mykal muttered. Solana was a good listener. Maybe she'd get Kael to open up, though he couldn't help but ponder the reasons why his Do'strath had chosen to shut him out.

"Give him time, Son." Lord Darrok seemed to read the self-destructive spiral of Mykal's thoughts. "Let him come to you when he's ready."

"What did they do to him? And to you?"

"Aerella knew better than to raise a hand to me without Daganver firmly in her hold." He looked pointedly at Eileen, and she lowered her eyes. "She demanded I relinquish my position to Eileen, but what she really wanted was to put her son in charge."

Because Eileen and Derron were betrothed, and Eileen loved him. That last part was a bitter pill to swallow, but Mykal couldn't stand to watch his father crush her beneath his scrutiny. "And Kael?"

"I only know what I heard." His father fumbled with the damp rag, but Mykal saw it for what it was—a way to buy himself time before sharing a hard truth. "Semal Leneris interrogated him every day. It wasn't gentle, and it wasn't brief."

Acidic water rose up Mykal's throat. His father's words conjured the most horrible images—Kael tortured, cut, bleeding. And Mykal hadn't been there. He'd left his Do'strath with those butchers for weeks.

Mykal toyed with Shara's ring, shooting a pulse of magic into it with his friend stark in his mind. A tug pulled him in the direction from which they'd come, lively and warm as the Fire in her veins. Wherever she was, Shara was alive. That, at least, was some consolation.

"Are you certain we'll be safe in Lur?" Eileen asked, the question directed to Lord Darrok. It was like they were children again, gathering at their father's feet while he sat in his armchair to recount their histories. Except back then, Lord Darrok had looked at his daughter adoringly, not as if she were an enemy. Eileen lowered her eyes, as if noticing the same, and Mykal couldn't stand the heartbreak she failed to mask. She deserved better from her family.

"Lur is neutral," Mykal explained. "Aerella has no authority there, and the wards on the Library will shield us from tracking spells." It was why he and Shara had chosen it as their rendezvous point. If everything had gone according to plan,

Jaero would have informed the Rising of their whereabouts and in a matter of days someone would've come to collect them. "We can trust the maenari's neutrality. They'll grant us safe haven while we reassess how best to return to Daganver."

Eileen offered a tentative smile before moving away to lean against a tree, wrapping her arms around her middle. Mykal made to stand when his father said, "You need to be careful about what you share with her, Mykal. I know she's our blood, and you want to trust her, but remember who raised her. For all we know, she'll try sending word to Aerella at the first opportunity. Going back for her was a mistake."

Mykal remembered Eileen's protests when he'd entered her room in the Embernest. He wasn't sure Eileen had chosen to escape with him or if it had been a forced decision once the guards barged into the room. Who would have believed her innocence if she'd been found speaking to a traitor to the Crown? "She didn't choose any of this. Not then, not now." Mykal stood. "Maybe if you behaved more like her father, she'd be happier to be free."

If his father had anything to say, Mykal didn't care to hear it. Let him add it to the list of reasons he was upset with Mykal. He strode to Eileen, though it was more a shuffle. Their shoulders brushed as he settled beside her. "Hey."

Eileen looked over at him and smiled. "You should rest."

Mykal was tired, but he couldn't help the nagging desire to spend time with his sister. They'd been together two days—more than they had since childhood—and they'd barely spoken three words to each other in that time. She needed space, but he also didn't want the distance between them to solidify. "I could use some company."

"I don't want to keep you from your friends."

Mykal ignored the churning in his stomach upon thinking of Solana and Kael speaking without him. "They don't have to be mine alone, Lele." Eileen's eyes widened at the nickname, and Mykal wished he could gather all the years they'd lost and crumple them like paper. "I used to call you that when we were little."

"I've never had a nickname." The corner of her lip turned upward. "I like it."

Mykal brought his finger beneath her chin. "I'm happy you asked about the Library earlier. You've never been there?"

"No, but Derron and Cassia have." A grin lit up her face. "She hates it, but Derron could spend hours there even if it got him into trouble. He likes to…" Her words trailed away, as if only now realizing what she was talking about and with whom. Eileen's shoulders slumped, her smile faded, and her silence returned.

Her somberness was like a stab wound. Mykal hadn't taken her away from the Argarys so she'd be unhappy. "You don't have to be afraid of speaking to me," he said. "I want things to be good between us. I want to know what your life was like."

"Even if Derron and Cassia were in it?"

"You'll never get me to like those bleached pricks." Eileen chuckled, and the sound caused Mykal's first genuine smile in days. "But I'm glad you weren't alone all those years, Lele."

Eileen studied Mykal's face for an endless moment, and whatever she found convinced her of his sincerity. She dove to his chest, and Mykal let out a surprised "oh" as his arms found their way around her. He held her tight, resting his cheek on the soft pillow of her curls.

For a while, he didn't feel like he'd failed completely.

38

Cassia

The forest sounds faded to the background, Cassia's attention wholly engrossed by her book even amid the carriage's jostling. Eileen had given her several for the journey, her only comment that Cassia would enjoy them. Now her cheeks flushed, having reached a particularly steamy scene. At the same time that she told herself Eileen would get an earful upon her return, she leaned closer, as if the pages could suck her in.

The wheel caught a bump on the path, making Cassia smack her nose into the book. She cursed, holding onto her seat until the worst was over. This journey would have been easier if she'd been allowed to travel on horseback.

For seven days, Cassia had no company but the twenty guards who only addressed her to inquire after her well-being or to inform her they were stopping. She'd have gone for fewer to keep the anonymity Derron had suggested, but the queen only allowed one of their plainer carriages. *Remember your duty* had been her parting words.

Cassia was no stranger to solitude, but being alone in a carriage was somehow more depressing than feeling lonely in a castle. Having no one to talk to left an open door for unpleasant thoughts. She couldn't help reliving her last moments with Derron and feel as if she'd made a terrible mistake. Once she returned, she'd make things right. Somehow.

The first two nights, she'd dreamed of the room. Ever since it had first spoken to her, the darkness had taken to striking up short conversations in its deep rumble, and those nights were no different.

Where are you, princess?

How would you know I'm someplace else?

Tell me.

I'm traveling, Cassia replied, stepping closer to the light. *Why don't you figure out where I'm going yourself?* She smothered her clever smile the moment it crossed her lips. This incorporeal voice was a figment of her imagination. What was she doing smiling at it?

Her dream ended abruptly, and she hadn't seen the room again. She wondered if she'd offended the darkness. Once she would have been glad for the reprieve, but the room had become a quiet place to retreat to when the real world turned dark and she'd grown strangely fond of the voice.

Yet neither her brother nor the room put her on edge as much as what awaited her in Heartstar, the seat of the Vynatis. Who would be waiting.

In those seven days, the landscape gradually changed. The bustling city receded in favor of vast valleys and fields bathed in white, purple, and gold. The rural side of Adara was charming, like a pretty picture one would hang on a wall. In the summertime, before her mother's coup, Cassia and her family would retreat to the countryside for a month to visit Grandmother Catlana in her large villa. For a mermaid who'd married into a Fire-wielding family, Lady Catlana was rather fond of the house. Cassia spent countless hours riding through the lavender fields of her grandmother's estate and often imagined living on a similar land once she married. It had been another life, when her prospects had seemed limitless.

Green seeped back into Adara's autumnal colors the closer she came to Tyrra, and fields gave way to dense forests and enormous trees. Oaks and elms, their branches so high and long they obscured the sky and curled over the forest path, created natural archways. Cassia could have sensed she was in Tyrra from the smell alone. Colorful flowers bloomed as if in the height of spring, filling the air with their fragrant scents.

The perfect territory for wild animals to build homes, and for shifters to hide in their midst.

Birds chirped as they nested within the trees or flitted about the thick foliage. Squirrels climbed over trunks and leaped from one branch to the other, and Cassia was certain far bigger animals more adept at hiding stalked her carriage. It was difficult to tell the true animals from the fae, but she doubted her arrival would remain secret for long.

The carriage came to a sudden stop.

Cassia set her book down and leaned outside the window. "Why are we stopping?"

"Stay inside, Your Highness."

The woman's wary tone stirred the princess's Fire. It tickled her fingers, ready to be summoned. The carriage and the guards on horseback obstructed her vision, so she perked up her ears, listening for any threats. The horses shifted their weight, visibly nervous. Cassia should have shared their fear—and perhaps a part of her did—but her heart picked up its beat. *Finally something exciting.*

Barks and yelps rose for the high grass. Cassia leaned farther out her window to track the sound's origin. Flashes of gray and black zoomed between the trees, the tread of strong paws around them. Steel whispered as the guards extracted their swords. Wolves came out of hiding and blocked the path.

Animals would have attacked the horses by now. This was an ambush of another kind.

"Sheathe your weapons."

Cassia almost slipped from her seat in her haste to draw back into the carriage. Her fingers dug into the plush pillows, her heart galloping.

Johan.

Johan was here.

"Lord Vynatis," one guard said, a man at the head of the party. "We weren't expecting an escort."

"How could you, when we were informed of our esteemed guest's arrival so late?" His haughtiness was just as Cassia remembered, if not sharper. "We've had rebel activity around these parts. I'll trust no one with her safety, including the lot of you."

Clopping hooves neared the carriage. Conflicting impulses rose within Cassia to lunge out one door to meet her former lover or to flee from the opposite side. She sat up straighter, flattening her gown, and leveled a cool stare out the window.

Cassia noticed his hands first—long fingers around a slender black stallion's reins. Thin silver bands adorned each one except for two with onyx gemstones on the thumb and middle finger. Those were new. Johan had never worn rings before, likely because Cassia preferred a plainer hand.

For all her attempts to brace herself, the sight of him was a blow. His kohl-lined hazel eyes were as magnetic as she remembered, as if she were looking at a tiger and feeling mesmerized and terrified at once. His hair was longer, grazing the top of his neck at the back and falling forward in dark brown waves to frame the sharp angles of his high cheekbones. It was like meeting a familiar stranger. "You look like you could use some air, love."

That was familiar. "Hello, Johan." She appraised the exquisite riding clothes, the rings, the kohl. Somehow, he made looking like a rogue elegant. "It's good to see you."

"Then come take a closer look." Johan backed up his horse, giving her space to open the carriage door.

"She's safer in the carriage, my lord," the guard said.

Johan turned the horse around so he could glare at him. "My wolves have an appetite for fresh kills, sir. You'd be wise to keep your next unsolicited opinion to yourself."

The wolves in question barked and licked their lips.

The guards lost some of their coloring, and even Cassia paled. The way the wolves had circled her retinue and their sizes led her to believe they were all fae.

Cassia stepped out of the carriage, glaring up at Johan. The result wasn't as vicious as she'd intended, for she had to squint from the sun. "Are you quite finished with the threats?"

"Keep me waiting and find out."

Cassia sighed and addressed the guards. "Saddle a horse for me. I'll ride with Lord Vynatis."

"No need. There's plenty of room on Kuro for us both."

Cassia couldn't help the flash of heat on her cheeks, her body tingling with anticipation. If Johan's determination to keep her close was any indication, maybe she wouldn't have a hard time convincing him to steal her away from Baramun. However, she couldn't risk any of the guards scribbling to her mother about her bad behavior. "I'm engaged."

"Then you'd better hold the reins to make sure you keep your hands to yourself."

"Are you going to ride with your back to me?"

Johan's smile was nothing short of devilish. "Why would I do that when my front fits so much better against your back?"

A cough came from one of the guards. There was no way her mother or Baramun wouldn't know about this. The idea of Baramun stewing in his temple had her recklessly accepting Johan's outstretched hand, even as she murmured, "I'm going to destroy you."

Johan's thighs embraced her hips, his chest aligning with her back as she settled onto the horse. He relinquished his hold on the reins to Cassia, and his hands brushed the back of hers. "We should at least wait until sundown, love." His lips grazed the shell of her ear. "Do you still ride as well as you used to?"

"My technique has only improved."

Johan's delighted laughter set off the butterflies in her stomach. "You're as sharp as ever, princess."

"And you remain a rake." Cassia couldn't help her smile, and though she had her back to him, she had no doubt he could sense it. This easy banter reminded her of their first meeting during Tyrra's Vernal Festival. She spurred the horse forward to a canter, only slowing when she put enough distance between them and her retinue to have a modicum of privacy. "I suppose I should thank you for saving me from that dreadful carriage."

"You suppose wrong. My reasons for wanting you on this horse are far from noble."

Heat swooped low in her belly. "My reasons for being here aren't all noble, either."

"Maybe you could enlighten me, then."

"Asharaya becomes more and more of a problem. My mother wants to know where the Head stands." Then, lower so only he could hear, "You wrote to me." His letter seemed to burn in her gown's pocket now that she'd acknowledged it.

His voice was soft as silk against her ear. "So, are you here for me or to do your mother's bidding?"

"I'm here because I could use a friend." She had no doubt he could hear how her heart thundered. "I found I have very few of those at home." Certainly not Baramun, who pressured her to claim his prize, nor Derron, lost and resentful as she hadn't seen him in years, nor her mother, who Cassia couldn't forgive. Not anymore.

Johan went rigid. "Did she hurt you because of the human?"

"No." Sorrow tasted like salt on Cassia's tongue. Korban was dead because she'd been selfish. Was she making the same mistake now? "But it's my fault he's dead. I shouldn't have started things with him, but I was missing you so much." She shut her eyes, swallowing back her tears. "I'm sorry. This is awkward."

"We weren't together anymore, Cassia. You didn't owe me anything." Johan's arms wrapped around her waist, and he tucked her closer to his chest. "I'm glad you came, princess. You're safe with me."

Cassia leaned her head against his shoulder, lulled by the horse's canter and the steady cadence of Johan's breaths behind her. For a moment, it was as if time had wound backward, and the years spent apart were nonexistent. All her worries began to disappear, like petals plucked from a daisy. Johan would help her. Protect her. Yet her body couldn't entirely relax, and she couldn't grasp why until a thought nagged at her.

Johan had avoided answering about Asharaya.

39

Derron

Derron leaned against the building, the straw hat he'd pilfered from a windowsill angled low over his face. If anyone were to look his way, they'd see a brown-haired man with sunburned skin. The hat added a touch of bored disinterest to his persona, and it made it more difficult for his reflection to reveal his identity. Across the street in the apothecary a blonde conversed with the shop's maenar.

Asharaya wearing her glamour.

They'd been traveling for three days, avoiding towns and main roads. It wasn't ideal, especially given Asharaya's injuries, but neither of them minded sleeping beneath the stars and eating what small game they could hunt. While evading tracking spells was impossible without renike, they took measures to throw off hunters. At the barn, they exchanged the palace horse with the mare that had taken a liking to Asharaya. She was a sturdy animal used to labor, which allowed them to ride together and avoid leaving a strong scent trail. Though the numerous Adarian rivulets provided plenty of water to drink, they avoided bathing to make it more difficult for any dog or fae to sniff them out, and they covered their tracks whenever they were forced to stop.

Avoiding the patrols, however, was getting difficult.

On the first day, Asharaya had sat ramrod straight on the horse to avoid her back touching Derron's chest. She'd lasted almost the entire ride before relaxing against him. Derron didn't fool himself into thinking she suddenly liked him. Her injuries were likely bothering her more than she let on, but the more they made contact, the more he marveled at the feel of her in his arms. Asharaya's shoulder was healing, slowly. What worried Derron was the wound on her side. Sometimes even standing drained the color from her face, and though she'd tried to hide it, her grasp on her magic—both fae and human—was fickle.

So they'd decided to enter the nearest town at risk of discovery. Without renike, it was only a matter of time until he was tracked, and with Asharaya's wound not healing, Derron doubted she'd be able to fight their pursuers.

He doubted she'd make it to Lur.

The opportunity to pass the gates presented itself with a caravan of performers. Asharaya climbed onto a passing wagon, leaving Derron little choice but to follow her lead. They'd waited in silence, and when the guards searched the wagon, Derron used his Song to trick them into seeing only costumes and makeup. The men had been two low fae, but a spell of dizziness had overcome him regardless. He'd used his ability too much these past days on minds far more difficult to control than humans. "We can't risk you dropping like a stone in the shop," Asharaya said. "I'll go."

"You're not much better," Derron countered.

"At least I'm not bleeding from my nose."

Some minutes later, the bell above the apothecary's door

chimed, and relief flooded through Derron as Asharaya strolled to him with a small bag beneath her arm, glamour intact. He pushed away from the wall. "Any luck?"

"No renike. We knew it'd be a long shot." This was a small town, and most of its inhabitants were low fae who'd have no use for the expensive herb. "Did you have to stare? A few minutes more and the maenar would have called the guards on you." Asharaya flicked his hat, and he caught it before it could tumble off his head.

"You were taking too long." Not a lie exactly, but he wouldn't admit to being drawn to her. The arrow that had pierced Asharaya had marked a break. At least they weren't trying to kill each other. Derron eyed the bag, an eyebrow rising. "Did you find the healing herbs I described?"

"Yes, and some leaves to prevent pregnancy. The maenar added them after I was forced to tell him you're my betrothed."

Derron snatched the bag. "Too bad the leaves will go to waste because you haven't Bled."

"Do you think about me Bleeding often, Adam?"

Derron couldn't help a grin at the haughty use of his fake name. "I've seen enough of your blood, Shana."

Their gazes remained locked, until a sudden gust of wind had Derron holding onto his stolen hat and Asharaya's hair whipping her face. She pushed it away, her attention going to her feet. A sheet of parchment had caught on her ankle. Before she could bend to retrieve it, Derron picked it up, and his stomach dropped. Asharaya stared at him from the page with a cruel expression, drawn almost to perfection.

She snatched it from his hands. "This is me."

"Keep your voice down," Derron hissed, hiding her with his body and launching a quick glance around to make sure they hadn't attracted unwanted attention. Fortunately, the street was deserted. Dusk was upon them, and by the scents coming from some of the homes, the villagers were getting ready for dinner. Derron ignored the low rumbling of his stomach in response.

Asharaya's knuckles tightened around the parchment. "It says I'm wounded, as if the bitch fucking knows I'm not healing."

Derron paused, his eyes landing on her wounded side, as if he could look through the layers of clothes and grime to her bandaged wound. "You're right."

"If there's a poster for me, there must be others." Asharaya frantically searched the walls. "Where did this come from?"

"Maybe they were handed out and discarded or hanging close to the guard's station. Either way, we can't waste time looking."

"But if there are others, it means—"

Movement from a nearby inn had them both spinning on the spot. Asharaya released a pained breath, and Derron's hands instinctively went to her elbows to support her. Three men stumbled out of the establishment, half drunk though the night was still young. "We should get out of here," Asharaya whispered. Her hair was back to being brown.

"Let's."

The sky was dark when they returned to the forest. This was a small town at dinnertime, which helped them sneak out with Derron only leaning on his Song once. Still, it had been enough for blood to trickle onto his lips again. Derron wiped at it with his sleeve before Asharaya could notice, though she was too focused on potential threats and masking her own discomfort.

The mare acknowledged their approach with a snort. Though she seemed calm, Derron brought a finger to his lips while they scoured their surroundings. When the coast was clear, he closed his eyes and thanked the gods for sometimes listening to his prayers.

Asharaya sat against a tree, and the horse approached her, sniffing her hair and nudging her head for cuddles. "Sweetie.

That's your name."

"Don't name the horse." Derron sifted through the herbs she'd acquired as he knelt beside her. Besides the leaves added by the maenar, there was everything he needed to properly clean the wound and stave off an infection.

"Why the hell not?"

"Best not get attached."

"And this is why she likes me more."

Derron couldn't help a small tilt of his lips, though he doubted she could see it in the dark. "Take off your shirt."

"You could be nicer about it," she said, grabbing the hems. "Turn around."

"I'm going to have to look at your wounds..." At Asharaya's glare, he sighed. "Fine."

Derron went to the satchel strapped to the mare's saddle, keeping his back resolutely turned on Asharaya. She shuddered when she made to pull up her shirt. He took two clean strips of linen and listened to the slide of fabric against skin. Derron couldn't remember the last time he was so aware of another person—of every sound, every pause. He swallowed past his galloping pulse. "I hope what we took from those farmers will be enough for the journey."

"I think we took enough from those people." A thud, followed by a relieved sigh. "You can turn around now."

Derron did, breathing slow to get his pulse under control. She was leaning against the tree, and though her chest was wrapped in linens, the amount of amber skin on display beckoned him to the feminine curves her leathers often concealed. He'd seen more of her in the barn, but he'd been too focused on nursing her back to life. This was different. She was awake, and warm, and maddening. Keeping his eyes trained on her face required more effort than he cared to admit. "We left them with a perfectly fine horse." Derron made to loosen the wrapping around her chest, but Asharaya swatted his hand away. "Take it off yourself if you must, but I need to clean the wound, Shara."

"Start with the other one."

Derron heaved a patient sigh and indulged her. He was careful with the bandage around her waist, aware of every sound she swallowed back when he moved too fast or the fabric chafed against her skin. Aware of every touch. The wound was only a slash, but it was still bleeding, and while the cut was a deep red, the skin around it was darkening. "This was from my mother's blade?"

Asharaya nodded, lips tight as she inspected the damage.

Derron poured some water onto the wound, his apology drowned out by Asharaya's hiss. He cleaned it as best he could, wishing his hands were cleaner, and then wrapped it. "I think it's poisoned."

"The blackened skin is pretty telling, Argarys." Asharaya closed her eyes, swallowing hard. "You wouldn't happen to know what kind of poison your mother is fond of?"

"I don't have the slightest idea. She's been keeping the new maenar busy." Derron handed her the herbs. "Chew them together. They'll help with the pain and swelling."

They sat in silence while Asharaya ate the herbs. Derron thought back to that moment in Maenar Errigen's study, trying to remember everything he'd seen, but his mind was only able to conjure the horrible green liquid that had served to blow up Heart. Though even if he did, he had no knowledge of poisons. Asharaya's best chance was with a maenar. In Lur they would know how to help her. The poison had been administered superficially, and the wound was small, but Lur was still so far away. They were so close to the Tyrran border, while Lur was farther north, deep into Adarian land.

Tyrra. Cassia had likely arrived in Heartstar by now. Like every high fae house, the Vynatis had a maenar at their service. Someone who could heal Asharaya. Cassia had no reason to help her, but she would shelter Derron. And Imiri Vynatis had been close to the Myrassar. Would she turn away Queen

Jaemys's daughter?

Shadows thickened around Asharaya and snapped Derron out of his thoughts. A bead of blood welled on her finger, taking several long seconds to heal. "What are you doing?" he snapped.

"You need to give your Song a break. You're bleeding from your nose now but if you keep this up, you're going to drop dead. I need you alive to get to Lur."

"Your wounds aren't healing. We can't rely on your vrah magic. You're not strong enough." Derron tossed the next strip onto her legs. "Lean away from the tree. I'll help you remove the bandage, and you can clean the arrow wound yourself."

Asharaya consented with a nod and scooted away from the tree, careful not to move too abruptly. Derron settled into the space she'd freed and carefully unmade the knot holding the bandage in place. When his fingers brushed against her warm back, he expected her to pull away. Instead, she stayed put, though he noticed the small shiver she tried to repress. This close he could smell a lingering scent of amber impregnating her skin. It brought up memories that went farther back than their most recent interactions, to quiet afternoons spent at the Embernest with Elon's nose stuck in a book and Asharaya concentrating on a drawing, hands smeared from pigmented colors. When she wasn't with her dragon, she'd been almost a constant presence at her brother's side, yet he hardly remembered Elon complaining.

Derron found himself slowing his movements. "Did you ever paint in Havanya?"

The stiffening of her shoulders gave away her surprise. Derron could picture her wary frown. "I didn't have the time to paint." Then, as if deciding she could concede more, she said, "I sketch."

"What do you sketch?" Derron brought the two ends of the bandage forward, handing them to Asharaya, who carefully maneuvered them around her breasts and gave them back to him to wind around her back.

"People, objects. Anything that catches my eye or that I need to understand." A pause. "Except you."

"Because you have me figured out?"

"Because I wouldn't let myself try." Derron blinked at her soft admission. "I didn't want to find out if the boy I knew had become someone I couldn't recognize."

The words snuffed the air from his lungs. After a final turn, the bandage came loose in his hands. Derron pulled it away, his gaze fixed on her shoulder and not daring to look farther. "I've been thinking a lot about that boy. About the girl you were, and the woman you are now." His gaze trailed the curve of her shoulder until it found the side of her face. Before he knew what he was doing, he brushed the loose strands of her hair to her other shoulder, marveling at their softness despite the journey's grime. He wanted to see her. He wanted her to know he was looking. "You've haunted my every dream ever since I left Merania. No matter how much I tried to shake you, thoughts of you followed me anywhere. My remorse made flesh."

"At least you made sure I didn't have daggers."

His mind flashed to the fragments of dreams in the Embernest gardens. To her look of shocked surprise, and later annoyed acceptance. "So you were there." The twinge of panic wasn't nearly as crippling as it should have been, but deep down he'd always known there was something more to those dreams. "I was beginning to wonder."

"I didn't think they were real until I realized you were in the city during the explosion."

"You saw that in a dream?" At her nod, he thought back on every image he'd seen of her. "Deimok. One of the last things I saw was him hurt. Is that true?" Again, she nodded, but didn't elaborate. "Shit."

Shara tipped her head back to look at him, her eyebrow rising inquisitively. "Is this the part where you tell me you fucked up again?"

He was tempted to push her forward. With how weak she

was, she might face plant into the dirt. "My guess is something went wrong when I saved your ass back on the *No One*. I entered your dream when I was under the effects of renike. It's a wonder I was able to slip into your mind at all."

"Shit." Asharaya straightened, but he didn't miss the flash of panic in her golden eyes before he could no longer see her face. "Can you fix it?"

"I don't know. Maybe if I enter your mind again."

"The last time you entered my mind when you weren't at your strongest, you apparently created a dream link between us. We're not risking that again." Shara paused, her expression turning thoughtful. "The dreams stopped after the Embernest. Maybe whatever link we had broke?"

"Perhaps." Derron wasn't convinced. "Or maybe we're both too weak for the magic to activate. Or perhaps it's triggered by distance."

"Are you sure you're not fishing for ways to stay stuck to my ass, Argarys?"

"I promise I don't want this link between us any more than you do."

Asharaya looked over her shoulder again. Did he imagine the small upward curve of her lips? "Maybe the maenari in Lur will know how to fix it. Whatever this is, it hasn't killed us yet. Let's focus on what we can control for now."

They lapsed into a silence not as strained as the ones that came before, reassured by this semblance of a plan. A week ago, Asharaya would have sliced his throat open, if not for everything he'd done, then to rid herself of his presence in her mind. Now she was giving him a chance. "Would you draw me now, Shara?" The name was barely a whisper, a slip of the tongue tearing him open.

"I..." Asharaya stilled, looking to a point between the trees. The mare's ears twitched and she raised her head in that same direction. Derron tuned his ears to the sound of footsteps and metal. Someone cursed about the lack of light.

A patrol.

This time it was Asharaya to signal him to quiet. She grabbed a dagger and sliced her palm. The shadows around her trembled like weakened things. Asharaya snarled quietly and squeezed more blood onto the ground, allowing the shadows to take more. The darkness swelled around them, forming a blockade through the trees.

"What—"

Asharaya shushed him. Derron glanced at his swords leaning against the tree. If he was quick, he could get to them. "Don't move," she whispered, as if reading his mind.

They remained like that for gods knew how long, encased in shadows. The sounds were muffled, as if coming through a thick barrier, but soon Derron could hear nothing at all. The patrol had moved past them.

The shadows slinked away, and Asharaya slumped against him, skin pearled with sweat. "I told you not to use the shadows," he said into her hair, though there was no bite to his words.

"I'm okay." She allowed herself another moment before pulling herself up. "Give me some privacy now."

Derron stepped away and kept his back to her. He'd seen Asharaya summon shadows with natural ease. That it would drain her like this now, when she hadn't even walked through them, only served to confirm his fears.

Four thoughts kept him company in the dark.

He and Asharaya were linked.

They'd almost been caught.

Lur was too far.

She'd allowed him to call her Shara.

40

Cassia

The seat of the Vynatis was a white mansion in the middle of a grove. Large elm trees stood on either side like ancient sentinels, their colossal forms shading the ground. Cassia and Johan traveled a full day to reach it, stopping only at night to rest. Being here again brought prickling tears to Cassia's eyes. Much of this journey felt like a homecoming—Heartstar was the place she'd imagined her future alongside the man she loved. Memories barreled through her, some more beautiful than others, all of them filling her with nostalgia. Cassia couldn't help a surprised gasp at the white rose bushes embellishing the estate's gardens. Johan had them planted in her honor, and when she imagined what had become of them, she often saw him tearing them from the ground, root and stem.

Johan had clearly held on to their past romance as she had done. This could really become her home. Yet caution reigned in her excitement.

"You're tense." Johan's hands hovered over her legs, drifting dangerously toward her inner thighs. "Do you need help relaxing, princess?"

Their relationship had been characterized by highs of passion and lows of stubbornness. Most times, they'd avoid each other after an argument until a force stronger than gravity brought them together. In those moments, the apology came in the form of a smile or a kiss rather than words. Other times, they could go on for days, pretending not to care while really devising a plan to make the other beg. Apparently, Johan had no trouble fitting back into their old habits. In a way, his wickedness helped her focus. "What should I expect?" The last time Cassia had been to Heartstar, she'd said goodbye to Imiri's only son. For all she knew, the Head hated her now.

"A delegation will be waiting to greet you with all the fanfare and obeisance you like. Everything has been planned to the smallest detail. When we received word of your visit, my mother could hardly sit still." The tip of Johan's nose grazed the shell of her ear. Cassia wished she could credit her loosening tension to his words, but distance hadn't made her immune to his touch. "She's very excited to see you again."

"She doesn't hate me?"

"On the contrary. She can't wait to have you all to herself, though not today. She's too competitive for that."

"Competitive?"

"My mother thinks you'll fall back into my bed by the end of the day." Cassia couldn't blame Imiri. If she had less self-esteem, she'd be riding his lap right now, horse, guards, and wolves be damned. "She'll lose, of course. I know you won't break so easily." His lips brushed her neck. "Three days sounds more reasonable."

Cassia twisted to glare at him. His devilish grin turned her core to molten fire, while the kiss of air cooled her skin where he'd touched her. "Not if you break first."

"That's a challenge I wouldn't mind losing, love."

As Johan anticipated, a small delegation waited upon the front steps. At the forefront of the group was Imiri Vynatis. Long dark hair framed her pale face. A stark line of kohl accentuated her slanted eyes with long wings. Beside her were several nobles Cassia remembered from her frequent visits, and Tyrra's young maenar, who was rumored to be one of Lady Imiri's many lovers. The gathered fae watched Cassia with an intensity equal to that of the wolves standing guard. She squared her shoulders at their scrutiny, refusing to cower like a bunny trapped between their jaws and a dead end. If the Embernest's court required wits, Heartstar's sought strength as well.

"Princess Cassia." Lady Imiri's red lips tipped in a pleasant smile. "Welcome home."

While Cassia didn't doubt the honesty of the Head's sentiment, her previous conversation with Johan also shed new light upon them. Having Imiri's blessing would make rekindling her relationship with Johan easier—but was it too easy? Cassia thought she'd have to beg Johan to move against the Crown and Makkan, yet neither he nor his mother seemed to care of Cassia's commitment to Baramun or the conflict that would ensue should she disregard her mother's orders.

Could they be already preparing for war?

The Vynatis would have to clear their stance on Asharaya Myrassar. As much as she hated having to serve her mother's interests, managing the threat Asharaya posed was in Cassia's best interest, too.

"It's good to be back." Cassia dismounted from the horse before anyone could help and walked into Lady Imiri's open arms.

"I was starting to worry you'd forgotten your way."

"Had I known you missed me, I would've come sooner."

After the rest of the nobles took turns greeting Cassia, Lady Imiri angled the princess toward the open doors. "You must be exhausted from your travel. The servants are preparing your room." At her words, servants rushed to fetch Cassia's belongings.

"Shall we pretend you haven't had the room prepared days ago, Mother?" Johan wrapped an arm around his mother's waist and pressed a tender kiss to her temple. Johan's features were a blend of his mother and whoever fathered him. The color of their eyes was nearly identical, though there was a glint in Johan's that equally drew Cassia in and kept her on guard. Liar eyes.

Imiri swatted him away. "You'll love the view," the Head said, and then addressed the six royal guards who'd followed them inside. "Princess Cassia is among friends. No need to be this close." Though her tone was pleasant, one of the men paled.

Cassia gave a subtle nod to her guards, who stepped back to give them privacy.

Satisfied, Imiri linked their arms and led Cassia to the staircase in the middle of the foyer. More than a princess's welcome, this had all the feel of a homecoming. The last time Cassia had been to Heartstar, she remembered a triumph of emerald and silver—colors favored by Imiri even for her clothes. Now, the carpets, the curtains, and vases adorning the foyer were an exquisite combination of rose gold, bronze, and gold. "How long will you be staying with us, Cassia?" Imiri asked.

"I'm not sure. Will that be a problem?" The words were meant for Imiri, but she found herself looking at Johan.

At the foot of the stairs, Imiri grasped Cassia by her shoulders. "Our home is yours. Your only mistake was leaving."

"You're smothering her, Mother." Johan eased Cassia out of Imiri's hold and tucked her to his side. "Cassia had a long journey. Let me see her to her room."

Imiri's red lips tipped up in a smirk. "Go on, then. I'm sure you two have a lot to catch up on."

As Johan led her up the stairs, Cassia marveled at the railing's polished wooden surface, reminiscing being backed up against it, flushed and exhilarated. Remaining skeptical was difficult when the slightest detail left her overwhelmed by longing and memories. "The roses are still blooming," she said. "I thought you'd get rid of them."

"It crossed my mind."

"I should've thrown out your letters."

"You kept them?" Cassia didn't miss the hitch in Johan's breath.

"It was my way of keeping you close."

Johan reached the landing before Cassia, and he held out his hand to help her up the last step. There wasn't a need for it, but Cassia couldn't deny herself the luxury of even this simple touch. Perhaps he craved contact as much as she did. "I couldn't let the roses die because they were all I had left of you." Johan's fingers tightened around hers. "You still smell like them."

They continued in silence down a large hallway. Silver lotus flower lamps jutted from the wall, matching the floral pattern of the wine-red wallpaper. Cassia's attention zeroed in on the large rosewood doors at the hallway's center. "This is the way to your rooms."

"This is the way to my hallway," Johan corrected.

Cassia glanced at him through her lashes as they stopped before the doors—the ones opposite Johan's. *You'll love the view.* Imiri Vynatis had a sense of humor.

The room was the mirror opposite of Johan's. A cozy sitting area welcomed her, large but not as big as her own quarters at the Embernest. Inside the bedroom, the bed was already turned down, and a bathtub filled with water likely enchanted to remain warm waited for her in the private bathing room. "It's perfect," she said.

"I remember what you like." Heat flared in every one of Cassia's limbs, and Johan, rake that he was, knew it. His nostrils flared, likely whiffing her arousal at his silky tone. "Do you want me to send some servants to help?"

Help me yourself. Cassia shook her head, not trusting herself to speak while her imagination peeled away his clothes one layer at a time. *Too easy*, a little voice in her head warned.

"I'll see you at dinner, then." Johan strolled out of the room, peeking back in before closing the door. "Think of me while you take your bath, princess."

41

Kael

After weeks of imprisonment, Kael soaked up fresh air as a sponge did water. The smallest things gave him the most pleasure—the red hues of sunset cresting the Library's high towers, the murmuring music of a nearby creek, the breeze carrying nature's scent to clear the stench of filth from Kael's nostrils. Like everyone else, he was anxious to get to Lur. Maybe then he'd shed the queen's voice, taunting that this was all a dream or the fear that he'd wake up beneath Semal Leneris's knives. That his tainted blood would soon cause his friends' downfall.

In the two-day trek to the scholars' city, Kael and Solana ensured that the path ahead was safe while Mykal carried his father. Kael would have happily let the vrah do what she did best while he helped his Do'strath, but Lord Darrok was a burly man from the waist up and Kael wasn't fit enough to shoulder his weight. Eileen stayed back, yet closer than before, and tracked Mykal's movements as if afraid he'd fall on his face.

"Mykal seems to have gotten through to her," Kael whispered in Havanian to Solana, though he doubted Mykal could hear anything lower than a shout over the blood pumping in his ears.

"He has a way with people when he manages to forgo his opinions," Solana commented with a small smile. "Do I sense disapproval?"

"She did nothing to help me or her father while we were prisoners." Kael fought to keep his voice low, though he couldn't help the venom in his words. "The Argarys treated her like a princess, while I was being carved open by Semal fucking Leneris."

"You don't trust her."

"Would you? She knows—and loves—them more than any Todrak."

Solana seemed to consider her words carefully. "I trust Mykal. He won't let his affections cloud his judgment."

Kael noticed the warmth in her tone. "I'm glad he had you. And Shara."

"I'm glad I had them, too. After Merania..." Solana stared ahead as if doing so might shield her from the memories. "There's no point in dwelling on the dead."

"It's okay to grieve, Lana."

"It's hard not to feel responsible. I left Xoro's body behind. He would have wanted to be laid to rest at sea."

"Xoro wouldn't have wanted you to die trying to get him out. For what it's worth, the Meranians dispose of the dead at sea, friend or foe. He died fighting beside the woman he loved, and he found rest. What happened wasn't your fault."

A thin line of silver lined Solana's doe eyes, shattering Kael's heart.

"I know Myk has been focused on my capture and Daganver, but now that we're together and his family's safe, we can track your brother. We promised we would."

"Finding Shara is more important right now." Solana cocked her head. "And you're still healing."

Kael's first impulse was to downplay his situation. Solana's quirked brow dared him to lie, so he released a shaky sigh. "I'll be okay." Sensing the prickly feeling of being watched, Kael glanced over his shoulder, where Mykal no doubt tried to catch their every word.

I'm fine, Kael shot down the bond.

Then stop shutting me out. There had been a time when Kael pleaded the same to Mykal.

They all halted as a large shadow loomed over them.

"We made it," Lord Darrok said.

"Lur," Kael and Mykal said in unison.

A small citadel surrounded the great Library for which the city was known. The white-stone structure resembled a keep, its central tower rising over seven hundred feet tall. Along the tower's walls were markings depicting Ilahara's history in a language long forgotten—Drakasi, according to some historians' reconstructions, who also claimed the Myrassar had aided the tower's construction with their dragons to make the imposing height possible.

Despite the late hour, the city gates were open to weary travelers, as was Lur's way. Apart from a scholar who paid them no heed, the streets were blessedly empty. Light spilled from a tavern's windows but no sounds came from within, meaning likely few patrons were stopping for the night.

Kael and the others halted at the Library's enormous oak doors. Before they could figure out where to ring, the hinges groaned as the doors opened to let them through. Torches illuminated a vast hall. Everywhere Kael turned shelves upon shelves lined with books greeted him. Tables were placed at even intervals, where the occasional maenar read late into the night.

"It's magnificent," whispered Eileen.

"Is it like this on every level?" Solana asked.

"This is the place where maenari train," Lord Darrok explained. "A portion is dedicated to their living quarters and their studies, but yes. The majority is the Library."

They entered a diamond-shaped hall. Moonlight bathed the space through the large windows, landing on a large oak desk in the middle of the room. Beyond it were more hallways branching out in opposite directions and a spiral staircase leading to the higher levels.

A young man in cream-colored robes emerged from behind the desk, his back bent by the weight of the books he lifted from the floor. A student. He didn't notice them until he set the books onto the desk and cleared his brow. "May I help you?"

"Maenar Alavin," Lord Darrok said. "I wish to speak to him."

Eyes widening, the young scholar gasped. The news of Lord Darrok's escape was undoubtedly reaching all corners of Ilahara. As the only ruling Head in a wheelchair, it wasn't difficult to identify him.

Solana casually brought her hand to her belt, a breadth shy of her dagger.

"I'll fetch him." The young man scrambled up the spiral stairs with impressive speed.

Once he was out of earshot, Solana murmured, "You should have worn glamours. I do not like the boy's reaction."

"We're here to seek the maenari's help. I won't enter their home with deceit." Lord Darrok leveled Solana with a stern look. "Stay calm, but be ready."

Eileen latched onto Mykal's sleeve. "Someone's coming."

A brown-robed man descended the stairs, followed by the nervous student who kept a respectable few paces behind. The maenar's brown hair was tied back in a short ponytail, highlighting his sharp jaw. The light dancing in his green eyes lessened his austere appearance. Both Kael and Eileen hummed appreciatively, to which Mykal knocked her toe with his foot.

"Friends." The maenar's voice was a nice combination of

gravelly and deep. "Welcome to Lur."

"Maenar Alavin," Lord Darrok said. "It's been too long."

"Indeed." The maenar sized them up and smiled. "You must be tired. I'll have rooms prepared for you." Kael released a relieved sigh, and Mykal began to thank him, but the maenar held out his hand. "Only for tonight. More aid would go against our vow of neutrality."

Lord Darrok nodded. "We won't take advantage of your hospitality."

"But father—"

"My son and his friend can share," the lord continued, cutting off Mykal. "Same for the ladies."

Mykal, Kael, and Solana exchanged a worried look. Shara knew to search for them in Lur. Without the maenari's aid, they wouldn't be able to hide here for long.

Maenar Alavin asked the student to see to the rooms and then addressed Lord Darrok. "We have a platform to take you up." Mykal relaxed at the words. "The queen has been searching for you, my lord." The maenar produced a parchment from the desk. Lord Darrok's likeness stared back at them, captured in full detail.

"Is mine the only poster?" he asked.

"The two young men also grace the walls of every town, big and small. Though you're not the only one she hunts, and that perhaps may be to your advantage." He pulled out two more posters.

The color drained from Kael's face.

Solana ripped Shara's poster from the maenar's hands, her grip tight enough to wrinkle the parchment. Mykal edged behind her, while Kael remained transfixed on his brother's likeness. The artist managed to capture the inscrutable look in his eyes—that hidden layer Kael had wanted to understand and that ultimately worsened the sting of Derron's betrayal.

Mykal glanced up from the poster. "It says here she's hurt."

"Is there any news of her?" Solana asked the maenar.

"Word has it Asharaya was injured during her escape from the Embernest. She hasn't been found yet, but Prince Derron knows this region and his mother well. I'm not surprised he's been able to evade capture thus far."

"Prince Derron?" Mykal asked, at the same time Eileen ripped the parchment from the maenar's hands. The way her brows crinkled closely resembled Mykal. His Do'strath's thoughts had gone quiet where Kael's were a hurricane.

Lord Darrok extended a hand to Eileen, who hesitantly passed along Derron's poster, a shadow passing across her face. "Derron Argarys has Asharaya, then."

"He doesn't have her, my lord. Derron Argarys is with Asharaya."

"Semantics," Lord Darrok and Mykal said in unison.

"What you call semantics makes all the difference to some." Maenar Alavin tapped a finger on Derron's poster. "Certainly to the queen."

Kael didn't know what to think. Derron had gone to great lengths to capture Asharaya, and now he was on the run—with her. He'd saved her. Did that put him on their side? Kael had been wary of the prince's help in the dungeons, but now he wasn't so sure.

"We'll speak more once you're settled," Maenar Alavin said.

"Has anyone come looking for us?" The maenar shook his head in answer to Mykal's question. The rebels Mykal was expecting had yet to arrive, then. Hopefully they would before they were forced out of Lur.

"Do you have anything that could shield us from tracking spells?" Lord Darrok asked.

"You won't have to worry about being tracked tonight, my lord. Our wards are strong."

A simple wheelchair was brought in for Lord Darrok, relieving Mykal of his father's weight. Maenar Alavin led them to a spelled platform, which took them to the higher levels dedicated to the maenari's lodgings. Three neighboring rooms had been prepared for them. Lord Darrok wheeled into one without a word.

"We'll have to move," Mykal blurted out. "Meet Shara halfway—and fast. Argarys wasn't supposed to be with her. She could be in danger."

"We are exhausted," Solana said, though she didn't outright disagree. The fright hadn't left her face since she'd heard of Shara's injury. "Take a warm bath. The last thing we need is for your muscles to tighten up after all the weight you carried."

"I'm fine."

Solana looked to Kael. "Make sure he behaves."

"Yes, my lady."

Mykal rolled his eyes. "I almost forgot how obnoxious you two are together."

Kael grinned, and Solana gave Mykal a playful slap behind the head. "We'll reconvene in the morning."

Mykal let himself be dragged to the nearest door, though both Do'strath stopped on the threshold. Solana stilled by her door as if sensing their attention, and looked over her shoulder, acknowledging them with a gentle smile before going inside. The sight of it was like sunshine after a thunderstorm. Warmth tingled through Kael's veins and collected in his lower belly. The feeling mirrored in the soulbond.

"Come on," Mykal murmured, lacing his fingers with Kael's and guiding him inside.

The room was barely big enough for the bunk beds stacked against one wall and the tub on the opposite side. Kael's throat closed. His cell hadn't been much smaller.

"Are you with me?" Mykal's fingers squeezed around Kael's.

"Yeah." Kael whispered, but the queen said otherwise in his head, so he concentrated on to the differences between this room and his cell—the smell of clean linens, the weight of Mykal's hand, the steam rising from the bathtub—until he could finally breathe again. "You're worried about Shara."

Mykal unfastened his cloak and placed it on the bottom

bunk bed. "The last time Argarys helped us, he had a dagger ready to stab us in the back. We've no reason to believe this time is any different."

"He saved her, though."

"Don't start."

"Derron tried to help me." Kael didn't have the energy to fight Mykal on Derron, so he wasn't sure why he was voicing his doubts. "Maybe this time it's different."

"He's the reason you were taken, Kael." Mykal cupped his face, pressing their foreheads together. "I don't want to fight. And Solana's right, we're exhausted. We need a clear mind to figure out what the fuck comes next."

Kael let out a small laugh, his fingers fisting Mykal's shirt. *Real.* "Okay."

Mykal drew him into a hug, kissing Kael's cheek, then the corner of his mouth. "Do you want to join me in the bath?"

The hidden promise in those words sent tingles down Kael's spine, but instead of soothing him, he locked up. He became suddenly aware of the brand hidden beneath his clothes and pushed out of Mykal's arms.

Mykal blinked. "I don't want sex. I only want to take care of you."

Kael hung his head, tears rising to his eyes. "I'm not ready yet, Myk."

"Okay." Mykal ran a hand through his hair, the thick strands sticking out at odd angles. "Then you take the bath first. I can wait."

"No."

Mykal's brows drew together. "You don't have to hide from me, Kael. I wish you knew that." He looked away, staring at a spot in the wall to hide the moisture in his eyes. "We're Do'strath. I should be the one helping you. I should be the one protecting you. And I know you need time, and that it's my fault if you're not opening up to me but I wish you would. It kills me that you don't."

"It's not your fault. It's me." Kael could hardly push the words out. "I don't want you to see me like this."

Mykal held out his hand, an offering for Kael to take when he was ready. "I promise you, I can handle it. Let me share the burden."

Kael swallowed back tears as he reached for Mykal's hand. That part was easy. Everything else—remembering, acknowledging the stain on his flesh and soul—was harder. "I'm tainted," he confessed. His fingers trembled as he brought them to the hem of his shirt.

Mykal's hands covered his, and Kael's tremors stopped. They stayed like this for a while, listening to each other breathing. Kael couldn't bring himself to look into Mykal's eyes until his Do'strath tilted his chin up. His immeasurable tenderness gave Kael the courage to lift his shirt and throw it over his head. He was filthy, and some of the nastier bruises still dotted his flesh, but what stood stark against his pale skin was the angry red welt of the queen's "A."

Mykal took in each mark before settling on the brand. Kael bit his lip to keep back a sob, shame falling over him like a bucket of mud. When Mykal's fingers brushed the brand's seams, Kael shivered and squeezed his eyes shut. His Do'strath's affection would turn to hatred at the violent reminder of who Kael was. The blood of Mykal's enemies flowed in his veins. Mykal likely regretted every kindness he'd doled out, every bit of trust, every kiss.

"You've been so strong." Mykal's voice shook on the last word, finally drawing Kael's eyes back to him.

"She said I belong to them." Kael shuddered at the memory, and the tears he'd fought to hold back poured out in a gut-wrenching sob. His legs bent, but Mykal was there to support him, holding him tight.

"You belong to no one," Mykal murmured in his ear, stroking Kael's hair as they cried together. "You taught me we're more than our families and our blood. Every time you chose kindness and compassion despite the sneers and the names people called you behind your back, you showed me we determine who we are. No one else. You took a lord's broken and opinionated son and made him a better man. One who dreams of a better world." Mykal reached up to dry his tears with gentle thumbs. "This mark isn't who you are. It says nothing about you, and everything about the woman who hurt you." He leaned forward, pressing a chaste kiss to Kael's wet and shaking lips. "I knew exactly who you were when I agreed to be your Do'strath. I knew it when I fell in love with you, and I want all of it, Kael. Every piece of you."

Kael wound his arms around Mykal and buried his face against his Do'strath's neck. Mykal's words didn't magically wipe away every hurt, doubt, and insecurity, but they eased a load off his chest. These were the words he'd imagined in his dark empty cell—no, better. Once again, Mykal reminded Kael he was worthy of love. "Please don't let me go in that thing alone," he mumbled against his Do'strath's skin.

"I meant what I said earlier. We can take it slow."

"I know, but I want you with me."

Their kiss was salty, slow, and wet, but it tasted of hope. Mykal had witnessed his shame and loved him all the same. The muscles of Mykal's abdomen flexed as Kael helped him out of his shirt. He'd seen his Do'strath's nakedness countless times in their long years of friendship, but he'd never let himself be aware of Mykal's beauty before. Not like this. On a subconscious level, he'd tried to protect the certainty of Mykal's steadfast friendship from the unpredictability of love, though even then a part of him had known his true feelings. Every time the idea of Raxan's hands on Mykal's body had driven him to anger, and whenever he blushed at Mykal's clever smirk, he'd known.

Heat gathered low in Kael's core, tightening his muscles as his fingers traced Mykal's chest.

Mykal covered Kael's hands on the line of dark hairs below his navel. "I realized we still haven't defined our relationship," he stuttered, a dark blush on his brown cheeks.

"We are, Myk." Kael smiled as he brushed Mykal's lips with his own. *We're doing it now.*

42

Cassia

After settling into her room and resting in a comfortable bed, Cassia received an invitation to dinner from Imiri Vynatis. Remembering the lady's fondness for the color, Cassia selected an emerald gown, and a young woman fixed her hair with little crimson beads that complemented it. She followed the Tyrran fashion, leaving her hair down if not for the small braids at the crown of her head and lining her eyes with kohl. On the dressing table, Baramun's necklace winked from its perch. She regretted bringing it, for the sight of it allowed doubt to creep in. Was she making the right choice? Was Johan still the man she used to trust? Was her rebellion worth the retaliation that would undoubtedly follow?

Cassia almost slammed the box shut, but another idea waltzed into her head. A challenge. Gods knew how driven the Vynatis could be when provoked.

She lingered in her room in case Johan would be courteous

enough to escort her downstairs. When it became obvious he wouldn't come, Cassia wasn't even disappointed. His resistance was reassuring in a way.

Light spilled from the open dining room doors. The long table was set for three at the far end of the candlelit hall, but there was no sign of Johan. Wrapped in a silver dress, Imiri glanced out one of the floor-to-ceiling windows overlooking the gardens. It seemed Imiri was aiming for a similar type of flattery with her attire.

"Looks like we're both dressed to please," Imiri commented as Cassia joined her. Her eyes dropped to the ruby necklace around Cassia's neck. "Impressive."

"Baramun's generous with his gifts."

Imiri clicked her tongue as she poured two glasses of amber wine—Tyrran, not Adarian, judging by the color and sweet aroma. Cassia would have to be careful. Tyrran wine wasn't only sweeter but stronger too. "Are you fond of His Holiness?" Imiri handed over one of the glasses. When Cassia didn't answer, Imiri raised a brow. "Shifters don't follow sensible whims. If you give him reason to think he owns you, you lose."

"Perhaps you should teach me how to play the game, then. I heard there was a bit of trouble at a wedding celebration. Two men were dueling for you."

"It's tedious when they start demanding exclusivity."

"Are they dead?"

"Johan handled it." It wasn't a straight answer, yet a dangerous thrill shot up Cassia's spine at the mental image of Johan's bloodied hands.

In Tyrra, it was custom for executions to be meted out in one's animal form, but no one had ever seen Johan's. Some claimed he couldn't shift, others that he was Imiri's most cherished secret weapon. Cassia was prone to believe the latter. Not even when she ordered him to confess in the throngs of passion did Johan reveal the animal lurking beneath his skin, but she'd sensed its power and might inside her. Whatever he was, Johan was no low fae.

"The Farwynd may have an impressive wingspan, but they're greedy lovers." Imiri's talk of Baramun made Cassia's skin crawl, as if her betrothed's presence were materializing in the room.

"Do you know from experience?"

"Don't answer that." Cassia's center of gravity shifted at Johan's presence. He joined them at the window and slid the glass from Cassia's hands. The innocent, if not overtly familiar, gesture was a message—everything that was hers belonged to him as well. Arrogant, territorial bastard. Cassia followed his maroon velvet sleeve to wide shoulders and a toned chest left partially exposed by his shirt's low neckline. The tips of her fingers tingled with the desire to touch him. He was all long limbs in perfect proportion and feline grace, and Cassia wanted to devour him. "Your adventures with the pigeons aren't fit for dinner, Mother."

"At that time, our diplomatic relations with Makkan were excellent."

"Is there trouble with Makkan?" Cassia asked.

Johan shrugged. "Border skirmishes."

"Is that why you were on the road yesterday?"

His gaze bore onto the rubies at her neck. "They'll soon remember to keep their feathers away from what doesn't belong to them."

"Is there anything I can do?" Cassia suppressed a gag reflex as she said, "I have influence with Baramun."

Imiri sipped on her wine as she glanced at her son, who remained preternaturally still if not for the tick in his jaw. "Let's eat, shall we?"

Servants poured into the room carrying trays. One helped Cassia to her seat, staring a moment too long. Like nobles, servants gossiped. Did they remember her time here, or had they heard of her tryst with a human?

Unbidden, the memory of Korban serving at her table and

throwing her a wink came to mind. The fool had always been too reckless, but his shameless flirtations had lifted her mood during tense situations. Gods, if only the servants would stop staring.

"You look rather pale," Imiri noted from the seat across from Cassia.

"No, I'm..." Cassia's words failed as Johan sat at the head of the table. He lounged like a king on a throne. Since when was he the one seated at the head of the table? "Fine," Cassia finished, realizing she'd been quiet. "Famished."

Johan met her gaze, and then his eyes slid to her necklace, the look positively feral. Cassia brushed a hand through her hair to bring more attention to the ruby.

"Have you told my mother the reason for your visit?" Johan asked, his tone clipped. "The queen doubts our loyalty."

"And here I was, thinking we'd given ample demonstration in the last war." Imiri speared her venison, blood pooling around the puncture holes. Did she ever spare a thought for the Myrassar king's brother? The queen had alluded that Imiri and Daemian were close, though Imiri never spoke of him.

"Apparently not." Johan tapped his fingers on the table. "Tell me, Cassia. What is it the queen wants?"

"Assurance that when the time comes, your armies will stand with hers."

"And what will Tyrra gain?"

"You need a prize to serve your queen?"

"Baramun got one." Johan's smile held no warmth. "Will she send precious Prince Derron to warm my mother's bed?"

Imiri chuckled around a morsel. "His face structure is quite impressive."

Cassia set her utensils down with a loud clang. "Forget my mother. Asharaya's return is a problem. What do you intend to do about it?" She should have directed the question to the Head, but her eyes remained fixed on Johan.

"I believe the queen capable of catching one girl with few

allies without the help of every Head, but we have eyes on the borders."

"So if Asharaya happens to cross into your territory, maybe you'll do something. Is that it?" Aware of Imiri's silence and scrutiny, Cassia leaned closer to Johan and placed her hand over his closed fist. "What if I were the one needing help? Not my mother. Me."

"You're the one who wants me to start a hunt for a young woman I've never met, then?" Johan asked. "Tyrran trackers may have a finer smell than most, but without tracks it's a wild goose chase."

"And if she gains allies, and the people rally behind her, what then? Where will Tyrra stand?"

Johan pulled his hand away. "A good leader doesn't stand behind names. If the people would rather rally in support of a stranger who spent most of her life with humans, perhaps there's a reason."

Imiri glanced at her son with evident pride, and though he spoke the truth, it nearly broke Cassia's heart. "If Asharaya wins, I'm as good as dead."

"Because you're so sure your mother's side is where you should stand?" Johan spread his arms. "This could have been our life, Cassia. She took this from us. She killed your human lover, promised you to a man you despise." He leaned closer. "Is the illusion of power she feeds you worth your blind loyalty?"

Cassia shot to her feet, chest heaving as if she'd run miles, skin burning with the promise of Fire. He was right about everything, but this wasn't about her mother. "I came here to ask for your help, but how can I when I can't trust you?"

Throwing her napkin on the table, Cassia strode out of the room.

Exhausted by the emotional bludgeoning, Cassia all but fell into the seat in front of the mirror and tore the beads from her hair, the crimson gems like drops of blood on the dressing table. A fitting metaphor of how she felt inside. Coming to Heartstar was a mistake. How many times would she get burned before she learned that playing with fire never ended well?

A knock on the door made her flinch. Cassia didn't move to open it, nor did she answer. Moments later, the door flew open and Johan forced his way inside. "Do you believe me a fool?" he growled, slamming the door. He was both a dream and a nightmare made flesh, with bloodshot eyes and disarrayed hair. Surprise zapped through her, followed by wrath. He had no right to be this devastatingly handsome while he hated her and she him.

Cassia stood to face him, arms crossed. "No, you're a brute."

"Leave, fuck a human—fuck ten humans, if it's what you want. I can live with that. But lying to my face?" Johan made a sound halfway between frustration and disgust. "If this is the woman you've become, you deserve that collar around your neck."

Cassia's hand flew to his face, but he grabbed her wrist before she could strike. "I haven't lied to you."

"You wear Baramun's gifts while manipulating me into fighting your mother's wars. I wrote you that letter because I care about you, Cassia. The woman I fell in love with wouldn't have weaponized those feelings."

"You stupid man." Cassia made to push him away, but his grip on her wrist tightened. "That shit about the war was an excuse to convince my mother to let me come here."

"And yet you doubt that I would keep you safe." Johan backed her against the wall. "The gods cursed me by making me love a wretched woman."

"Fuck you," she growled. "I'd choose you a thousand times if I could."

"Then why don't you?"

"Because I can't be with you if I'm questioning your loyalty."

"My loyalty is to you." Cassia's leg tangled around his,

dragging him closer. Heat spread at his words, his nearness, his heavy pants against her lips. "I would rain ashes on Ilahara for you. Asharaya, your mother, mine. None of them matter. Only you." His free hand circled her throat, gentle, but firmly holding her still as he drew close and took in her scent. "He hasn't claimed you," he hissed. "Is he buying you with jewels until Aerella gives him permission to fuck you?"

A shudder worked its way down Cassia's spine, his dominance liquefying her core. "I'm not his to claim."

Johan pinned her arm above their heads, aligning their bodies. This close, his growing hardness pressed into her belly, eliciting Cassia's greedy sigh. "You're mine," he whispered in her ear, his soft sigh a promise. "Our souls are bound, Cassia Argarys. I need no one's permission but yours."

Cassia ached with need. When he spoke like that, giving substance to her every forbidden dream, she couldn't hold on to reason. Her body chased what she craved, arching in silent demand.

Johan growled into her ear, the sound more animal than fae. He lifted her as if she weighed nothing, hiking up her gown to free her legs and her sex. Moisture glistened between her thighs, the scent of her arousal impossible to mask. As she fumbled to free him from his pants, Johan moaned against her jaw, nipping at her skin hard enough to leave a red bloom that would fade by morning. "Say the words, Cassia." His tongue traced a bare spot on her neck. The touch echoed between her legs, and Cassia groaned in a mix of pleasure and frustration.

Her fingers skirted the silken heat of his cock. "I want you. Now. Always."

Johan spread her legs wider and pushed inside. Cassia cried out, and he released a satisfied breath, as if he'd been holding it in since the moment they'd parted. She sighed into the hollow of his shoulder as he stretched and filled her. Johan allowed her a moment to take it, and then started moving, pounding her against the wall with each of his powerful thrusts. More than making love, this was a battle. As if he wanted to punish her for leaving and doubting him, and himself for wanting her still. His relentless rhythm allowed Cassia little respite, but Johan had never been one for gentleness.

"Gods, how I missed you," she whispered into his ear, biting his earlobe, begging him to keep going. Faster. Harder. In that moment, there was only the two of them, the rightness of his body moving into hers, claiming her.

The fire between them kept building with no end. The more he took, the more he gave, the more she craved. She clawed at the back of his shirt as if to shred through the fabric and feel his skin. His fingers dug into her legs, her hips, her ass. "I missed this," Cassia panted. "I missed us."

Too soon, Cassia's body locked up and built to her climax. She grabbed the curling locks at the nape of his neck, relishing in his quickening pace as he chased his own release and in the nonsense he murmured into her skin. That he loved her. That he wouldn't let her leave. "You're mine." A nip at her pulse. He whispered it over and over, a prayer as his hand dragged to her inner thigh, finding her clit.

Cassia shattered, not even trying to keep her voice low as her orgasm ravaged her. Johan's release followed moments after. He came with a growl, sliding his fingers beneath Baramun's necklace and tearing it off her neck. Cassia leaned back against the wall, feeling weightless and liberated, her chest heaving as he emptied himself inside her.

Rubies rained around them as Johan pressed a soothing kiss to her chin. A trick of the light brightened his eyes from hazel to yellow. He licked down the column of her neck. "Not my bed," he whispered against her skin.

The bet. Imiri's only mistake had been assuming they'd have sex in bed.

She pushed Johan away. "Get out," she ground out, though she couldn't help the hint of amusement in her tone.

Johan gripped her chin between his fingers. His lips grazed

hers, and Cassia's lids fluttered shut, but instead of kissing her, Johan released her and set her down. "Thank you for your insight, princess." Cassia's eyes flew open in time to see him adjust his pants and walk to the door. "The Head will have a proposition for you in the morning."

43

Shara

Shara's hold on the horn of Sweetie's saddle tightened as a new wave of dizziness overcame her. She was hyperaware of the sweat collecting in her palm, the leather chafing against her skin with each one of Sweetie's swayed steps. Moisture from the nightly rain clung to the air, but Shara garnered no comfort from it. She was warm—too warm—and every movement sent new licks of agony through her body.

"There's a lake up ahead," Derron said. "We could stop there to rest and bathe. We need to get some of this dust off you if we want to keep your wounds clean, and we need to keep your temperature down."

"If we bathe we make it easier for the hounds to pick up our scent." Shara hated how even her voice reflected her weakness. Derron's herbs helped, and he was surprisingly adept at dressing her wounds, but even that couldn't change the hard truth. The cut from Aerella's sword wasn't healing, and whatever poison the bitch had laced her blade with was winning the fight against Shara's magic. It shrank back a little more each day, her Fire lost to the fever and her shadows as slippery as oil when she didn't have Derron's herbs numbing the pain.

"Do you want to see your friends again?"

Of course she did. Ever since they'd come across those wanted posters, Shara's mind spiraled further into darkness. Had she missed her friends' posters, or was Aerella not searching for them because they'd already been caught? That fear haunted her, and even in her nightmares Shara's friends were locked behind bars—or worse. That morning, she'd dreamed of them being dragged onto the executioner's block where Sanda was murdered—Mykal first, then Kael, and finally Solana. Shara had shoved her way through the crowd, but the more she did, the more distant the platform became.

"Making me clean isn't going to stop this," Shara rasped, nausea rising. "The poison is going to keep spreading, no matter what we do. I need a cure, not a lake." *I need Solana, not Aerella's son.* Solana knew her way around poisons best. Shara had always taken to weapons and counted on her magic—even that sliver of it she'd held onto in Havanya—to get her out of trouble. Fevers, swelling, hallucinations—these were common symptoms of many kinds of poisons. But one that could fight off magic? Shara had never heard of such a thing. Apparently neither had Derron. "I want to keep going."

A new wave of dizziness struck her, and this time she didn't have enough strength in her fingers to hold onto the saddle's horn. Shara's grip slipped, and only Derron's arms around her kept her on the horse.

"I'm just trying to help, Shara." Derron's whisper against her ear made the hairs at the back of her neck rise. "The water won't cure you, but it'll keep your temperature down. We need to help your magic fight off the poison for as long as we can."

Shara went limp against Derron's chest. "Are we close to Lur?"

He took a moment to think about it. "Three, maybe four more days of travel if we don't stop too often."

"That's a lot." If her magic gave up, how long would it take the poison to finish her off? She'd die away from her friends, away from Deimok. Derron tightened his hold on her, as if he could sense the dark turn of her thoughts. "You really think the water will help?"

"I do."

"Okay." Shara shut her eyes as tears built behind her lids. "Take me there."

Derron steered Sweetie into thick foliage, using one of his swords to move away the ferns as they progressed deeper. Minutes passed before Shara made out the gentle babbling of water nearby. From the corner of her eye, Derron's lips tilted into a small smile—not a self-satisfied one. Simply relieved. Every new day reshaped her awareness of the prince. By their fifth day of travel, Shara had gotten better at reading his silences and perceiving his changing moods, like when his curious staring grew more intense, or his arms wrapped a little tighter around her on the horse. Each time, she felt less trapped and more protected. That, more than anything, unsettled her.

Once past the tall grass and line of trees, a wide expanse of water greeted them, the color so clear it reflected the gray clouds above. Derron dismounted and held out his arms to help Shara. She narrowed her eyes, and he let out a patient sigh, lifting his eyebrows but otherwise unmoving. "Unless you want to fall," he challenged.

Shara ignored her pride and accepted his help. Her feet hit the ground, the reverberations shaking her skull.

"Do you need help undressing?" Shara stepped out of his reach, and Derron chuckled. "As I thought." He unstrapped his swords and set them against an elm tree, and then began unbuttoning his leather vest.

Shara's eyes bulged as he cast it to the ground. "What are you doing?" She averted her eyes as he flung his shirt along with it.

"I'm filthy." Derron removed his boots. "And you need someone to make sure you don't drown." Derron flashed Shara a boyish grin over his shoulder as his hands went to his breeches. "I won't look."

Shara took cover behind the tree, careful not to look at a naked Derron as he ambled to the lake. She removed her belt of daggers and her boots, holding onto the trunk to keep from falling over, when she realized she couldn't hear the sounds of a body treading water. Shara looked to the lake.

No sign of Derron.

She hurried to the water's edge. "Where in the Dragon's name are you?"

Derron broke the lake's surface, and Shara's heart jumped out of her chest. He'd been as quiet as a shark, though he looked less predatory and more content. His eyes were closed, as if savoring each second spent in the water, which also meant he missed the way Shara flushed. The water lapped against his stomach, gifting her few peeks of his sculpted abs. That still left an ample view of his broad shoulders and muscled arms. Droplets clung to his skin and captured the light, teasing Shara to follow their downward trail along his body. She'd seen much more in Merania, but she hadn't let herself appreciate the view when she'd perceived him as a threat.

She'd spent countless hours on a horse with all that pressed onto her back.

Sweetie's whinny had Derron's eyes spring open before she could retreat. His alarm quickly became amusement. "What are you doing?"

"You vanished. I thought you drowned." Shara cleared her throat. "I think one of us has to keep watch."

"Are you nervous, Asharaya?"

"I'm being reasonable."

"Everything we need to watch is here." Derron's grin widened proportionately to her scowl. "And if anyone were to find us, my Song will keep them still long enough for you to protect me."

"Granted you don't hemorrhage," she quipped. Had he just painted himself as the damsel? Shara couldn't help the smile tugging at her lips. Perhaps it was the fever, but his playfulness piqued her curiosity. Her hands went to the hem of her shirt, and Derron's eyes followed. "You said you wouldn't look."

Slowly, she raised her shirt over her stomach, exposing her heated skin to the fresh breeze. Derron watched like a wolf tracking his prey, turning only when her shirt reached the lower curve of her breast. She couldn't explain why the privacy disappointed her.

Shara stripped and made quick work of setting aside her things before stepping into the lake. The freshness prodded at her sensitized skin, and it took a few steps to gather the courage to dip her head. She wiped away the drops weighing down her lids. "You can turn around now."

Derron walked closer, and she flinched when his hand came around her elbow. The salt of his skin invaded her senses. The cobalt of his eyes bled into the silver, as if reflecting the water's color. "How are you feeling?" he asked.

"I don't need help."

Derron released her. "Okay." The hitch in his voice tugged Shara's attention to where the water parted around his hips. A glimpse of thick skin had her putting some distance between them. She ventured farther out so she could stand up with the water lapping at her collarbone.

Soft splashing at her back alerted her to Derron's approach. When she could sense his heat, she said, "You enjoy the water."

"It's my Meranian side."

"At least you don't look like a shark like that pompous asshole Andren Nahar."

Derron let out a small laugh. "I'm going to touch your forehead." Something in the way he waited patiently for her consent quieted her protest, and she nodded. Derron dipped his hand into the water and brought it over her head. The water gently trickled down her hair, and she tilted her head back. The drops were cool against her skin.

Derron seemed to sense the tension leaving her body, for he lapped more water and let it wash over her hair. He then threaded his fingers through her tangled strands and across her forehead, dabbing it gently with more water as he saw fit, all the while staying behind her. Soon, the fever's heat dimmed, and a new warmth spread at her back, like an impression of the prince she couldn't see.

Derron found the shorn tips of her ear, a silent question hanging between them.

"I arrived in Havanya shortly after a brutal reaping," Shara said. "Many died. Hundreds of children were stolen—most of them destined for Ilahara. It wasn't a good time to be a fae among humans. At first, Solana made me glamour my ears even to her father, but when my magic began to weaken, the Vrahiid found out the truth. To keep me safe, he cut them." Shara could hear the echo of his unsheathed dagger, the heat of the incandescent blade. Her body locked up at the memory, but Derron's thumb grazed the scarring, gentle, soothing. "The tips grew back a few times, and we had to do it again until they stopped." Derron shuddered. "By that time, what little magic I had only healed most of the scarring. Still to this day, I can't stand to look at them."

Derron tucked a strand of hair behind her ear. "Your scars made you stronger. Both the physical ones and the ones you carry inside."

Shara looked at him over her shoulder. *Dangerous*, a voice warned in the back of her mind, but then Derron's lips tipped up in a reassuring smile, and all her caution swam back to shore. "Better?" he asked.

"Yes. How?"

"The Ilah's magic flows through the land and into the water. It won't heal you, but I was hopeful it would help. Later we can fill our canteens, and if I ration how much water I take, I could use it to clean your wound and cool you down."

Shara twisted to face him. Thin scars a shade lighter than his skin peppered his chest, visible only by standing close. They were likely mementos from the sirens in Eathelin, yet another time he'd protected her. "Why are you still helping me? You know as well as I do that unless we find a cure, this is only going to get worse. I'll slow you down." And yet, despite what she was suggesting, she leaned forward, closer to him. "You don't owe me anything."

"I want to do right by you this time." Derron visibly swallowed, his eyes searching hers. "We were friends once." The same words she'd said in Merania thrown back at her with disarming gentleness. "I never gave much thought to how things could've been, but lately it's all I can do."

Shara's eyes bounced from his intense gaze to his parting lips. Derron moved closer, their chests almost touching, and his hand came up to caress her cheek. His fingers brushed away the strands of wet hair plastered to her face as he angled her head up, his intent shining in his eyes.

Heart pounding, Shara slinked away. If not for her body's awareness of all the places it had touched his, the moment with Derron might have been a dream. She sloshed back to shore, resolved to move past this incident and never look back on it again. "We should get back on the road while we still have daylight."

"We could wash our clothes first. At the very least yours."

"We're moving now."

Derron didn't protest further. They dressed in silence, the unexpected vulnerability in the lake almost as tangible as the tree between them. He didn't say a word even as he strapped his swords to his back and went to scout ahead for trouble, and for once she didn't question whether he would return. The Derron in the lake had been true, so eerily familiar that she'd allowed him to touch her like that. That she'd lowered her guard.

Shara walked up to Sweetie, untying her from the branch, when movement in the foliage had her reaching for her daggers. Derron barged into the camp with hurried steps, glancing over his shoulder. "There are Argarys soldiers patrolling the forest. I counted four, but there could be more."

"If they're this close, we won't be able to outrun them."

"We can use my Song, but its effect will depend on how many there are."

"Stop relying on that damn Song. It's hurting you." Shara extracted two daggers from her belt as she stepped around him.

Derron grabbed her arm, lips pressed in a determined line. "It's too dangerous."

"You underestimate me if you think I need your Song to do my job."

"And you overestimate your strength."

"I'm better now," she insisted. Neither one of them backed down. Her eyes darted to his hand still around her arm. "Watch my back."

Derron capitulated beneath her resolve. His grip tightened before he released her.

They took a longer route to creep up behind the patrol. Despite his bulk, Derron was stealthy, and the forest undergrowth barely made a sound beneath their feet. The weight of her blades was grounding. The fever receded with the water's healing touch, but her wounds would leave her winded if she needed to parry against a heavier opponent. She'd have to favor stealth and speed.

Derron raised a finger to his lips. Shara followed him behind a bush's cover, peeking between the leaves. Four men. Disposing of them would be quick if they timed the attack right.

"Don't use your Song unless it's necessary," Shara whispered. "Don't hesitate, and don't play the hero."

"Anything else?"

Shara rolled her eyes, collecting a handful of dirt.

As she crept out of hiding, the man at the head of the party stopped in his tracks. "He's close," he said. This patrol must have come from the Embernest if they were tracking Derron.

Ignoring the way her wounds pulled, Shara lengthened her strides, light on her feet. The man at the party's rear turned. His lips parted, but Shara thrust her dagger into his throat, and his warning drowned in a gurgle of blood. Her cover exposed, Shara threw the dirt into a second guard's face and spun with the momentum of removing her blade from the other's throat. She slashed the man's chest and then sliced into his exposed neck. It wasn't clean, but it was deep enough, and the man dropped to the ground, lifeless.

Derron had handled the other two. Blood splattered his face, his expression cold as he pushed his sword deeper into his opponent's chest. The fourth man was already bleeding out a short distance away.

"You didn't play the hero," Shara said, praising him as he pulled free his blade. Derron didn't look at the man as he fell to the ground, but his jaw was tight and his eyes dark. "They were going to murder you. Don't feel guilty for saving your hide."

"We should hide them in case someone comes looking."

Shara crouched beside the man nearest her and tugged loose his coin pouch.

"What are you doing?"

"Dead men have no need for coin, but we do."

Derron's gaze landed on the ground not too far from Shara. He stepped over a body to inspect whatever caught his attention—a small glass vial containing what seemed to be blood. Shara knew loss well enough to recognize it. Aerella was her villain, but she was also Derron's mother. It couldn't be easy for him to have to choose between his family and justice, to run away from his own blood and witness the lengths his mother would go to dispose of him. In another life, she might have comforted him. "If she's using blood to track you, it means she's close."

Derron ran a hand through his damp hair, muttering a

curse. "We're never going to make it out of this alive."

As much as she shared the sentiment, that same restless urge that had blinded her in the Embernest was making itself known again. If she found Aerella, she might have another chance at ending this war before more lives were lost. And with the poison eating away at her, she might have a better chance finding Aerella than making it to Lur. "What if she has the antidote?"

"It's a possibility, but if she's out of the Embernest, she's doing so with an army. You and I won't get to her alive."

"And if she has my friends?" Shara couldn't hide the shaking in her voice, her worst fear made all too real once voiced. "We can't be sure they made it out of the Embernest, and we haven't seen any posters for them."

"We didn't spend nearly enough time in a town to know that." Derron countered, grabbing a dead man by the ankles. "It's too dangerous, Shara. We'll have better odds in Lur."

Shara let the argument drop as they worked together in silence, Derron's gaze like a brand on Shara's skin and Shara resolutely focused on the task at hand. The moment at the lake faded like a distant memory, her thoughts a dark cloud blinding out the sun. What was Aerella doing away from the Embernest? As big a threat as Shara was—even with Derron in tow—she was still only one person. It made sense for Aerella to send men after her, but she wouldn't leave her stronghold unless something bigger was at play. Had she received word of what happened in Daganver? Was she marching north?

Deimok, please tell me you're safe. If only the words would travel to the other end of the bond. Her dragon was too far away to sense. "We should try going to another town on the way to Lur," Shara suggested. "We still need renike."

And I will find out where Aerella is and what she's up to.

44

Cassia

Cassia's first night in Heartstar was restless. A bevy of doubts and emotions had kept her up most of the night, and when she managed to sleep, it was only to return to the room. Cassia screamed into the dark, asking it why it had abandoned her for days, but the darkness remained silent until she calmed, sliding down against the cavern walls.

When a maid roused her in the morning, Cassia's back was sore, as if she'd spent the night against the wall in her dreams rather than in the comfortable bed where she now lay. A plate of raspberry tarts and a glass of milk sat on a tray at the foot of the bed. Despite her bone-deep weariness, Cassia managed a smile. This was Johan's doing. He was a doting puppy after making love, especially when the sex was that intense.

Cassia made to reach for the tray, but the maid beat her to it. She was young and pretty, with blonde locks tucked into a tight bun. Her bosom was bound in a way that seemed painful.

"You were here last night as well. You helped me prepare for dinner."

A small blush colored the girl's cheeks, and she subtly dipped her head. Sometimes Cassia forgot how quiet humans were. Being with Korban had loosened her tongue around them, but not the other way around.

Cassia was undeterred, though the reason eluded her. "I like what you did to my hair yesterday."

"Thank you, Your Highness." Although she spoke softly, the maid's voice was clear as a bell. "Lord Johan and his mother are both unable to attend breakfast this morning. I was asked to see to your needs."

"What's your name?"

"Coraline, Your Highness."

"How old are you?"

"Nineteen." Coraline glanced at the tray. "Lord Johan said you're fond of raspberry tarts. He had the cooks prepare them especially for you." Her tone sweetened, and her blush darkened. Unsurprisingly, Johan had admirers among his staff.

The first bite made Cassia's growing headache almost bearable. Johan remembered her fondness for the raspberry's contrasting taste. Not too sweet, not too sour. *Like you*, she imagined him saying.

A knock on the door had Coraline going into the other room. Cassia allowed herself a small, pleasurable moan as she savored the tart. Something about Tyrran food made her fall deeper in love with the region each time.

Coraline returned moments later, hands folded neatly at her front. She must have heard Cassia's ecstasy because the girl struggled to hold back a smile. "The Head would like to see you as soon as you're done with your breakfast."

Cassia wished she'd had a better night's sleep. Imiri would no doubt try to handle her, but it was best not to delay the inevitable. Though her instinct was to trust Johan, Cassia would hear what the Head had to say to see if she could place her future in the Vynatis's hands.

A Tyrran guard led Cassia down the familiar path to Imiri's study. Four more guards from her own entourage followed close behind. Suspicion infiltrated every interaction between the Argarys and Vynatis guards, which culminated in an intense stare down outside the study's door.

A hushed conversation came from within the room, the low chatter indistinct. It stopped altogether when the Tyrran guard knocked and opened the door. "My lord, Princess Cassia is here."

My lord?

Without waiting for a formal invite, Cassia sidestepped the guard and entered, her guards at her heels. Johan leaned against the desk, framed by the stunning vista of Heartstar's lake at his back. Cassia might have spent more time enjoying the view—especially when her body tingled at his nearness, as if his hands were still all over her—if not for the fact he wasn't alone. A petite beauty stood beside him, regarding Cassia with a devil's smirk. Raven-black hair framed a soft, round face and faded into a plum hue that grazed collarbones left partially exposed by a too-large man's shirt tucked into high-waisted breeches.

"Your Highness," the stranger crooned, bowing with a flourish. Necklaces dangled out of the shirt's neckline. "Lord Johan's lengthy description of your beauty doesn't do you justice."

Johan cleared his throat. "Princess Cassia, this is Sera. They're an adviser to the Tyrran court."

The fae bowed, but Cassia's lips thinned. "I don't remember seeing you before."

"I wasn't here the last time you graced Tyrra with your presence."

"That'll be all, Sera," Johan said. "We'll talk later."

When Sera bowed to Johan, the gesture was full of fond mockery. Cassia couldn't decide if she found the fae endearing or troublesome. Perhaps both. They flashed her another knowing smirk before leaving the room. "I'll leave the door open for you, gentlemen," they said over their shoulder.

Johan eyed Cassia's guards, then gestured with his chin toward the door. "Wait outside."

The guards bristled, waiting for Cassia's confirming nod before filing out.

As soon as they were alone, Johan asked, "Did you like the tarts?"

"Are you warming your mother's seat or is there something you wish to tell me?"

"I thought you'd be in a better mood this morning, love." Johan gestured to the chair beside him with a flourish. "Those guards will be reporting on your every move."

Cassia took the seat he offered, sinking into the plush chair. "I trust the correspondence going in and out of Heartstar is being monitored?"

"I have eyes on it."

Cassia turned to the window and allowed herself a moment to marvel at the view. Giant oaks framed the scene on either side of the lake, creating a wonderful illusion of lights and shadows with their large roots. Like many things at Heartstar, Cassia had fond memories of the lake—of afternoons spent bathing in the sun and drinking in Johan's company, of swimming naked and making love under a maple tree. "Your mother asked to see me."

"The Head asked to see you." Johan moved behind the desk to sit in the armchair. "Don't disappoint me, love. You're far too observant for that."

Johan was in the Head's study instead of his mother, sitting in her armchair as if he owned it. At dinner he'd sat in Imiri's place, and the proud woman said nothing. Cassia clenched her fists in her lap, where he couldn't see them. Not that it made any difference, judging by his clever smirk. "You're the Head."

"The murderous look in your eyes is more enticing than I

anticipated."

"How long has this been going on?"

"Not long." Johan leaned back, fingers tapping on the desk. "When word of Asharaya's survival reached Tyrra, Mother proposed it and I accepted. She isn't fond of being caught in the middle of another war between the Argarys and the Myrassar."

"So the complete and utter disinterest we've received from Tyrra was your doing." Cassia eyed the stack of papers within reach and was tempted to thrust them at him. Johan must have seen the intent on her face, for his grin widened. "You said you didn't care about Asharaya, yet you acted with deceit. You're waiting, calculating the risks and weighing the advantages. I know you despise my mother, but I didn't think you'd risk hurting me. That I'm here now, at odds with my mother, is an outcome you couldn't have foreseen."

Johan regarded her as if considering his words. There was something he wasn't saying, a secret lurking behind his liar eyes. "A quarter of our forests were burned during the Uprisings. Homes were ransacked and people killed in your mother's name to quash whatever loyalty to the Myrassar was left. So, yes, I'm stalling, but only because I will do anything in my power to save my people from another war until it becomes unavoidable."

Cassia swallowed past the sudden knot in her throat. Johan's heart was in the right place, and here she was, dropping trouble on his doorstep. If she stayed with him, the queen would retaliate. Makkan would not sit idle. She looked down at her hands so he couldn't see the tears veiling her eyes. "Perhaps coming to you was a mistake."

Johan stood and rounded the desk to kneel in front of her. Cassia's heart cracked down the middle at the determination on his face. "Don't go back. I don't care what your mother promised Makkan. You're not property to be bought and sold. I can keep you safe."

"She tortured and killed a man because he was a

distraction. She'll do much worse to you. She'll destroy you, and Makkan will help. There'll be nothing of Tyrra left to regrow."

"Let them come."

Cassia rose to her feet, hopeful and restless and terrified. "You'd stall aiding your queen, but you'd bring war to your doorstep for me?"

Johan's arm wound around her waist, drawing her close. "Every day for two years I've had to talk myself down from coming to Adara to take you back. I kept telling myself the best thing I could do for you was let you go." He grazed her cheek with his thumb. "My place is by your side. I'll do whatever I must to make you see that yours is by mine."

"Johan, you can have anyone you want—"

"There's only ever been you." Johan leaned closer, and Cassia's heart fluttered. "It will always be you."

Cassia desired nothing more than fighting for a future in which he was hers forever. And yet when she opened her mouth to say the words, Korban's mutilated body flashed before her eyes, the message carved into his flesh echoing in her ears in her mother's voice. *Hide your heart.*

Losing Korban had shattered the part of her capable of feeling any sort of joy—the part that had started piecing itself back together the moment Johan rode back into her life. If anything happened to him because she was reckless, she wouldn't survive it.

A raven rapped against the glass. Cassia stepped back, the dregs of their shared tension coiled in her chest. Johan let the raven inside, and the bird flapped to its designated perch by the desk.

"I'll leave you to your affairs."

"It's a message from Adara."

Blood rose to Cassia's face and pumped loud in her ears as Johan unraveled the parchment. Her eyes followed his as they skimmed the words. "It appears the queen has burned down a quarter as a message to the rebels."

Relief washed over Cassia. Her mother wouldn't be sending correspondence on her dealings to the Heads of Ilahara. The message didn't come from the Embernest but rather from a Tyrran spy. Once the feeling abated, Johan's words sunk in and the cool balm on her nerves hardened to ice. "She what?"

"You sound surprised." Johan cut her a glance over the letter. "Weren't you commenting on your mother's penchant for blood moments ago?"

"She wouldn't be that stupid." No point arguing in favor of her mother's empathy. "The people could cower, but they could just as well rise against her. She'd be doing the rebels a favor." Johan raised a brow, as if baiting her to deny reality. Cassia's mind numbed. "How many?"

Johan didn't answer, his attention back on the letter. "Shit."

"What is it?"

He extended the parchment. Cassia snatched it and held it in both hands, but it didn't quell her shaking. The further she read, the deeper the cold seeped into her heart.

The dungeons breached.

Asharaya spotted in the Embernest.

Derron gone with her. An enemy of the Crown.

Cassia's knees buckled the third time she read the words condemning her brother. She was vaguely aware of Johan catching her and leading her to his armchair. Her vision blurred and then blackened. Fire surged to her fingertips. She imagined burning the letter, burning time and space to go back and slap her brother out of his lunacy. If only she'd been there—she could have stopped him from doing something so stupidly brave. And for what? For the very woman who threatened their lives. If Derron were standing in front of her now, she'd shove the parchment down his throat and have him choke on it.

His love for the Myrassar had seen him hurt once already.

Now, their mother was out for blood. Derron wouldn't survive her reckoning this time.

Once again, Johan knelt in front of her. "Tell me what to do."

What she wanted was to wrap her hands around her brother's throat and then hide him until everyone forgot who he was so he might survive to see his hundredth year. She could track him, but so could the queen. *I found out how we can evade tracking spells.* Cassia closed her eyes, pulled down by dread and filled with relief.

Her eyes were lined with scorching silver. "We need to find him before she does." *I need to save him.*

Johan nodded. "I can put some of my own on his trail."

"I can give you my blood, but there's a chance it won't work."

"A shifter doesn't need tracking spells." Johan stood and leaned against the desk, rubbing his chin. "I made arrangements to leave Heartstar tomorrow. There's been some unrest near the border. I'd rather look into it before the queen intervenes. I could lead the search myself."

"What about your responsibilities here?"

"My mother can take over while we're gone."

Cassia shot to her feet. "I'm coming with you." Then she realized Johan said *we*. He'd already counted on her being there, not relegating her to the sidelines while her brother was most likely fighting to stay alive. She grabbed his hand. "Thank you."

Johan pressed a kiss to her forehead. "Always."

45

Mykal

Rain pelted down outside the window of their small room in the Library. Wind raged, and thunder lit the twilight sky. The sounds carried through the stones, low and hollow like a ghost's wail. Drafts slithered in through fissures in the wall, but Mykal didn't mind. It gave him an excuse to wrap more tightly around Kael's naked body. They hadn't gone further than kissing and exploring their new intimacy, both inside the bath and in the lower bunk bed, but Mykal wanted to learn every one of his Do'strath's sounds.

Kael rolled in Mykal's arms with a sleepy chuckle, their chests aligned, and Kael's head comfortably nuzzled beneath Mykal's chin. The warmth of his Do'strath's Fire-heated skin enveloped him.

"Have you slept at all?" Kael whispered, pressing a kiss to his throat. Such touches would forever feel like a daydream.

"Not much," he confessed, bending his head as Kael's tipped

up. Their mouths grazed. "I didn't mean to wake you."

"I don't need the bond to know how loud your thoughts are." Kael's breath brushed Mykal's lips and made him shudder. "What are you thinking?"

Where to begin? Mykal's worries were as interlocked as the links in chainmail. He counted the days since he'd left Daganver, wondering if his mother and Luna were safe and whether other cities had been freed from Adarian invaders. And then there was his concern for Makkani spies spreading word of the events at Frosthead Hall. If they'd ambushed Deimok during the battle, they could infiltrate Daganver again.

Next came Shara. Missing her surprised him. He conjured up her loud opinions to fill her absence, expecting to find her scrutinizing her surroundings with that disturbing Deimok-like stillness, only to be disappointed when she wasn't there.

And then there was Kael. While he slept, his nightmares barreled in chilling flashes down the bond—blood streaming down a drain, a pale hand guiding a knife into Kael's flesh with a butcher's practiced precision, the queen's impassive expression as Kael screamed. Now that he'd let Mykal see the extent of what he'd endured, Kael was no longer hiding those horrors from the soulbond. Mykal was grateful, though his resentment for the Argarys had never been so bitter. None had made an effort to help Kael. Not Vaemor, the wretched man who'd fathered him. Not Cassia, the shallow princess who refused to acknowledge Kael's existence. Only Derron, who Kael said had visited him in the dungeons and given him food and herbs for his injuries.

Derron, who'd also saved Asharaya and had shown Eileen so much kindness that she now believed herself enamored. Mykal didn't know what to make of it.

But he shared none of that with Kael. Not now, when despite his nightmares he relaxed in a way he hadn't since they'd fled Adara, and there was true smile on his face.

"I'm thinking," Mykal said, as his hand trailed down Kael's

side, "this might be the last night for Dragon knows how long that I'll get to be naked with you." Their lips brushed again. "I'll miss this."

Their mouths met, hard but unhurried. Kael's sleepy moan had Mykal's cock twitching. Dragon, Mykal wanted to deepen the kiss, ease Kael back and explore every part of him, but a knock on the door put a stop to his mounting desire.

A scholar, informing them Maenar Alavin wished to see them.

The last time Mykal was summoned to a private study, his father showed him a bloodied note from a maenar that changed his life forever. He didn't know what to expect now.

As he and Kael walked through the vacant halls to Maenar Alavin's study, Mykal's thoughts wandered again to Shara. Self-loathing wasn't far behind. He owed Shara for Daganver's freedom and the luxury of Kael's embraces, and he'd repaid her by leaving her behind. This is what he got for following her reckless plans. If Derron Argarys hadn't gotten to her, would Aerella's arrow have killed the last Myrassar, or would his friend be rotting in the usurper queen's dungeons? Was she any safer alone with the harpy's son? A part of him hoped Shara had gutted the prince, but that wasn't a likely outcome if she felt she owed him her life. All they could hope for was that the two had parted ways and that they'd find Shara soon. His queen wasn't safe in an Argarys-ruled Ilahara.

Lord Darrok was the only soul in the maenar's otherwise empty study. The lord barely deigned him worthy of a greeting, and Mykal shrunk into himself. He looked over his father's shoulder, imagining Rendal's silhouette etched against the study's bare walls. Rendal, who'd been so faithful to his father's teaching as to become his shadow. He wouldn't have gone back for Eileen or lost the last Myrassar. If only to please the man he respected above all others, Mykal might have done the same, once.

Before meeting Asharaya.

Fuck the old grouch, she'd say. *I'm not his puppet and you're not my keeper. If you'd acted any differently, your frozen balls would be hanging around your neck, and I doubt Kael would appreciate that.* Dragon, he missed her.

Lana isn't here, Kael said.

She must be on her way.

That had been ten minutes ago.

Maenar Alavin's study was minimally furnished. Even the desk was bare, either deliberately or because the maenar simply spent little time in the room. The sprawling bookshelf behind the desk with the maenar's private collection was the only thing worth notice. Hundreds of books lined the shelves in neat, orderly rows. Unlike Lord Darrok, who cataloged his books by themes, the maenar seemed to favor height. They were mostly academic tomes on alchemy, anthropology, and geology.

Kael squeezed Mykal's shoulder. *Stop fidgeting.*

I'm not. Mykal then looked at his foot beneath the desk and realized how furiously he'd been shaking it. *What's taking so long? He'd better not be conditioning his hair.*

Maybe he is. His hair looks soft enough.

As if summoned by their brief exchange, the door sighed on its hinges and in fluttered Maenar Alavin. He looked refreshed despite the early hour, and more handsome than anyone had a right to be when wearing a maenari's brown robes. The hair fallen free of his short ponytail flowed as if caressed by an invisible current.

"Thank you for joining me," the maenar greeted as he pulled out his armchair. Even that barely made a sound, as if the universe were determined not to disturb the even-tempered man. "I know the hour is unseemly, but I would rather speak of this without an audience. I mentioned yesterday that I couldn't extend the Library's hospitality further. However, I—"

The door burst open, and Solana stormed inside. "Why was I not summoned?"

A scholar peeked in, the yellow undertones of his skin gone

pale. "I'm sorry, Maenar Alavin. I-I tried..." The poor boy—still likely in his teens—squeaked at Solana's murderous glare. It must have been the most terrifying thing he'd ever seen.

"It's quite all right, Lyan. You may go." Kael and Mykal exchanged a look, and then together turned to a stunned Maenar Alavin. "I didn't think a human needed to be summoned to discuss fae matters."

Mykal winced.

Solana slammed her hands on the maenar's desk. He was lucky the wraith hadn't chosen to stab him instead. "This human is not a servant, and she demands to be informed when a meeting is called with her associates."

Movement on Mykal's right had him peering at his father, who bent his head forward to hide an amused smile. "What was it you were trying to say, Alavin?"

"Apologies." Maenar Alavin cleared his throat, the confusion not quite leaving his face. The maenari had no servants, but even the best-intentioned fae often overlooked humans. "As I was saying, I cannot let you stay in the Library, but you are my friend, Darrok. I would not see you harmed if I can avoid it."

"What exactly do you have in mind?" Lord Darrok inquired.

"We've recently been able to obtain a sample of crystallized lava from the Burning Sea."

Mykal blinked. *Did he pull us out of bed for a lesson in lava rocks?*

Myk.

"Our studies revealed the rocks have certain magic-repellant qualities, much like those rumored to be possessed by dragons. Worn as bracelets, you'll become undetectable while still being able to wield your magic."

Behind the ebony skin and stone-hard face, Mykal imagined the cogs in his father's brain turning, twisting this new information into a strategy they could wield. "How many?"

"I can only give you six."

"I need more."

"Even if I had the resources, I'm already exposing myself and those under my care enough as is. I can help you leave this Library, but I will not have the maenari involved in the war."

"Why six?" Mykal wondered aloud. "Counting Asharaya, it's only five of us."

"Asharaya isn't alone."

The jolt of Kael's surprise rushed down the bond, and Mykal's head filled with static noise until a mirthless laugh bubbled out. "You want us to give one of your fancy bracelets to Derron Argarys? He's done one good deed and we're already counting him among our friends?"

"Myk," Kael cautioned.

"This is insane." Mykal abruptly stood. "I've already been on the other end of one of the prince's heroic deeds, and it nearly got us killed." The bond went cold with Kael's fear, stilling Mykal's tongue. "We can't trust him."

"I've had the opportunity to meet the prince many times over the years." Maenar Alavin's hands flattened on the desk, the gesture slow enough to be deliberate. "He isn't the monster you describe."

"To his friends, perhaps, but Asharaya isn't one of them. He's tried to kill her before."

"If your father ordered you to kill Derron Argarys, would you hesitate?"

Mykal bared his teeth. "We're not the same."

"Defying family is never easy. Some need more time than others."

"I am tired of talking about Derron Argarys," Solana snapped, turning to Lord Darrok. "Why are you saying nothing? Have you suddenly decided to trust him?"

"Having the prince on our side may work to our advantage."

Mykal could hardly believe his own ears, and he turned to Kael, finding the same surprise on his Do'strath's face.

"What if you are wrong?" Solana asked. "My sister is not a

pawn for you to do with as you see fit. Do you even care about her safety?"

"Asharaya is all I have left of Jaemys." The lord's hands tightened around the armrests of his chair. "And Gailen. Her safety is my priority."

"Fuck you," Solana spat. "The moment you sent your son to find her, you endangered her. I curse the day you found her."

"Lana," Mykal and Kael called after her, but Solana stormed out the door.

Lord Darrok sighed, and then turned back to the maenar. "You say you want no part in this war, but if Aerella finds out you provided us with these bracelets, the robe you wear wouldn't protect you from her wrath. You know as well as I what happened to Maenar Elvik." Lord Darrok reached for the maenar's hand. "We are bound by a long friendship, you and I, but I would not fault you if you looked after your best interests."

"Elvik was my friend too. My mentor." Maenar Alavin squeezed Lord Darrok's hand. "He would want me to help you, and to help her."

Asharaya's name didn't need to be spoken aloud. Mykal hung onto his father's silence. They all seemed to.

"How long until you can get us those bracelets?" Lord Darrok finally said.

"Give me an hour." Maenar Alavin stood. "Help yourself to some breakfast in the meantime."

Neither Solana nor Lord Darrok followed the Do'strath to the great hall for breakfast. Though Mykal's appetite was nowhere to be found, he was determined to make sure Kael ate his fill of honey bread rolls. Kael's sweet tooth was notorious in Daganver, so much so that the cooks often set aside extra helpings of desserts in case Kael made any late-night visits to the kitchens. Mykal indulged in the sight of Kael's blissful expression and his soft, appreciative moans. It was as if they'd gone back to a time before Maenar Elvik's message, before Aerella tried to break Kael. This moment was a pocket of stolen time where they could be carefree, where Mykal could focus on how the man seated across from him was the center of his universe. He wanted desperately to soak it in before reality ripped it away.

The third time Kael left the table for a refill, he returned with two plates. "One is for Lana," he explained.

Mykal toyed with the crumbs on his plate. "I think she's struggling more than she lets on. She hides it better than most, but this is taking its toll. First, she lost Xoro, and then her gift. Now Shara."

Kael frowned, swallowing a bite of his bread roll. "What happened to her gift?"

Mykal struggled not to swipe the crumbs from Kael's plush lips. "She hasn't summoned a single shadow since the siren attack, and not for lack of trying. It's as if her goddess just vanished. No matter how much Solana makes herself bleed, she won't show." The memory of Solana's scarred arms tamped down Mykal's amused smile. "I'm afraid she'll push herself too far."

"She'll feel better once we reunite with Shara." Kael took Mykal's hand across the table. "And once we track her brother—"

"I don't know if there's anything left to track." Kael's hold on his hand slackened at Mykal's confession, his expression somber. "I tried tracking him on my own. I couldn't find a trace."

"It doesn't mean he's dead. You know distance weakens our magic. We'll track him together once we leave the Library."

When Eileen joined them on her own, the Do'strath decided to bring Solana some breakfast. The wraith didn't open the first time they knocked, or the second. Mykal and Kael stood outside the door for five minutes before she padded with soft footsteps to the door.

"What do you want?" Solana said in Havanian as she opened the door. She'd nicked her thumb to smear a line of blood from her bottom lip to her chin.

"Did you make me wait five minutes because you were praying?" Mykal snapped at the same time Kael said, "We only wanted to see if you were okay."

She paced back into the room but left the door open for them to follow her inside. The room was the mirror opposite of theirs, with the same plain stone walls and bunk beds, but the strong floral scent was entirely feminine and somehow welcoming. Mykal's eye wandered to the bathtub, still wet from the latest bath. Did either of the women like to luxuriate in the water? He imagined Solana's slender fingers grazing her arms as she lathered her skin with soap, and then doing the same with the space between her small breasts. When he pictured her hand falling below the water's surface and his balls squeezed, he blinked the daydream away.

"In my heart, I know Shara is safe, but I can't sit still and do nothing, especially knowing she's with that man." Solana ran a hand through her unbound hair, the cascade of straight black locks down her back unusual since she always kept it braided. "I hardly slept last night thinking about her, alone and hurt. I wanted to leave but I don't know where we are or where to look. I've never felt this helpless, or this useless."

"I hope you would have had the foresight to leave a dagger behind so we could track you when you inevitably got lost." Mykal picked up a honey bread roll from the plate and offered it to Solana, who took it with a scowl. Mykal then switched to Ilahein. "If there's anyone who knows how to survive against impossible odds, it's Shara. If Argarys tried anything funny with her, I'm sure she's already strung his corpse to the nearest tree. It won't be much longer now until we find her." He ripped a piece from Solana's roll and plopped it into his mouth before she could swat his hand away.

"I don't think Derron's going to betray her now." The words

rushed out of Kael as if he'd been trying to hold them in. He flushed at both Mykal's and Solana's attention. "The queen's hunting him openly. She's not the kind to flaunt her dirty laundry like that unless he gave her reason to. I think he regrets things."

"I hope you're right." Solana lifted a hand to Kael's cheek, and Kael's joined hers. Not long ago, the exchange would have driven Mykal mad with jealousy. How Kael's gaze followed the lines of Solana's face to her lips, and how Solana's thumb stilled at the corner of Kael's mouth.

Mykal's stomach churned, accompanied by a pulsing in his crotch.

The feeling wasn't wholly unpleasant.

Racing footsteps echoed outside the door, interrupting the moment. Solana produced a dagger from Dragon knew where as Mykal formed some from his Ice, taking a stand between Kael, Solana, and the door. It was only sheer luck that he didn't let one fly when the door banged open and Eileen's terrified face peeked into the room. "What happened?"

"Riders," she panted. "Argarys soldiers."

They rushed into the hallway. Dawn was an unusual time for anything but an ambush. How had Aerella realized they'd be in Lur? She couldn't have found their tracks through the mountain pass so soon. Mykal's turmoil mixed with Kael's anxiety down the bond. The chances of capture were high. Mykal would be damned if he let anyone lock Kael in a dungeon again.

Lord Darrok spoke urgently with Maenar Alavin.

"How long do we have?" Mykal asked.

"Not long," the maenar replied. "The Library is outside the queen's jurisdiction, but they can set up a perimeter to keep you inside."

Unless Aerella orders the Library burned to the ground.

"We'll need horses," Lord Darrok said.

Mykal followed his father's hands to the black-beaded bracelets in his lap, which Lord Darrok then handed out to each of them. The rocks were rough and warm, veins of red gleaming through the black, like the sheen of Deimok's scales. The maenar also slid a satchel off his shoulder and held it out to Mykal. "These are Myrassar journals. Elvik brought them here for safekeeping after the Coup. He'd want Asharaya to have them."

Mykal had once thought Jaemys's necklace was the last heirloom of the dragon riders, and now the king's ring sat on his finger and their journals were within his grasp. Were there more heirlooms hidden in Ilahara, unbeknownst to all but their keepers? Curiosity lulled its sweet song, as incessant as Daganver's flurries, but the maenar was right—Elvik would have wanted Asharaya to have them. His friend deserved to be the first to read her family's words.

Quick footsteps sounded through the hall, and the group spun toward the approaching sound. Ice condensed in Lord Darrok's hands, and Solana's fingers lingered a breadth shy of her blades. Mykal held his Ice daggers tighter.

A young scholar bounded into the hall, clutching at his heaving chest as he sagged against the wall. "They're here," he croaked.

Mykal's heart lurched, and Kael's echoed twice as fast.

"We're out of time." The fear in the maenar's eyes was another novelty Mykal could have done without. "Get to the stables and take as many horses as you need. Follow the path east to the hedgerows. There's a gate there that leads off the main roads. I'll buy you as much time as I can."

"Thank you, Alavin, for everything," Lord Darrok said. The two men shared a quick embrace.

"Good luck, old friend."

In the Library's tense quiet, voices rose from the lower levels. One belonged to Maenar Alavin, the other to a woman. The voices echoed too much to follow the conversation, but the words "stairs" and "search" had the hairs at the back of Mykal's neck rise.

Lord Darrok gestured to a room at the end of the hall. They all moved in tandem, careful to make as little noise as possible. Mykal, Kael, and Solana made a straight line for the narrow window overlooking the main gate, while Lord Darrok remained behind the door, peeking through an open sliver. The heavy rain made it hard to see more than a few feet ahead. Maybe if they could fit through the window, he could create some sort of slide to the courtyard. They'd have to abandon Lord Darrok's chair, but once they reached the stables, carrying him wouldn't be an issue.

"How many Argarys horses?" Lord Darrok inquired with a commander's even tone.

"Six." Mykal clung to his father's steadiness to find his own battle calm amid Kael's turmoil. *Stay with me*, Mykal begged down the bond. Kael's chest heaved, and his limbs shook with the effort to keep it together. *We're all right.*

Solana pawed the edges of the window, assessing its size. She might have been able to slip through, and maybe Eileen, but Mykal wasn't sure about himself, Kael, and Lord Darrok. At Solana's silent question, he shook his head.

"The shadows, then," she suggested. Mykal's hand flattened atop hers before she could cut her skin. He was suddenly back on the *No One*, watching Solana inflict cut after cut upon herself to pay in blood for her goddess's help. The toll of carrying five people wouldn't be as high, but since the Maiden refused to heed Solana's summons, Mykal wasn't willing to risk it. At the light pressure of his palm against the back of Solana's hand, her eagle-sharp focus softened. "What if it works this time?" she asked.

"We don't have time to play your goddess's games. I need you."

Solana's lips parted, and Mykal became all too aware of her hand beneath his.

"All right," she conceded. Determination shone in the black depths of her eyes. "You'll need to be my eyes."

"What are you planning?" Kael asked.

"Trust me." She didn't look away from Mykal, as if uttering a question meant for him. Once he gave his answer, there would be no going back. It was like standing on the edge of one of Daganver's steep cliffs, the feeling of vertigo both terrifying and thrilling. "Tell me what you need."

"They're in the hallway," Lord Darrok warned.

"Move away from the door," Solana ordered. To Mykal's surprise, Lord Darrok obeyed.

Solana positioned herself behind the door, Mykal taking a place at her back. Judging by the footsteps and the sounds of opening doors, there were at least two riders in the hallway.

"Can your Ice work as a mirror?" she asked.

A rectangle of Ice formed on Mykal's hand, small and light enough to be manageable with one hand. Solana collected it gingerly and opened the door a sliver more. She angled the Ice to peer into the hallway. The image was blurred and fractured but served its purpose.

Minutes ticked by when no one made a sound, the tension thickening as the riders drew closer to their door. Like a predator closing in on prey, every line of Solana's back was taut against Mykal's front.

A man disappeared into the opposite room.

A woman neared their door.

Solana slipped the glass into her belt and adjusted her grip on her dagger. Blue frosted Mykal's fingers, his palms slickening with nervous sweat as the footsteps stopped.

Mykal inhaled, and the rider nudged open the door.

He exhaled, and Solana lunged, swift as an adder and graceful as a dancer. Her knife jutted into the woman's chin, and a second blade severed her throat before she could voice her alarmed cry. The woman's body slackened with a wet gasp, blood spluttering from her mouth. The wraith's face was a breadth away from her victim's as she eased the body onto the floor, gentle as a lover.

Right as the second rider appeared at the door.

Mykal's hand shot forward, an Ice spear releasing from his palm in time with the jackhammer jolt of his heart. The weapon rammed through the man's middle, sending him flying across the room. He was dead before his body hit the wall, his hand still wrapped around the sword he'd been ready to unsheathe.

For a few moments, no one moved. Only Solana's eyes flicked up to meet Mykal's, both of their chests heaving.

"Good work." Lord Darrok's small compliment lightened Mykal's heart.

They left the wheelchair in the room and Mykal carried his father down the stairs, with Eileen at his heels. Solana and Kael flanked his sides, the former gripping her bloodied daggers and the latter brandishing Mykal's sword. Mykal attuned his senses to his surroundings, fishing for the sounds of footfalls from the higher levels and voices from below. If there were six horses in the courtyard, there were likely four more riders somewhere in the Library.

"Why don't we go to my study so we can speak more calmly?" Maenar Alavin asked.

They stopped at the last bend of the spiral staircase, their view of the diamond-shaped hall mostly obstructed. Mykal could only see the feet of the fae—two guards, Maenar Alavin, and judging by the robes, one scholar, likely the one who'd warned them of the riders' arrival. The dim light spilling from the windows stretched their shadows across the floor.

"Very well," someone said.

"I will require no more assistance, Jylian, thank you. Get some rest before the day begins."

As the riders followed Maenar Alavin, the group retreated several steps to remain hidden until the study's door clicked shut. This time they didn't bother with stealth, rapidly descending the final steps. The scholar—indeed, the one they'd seen before—startled at their sudden appearance.

"The stables, Son," Lord Darrok thundered. "Now."

The maenari's stables consisted of a dozen draft horses. The massive creatures wouldn't be the fastest, but they were durable, reliable, and surefooted on any terrain. They selected a mare for Mykal and Lord Darrok, another for Eileen, and a gelding for Kael and Solana.

Kael helped Mykal lift Lord Darrok onto the horse while Solana and Eileen saddled the remaining two. As soon as everyone was mounted, they galloped out, following Maenar Alavin's instructions to find the secondary exit.

Heavy winds blew at their heels, pushing the pelting rain away from their eyes. Thunder silenced the synchronized clopping of hooves, and soon the hedgerows came into view. Tall walls of green leaves and white hawthorn blooms delimited the Library's grounds. Some wayward branches twined around the wooden gate's pickets, giving it a fairy-tale look.

Safety seemed within reach.

"There they are!"

The staccato of Mykal's heart beat in time with his dappled mare's heavy breaths. Hoofbeats exploded at their heels and the shouts of riders broke through the rain's music.

"They were waiting for us," Kael cried out.

Lord Darrok flung out his arm, Ice bursting from his palms to envelop the wooden gate. With a snarl, his hand closed in a fist and the Ice exploded, shards of Ice and wood shooting in every direction. The horses hesitated, startled by the sound, before barreling through the opening and down the road.

Mykal squeezed his legs around his horse's sides, twisting to face their pursuers, who were drawing closer. He released the reins and pointed his hands skyward, directing his magic toward the rain that kept pouring down upon them. Eileen must have understood his intent, for she too released her grip on her horse. Lord Darrok followed. A tingle gathered in Mykal's palm, the frost spreading along his fingers and spearing out in a beam of blue light. His father's and sister's magic joined his, and within moments the sheet of rain solidified into a wall. The last thing Mykal saw was a rider's startled expression, and the horse's terrified eyes as it reared on its hind legs and whinnied.

They followed the road until they reached a patch of forest. The fear of pursuit followed Mykal for hours, feeding adrenaline into his body and keeping him tense and alert, until froth gathered at the mare's mouth and he finally allowed her to slow down.

The rain eased to a drizzle and the sky lightened to an early morning gray. His clothes clung heavily to Mykal's body and a wet chill settled deep into his bones, but they were safe.

Safe.

Eileen and Kael slowed alongside him, their horses as exhausted as Mykal's. Kael patted his gelding's buckskin neck as the animal's lips twitched around his bit, and Eileen's mare lowered her head, eyes drooping.

"What's the plan?" Eileen asked.

Mykal toyed with the dragon around his finger, the ring warm in spite of the rain. For a moment he couldn't think, stuck on what was happening in Lur. He had to trust the maenar would find a way to protect the scholars, or that he'd poisoned the Argarys scum and buried their bodies where no one would ever find them. Hopefully by the time Jaero's rebels arrived at the Library, it would be free of Argarys threats. Things hadn't gone according to any plan, but returning would only put the maenari in more danger. There was only one thing they could do.

"We find cover. The horses need rest, and so do we." Mykal said. "Then we track Shara."

46

Derron

After their run-in with the patrol, Derron could hardly sleep. When he wasn't imagining his parents bleeding into dozens of vials, he was alerted by any moving shadow or sound. His mind conjured threats that weren't real, forcing him to keep his swords at his side rather than sheathed into their scabbards. More than for himself, Derron feared what might happen to Shara if they were captured—if she didn't first figure out he was leading her in the wrong direction and disembowel him for lying to her.

The streak of bad weather these past two days wasn't helping them make good time, but it was effectively covering their tracks. To recover time lost, they reduced their resting time, which hadn't been a lot to begin with. Derron often dozed off while on the horse, sometimes smacking his head against Shara, who teased him about it when she was in good spirits. Her voice kept him awake, but it also relaxed him so his eyes drifted closed.

They stopped at the outskirts of Dragonside, a big town close to the Tyrran border. It was their best bet to get renike fast. Leaving Sweetie in a clearing to graze, Derron and Shara sheltered behind a forest outcrop, which gave them a good view of the town's entrance. Guards stationed at the walls were holding a mirror to anyone going in and out. Derron looked to the sun. They were an hour from sundown, two at most. "Are you sure you can use your shadows?"

"I told you I'm fine five times already." Indeed, Shara's face had lost some of its coloring, but she wasn't shivering, and her temperature seemed adequate for a Fire wielder, but that could change at any moment. There was no telling how long her body would hold out before succumbing to fever and pain.

"Can we slip in and out without anyone the wiser?"

"I can get us past the guards, but when I'm using my powers I can only track shadows. It's no reliable way to navigate an unfamiliar environment. We'll have to glamour once we're in."

More magic. Their plan was shaky at best. "Activities cease at nightfall. We'll have a hard time stocking up on provisions."

"If we were law-abiding citizens working during business hours, yes. But if we find the apothecary, I can take care of the rest."

Derron tutted. "Little thief."

"I have no choice but to be one to protect your high-maintenance royal hide."

"Whatever would I do without you?"

"You'd die of boredom." Shara leaned back against the rock. "Realistically, you'd be in the Embernest, in a comfortable room with servants at your beck and call. Given the time, you'd be getting pampered and readied to go out and fuck an artist or two before bedtime."

"You've given my proclivities much thought."

"Am I wrong?"

"I've had some lovers who also happened to be artists," he

confessed. "But not as a regularly as you make it sound."

Her voice turned somber. "Were any of them hurt in the explosion?"

Derron's throat dried at the memory. He could almost hear the cries, taste the ash on his tongue. "I hope not. One was long gone before it happened." At Shara's questioning gaze he added, "I suspect she's a rebel. She wouldn't be surprised I turned rogue."

"She'd be the only one." Shara's eyes found their way back to Derron's face. "Do you regret it?"

"I'm a fugitive, hunted and tired. My family hates me." His chest ached at the thought of Cassia, yet he didn't lose hope that she might forgive him and understand. His desperate dash for Tyrra hinged on that. "I may not be in control, and the chances of me surviving are bleak, but regret never crossed my mind."

"It gets easier with time, Derron. You just need to find a new purpose."

Their gazes locked, Derron's throat thick with an emotion he couldn't place.

Sounds of hoofbeats had them crouching low behind their shelter and looking back at the city gates. Riders made for the city, some wearing blue and silver jerkins, others silver armor crusted with dust. A silver flame flapped on a blue flag upfront and was sewn onto the saddles and vests of the women and men in the company. There must have been close to two dozen—too many for a simple patrol. The ones at the front dismounted to talk to the guards, while others lingered or filed into the city after passing inspection. Derron and Shara were too far away to hear anything aside from boisterous laughter and indistinct chatter. These soldiers weren't here for them, but they remained a problem.

"No way we're entering Dragonside now," Derron said, barely unclenching his jaw as he spoke. "It's too dangerous."

"They must have split off from a larger group. Looks like they've been marching for days."

"They're likely heading north. My mother expects Lord Darrok to be making his way home."

Shara grabbed Derron's arm, delight entering her eyes. "If we follow those soldiers, they'll lead us right to her. We could end it all. Now."

"How?" Derron almost shrieked. "You keep forgetting the army ready to kill us."

"And you keep forgetting I'm an assassin."

"You're not an assassin anymore, Shara. There are people who want to see you as queen."

"What queen will I be if I hide like a coward? If I don't act upon an opportunity that could spare hundreds of lives?"

"A smart one," Derron hissed through his teeth. "Even if you weren't wounded, and even if you manage to kill the queen, you won't make it out of the camp without backup. The soldiers will kill you, and I don't see your dragon anywhere. He won't be there to save your ass this time."

Her gaze shuttered at the mention of Deimok.

"Shara." Derron gripped her chin and forced her attention back to him. "Our best chance is to get as far away from these soldiers and the army as we can. Stealth is not the answer."

Shara sunk her teeth into her lower lip, looking back to the gates. Derron found himself drawn to her mouth. For a moment, he imagined it was his teeth sinking into the soft flesh. He ripped his gaze away, a flush rising to his cheek.

"You're right," Shara said, wholly unaware of Derron's fluster. "We need to be smart about this."

"Good." Derron lifted himself out of the crouch and helped Shara up, noticing how she grimaced through the pain. *I'll get that poison out of you if it's the last thing I do.* "Let's get going before we're seen."

47

Shara

Walking away from Dragonside was one of the hardest things Shara ever did. It went against every instinct, everything she'd learned in her years as a vrah. Knowing Aerella and her army were close meant she had a purpose and opportunity to study her patterns for the perfect time to strike. But Derron was right—she was no longer just a vrah. More than her revenge was on the line now. Her friends, the people of Ilahara—they all counted on her to make the right decisions. To think like a queen. A queen would take things slow, gather her allies, and attack when she had all the best weapons at her disposal. She needed those allies, and she needed her dragon. Going to Lur was the right call.

At least, she hoped it was.

Doubts crowded Shara's mind as she and Derron returned to Sweetie. Would they be able to find another town before they reached Lur? Not having the protection of renike to cloak

Derron from tracking spells was a greater risk than ever if Aerella was as close as they suspected, and the herbs they'd purchased at the last apothecary were already dwindling. The more days that passed, the more Shara relied on them to stay upright and to keep a hold on her magic. The herbs wouldn't last the rest of the journey to Lur, and if the poison kept advancing at this rate, neither would she. Was she making the right decision?

"I think it's dark enough that we can stop for a bit." Derron pulled on Sweetie's reins, assessing the area. "It's probably best if we keep riding, but we won't get far if we're exhausted, horse included."

"Let's scout the area, then we rest," Shara suggested. She was in no mood for surprises from Aerella's hunters.

"You can get a head start if you want." Derron gracefully slid off Sweetie's back and held his hands out to Shara. For once, she accepted the help without fussing.

"I don't need a head start to be a better lookout than you," Shara teased.

"I don't doubt it, but nature calls."

Shara snorted, and a pleased smile stretched over Derron's lips. Heat pooled low in her belly, slow and insistent. The longer Derron held on to her, the harder it was to suppress the memory of his hands cupping her face at the lake. What would he do if she did the same? The irrational craving to draw the shape of that distracting, disarming smile overcame her. She imagined her fingers on his mouth, the warmth of his breath against her skin. How would it feel against her lips?

Derron must have noticed the direction of her thoughts. His eyes darkened, and his fingers pressed a little harder into her sides.

She pushed him away, ducking beneath his arm to walk past him. "We meet back here in ten minutes."

Every step she put between herself and Derron made it easier to draw in air, but she could do nothing against the empty, nauseated feeling ravaging her stomach. She was only half focused on her surroundings, aware enough to flinch at any unexpected sound but lost in the turmoil of her own scattered thoughts. The first days of their journey, she couldn't even look at Derron as he changed the dressing on her wounds without being reminded of his treachery. Of his mother's vicious eyes as she shot her. She couldn't pinpoint when that changed, or why she no longer flinched away from his touch. Dragon, she'd even let him grip her chin without biting off his fingers.

As if she trusted him.

As if they were friends.

As if she wouldn't stab him if he tried to kiss her.

Shara's pacing led her to the edge of the forest, the outline of a dirt road visible beyond the thicket. She pushed Derron from her mind and advanced slowly, her hand close to her daggers in case she needed them. A roadside inn stood on the opposite side of the road, a single horse fastened to the post outside the small, two-story cottage. The only visible light came from the windows of the lower floor, and a slow curl of smoke rose from its chimney.

Would the innkeeper know about Aerella?

Shara looked over her shoulder for signs of Derron. The ten minutes were almost up. If she returned to their meeting spot, would he agree to visit the inn? Unlikely. He'd probably warn her that it was an unnecessary risk. But wouldn't it be better to know Aerella's intentions? It would give them an advantage once they reunited with Mykal and Lord Darrok.

Summoning her magic was like pulling water from a well. Shara grimaced against the spike of pain flaring in her wound but pushed through it. She willed her eyes to darken to brown and her face to lighten and fill out—a slight glamour that wouldn't require too much energy. Yet her knees quaked as she walked to the inn. *I won't take long.* She raised the hood of her cape.

Inside, the inn was deserted save for a man busy polishing

the counter. The smell of warm stew roused the angry bear slumbering in Shara's stomach. The grumbling was strong enough to cause an ache. All she could remember eating in the past two months were hastily roasted game, frost-covered berries, or slimy sailors' slop.

She cleared her throat to attract the man's attention—who she assumed to be the innkeeper. "I need a room," she lied, hoping it would be a less suspicious conversation starter at this time of day. "Also, a portion of whatever you're serving tonight."

The innkeeper assessed her silently, his expression unreadable. Shara held still under his scrutiny, fighting the instinct to reach for the comfort of steel hidden beneath her cape. "Are you alone?"

"For tonight. I'll be meeting up with my husband tomorrow."

"Where are you headed?"

Dragon, he was a suspicious grizzly. "Do you ask all of your customers so many questions?"

The man gave her an odd look, then dropped the rag onto the counter. "I'll get you some stew."

Shara faked an interest in the bottles and jars lined on the shelf as she waited for him to return with the food. Hidden in the semi-darkness was a stack of papers of which she could only read the hefty sum written in bold. Wanted posters. She stretched over the counter to get a better look, her wound screaming in protest. Already drops of sweat were dampening her brow, but she had to know if her friends were on those posters.

The kitchen door opened and Shara straightened, swallowing back a grimace. The man narrowed his eyes, his gaze going to the shelves as he set the plate in front of her. "Why haven't you hung those?" she asked in a small voice.

The man made a gruff sound as he grabbed a cup and filled it with water. "Which side are you on?"

"You first."

"My brother lived in the capital, in the district the queen blew up. He didn't make it."

A lump formed in her throat. "I'm sorry." The words wouldn't lessen the man's loss, or explain why his brother had to die as collateral damage in a war that had nothing to do with him, but the innkeeper seemed to appreciate them regardless. Shara's hands, instead, turned clammy. She didn't know what the innkeeper's brother looked like, but she imagined a man with a similar tan and dirty blond hair working the markets, saw him laughing one moment and screaming as he burned the next. "So, you're with Asharaya?"

"Asharaya is no better than Aerella." Shara flinched, the spoon threatening to drop from her grasp. "Spent a lifetime away with those humans only to come back and hide. King Gailen didn't hide when Aerella attacked. He fought and died with honor."

Shara carefully took a spoonful of the stew. It might have been delicious if not for the bitter taste coating her tongue. The dampness on her brow was spreading down her temples. The room suddenly felt too small, too tight. Was this what people were saying about her on the streets? That she was a coward? That they were no better off with her than they were with Aerella? In that moment, it hardly mattered that she'd gotten none of the answers she'd come in here for. All she wanted was to prove this man right, bound off that damned barstool and flee—flee this inn and this continent that had dragged her back by force and now rejected her.

"You should hang those," Shara said after a moment of silence. Perhaps the man loathed her, but she wouldn't have him die a fool's death like Sanda. "The queen will think you're a Myrassar sympathizer if you don't."

"What's the matter with you?" the man asked, his thick brows furrowing. "Why are you sweating, girl?"

The door opening saved Shara the effort of coming up with a lie, but her relief was short-lived. Throughout the otherwise silent inn, something metallic accentuated the approaching footsteps. Steel. Were they bounty hunters or soldiers? Either way, they were likely in Aerella's pocket, or else they wouldn't be walking around with an arrogant swagger.

Shara forced herself to take another spoonful of stew, tracking one of the newcomers from the corner of her eye as he stood to her right. His companions stayed a step back, their whispering unintelligible, though their soft snickering set her on edge.

"Got any more of that stew for us, sir?" the one on her right asked.

Hesitantly, the man nodded. "Why don't you and your friends take a seat at one of the tables while I get you some?"

"We're fine where we are."

The innkeeper shot Shara a look, his mouth dropping into a frown. Maiden help her, he was worried. She didn't care to find out what looks the strangers at her back were giving her. The slick feeling spreading down her body from their attention alone was enough.

Her grip on the spoon tightened when someone at her back moved. A moment later, her hood was yanked down, and it was all she could do to keep still. *Don't react. They'll grow bored eventually.*

"You have pretty hair." This second man picked up a lock of her hair, and despite what she'd told herself, Shara jerked her head to the side to force him to release it. "Easy, darling. I'm only making conversation."

The innkeeper banged a hand on the counter. "If you can't leave my customer alone, you'll have to find your supper somewhere else."

"A customer, eh?" The one who'd touched her hair said. "And is your customer here alone? Unusual, don't you think, for a pretty thing like this one to go around all by herself?" The prick stroked her hair again, and this time she couldn't hold back a shudder. Her nostrils flared, and the slickening of her skin was hard to ignore. She needed to find a way out of this fast, before her body betrayed her identity. "Are you alone, sweetheart? I can keep you company, if you'd like."

"I'd rather keep company with a horse," Shara said through gritted teeth. "Touch me a third time and I'll make you wish you hadn't."

The man chuckled. "She has fire. I like it."

"Are those the queen's wanted posters?"

Shara's eyes bounced up to the innkeeper, who seemed to have paled in the span of a moment. She didn't dare acknowledge the man standing beside her—the one who'd asked for the stew—lest he see the fear written on every line of her face.

"The queen demands those be hung in every inn. Refusing is an act of treason."

"He was about to," Shara blurted. "He set them down to get my stew when I came inside. Isn't that right?" She nodded encouragingly at the innkeeper. *Don't deny it. Please, hang those fucking posters.*

The innkeeper sighed, resigned. "This is my inn. I hang whatever the fuck I want."

"Then you're under arrest."

Shara sprang from the stool, latching onto the man's arm before he could unsheathe his sword. She could do nothing to stop the other two men rounding the counter, however. "Please, don't do this. They're just fucking posters. They don't mean anything."

The man pushed her away as if she were a pesky child, and Shara stumbled hard into a chest. A breath that smelled like liquor fanned across her cheek. "Don't fight, sweetheart. It would be a shame to have to arrest you too, when we could be enjoying each other's company instead."

Shara nearly threw up at the allusion. Her elbow found a home in his gut, and while he sputtered for air, she spun with her dagger in hand and slashed a cut across his cheek. "I warned you not to touch me," she spat, her chest rising and falling with rage and exertion. She was already tiring and no closer to getting out of here. No closer to helping the innkeeper.

"You little bitch." The man righted himself faster than Shara could counter. The back of his hand struck her cheek with enough violence to knock her off her feet. Shara went down with a yelp, her mouth filling with copper, and crashed into the counter. Her head banged against the hard wood, and for a moment her vision blackened and her ears whistled. Then the pain began.

"Fuck the gods," he cursed. "It's her!"

Vision still hazy, Shara raised her hand. Her fingers were once again brown. She'd lost the glamour.

One of his companions grabbed the man closest to him, his movements jerky as he put a small blade to the man's neck. "What the fuck are you doing?"

"Nobody move or your friend's dead."

Shara's chest expanded with a pained breath.

Derron stood at the entrance, swords at hand, pale hair almost white in the dark. His jaw clenched in concentration—or perhaps irritation. A drop of blood dribbled down from his nostril, and in the moment of shocked stillness, his silver eyes assessed Shara's state before returning to the men with simmering fury.

"We don't wish to hurt you, Your Highness," one said.

"The feeling isn't mutual."

"Come peacefully and we'll see you home safely."

"So that my mother may execute me?" Derron unsheathed his swords. "I don't think so."

Fighting her body's heaviness and the painful flares at her hip and head, Shara took advantage of Derron's arrival and the distraction of the men to arm herself. She extracted a second dagger from her belt and slowly, silently, put her feet beneath her. They couldn't count on Derron's Song holding for long, not if he was already bleeding.

The asshole who'd been pestering her looked in her direction when she pounced. It wasn't neat, but her blade cut a deep line in his throat and he went down choking on his own blood. A second guard deflected the dagger she threw his way by a hair's breadth.

The man under Derron's influence slit his companion's throat, and a moment later Derron was on him, driving his sword deep into the man's stomach.

Three down, one to go.

The remaining soldier moved to tackle him, but Derron skirted out of reach. He adjusted his grip on his sword when Shara grabbed a stool and hefted it off the ground with a snarl. She crashed it into the man's back, losing her balance. Splintered wood rained down on her as she toppled to the floor. She cradled her middle, gasping at the onslaught of pain from Aerella's cut.

Derron skewered the man on his sword, and all was silent save for a rattling breath and the gurgle of blood. He pushed the man away, sword still embedded in his stomach, and rushed to Shara, dropping to his knees at her side. "Are you hurt?"

"I'll be fine," she reassured him as he gently cupped her chin and angled her face up. The blood splattered on his face complemented the rage simmering in his silver eyes far too well. "I'm all right, Derron."

"You could have been hurt," he hissed.

"You had perfect timing." She brought her hands to his and led them away from her face, squeezing his fingers. "Help me up."

Once on her feet, she sagged against Derron's chest. His hold around her waist solidified, though he was careful not to touch her abdomen. For a single moment Shara allowed herself to close her eyes and take in the strong scent of forest, sweat, and blood emanating from Derron. His heart was still racing from the fight, and every one of his muscles was tense and primed for violence. And yet, he still managed to hold her with such gentleness.

"What am I to do with you?" he asked, and it took her a moment to realize he wasn't speaking to her. "I should shatter your mind right now."

Shara pressed her hand to Derron's chest. That touch alone tore his attention away from the innkeeper. Dragon, she'd never seen him look quite so feral, like he was a moment away from razing this inn to the ground if he so much as smelled a new threat. His eyes were trained on her face, dark and furious. Heat swirled in her lower abdomen. "He won't report us," she whispered. "Let him be."

"Asharaya Myrassar and Derron Argarys in my inn." The innkeeper sagged against the shelves at his back, the bottles rattling. "You saved me."

Shara pointed a finger at him. "Hang those fucking posters. Next time you decide to play the fool, I won't be around to save your ass."

"Those things I said—"

"You meant them," Shara interrupted him, and the man's shoulders slumped, his stunned expression turning somber. "And you're right about all of it except one thing—Aerella and I are not the same. And if you give me the chance, I'll prove it." She stepped away from Derron and stumbled against the bar. "What do you know about Aerella's army?"

"The queen is marching north. Last I heard she was headed to Oakwood."

Dragon, what she'd give to have her journal again and the map of Ilahara she'd drawn to it. She looked over her shoulder at Derron. "Do you know where that is?"

His mouth thinned into a fine line. Oh, he was furious, and she had no doubt she was scheduled for an earful once they were alone again. Every bone in her body hurt, but the prospect of arguing with him, fighting for the upper hand, had a flutter starting low in her belly and a smile tugging at her lips. She had to force her gaze back to the innkeeper when he cleared his throat. "I don't have other guests and it's looking like it'll be a cold night. You can stay here, if you'd like."

Shara turned back to Derron, seeking his opinion. It wasn't wise to stay too long in one place, and there was the risk that someone would notice the missing soldiers and come looking, but she could use a comfortable bed to regain some of her strength. If not for the whole night, at least for a few hours.

As if reading her mind, Derron nodded to the innkeeper. "Just for a few hours."

48

Shara

Once the innkeeper dropped off a tray with more stew and a pitcher of water, Shara sagged against the closed door. The drops of perspiration on her forehead tickled her skin and captured the chill clinging to the room's walls. The furnishings consisted of a small desk by the closed window, a rickety chair, and a bed barely big enough for two. It was a sleeping arrangement fit for a queen after all the days spent on the forest floor. She couldn't remember the last time she'd slept in a proper bed. Holding a hand against her thigh—which had stopped bleeding, though it still ached like needles were stuck beneath her flesh—Shara shuffled to the window and threw it open, welcoming the cool breeze against her heated skin. All the while, Derron's inquisitive gaze followed her, his silence thickening the air. "Let it out, Derron."

"What's the point? You know what I'm going to say."

"I know how it looks, but I wasn't planning on going to the

inn. I came upon it by chance, and there was no time to go back and find you." She leaned against the windowsill, happy to surrender some of the weight from her wounded side. "We know more now than we did a few hours ago. It's a good thing. Now we know which city to avoid if we don't want to run into Aerella, and we know where to start hunting her down once we find Lord Darrok and the others."

Derron's footsteps announced his approach. He gently grasped her shoulder, and Shara didn't resist as he spun her around. Her attention snagged on the lock of silver hair that fell into his face, the single detail making him look like a handsome rogue plucked from a romance novel, especially with the hint of violence that hadn't completely left his features. Derron wiped her forehead with gentle fingers. "They could have killed you."

"But they didn't." *I can take care of myself.* Instead of saying it aloud, she surprised herself when she murmured, "You came for me."

"You still doubt I would?" Derron's hands lowered to her waist, his fingers curling into her hips. "You maddening woman. Sometimes I can't decide if I want to fight you or..."

"Or?"

Derron's gaze dipped to Shara's lips, and though she tried to fight it, her own gaze dropped to his mouth. "How's your wound?" he murmured.

Shara didn't trust herself to answer. In truth, she didn't think she could. All the heat in her body went south and gathered beneath Derron's palms. She became hyperaware of their closeness, of the shape of his fingers holding her firmly, of the breadth of his chest. Bright-eyed and flushed, he seemed incapable of stopping his hands from kneading her hips. Not even during the long hours spent riding together had he dared to touch her like this—not even when they were naked in the lake. Now that he was, Shara couldn't stop the images taking shape in her mind. His hands traveling lower, those long pianist fingers slipping beneath her leathers and finding the pulsing heat between her thighs.

A strangled sound came out of her, and she yanked a dagger from her belt, pressing it into his neck before the last shred of her sanity dismantled. She desperately wanted to feel in control again, to gather the threads of her unraveling self while there was still time, and she could only do so with the reassurance of a blade between them.

Derron stilled, his throat bobbing. "Your blades don't scare me."

"You're deflecting," Shara said, her voice shaking. "And you're trying to confuse me."

"Maybe you're the one confusing me."

"I'm not the one who tried to kiss you. Twice," she snapped, pressing the blade deeper. Shara didn't realize she'd stepped closer until her breasts went flush against his hard chest, so close she could feel him expand against her with every inhale. Dragon damn her, she wanted to feel his strength beneath her hands. The temptation to give in was maddening, made worse by Derron's arousal mixing with her own. She could feel the evidence of it prodding against her thighs, growing harder. "You weren't acting like yourself at the inn."

"I was afraid." One of his hands covered hers—the one holding the blade. "When I didn't find you at the rendezvous point, I didn't know what to think, and when I found you here." He slowly pushed the blade away from his throat, his eyes never leaving hers. "With those assholes..."

The dagger clattered to the floor. Derron backed Shara onto the desk, and her free hand came up between them, stretching across his chest. His heart was thundering, matching hers with its erratic rhythm. "Were you worried because you want to fight me?"

"I don't want to fight right now, princess." Derron lowered his lips, his next words brushing the shell of her ear. "I want to fuck you."

Their faces turned together, and the last shard of her

resistance splintered at the crash of Derron's lips on hers. The kiss was a clashing of blades, their mouths devouring, punishing in their hunger. Teeth scraped against lips in a battle for dominance where neither seemed willing to bend. Shara's hands slid down along his chest, squeezing between their tightly pressed bodies to slip beneath his shirt. She'd always thought his skin was fresh as a forest stream, but now he was all fire, calling to her most primal instincts. Her fingers flexed against his bare skin, the hard muscles of his stomach making her toes curl. Everything was happening so fast, forbidden enough to be exhilarating, so wrong it almost felt right.

She was kissing Derron Argarys, and she never wanted to stop.

A sound of protest slipped past her lips when he leaned back, his smile more dazzling than ever with his mouth glistening and swollen. She took the opportunity to remove his shirt, and then Derron was kissing her again, one hand braced behind her head, and the other cupping her thigh, lifting her on the desk. "I need you closer," Shara demanded, granting him access to her neck. Every place he didn't touch buzzed with the need for attention. For worship. It had been so long since anyone touched her like this.

"Let me touch you." Derron's raspy tone sent shivers down her body, pebbling her nipples.

"Dragon, yes."

With a sharp jerk of his head, he removed his mouth from her neck as if it cost him, tugging at her shirt to lift it over her head. Derron groaned, his cock twitching against Shara's thigh. "Gods, Shara." His mouth was on hers, and then descended onto her jaw, her neck, her collarbone in ravenous strokes of his lips and sweeps of his tongue. Derron kissed the space between her heavy breasts and followed one's curve with his tongue while cupping the other in his hand. He sighed against the sensitive peak before closing his mouth around it.

Shara squeezed her mouth shut, but it didn't stop the

whimper echoing in her throat. Her hand found the silken strands of his hair, and she fisted it as her back arched to press her breast harder against his face. Pleasure skipped along her spine, pooled in her core. Her legs wound around his middle, and she dragged herself to the edge of the desk to feel his length against her sex.

Closer, her heart screamed with every heightened beat.

Shara fumbled with the strings of his pants, fingers trembling each time they brushed his bulging erection. As Derron moved to her other breast, Shara slid down his pants, using her legs when her hands could no longer reach. Her fingers explored the strong muscles of his thighs, the deep cut of his Adonis belt. She followed it back to his round ass, squeezing as she pushed him hard against her. Her hips lifted of their own volition, chasing release from the pressure building in her core.

Derron ripped away to yank down her pants. Shara shimmied, heedless of the tight pull of the skin around her wound, and helped him remove them. His mouth greedily tasted her abdomen, dropping lower and lower as he slid the pants down her legs. "That scent," he groaned, right before his tongue swept down her center.

Shara moaned his name as her hips bucked off the table, but Derron's hand on her stomach kept her right where he wanted her. She spread wider, baring herself to his sinful claiming. The spill of his moonlit hair on her thighs nearly undid her. Shara gripped it, her tattooed leg winding around his shoulders for purchase as she met each stroke of his tongue with a lift of her thighs, wanting—needing—him deeper. The image burned in her mind, a painting given life in candlelit contrasts. His pale head bent between her amber thighs, and the black dragon inked on her skin wrapped around him, caging him in.

"You taste too sweet for reason," he whispered against her, mouth finding the swollen bud of her clit. When he sucked her into his mouth, Shara screamed in ecstasy, bending back. The mounting desire seemed endless, no matter how much he took and gave.

"I hate you." Shara kicked him away, and Derron stumbled upright. His mouth glistened with her moisture, and a sound akin to a growl rippled up her throat. She lunged for him, their mouths crashing hungrily, as she guided him to the bed.

They dropped in a tangle of limbs, Shara straddling his hips and pushing him into the mattress before he could think to flip them over.

"The moment you showed up in Havanya, everything went to shit." Shara kissed his jaw, his neck, nipping at his pulse. His body had been molded from her forbidden fantasies and reckless dreams.

"Show me how you hate me."

Shara sat upright, hands braced on his chest, and rolled her hips. "Do you ever think about what would have happened without the Coup?" she asked as she positioned him at her entrance.

"I do." His fingers dug into her outer thighs and dragged up to her hips.

"This would have happened." Shara eased him inside her, eliciting a moan from Derron, and a gasp from the very heart of her. He stretched her almost to the point of pain, sinking deeper with every sway of her hips. "I would have had my way with you eventually." Pleasure washed over her, overriding reason, urging her to move, to take. "Dragon, Derron." She bent over him as she increased her speed, the new angle taking him deeper. Her nipple bounced against his lips and his tongue skirted her pebbled brown bud.

"I wouldn't have let you marry Todrak." Derron watched her as if she were a dream taken form and not a wanton vixen unraveling in their shared bliss. "I would have killed to have you."

"Show me how you want me."

Derron gripped her sides and slammed her into the pillows. Their mouths clashed, their kisses hard enough to bruise. The slide of their naked bodies ignited fires beneath Shara's skin. He was everywhere at once, invading her soul with every touch.

Derron thrust inside to the hilt. Shara screamed with abandon, arching beneath him. She could hardly remember her own name. Her world narrowed to Derron's weight pinning her down, the feel of him slipping in and out of her, his grunts fanning against her lips. The room filled with the music of their sighs and the rhythm of the bed's steady thump against the wall. Shara careened closer to the edge as Derron hit her most sensitive nerves. When she was close to falling, Derron kissed her, long and so sensual Shara's toes curled. His long fingers slid between them, finding her clit. "I'd still kill to have you," he whispered, nipping at her lip.

Stars burst in the back of Shara's eyes as her body seized and she shattered in his arms.

49

Kael

After two days of unusual bad weather by Adarian standards, the sun was finally shining in a cloudless sky. Leaning against a market stall, Kael squinted against a ray of light filtering through the hole in the tent while Solana chatted with the stall's owner as she prepared their order. Kael hid his silver-blond hair and the rounded tips of his ears with a glamour, and Solana kept her hair down to pass as fae. The woman hadn't questioned her accent, instead asking her if she were a southern Adarian.

Lana knows how to pick them, Kael mused down the bond. *This woman is a busybody.*

Five stalls down, Mykal was stocking up on blankets. *Did she get any interesting news, at least?*

Nothing about Shara or the queen.

Once they'd left Lur, Kael and the others hadn't dared stay more than a few hours in one place. They'd managed to slip past patrols undetected, though Solana's stealth had helped them out in a few narrow escapes. A tracking spell revealed Shara was still south of them, far closer to Tyrra than they'd have liked. Gathering information was a way of putting their minds at ease—especially Solana, who was held together by the hope that her sister was safe.

Avoiding the main roads, they traveled in Shara's direction until they reached a mountain range marking Adara's northwestern border with Tyrra. Shara's ring grew warmer with each new spell, reassuring them she was alive and that they were getting closer, albeit slowly. The safest bet to avoid patrols was traveling close to the mountain, so they'd risked stopping by this hamlet to stock up on supplies.

Solana's gasp drew Kael from his silent conversation with Mykal. The merchant had just announced the sum, and judging by the indignant flush on Solana's cheek, it was one they couldn't afford. "I did not realize you baked bread with gold in these parts." Solana's collected demeanor vanished in the heated argument. She gesticulated wildly, and Kael's attention caught on her movements. He should have helped with the negotiations, but an errant beam of light turned her brown eyes honey-gold, successfully clearing his mind of anything but that particular shade.

Still got eyes on my sister?

Mykal's voice zapped him back to focus. Eileen's thick curls were easy to spot in the crowded market. She was a few stalls ahead, chatting with a young tailor. *She's doing fine.*

"You drive a hard bargain, miss. I wish you and your husband safe travels."

More than a wild lioness, Solana now resembled a sweet kitten as she took the bag with one hand and tugged Kael closer with the other. Her smile was radiant, obscuring the sun and denying Kael the ability to breathe. He lasted all but a minute, in time for them to be out of earshot. "Did you say we were married?" he asked, slipping into Havanian. Using the human language was second nature around her, much like when he was with his mother or the other servants of Frosthead Hall. The Ilahein humans had adopted the fae's traditions, yet they held onto the language of their ancestors. Most fae didn't bother learning Havanian, making it a convenient means of communication.

"No." Solana inspected the bag's contents as if to ensure that she hadn't been swindled, and then looked up, still smiling. "I wonder what gave her that idea."

Kael's insides liquefied, his lips pulling into a mirroring smile. "I can't shake the feeling I'm being made fun of."

"Did I say it was your fault?"

Kael wished he could distill this moment of mirth and preserve the smile on her face. Too many bad things had happened to her in a short amount of time, and there was still the matter of her brother. The Do'strath were waiting for the opportunity to practice a tracking spell, unbeknownst to Solana in case the results were as grim as Mykal's first spell insinuated.

"I may have been too close for comfort," Kael admitted. "I was afraid the ruse wouldn't work." He'd been ready to step in to avoid any unpleasantness, though that was hardly the reason he couldn't look away—and the stall's owner had seen right through him. "You were right, though. Your methods for gathering intel are unmatched."

"There's more to being a vrah than killing. We learn how to be inconspicuous, blend in." Her gaze swept over the stalls and then zinged back to a specific spot. Kael followed her line of sight to Eileen talking to a handsome young man. The dust on his cloak revealed he'd been on the road for a while—a traveler. Solana beelined for them, starting an anxious flurry at the mouth of Kael's stomach. Had she noticed something he hadn't? Was he a guard? Were they in danger?

Kael, what's wrong?

There's a man talking to Eileen. Solana reacted strangely. We're going in.

I'm coming.

Solana reached Eileen seconds before Kael. She yanked Eileen back, squaring against the shell-shocked stranger. "What are you doing here?" she demanded in Ilahein, right as he asked, "Weren't you supposed to be in Lur?"

"You know each other?" Kael studied the fae more closely. He was tall and lean, with gray eyes, brown skin, and dark hair.

"You're supposed to be in Daganver," Solana plowed on.

Kael filed the information as Mykal caught up to them, surprise flaring down the bond. "Jaero?" he said aloud, and to Kael, *He's the rebel I told you about.*

The fae—Jaero—blinked at Mykal's disguise and raised his hands, placating. "Let's find someplace private to talk."

Jaero knew the owner of the one tavern in town—a man who asked no questions and had zero tolerance for guards. This was a frequent stop for rebels crossing into Adara through the Tyrran mountain pass. Still, Kael, Mykal, and Lord Darrok didn't forgo their glamours. The space was small—like everything in this town—and empty, with only six round wooden tables matching the other furnishings. They chose one close to the secondary exit that would offer a quick escape and privacy in the desolate tavern. The owner brought drinks, but nobody reached for theirs.

"I take it you've heard the new song," Mykal stated, shrugging at Solana's disbelieving glance.

Jaero grinned. "Yes, I've heard it. The new reprise is interesting."

Lord Darrok tapped a finger on the table, while Eileen asked, "What are you talking about? What song?"

"The song is Shara," Mykal explained in a hushed tone. "The reprise—"

"The prince," Jaero supplied.

"We don't have time for codes," Lord Darrok interrupted,

his voice low but decidedly more feminine thanks to the elaborate glamour he wore. "I understand you have news from Daganver."

Jaero leaned closer, drawing everyone in without uttering a word. "The liberation is proceeding successfully. Some of the smaller towns close to the Makkan border have been more difficult to get to, but word of what happened in Frosthead Hall spread fast. Asharaya had us send word through our network. Ares reached areas we couldn't. It saved us a lot of time."

Who's Ares? Kael asked.

The rebel seer.

"I've never seen the people so determined. Without Aerella's emissaries giving orders, the soldiers don't stand a chance."

Mykal seemed like he might grab Jaero by the collar if not for Solana holding him back. "What of my family?"

"Safe."

"And those who were to meet us at Lur?" Solana asked.

"The proceedings in Daganver kept many of our people engaged. Once the tide was in our favor, I moved ahead to meet you. We'll reconvene with the others in Tyrra, and from there we'll take the Veins."

"I'll explain later," Mykal said to his father and sister. He'd already told Kael about the secret underground passages beneath Daganver and Tyrra.

"We need to find Shara first," Solana interjected.

"Agreed," said Mykal. "But we must arrange for my father to go home before the queen discovers what happened in Daganver. We won't be able to contain the news for long, ravens or no ravens."

Jaero nodded his agreement. "Once we find the nearest Veins, it's all a matter of crossing the right portal. He'll be in Daganver within days. The lady can join him, if she wishes." He inclined his head toward Eileen with a charming smile, which she reciprocated. "Meanwhile, we look for Shara."

"We?" The Do'strath and Solana chorused.

"I'm coming with you." Jaero leaned back in his seat with a shrug. "We can use the Veins to get back, and I'm the only one in this group who knows where to find them."

He has a point.

Mykal slumped. "Fine, but no funny business. Shara is the priority. If your commitments slow us down—"

"Finding her is paramount for us as well. Trust me, I won't be in your way."

Lord Darrok rubbed his chin, the gesture so familiar that for a moment Kael could see him through the glamour. "Taking the mountain pass through Tyrra will save us time."

"It's a straight path to Tyrra, and it's narrow enough to allow cover."

Kael, Solana, and Mykal exchanged a glance. "The sooner we leave, the better," Mykal said, voicing their silent agreement.

They all turned to Jaero. "I was coming to you. I have no business here."

"Then it's settled," Lord Darrok intoned. "We'll see to our needs and leave soon after."

50

Cassia

Cassia curled her fingers around the bead of blood blooming from her finger. She closed her eyes, summoning the silver thread that connected her to her family. Two threads glowed in her mind's eye, warming the center of her chest where she imagined her magic originated, as they had been for the past two days. One was her brother, which she knew thanks to something that went beyond magic. The other was not hard to guess, though they'd received confirmation among the villagers they met.

The queen was on the move.

Every mile brought Cassia closer to both, and her urgency to find Derron grew. That she could still track him reassured her that he was alive, but she was filled with no small amount of dread. If Cassia could track him, so could their mother. Cassia could hardly eat with that knowledge in mind. Johan had sent his best trackers ahead to hunt for any whisper or trail of

Derron's whereabouts. And Asharaya's. Saving one would likely mean saving the other, and though Cassia was no fan of the Myrassar princess, she would tie her to the back of her horse if it meant Derron would follow.

Though most of Johan's trackers were not with them, a small party still accompanied them. No soldier worth their salt would allow the Head to traipse alone without an escort, more so when the princess traveled with him. Most were shifters—wolves and wild cats—who traveled in their animal forms, but there was one woman who had the rare Tyrran ability to manipulate plants. Her gift became most valuable when creating shelter for the night. Cassia's guards had also followed her out of Heartstar, and though their role was to protect her, she felt safer around the wild animals. As long as there was the possibility that they would report her movements to her mother or be an obstacle to saving Derron, they were a problem.

One that she would have to solve. Soon.

Cassia had grown distrustful of every bird flittering about or chirping within the trees. Despite ordering every avian creature shot down in Heartstar, Johan had killed only three during their journey, likely wary of Cassia's guards' watchful eyes. Something about the scent set fae apart from real animals, a subtlety Johan seemed to be among the few to identify, even among his fellow shifters. It made sleeping easier, but it didn't entirely lessen the tension draped over Cassia's shoulders.

Then there was Sera. The purple-haired fae traveled on Johan's opposite side, their horse level with the Head's as if they were equals. Friends. Cassia wasn't jealous—especially since she rode on Johan's other flank—but she grew curious about them. Somehow, this stranger had climbed up Tyrra's social ladder and into the Vynatis's good graces in the two years she'd been gone. Was it wealth, power, or beauty that had brought them so high?

Though chatty and friendly in their treks or around the campfire, Sera revealed nothing about themselves. Not that

Cassia had asked outright, sensing that her prodding wouldn't be well received by Johan. It was in the way he observed every interaction carefully in those rare moments Cassia and Sera were alone. What she didn't know was which of the two he was protecting.

"Are we going in the right direction?" Johan asked.

Cassia nodded. "He's getting closer to us."

"Maybe he's coming to Tyrra. To you."

Cassia tasted tears at the back of her throat. She hardly believed Derron would seek her out after their last conversation—after the things she'd said or implied. And yet a part of her couldn't help but hope that Derron was coming to her, because he knew that if put to the choice, Cassia would damn everything to stand by his side, always.

"A storm's coming," Sera noted now from their spot on Johan's opposite flank.

Cassia frowned at the sky. It wasn't the brightest day, but nothing about it hinted at rain. "How can you tell?"

"I have a sense for these things."

"You mean a scar?" Both Semal and Derron lamented an ache whenever the weather turned for the worst.

"We're almost at Oakwood," Johan cut in. "We'll find cover once our business there is done."

The two towns and the occasional home in the woods they'd passed in the first day of travel hadn't revealed anything alarming aside from the rumors concerning the queen's march north. The Tyrrans welcomed their Head with wide smiles, food, and drinks. Their hospitality extended to Cassia, though not with the same friendliness. Johan listened to the people's troubles and took note of their needs. The townsfolk whispered of unrest close to the border in the wake of what had happened in Adara at the queen's hands.

Which explained the tense set of Johan's shoulders now. Oakwood was one of the main Tyrran towns because of its proximity to the small mountain pass dividing Tyrra from both

Adara and Makkan on its northeastern border.

"I would advise against it," Sera said. "The storm is close. We should find shelter."

"It'll put us a day behind."

"Perhaps there is a reason for that. Do not question fate, my friend."

Cassia expected Johan to insist, but he didn't press the matter. "We'll proceed a little longer and then find a good spot to set up camp."

"But my brother—" Cassia began.

"We won't find him today, Cassia. Not with the storm."

"But you don't know it's going to rain."

"Sera's never wrong."

Cassia studied Johan's profile, noting the worried creases between his eyes, and the fight drained out of her. "Did my mother give you reason to worry?"

"The queen has voiced her concern regarding the rebels in a letter not long ago. It was implied she'd intervene should she find our response inadequate."

"It's within her right as queen." Cassia's insides clenched with unease. "Though I shudder to think what she might deem a fitting punishment."

"Most unrest comes from the border towns, the ones closest to Adara and Daganver." Johan raised a brow. "For obvious reasons."

"The Todrak are notoriously anti-Argarys, and the Adarians either hold on to the memory of the Myrassar or simply hate my mother."

"Too much power in the hands of one individual is a dangerous thing," Sera commented lightly, as if still discussing the weather and not the queen of Ilahara. The instinctive urge to defend her mother surged hot and sudden. Cassia clenched her lips to stop venomous words from spilling out.

"Would you rather have someone who hasn't seen Ilahein soil for fourteen years sit on the throne because some fire-breathing monster said so centuries ago?"

Johan chuckled as Sera said, "Centuries ago, fae died by the thousands beneath the dragons' wrath—"

"Sera," Johan cautioned.

"—and that only stopped because 'some fire-breathing monster' deemed one man just. One man who started a dynasty that brought about an age of enlightenment," Sera continued in that smooth tone that made it difficult to discern facts from sympathies. "But it's true not all Myrassar were benevolent. As I said, too much power in one individual."

Cassia considered their words. "A council of leaders would hardly fix things. Most fae are fickle beings. Sooner or later, someone would overpower the rest."

"Perhaps."

A short time later, dark clouds rolled in, and thunder boomed in the distance. Sera had been right about the storm.

They made camp a few miles north of Oakwood, closer to the mountains delimiting the Tyrran border. Rain pelted their magic-built refuge for most of the evening, making it difficult for any conversation to carry over the storm. Johan stared into the fire most of the time, the flames dancing in his hazel eyes and almost turning them gold. Cassia found herself staring, half wishing to see the color seep into his iris. *Show yourself*, she silently pleaded, as if she could reach whatever animal hid in Johan.

Then finally, as if he'd heard her, Johan's gaze strayed to her, stirring a fire in her core.

Later, they met in their shared tree-made tent, lips clashing the moment the branches serving as a flap divided them from the rest of the party. They tore at their clothes and gripped onto each other as if starving for pressure, for friction. Johan didn't waste time bending her onto their blankets, and Cassia let herself be dominated, chasing release.

Tingles skittered up her spine when he aligned himself to her entrance from behind, and almost collapsed beneath the onslaught of pleasure-pain when he entered her. Johan's animalistic growl reverberated down the length of his body and through hers. Her core clenched around his cock.

"Fuck, yes," Cassia cried, fisting the blanket.

Johan's grunts and the sound of flesh slapping flesh were sweeter than any music. Her knees trembled with the effort of keeping upright while their bodies rocked together, his weight a delicious, burning pressure on her back. He wasn't gentle, but Cassia didn't want gentle. Her need to feel something—anything—that wasn't the overwhelming concern for Derron's welfare and his clear need of a distraction had brought them to this point.

"Your hips have gotten softer with the Bleeding." His tongue followed the pointed shape of her ear until he reached her lobe. "I love how you feel, Little Ember." His teeth nipped at her skin, followed by a soothing sweep of his tongue. "And how you taste."

Her climax built with each of his thrusts, his cries growing louder and her body clamping around his cock as he pounded in and out. Johan's rhythm increased, guiding her over the edge, a hand sliding down her stomach and between her legs.

Cassia climaxed loud enough that she doubted the storm drowned out her voice. Johan's release followed shortly after, his head dropping against her shoulder as he panted heavily against her skin. Boneless and satisfied, Cassia fell on the furs and twisted beneath him, pulling him down with her. "Little Ember," she cooed, guiding his mouth to her smiling lips. The endearment sounded familiar, though she couldn't place it. He'd never called her that before. "Do you think the guards heard us?"

Johan looked at her with heavy lidded eyes and gave her lips a sultry lick. "I want you again."

"This isn't funny. If my guards are spies in my mother's

employ, this will blow up in our faces before either of us is ready."

"I never said it was funny." Johan started a slow descent down her body, sending licks of pleasure pooling in her core. Cassia arched beneath his mouth and hands, burying her own through his hair, and opened up for him when he came dangerously close to where she wanted him. He pressed a kiss to her thigh, his arm draped over her belly. "You don't have to worry about your guards." Another kiss, closer to her inner leg. Cassia spread wider, emitting a sound close to a kitten's purr. "I'm handling it." Another on her lower stomach, barely above her sex. "For now."

"What does that mean?"

"It means I'm having them watched." His hazel eyes seemed to flash gold as he looked up at her from his position between her legs. "But you know what you have to do, Little Ember."

Cassia fisted his hair and drove his mouth to her center. Perhaps she was ignoring the problem, but she first had to blow off some steam before she could face the consequences of her decision.

When night fell and the rain stopped falling, Cassia left the tree-branch tent created by the caster in the group, moving slowly so as to not stir Johan from his sleep. The storm had taken the clouds with it, blanketing the sky with hundreds of luminous stars. For a while, Cassia kept her head tipped up in wonder, until the kink in her neck made her look away.

Sera leaned against a rock, stargazing. Cassia's boots squashed against the wet grass as she made her way to them. "Couldn't sleep?"

"The stars are excellent listeners," Sera said.

Cassia peered up at the sky and then back to Sera. She would have considered it a joke if they hadn't spoken with their usual soft note. "You talk to them?"

"Don't you talk to the intangible because it gives you comfort?"

Her mind went to the darkness, to the solace of the room in her moments of despair. "Sometimes." She sat on Sera's rock—not on the ground, lest she got her riding clothes stained with wet grass. "What are you, Sera?"

"I'm many things."

Cassia sighed and looked down at them. Sera had their hair tucked behind their ear. A round ear. "You're a half-breed."

"Does that surprise you?"

"I assumed you were a noble of some sort. Rich."

"And my kind isn't allowed such commodities." Sera played with a blade of grass. "Luckily not all in Ilahara are so short-sighted."

"So, you are a noble."

"I didn't say I was."

"You confuse me."

Sera glanced up at her with a devilish grin. "You're only confused because you think inside a box."

"A box?"

"A box of your expectations, your preconceptions. Your experiences, limited as they are. You find comfort in what you know."

"Doesn't everyone?"

"What happens when what you know is a lie? What grounds you then?"

Something about Sera's words made Cassia think about her mother. She imagined a barren field, with her mother standing opposite her, a line etched between them. Only the line wasn't a line, but a crack in the earth's foundation. Small spiderweb fissures starting from the day she'd hurt Derron, which had slowly opened into a void.

She wants you as a pawn. The familiar voice didn't belong to this realm. She'd only ever heard it in her dreams. Perhaps she was dreaming. A strong pinch on her arm confirmed she was well awake.

She's hunting your brother. You know what'll happen if she catches him, the voice continued, so real that Cassia almost turned to see if it were whispering in her ear.

Sera regarded her curiously. "What troubles you, princess?"

Cassia didn't know what compelled her to speak. "I'm afraid of what I could become with time." Her eyes trailed to the tent, where Johan was sleeping, her mind flashing to their earlier conversation. "Victory comes with sacrifice. The only way to acquire power is having the guts to take it. Use it. Emotions can be exploited. They make you weak."

"Show your power, hide your heart."

Surprise burned through Cassia. "How do you know that?"

"You're afraid of becoming like your mother."

"There are moments I think like her. Moments I might be like her."

"It's your actions that define who you are, princess." Sera's smile was kind, patient. "You decide what to do with the things she taught you, not her."

"And if those lead me to do terrible things?"

"Ask yourself why you're doing those things, and if the price is worth it."

Johan emerged from the tent, scanning the trees. Alerted by their Head, the wolves and wildcats bristled and rose, some emitting low, threatening growls. Cassia couldn't see any threat, but that didn't mean there wasn't one. Her metaphorical hackles rose in response. Exchanging a worried glance with Sera, they made their way to Johan. "What's the matter?"

Johan grabbed a bow and a single arrow from a startled guard. Cassia had only the time to see a swallow darting from the trees before Johan shot it down.

Once the bird hit the ground it transformed into a naked man. Another spy. The arrow had found its mark straight into the heart. Bewilderment crossed the guards' faces. None had sensed the small bird but Johan, and he'd been sleeping in his tent. Sera stared at the dead man, eyes unblinking. Were they in shock?

"Damn Makkani spies," Johan said, seething. He noticed Sera the moment they blinked out of their stupor. He walked over to them, and they exchanged a brief, whispered conversation before he addressed his people. "If High Keeper Baramun and his brothers want to fight, then they do it the shifter way. Face to face, not through subterfuge." The Tyrrans made their agreement manifest either through nods or shuffling paws.

Johan turned to Cassia, eyes blazing. Again, they looked more gold than hazel. *Time to choose, Little Ember*, he seemed to say, only that Cassia could almost hear the words and they sounded like the darkness.

A sensation akin to a phantom touch, a caress along the nape of her neck, seemed to push her encouragingly. Subtle, but tangible enough to make her hair stand on end. It was impossible to believe she'd imagined it. *Is it you?* Cassia's thought was a whisper. *You're not real.*

First you accuse me of lying and now you deny my existence? The darkness sounded amused.

Cassia's heart fluttered in her chest. Was it relief? Distress? *If you're real, where are you?* She looked through the many shadows, trying to discern her darkness from the night.

The darkness remained quiet, as if waiting.

Cassia met Johan's gaze again, and then she looked to their company, their faces illuminated by the perseverant light of the campfire. All twenty of her guards were accounted for. Perhaps there was a good man or woman among them, but Cassia couldn't tell apart those she could trust from those who would divulge her secrets. All of them had been selected by her mother. Had sworn fealty to the queen.

She could have them swear oaths to her instead, but could she ever trust a turncloak?

Cassia nodded to Johan, who turned to his shifters.

"Kill them," he ordered.

The Argarys guards had barely the time to register what was

happening before the wolves pounced. The ones who had time to draw their swords were either felled by the wildcats or strangled by wayward branches and vines. The metallic stench of blood and the sounds of dying wails and tearing flesh coated the night, but Cassia fought the impulse to turn away from the slaughter. *Have the courage to see your decisions through, no matter how messy.* Another one of her mother's lessons. She shoved the flicker of remorse deep and locked it in a dark place in her mind she wouldn't visit if not for the dreams—in the room, with the darkness that had become her companion. A shadow of a friend.

Another feeling flickered inside her, like a cat arching its back against her leg. Purring. The darkness was pleased.

If she could sense the darkness, could others sense it, too?

Johan wrapped his arm around her middle and pulled her closer. "Regrets?"

"The price is worth it," Cassia said, her tone steady. "This is only the first step in claiming our life back."

Johan pressed a kiss to her temple and then issued orders to his shifters. Some would dispose of the bodies, while others were to scout the mountains before they set off for Oakwood come morning. Cassia watched his every movement as one might watch a flame—fascinated, yet unfocused—her mind drifting back to the deep rumble in her head, to the flash of bronze she'd seen in her dreams.

Little Ember.

An odd thought began taking form in Cassia's mind. "Who are you?" she whispered.

She'd referred to the darkness as a person.

Johan turned to look at her, his lips stretching in a lazy smile.

His eyes glinting gold.

I think you know.

51

Derron

Derron and Shara slinked out of the inn in the dark hours of the night, taking Sweetie and one of the horses left there by the now-dead men. The remaining three the innkeeper would do with as he pleased. If he resold them, they would more than cover the cost of the room, the food, and the inconvenience. They pushed their steeds hard and fast to put miles between them and the queen's armed soldiers, keeping to the thick vegetation and away from the main roads. To the animals' merit, they'd endured it without breaking speed, even when their coats glistened with sweat and foam frothed at their mouths.

Derron's hope and dread grew the closer they got to the Tyrran border. He was riding toward what would hopefully be safety, but there were so many variables he couldn't predict, like how Cassia would react once he showed up with Asharaya or if the Vynatis would shelter them out of sympathy for his sister and to honor their past ties with the Myrassar. If anything, the neutrality shown thus far hinted at discontent with the queen, and if the enemy of the enemy was a friend, it stood to reason they'd help. Derron was willing to make any promise if they'd at least allow their maenar to treat Shara.

Shara. She was perhaps the biggest variable of all. Derron couldn't imagine she'd be happy to learn he'd lied to her, but once she saw the merits of his plan, she might understand why he acted as he had. Perhaps she might even forgive him. Her anger he could tolerate, but imagining a reality without her was becoming harder each day. His mind went back to how much he enjoyed sex with her and wanted to do it again. *I don't want to lose it. I don't want to lose her.*

Gurgling water announced their arrival on Tyrran land. Their horses whinnied at the sight but both Derron and Shara tugged on the reins to keep them steady. The large river was one of the four branches of the Artery—the body of water born from the Ilah's roots. In the dusky light and the shadows cast by the forest's trees, the water's sapphire hue was tantalizing, its gurgle as enchanting as a siren's song. If they followed its course upriver, they'd eventually reach the magical tree source of Ilahara's magic.

Shara cast a questioning look Derron's way. "Is this the Artery?"

"It is."

"I know most of Ilahara's rivers branch from here and that magic is less concentrated farther from the Ilah, but won't it be dangerous for the horses to drink directly from the source?"

"These horses were born and bred here. They've built a tolerance thanks to the limited quantity of magic in their water and food. The Artery is only dangerous to humans who haven't lived long in Ilahara. At least, I've never heard or seen magic change those who were born here, other than reducing the incidences of sickness."

Appeased, Shara dismounted and left the mare free to

approach the water. Derron did the same, whispering soothing words to his horse and kissing the animal's nose before releasing him as well.

Without the horses as buffer, Shara's proximity was more tantalizing than the Artery's shimmering waters. Their passionate night at the inn irrevocably altered the balance of their truce. It hung between them, weighing their tense silences in between brief, practical conversations. Derron's body prickled with awareness every time she looked his way, as if her gaze was a physical caress. Did she think about how it had felt? Did she look at his lips and remember the taste of his kiss? Derron couldn't get it out of his mind. He couldn't look at his hands without feeling her skin beneath his fingers, nor could he stop remembering the feeling of his hair clutched between her fingers as they kissed.

"These waters changed Ilahara's first human settlers, back when the continent had been a wild land ruled by dragons," Derron started. "If the lake gave you some respite, this might help you get some strength back."

Shara crouched by the river, grimacing. She'd hardly seemed bothered by her wound when she'd been in his arms, but now Derron couldn't help wondering if he should have been gentler. "Did I hurt you?"

She flashed him a surprised look as she brought a handful of water to her lips. "If I didn't like it, you would know."

Derron's cheeks flushed. "You know what I mean."

Her clever smile was only partially hidden by her hands. Derron watched for any sign of improvement, a weight beginning to lift off his chest when she closed her eyes. Now that some color was returning to her face, he realized how ashen her skin had been moments before. Still, strain lined the corner of her eyes and mouth. "You need more."

But Shara let her hands fall to her sides as she stood, her gaze lost in the river's depths. Derron approached her, meaning to touch her shoulder reassuringly, but the sudden sound of her voice stilled his hand. "Where do we go next?"

Something in her tone put him on edge. "We need to cross the river."

"Past the Artery."

"If you're nervous, I can carry you across."

Shara turned to face him, a new tension written in the crease of her brow and the straight line of her mouth—a mouth that had been smiling for him moments before. "If I remember my geography right, Lur is nowhere near the Artery."

Derron's insides turned heavy and dropped like a stone in a deep well. They were still plummeting when he said, "No, it isn't."

Shara took a step back. "You're taking me to Tyrra. To your sister."

Derron made to bridge the gap between them, but Shara took another step back, her gaze hardening, her jaw clenching. She looked so much like her dragon in that moment that Derron was momentarily petrified. He didn't doubt he'd already be dead had she had the ability to maul him in a single bite. As it was, he was surprised she hadn't skewered him with one of her daggers. "You're dying, Shara. Lur is too far."

"I would have made it."

"You can't know that." Derron brought his hands together pleadingly. "It's more likely the poison would have finished its course before we ever saw the Library's tower."

"You lied to me."

"You would've never agreed."

"I should've known better than to trust you after everything you've done. You will always do what serves your best interests."

"That's not fair. I've done everything in my power to keep you alive and safe."

Shara scoffed and shook her head, and the next moment she was storming to her mare.

Derron took off after her, matching her stride. "Shara,

please, you'll never make it to Lur."

"And whose fault is that?" Shara turned with such viciousness that Derron instinctively jerked away, expecting the arch of a blade that was not there. "I'm closer to my enemies than I am to my friends. To my own sister. I've been traveling through the woods imagining the most horrible things, and every time I've tried to learn what's become of them, you were there to make sure I wouldn't."

"That's not true."

"You stopped me from finding the wanted posters."

"Because we didn't have time. Shara, you agreed with me."

"You made sure I would agree with you."

Derron reared back as if slapped. "I didn't use my Song on you."

"No, but you might as well have."

Shara spun for Sweetie, but not before Derron caught the tremble of her lip. The sight emboldened him to reach for her hand as she mounted the saddle. Shara made to pull free, but Derron only wrapped his fingers tighter around her wrist. "I want to stop my mother from doing any more harm." Derron jerked on her arm, forcing her to look at him. His gaze searching hers, voice breaking, he said, "And I'd prefer not to do it alone. To do it with you."

Aside from the river, the silence was so dense one could have heard a pebble skip. Derron's breaths were short, as if he were hanging off a mountain's edge rather than on the arm of the woman he'd sworn to protect. The woman he cared for more than he should.

Shara shook her head, her face contorting with rage, with pain. Silver lined her golden eyes. "How can I trust you to fight by my side if you keep deceiving me at every turn?"

Something cracked inside Derron. "Shara—"

Her foot connected with his middle right as she pulled on Sweetie's reins. The mare whinnied and rose on her hind legs, and Shara shoved him away with the momentum. Derron stumbled back, his foot connecting with a rock. Suddenly he was on the ground, his ankle and backside aching but not as much as the pain blooming at the back of his head. He'd hit a tree. The horse took off, and Derron called out Shara's name. Darkness swam in his vision.

Her figure on a galloping horse was the last thing he saw before his vision blurred, and he closed his eyes with her name on his lips.

52

Shara

Shara was in desperate need of a new plan, but thinking rationally was a feat easier said than done. Tyrra was much farther west than she should be. It would take weeks to retrace her steps and find her way back to Adara—and this was hoping she wouldn't lose her way. Without a map or Derron to guide her, she might as well be ambling in the dark. Dragon and Maiden help her, how foolish she'd been to trust him, to lean on him as if he could ever be her ally. To let him in. No good would come from dwelling on how naïve she'd been or letting her time with Derron haunt her. She had bigger problems on her hands, the first being the damn poison slowly killing her.

The herbs left in her satchel weren't nearly enough to last her weeks. Even if drinking the Artery's waters had eased some of her pain, it was a temporary fix. The skin around her wound was darkening. She didn't need to know what Aerella had used to understand that wasn't a good sign. Shara had no clue how close she was to a town, or any idea how she would get inside one on her own. The last time, Derron's Song had made all the difference.

Derron, always Derron. Shara cursed the day he'd been put in her path.

If Aerella's patrols and hunters didn't find her first—a concrete risk—the poison would kill her before she ever made it to her friends in Lur. But maybe she could make it to Oakwood. Who would stop her now from going after Aerella? Shara mulled over her odds in the sleepless night following her split from Derron, the idea of seeing him in her dreams keeping her awake as much as her whirring thoughts. She wished Solana were here to offer her clear-minded counsel, or that Mykal would spring from the foliage to bicker with her about the absurdity of her plan. "It's a suicide mission, Shara," he'd say, and perhaps he was right. This time, Shara didn't have Deimok giving her confidence or Jaero and the rebels ready to fight with her—for her. She was alone, with no one to turn to but Sweetie's disinterested ear. In the quiet her anger stirred. The odds weren't stacked in her favor, whether she searched for Aerella or died on the way to Lur. Would she go down as the last Myrassar felled by poison, or would she play her part in Ilahara's new song, even if she might not live to see it to its conclusion?

Shara knew her answer.

Not knowing which forest paths to take to Oakwood, she had no choice but to make use of the main roads and hope a sign would point her in the right direction. From what she surmised, this trail was mainly used by traveling merchants. She kept her hood raised, limiting glamours to those times when she encountered company on the road. To draw as little attention to herself as possible, she opted for manly features, even if holding such an elaborate glamour for long was more taxing on her instable magic, and every eye turned her way spiked up her pulse.

If Daganver was trapped in eternal winter and Adara was blessed with summer's warmth, Tyrra was kissed by springtime. No wonder it was referred to as the land of rivers and flowers in bloom. Colorful buds grew around trees wherever one looked, filling the air with fragrance. To think that so much beauty was the nursing ground for some of Ilahara's most dangerous predators and cunning spies. Even the smallest critter scurrying on the roadside had her tense, the curious ones stopping to stare most of all. What made Tyrran shifters different from regular animals? If Shara had ever known, the answer had been snatched away by the hands of time. *Derron would know.* For a moment she forgot he'd tricked her. Her seat on Sweetie's back felt empty without his solid body behind her, her thoughts loud without his voice to fill the quiet.

You don't miss him, Shara. Stop thinking about him.

Shara knew she was getting closer to Oakwood when the number of patrols along the side of the road increased. Her skin became clammy with more than just perspiration from the increasing discomfort of her wound, her eyes scanning the soldiers warily from under the safety of her hood. Sweetie tugged on the reins as if she could sense Shara's growing agitation. A mounted guard looked their way.

Shara leaned over her horse's neck. "Please, Sweetie. Behave."

The guard's curiosity lasted all of a minute, but the knot in Shara's stomach persisted. From the forest, the baying of hounds echoed. The trackers were scouring the forest, likely carrying more of Aerella's blood to search for Derron. How far had he been from Heartstar? Had he already reunited with his sister?

It's not your business. Stay focused.

It wasn't until nightfall that she finally came upon the wooden sign welcoming travelers to Oakwood—and the border patrol stopping everyone trying to get through. Shara tugged on Sweetie's reins and led her off the road and onto a forest trail, feeling the gaze of one of the foot soldiers on her. Sure enough, the telltale clinking of his light armor followed her into the forest.

Shara's hand ventured beneath her cloak. She cleared her throat to cover up even the smallest whisper of steel as she extracted the blade. "You've been a good companion, little lady," she murmured to Sweetie. The tip of the blade sank into Shara's palm, and she winced. "If I survive this, I'll find you again. I promise."

Around Sweetie's legs, the shadows thickened like the beginnings of a foggy trail. Shara dismounted, making a show of checking the saddle's bindings as she opened the pouch and produced the last strands of herbs. She stuck them in her mouth, munching as she tracked the foot soldier's approach. Too close to slip through the shadows undetected. *Shit.*

"Hello, sir." Shara didn't trust herself to also glamour her voice, so she hoped her low baritone was convincing. "Would you mind keeping an eye on my horse while I go behind that tree?" She patted Sweetie's flank. "She's fearful, this one. Especially with all these dogs around, but nature calls."

The soldier looked younger than her by a couple of years. Appearance didn't mean much when it came to the fae, but the way his posture relaxed belied his inexperience. *Turn around, you fool.* Was Aerella already drafting green soldiers for the war? Would he listen to her if she gripped him by the collar and told him to go home?

"Sure thing," the young man said.

Shara plastered a fake smile on her face, tremulous as it was. The soldier was only a few steps away now, his attention on Sweetie. "I'm sorry," she whispered when they were shoulder to shoulder. By the time she realized she'd spoken with her own voice, her dagger was already deep into his carotid artery. She pushed away the guilt, detaching from her actions as she accompanied the young man's body to the ground, holding him until he stopped spasming.

The body hidden within the nearest bush, Shara slapped Sweetie's rear to urge her deeper into the forest and walked back to the main road on foot. The shadows tripped after her like eager puppies around their owner's ankles. She remained within the foliage, mapping out her surroundings. Once she identified a decent blind spot, she stepped into the darkness and let the shadows lead her into Oakwood.

The little town of Oakwood had merged so deeply with the forest, it was hard to imagine it hadn't sprouted from the earth alongside the trees. Huts emerged among the clusters, stables or small workshops taking up the lower levels. Some of the houses jutted from the trees themselves, moss spreading along roof shingles and lining the picket fences of gardens and orchards. Lonely candles flickered behind glass panes built into the oaks' broad trunks as horses' hooves echoed on the stone-studded path.

For the following hour, Shara wandered in search of information on Aerella's army. A couple of drunkards outside the inn complained about how much the men's incursions into town had cost them—they were likely shop owners pressured into giving their wares to Aerella's men free of charge. From the gossip in the streets, she discovered the army had made camp nearby. Sure enough, she spotted the first tents after a short walk to the other side of town nestled beneath a hill. With only a small inn and a shop or two for essentials, this part of Oakwood wasn't as crowded as the rest of town. She only had to wait a minute for the road to clear to use the shadows to take cover behind a tree, where she'd have a better vantage of the camp.

If the streets were nearly deserted, the camp was buzzing with men exchanging drinks around campfires and laughing raucously at their bawdy jokes. Some led women into their tents—human bed slaves, most likely, given Ilahara's lack of brothels. No sign of Aerella and her general, though the usurper's tent was distinguishable from the rest—larger, the canvas a vivid silver and blue.

If she had to guess, the queen wasn't staying in her tent. Why else would soldiers be surrounding the inn? And most importantly, how would Shara get to her while avoiding detection?

A short while later, as if in answer to her question, a young woman in a simple woolen skirt and blouse stepped outside, a brass bowl tucked beneath an arm. A soldier followed after her.

Here was the opening she was waiting for.

Heart thundering like a drum, Shara sliced across her palm and pulled the shadows to her. Tree by tree, she followed the woman's procession through the forest. Water dripped over rocks nearby, filling the forest with its enchanting melody. It was there that the woman stopped, kneeling on the creek's mossy banks to fill up her bowl. The guard stopped a few feet away—right underneath Shara's tree.

Shara slipped into the shadows a final time to emerge from the elm's large shadow etched on the damp soil. She snuck up to the guard's back on silent feet, teeth clenched against the ache even the smallest lick of the breeze caused against her sensitized skin. One hand clamped hard on the guard's mouth, while the other whizzed across his throat, the dagger cutting a deep line that severed straight through the vocal cords. Then, Shara pounced on to the woman, locking her neck in the crook of her elbow and squeezing until she lost consciousness.

Slipping into the glamour was easier with a model to imitate. Shara lightened her hair to wheat blonde and her skin to a pale, freckled complexion. Then she switched out her clothes with the young woman's, fastening the daggers to her thighs and hiding them beneath the skirt. She filled the brass bowl with water before returning to the inn, praying no one would notice the guard's absence or the limp she wasn't quite able to hide.

Inside, a fae woman behind the counter shot her a disinterested glance before focusing her attention back on the three soldiers seated at the bar. Shara clutched the bowl tighter and headed up the stairs, gaze fixed on her hands to make sure the glamour held. Every step up shot new pain into her side, and her teeth ached with the pressure of her bite to keep from whimpering. *Just a little longer.*

Outside one of the rooms a guard stood watch, and he turned at her approaching steps. The hairs at the back of Shara's neck raised at his scrutiny. She glanced at the water in her bowl—at the reflection that would give her away. "Where's Rolan?" the man asked.

Crap. How was she getting out of this one? If the man looked into the water, she'd be done for. And if she spoke, her disguise would be forfeit.

"He snuck off again, didn't he?"

Shara wasn't one to look a gift horse in the mouth. She nodded, hoping it would be enough to please the guard. "Fucking obsession with that baker girl's gonna get him killed one of these days." He had the decency to knock on the door for her. "The servant's returned, Your Majesty."

"Let her in." Shara's blood curdled at the soothing tone of Aerella's voice. It was an effort to keep her lip from curling into a snarl.

"Don't make word of Rolan to the general, you hear?" the guard warned in a low hiss.

Once again, Shara limited herself to nodding and stepped into the usurper's room.

53

Kael

Wood snapped in the fire at their makeshift camp. After a full day trekking through the mountain pass, they still had a ways to go before its end. There, a small group of rebels dressed as traveling maenari waited to lead Lord Darrok north to Daganver. The mountain provided plenty of spaces to hide and ambush pursuers. Hopefully, this shortcut would also allow them to intercept Shara soon. A quick tracking spell revealed she'd passed the Tyrran border. Jaero led their small company with the surefootedness of someone who'd traversed this mountain path many times. The tension was palpable in their careful silence, in part due to the journey's dangers, but much of it hounded them since before the mountain. Besides their collective worry for Shara, there was the strain within the Todrak. Lord Darrok seemed more amicable toward Mykal, but he barely said a word to his daughter. Despite Mykal's attempts at bonding, Eileen seemed more at ease around Jaero—a stranger who wouldn't judge her—than anyone else. The problem wasn't Mykal, but Kael. Eileen could barely look his way without her gaze darting elsewhere, and Kael wasn't putting much effort into making her feel welcome. While a part of him wanted to try for Mykal's benefit, another couldn't forget she'd been a guest of the Argarys while he'd been their prisoner.

On their second night in the mountains, they found shelter in a small opening—not quite a cave, but it offered enough cover. Lord Darrok chose to rest against the far wall, falling asleep almost instantly while the others built a fire.

"Shouldn't he eat something?" Eileen whispered. A small flush rose to her cheeks when she caught Mykal's surprise at her concern.

"We'll make sure he does later," he reassured her.

Kael lit the fire with a flick of his fingers. Solana made to grab the hare she'd hunted earlier, but Jaero beat her to it. "Let me," he said, and then gestured to the growing flames. "Enjoy the fire. You look like you need it."

Solana frowned, watching him as he sat by the fire to skin the animal, but didn't protest. "I'll be right back," she said, and the Do'strath tracked her movements across the cave until she kneeled in a shadowed corner to pray.

Eileen's gaze flickered from the wall to the fire, as if debating whose company would make her less uncomfortable. In the end, she chose the fire and sat next to Jaero. The rebel greeted her with a kind smile that seemed to ease some of her tension despite his gruesome task. Kael wished he could feel the same around the newcomer in their fold. Jaero didn't reveal much about himself. Was it a professional habit to be this secretive? Was he simply modest, or was he hiding something? His instincts told him Jaero could be trusted, but his mind warned caution.

You're beginning to sound like me, Mykal teased down the bond, though he watched his sister whispering with Jaero like a hawk.

A few minutes later, Solana took the empty spot the Do'strath had left between them and scooted close to the fire, rubbing her hands and holding her palms up at a safe distance. Blood still dribbled from a small cut on her palm. Kael pressed his shoulder to hers to offer some of his Fire's warmth while Mykal's attention fixed on the stained handkerchief she'd dropped next to his knee. "In Daganver, the few humans who remember Havanya complain about the cold," he said, voice low as to not disturb Lord Darrok's rest.

"We aren't familiar with it at home." Solana snuck a glance at Mykal, who tugged at the collar of his shirt, and bit her lip to hide her amusement.

Kael leaned back on his elbows, keeping his leg pressed to Solana's side as he grinned. "The weather here is nice. Right, Myk?"

Mykal scowled. "Sure, if you like melting."

Kael and Solana laughed, but then he remembered Lord Darrok and quieted. Solana's soft laughter echoed in the small space before she too fell silent. Kael traced the shape of her smile with his eyes and then shifted his attention to Mykal, who watched them fondly. The sight stirred warmth within Kael that was a magic all its own.

The spell dissolved when Lord Darrok murmured in his sleep. Sadness crept onto Eileen's face as she looked at her father, and Mykal, whose mood seemed to undulate based on his sister's reactions, stared into the fire. For a moment, everything stilled but the sound of the crackling flames. Even Jaero stopped his work, as if sensing the tension. He glanced between the Todraks, and then nudged Eileen with his elbow. "Have you ever cooked your own food, princess?"

Eileen blinked several times in astonishment. "I'm not a princess—and no, I haven't." Her cheeks darkened as she scooted closer. "But I can learn."

Jaero slashed a grin. "Watch what I do." He launched into a demonstration on how to prepare an animal for cooking. Eileen observed with equal parts fascination and revulsion. Kael wondered if she realized Jaero was only subjecting her to this to keep her mind busy. *Perhaps my instincts weren't wrong after all.*

As if campfire bonding is going to fix things.

Solana nudged Mykal's foot, drawing his attention. "It's not her fault she was raised away from you," she whispered in Havanian.

Kael snorted at Mykal's flabbergasted expression, earning a cursory glance from Eileen. "I didn't say anything," Mykal protested in Ilahein, matching her low tone.

"I don't need a magic bond to know what goes on in that thick skull of yours." The fact Solana could read his Do'strath as well as he did filled Kael with an odd sense of relief. "In your heart you know she can't help who she loves." She pinned Kael with an intense stare. "Nor should you blame her for adapting to survive." The words landed like a punch to the gut, summoning something that was very close to guilt. "Once you make peace with that, all will be better."

"The Argarys are the monsters who took her. It's..." Mykal blew out a breath.

"Fucked up," Kael finished. His thoughts dragged him to the family he didn't know. To his father, who'd come once to his cell to mock him. To Cassia, who'd been a sister to Eileen but hadn't deigned to see him once. To Derron, who'd been the reason Kael was thrown into those dungeons, but who'd also tried to help. Derron, who'd saved the woman he'd been meant to kill. "Do you think they're safe?"

"The tracking spell is working. So, she's alive."

"I'd know if she were hurt." Solana brought her hand to her heart. "Shara may not share my blood, but she's still my sister. If her family were to return from the dead, I know her love for them wouldn't erase her love for me. And it would be the same if I were ever to reunite with my brother." She squeezed Mykal's hand. "Life, love, family—it's all blurred lines. Not everything is black and white."

Jaero furtively watched the scene, looking away when he noticed Kael's attention. Solana's earnest tone might have captured his interest, or maybe he could understand Havanian. With him being a rebel, Kael wouldn't be surprised.

Mykal swallowed and disentangled his hand from Solana's. "The fire needs more kindling. I'll gather some twigs."

One look, and Kael was standing too. "We'll be right back."

His Do'strath marched several feet away from their refuge before stopping. Mykal paced the same three steps several times over, running his hands through his hair and then gripping it. "We need to find him," he finally announced. "Solana's brother."

"You want to do it now?"

"I can't look her in the eyes knowing she might never see him again and I'm hiding it from her. You saw her. She's so hopeful. And good. I want to give her closure."

Kael nodded, though his insides knotted with dread. If Mykal's first spell had been correct—if Solana's brother was dead—how could they possibly tell her? The thought of causing her more grief was like a stab in the gut. She already had enough on her plate without adding her brother's uncertain fate to it.

"Did you get it?"

Mykal opened his palm in the space between them, revealing Solana's bloodied handkerchief. "This should work."

Kael wrapped his hands around Mykal's. Their breathing slowed and synchronized as they burrowed into their magic, finding the threads of the tracking spell. They focused on Solana, on her essence, and willed the magic to find a similar signature. Someone who shared her blood.

For the longest moment, the threads remained cold. Kael opened his eyes to Mykal's concerned gaze. *We need to go deeper*, Kael said. *We should at least be sensing her father.*

Unless something happened to him since we last saw him.

Kael dove deeper into the spell, Mykal's magic following

close behind. Their Ice and Fire wove through Solana's threads. *Her brother. We need to find her brother. Dragon, please let him be alive.*

The handkerchief grew warm in their hands, the sensation traveling up their arms and seeping into their chests as the spell took hold. A cold silver thread came to focus in their minds' web—distant. If they followed it, it would undoubtedly lead to Havanya and to Vrahiid Dougas. A glow radiated behind it. The Do'strath reached for it, feeling its warmth. This thread had been concealed, as if the magic wasn't certain this was what they were searching for, but now it was near blinding in its radiance.

"It's close," Mykal murmured.

Kael laughed joyously. "Her brother's alive." He squeezed Mykal's hands. "He's here, in Ilahara."

"Shara's in Ilahara too, and the spell isn't nearly as warm. This is too close."

Kael's hands fell away as Mykal followed the spell's pull, holding the handkerchief as if it were a compass. Mykal's doubt was palpable down the bond. Could they have accidentally tracked Solana instead of her brother?

It doesn't feel like Solana, said Kael.

Mykal stopped at the cave's entrance. Inside, Jaero was preparing to roast the hare over the fire. Solana held her hands out for warmth, but Eileen was sitting beside her now. The two were talking, and by the look on Eileen's face, she was enjoying the conversation.

Kael frowned when Mykal didn't move, doubt rearing its head again. *Did we fuck up?*

In response, Mykal offered the handkerchief. The moment Kael grasped it, the spell tugged him toward the cave's interior, growing warmer as his eyes swept over Solana. Yet the tug persisted.

Kael followed the pull to the left.

"Jaero?"

Three sets of eyes turned to Kael, startled and confused by

his sudden outburst. Solana looked from one Do'strath to the other, concern creasing her brow as she saw their shocked faces. Kael wanted to reassure her, to wipe those lines away and put a smile on her face instead, but words eluded him. He and Mykal hadn't messed up the spell—it had led them here.

To Jaero.

How could he possibly be Solana's brother? He's fae.

The questions swirling in Mykal's head belonged to Kael as well. There had to be a mistake, and yet how could there be? The tracking spell had recognized Solana's blood.

There could be another explanation, Mykal rationalized. *Maybe one of Solana's ancestors was taken to Ilahara and mingled with fae.*

Jaero's brow quirked. "Yes?"

The more Kael stared, the more he recognized similarities he hadn't bothered to notice before: The shape of his eyes, the bridge of his nose, his chin, the silky quality of his hair, the skin tone. Now that he knew the truth, he couldn't unsee those distinguishing features that marked Solana and Jaero as siblings, as unfathomable as the notion was.

He's not a half-breed, Myk. His ears are pointed.

True, but we don't even know how old he is. For all we know, he could be Solana's great-grandfather. There was an edge of panic in Mykal's voice. *We need to be sure before we drop this on Solana. If the spell is wrong—if we're wrong—it'll destroy her.*

A rock skidded not far away. The sound had been soft but sudden enough to startle Lord Darrok awake. Mykal and Kael spun. With a wave of his fingers, Kael took out the fire while Solana stalked to them at the cave's entrance. They hid behind the rock wall while waiting to discover the origin of the noise.

"Is someone there?" Lord Darrok asked, his voice soft. Jaero and Eileen rushed to him—Jaero quieter than Eileen—to hoist him up.

"I can't hear anything," Mykal said. *But I smell something.*

Kael smelled it too, and he chastised himself for not noticing it sooner. He tapped his nose for Solana's benefit and she nodded her understanding. Whatever lurked about was silent on its feet. A predator, perhaps.

"I will see what it is." Solana made to leave their shelter, but Mykal held her back.

"We're crossing into Tyrra. We're lucky if whatever's out there is just an animal," he hissed between his teeth. "I'll go." He glanced at Kael. *Stay back with them.*

Solana yanked back her arm. "And if it is not an animal?"

"Your faith in me is astounding."

"We stand together," Solana insisted. Kael stepped beside her in silent agreement. They wouldn't separate again. Whatever the threat, they had a better chance of facing it together.

Mykal sighed, only half annoyed. The twinkle in his eyes matched a subtle glow down the soulbond. "Very well then, but I go first." He turned to the others. "Stay close. If there's trouble, get to the horses."

Mykal stepped out of their refuge, Ice coating his fingers. He scanned the mountain's wall. *There's definitely something here, though I can't see it.*

Solana understood the meaning behind Kael's tense nod and followed Mykal with dagger in hand. Kael motioned Jaero and Eileen to stay put as he reached the others. They stood with backs to each other, scanning their surroundings. Kael listened for the subtlest shift, but it was his nose picking up the threat. Earth and grass and a feral scent that could only belong to an animal. Perhaps a wild cat.

A breeze carried other scents similar to the one Kael had singled out. Large animals prowled the mountain, too close for comfort. His skin prickled as the distinct signature of magic impregnated the air.

"Not animals," Mykal murmured.

A rock tumbled down the mountain's rocky wall. Jaero and

Eileen came out of the refuge with Lord Darrok between them. Mykal ushered them to his side as large shapes emerged from their hiding spots. The beasts descended the steep mountain on both sides of the path, herding Kael and the others into the middle. Kael's attention snagged on the paws first as they stalked forward with lethal grace. Large cats, most with the pointed ears and gray-and-tawny fur of lynxes, but there were several spotted coats among them. Leopards.

Kael's heart beat loud in his ears. He'd seen his share of wild animals in Daganver's snowy forests. Though most were big, they weren't as bulky as the ones surrounding them. Tyrran shifters. Down the bond, Mykal readied his Ice to strike.

"I wouldn't do that."

Two mountain lions descended the rocks with graceful leaps. Their large paws were near silent as they touched the ground, and even more so as they prowled closer. Green eyes glowed in the dim light, filled with a predatory intent almost as frightening as the menace of their bared fangs. Following behind them, as surefooted and nimble as the predators, was the fae who'd spoken.

Mykal cursed. He didn't relinquish his hold on the Ice, but neither was he foolish enough to strike. The fangs and claws would reach them before Mykal and Kael could so much as land a blow if the man commanded it.

The mountain lions flanked the fae and stalked forward alongside him. Moonlight shone on the deceptively lithe and slender lines of the man's body, and on the nobleman's clothing he hadn't forsaken even for the hunt. Everything about him— from the lace on his shirt to his leisurely walk—fit the image of a bored nobleman. Everything but the predatory gleam of his hazel eyes, so similar to that of the shifters even in his fae form. The imprint of his magic was crushing, though there was no sign of the animal lurking beneath. None had ever seen it, though all knew to fear it.

Kael muttered a low curse as dread turned to acid in his

stomach.

"Friends," Johan Vynatis crooned. "You're quite a long way from Daganver, wouldn't you say? Let us offer you Tyrra's hospitality." He gave them all a wicked smile. "I insist."

54

Shara

"Put it on the table."

The usurper queen reclined on the bed, the covers only partially concealing her form. Beside her, General Leneris lay in a similar fashion, his scarred chest on full display. Their state of undress and lack of modesty left little doubt as to what had occurred between them. Shara hid any hint of surprise from her face lest she raise suspicion, though she wondered if Derron was aware his mother's closest adviser was also her lover.

Not the time. What she needed was a plan. She'd not considered the possibility of Aerella having company—and the general, at that. Attacking the queen and coming out unscathed wouldn't be easy.

The room was scarcely furnished, with a round table and four chairs at its center and a mirror in the right corner. No windows, no adjacent bathing room. The space was hardly fit for a queen, but at least the mirror and the water in her hands would be the only reflective surfaces for Shara to worry about.

Careful to disguise her limp and discomfort, Shara walked to the table. In her peripheral vision, General Leneris spoke to the usurper in sign language. "We cannot linger any longer" was the queen's reply. "The situation in Daganver is too dire. I need to regain control before Darrok Todrak has time to bring order to his forces."

Aerella knew what had happened in Daganver. *Shit.*

Shara set the bowl on the table, her heartbeat pulsing in her ears.

"We have enough people staying behind to locate him."

Shara wished she could understand what the general was saying.

"My son is trapped. It's only a matter of time until he's brought crawling to my feet."

Derron.

"I wouldn't be surprised if he were delivered to me today. He's close." The general spoke again, and the queen rose from the bed, obviously irritated. "Don't start this again. I need you by my side." She strode to the table with every curve on full display. Eyes averted, Shara stepped away from the bowl like a demure human, tucking her hands beneath the folds of her skirt to hide their shaking. The hair at the crown of her forehead was damp with the effort of holding the glamour. "I would be hunting him myself if I didn't have bigger problems on my hands. You."

Shara's gaze snapped to the usurper.

Aerella's stare bored into her. Shara wasn't sure if she'd imagined her brow creasing. "Fetch my robe."

Shara nodded, taking a moment to scan her surroundings. A servant would know where to find the queen's robe. Normally it would be in an armoire or dresser, but there were none here. Maybe it was at the foot of the bed and Aerella was too lazy to grab it herself.

Shara found it hanging behind the mirror.

"When I march against Daganver, my general will be on my right leading my army, not running after my errant son. Let the soldiers fetch the traitorous rat, and I will deal with him accordingly once he's returned to me."

Shara's footsteps echoed in the following silence. The closer she came to the mirror, the more her agitation grew. If either the general or the usurper caught a glimpse of her reflection, her ruse would be forfeit. If she was meant to die, she refused to go without taking Aerella with her.

"If she's still alive, that is. Maenar Errigen assured me the poison would snuff out her magic."

They were talking about Shara now. The usurper's confidence in her death almost made Shara laugh. *This is the last time you'll underestimate me.*

Shara winced as she reached for the robe, and she bit down on her lip to hold back a cry. After finding her bearings, she brought the robe back to Aerella, who watched her expectantly. Even the general's eyes were on her now, though he remained on the bed.

Shara held the robe out for Aerella.

Aerella shrugged into it.

Then she twisted, grasping Shara's hair in one hand and her arm with the other before Shara could react. Shara cried out, her middle slamming against wood as the queen shoved her onto the table, holding her face over the water. Her true reflection stared back at her and the usurper, whose lips spread in a murderous grin. "I should have known a little cockroach like you would find a way to cheat death yet again." Aerella shoved Shara's side against the table, right over her wound.

Shara bit her tongue in an effort to stop from crying out. Copper filled her mouth.

The general, who'd flown out of bed, was pulling up his pants.

Shara would be dead soon.

"Where did you leave my son?" Another push elicited a

small cry from Shara. Hot, sticky blood oozed from her wound, tainting the maid's blouse. "I know you didn't bury him. He's still alive."

Shara's free arm was wedged at an odd angle between her body and the usurper. On her wounded side. Stars danced in her vision, but with a grimace she managed to twist it free and slam her elbow hard into the queen's stomach.

The two women crashed to the ground, Aerella dragging Shara down with her. Shara kicked out of the usurper's hold and scrambled back and out of reach.

The door burst open, the guard stationed outside storming in with his weapon drawn.

Semal Leneris charged with his sword, but Aerella was faster, shooting a spear of fire against Shara.

Out of instinct, Shara lifted her hands.

The magic in her veins sparked. Detonated.

Fire engulfed the room. Shara was hardly able to glimpse Semal throwing himself over Aerella and the usurper lifting her hands before the ceiling crashed over them. The guard's anguished scream was drowned out by falling wood and stones.

Shara rolled underneath the table and curled in on herself, hands protecting her head. A beam fell from the roof, punching a hole in the spot where she'd been moments before. Its weight made the table cave in. Shara was squashed to the ground. Agony tore through her.

Then the floor collapsed.

When Shara came to, it took a moment for her eyes to adjust to the darkness. She was beneath a pile of debris. People were shouting, the words indistinct through the roaring fire. Shara coughed and tried to ease the weight off her wounded side, but she was stuck.

"Find the queen."

"We need more water!"

"It's going to burn the whole town!"

Shara couldn't stay there. If she didn't die crushed or

suffocated, someone would find her and she'd still end up dead. Coming to this forsaken town had been a mistake. Dragon, she never stopped messing up.

Gritting her teeth, Shara kicked her ankle free from under a beam. She crawled on her elbows, dragging herself inch by painful inch out of the rubble and toward the light. Everything hurt, the flesh beneath her arms and knees tearing against rocks and wood. The blouse clung onto her side, where her poisoned wound wouldn't stop bleeding.

Then she was out. Turning on her back, Shara squinted against the light and sucked in a lungful of air. It was so bright, and yet it was the middle of the night.

Shara slowly brought herself up into a sitting position, taking in the destruction surrounding her. Towers of fire engulfed tents, trees, and buildings. Screams resounded from burning pillars—people. People were burning. Others were scrambling to salvage what they could and to stop the fire before it could spread further into town. Children's cries and the stench of burned wood, grass, and flesh saturated the night.

Shara bent to the side and dry-heaved.

"There's someone there."

"It's her—Asharaya!"

Shara stood and wielded two daggers, the movement slow and not as fluid as she would have liked. She was in no shape to run, but she wouldn't stand around waiting to be slaughtered by Aerella's soldiers. There were more than two dozen rounding on her, all with swords in hand, the others either too preoccupied with finding Aerella and taming the fire or too dead.

Sweat trickled down her temple. She tightened her hold around her daggers.

Then the soldiers stopped.

It wasn't natural but rather a complete cessation of movement. They froze mid-stride, like living statues, their lifting chests and slow blinking the only signs they were alive at all.

And behind them all, making his way to her, was Derron.

His skin was ashen against the ghastly backdrop of the burning night. Veins pulsed at his temples and around his neck, and blood trickled out both his nostrils. The closer he came, the more his tremors became evident. He strained as if he were holding back a flood with a rickety wooden door rather than a dam.

"You need to go," he said, voice strangled.

"Why did you follow me?"

"Don't argue with m—" Derron bent over, and Shara rushed to his side to keep him upright as he spat blood. It splattered his chin, leaked from his eyes. "I can hold them," he rasped. "Go."

"Not without you."

"You're not listening."

"You're not listening." Ignoring the flare in her side, she wound his arm around her shoulder. He'd followed her here, knowing there were hunters on his track and that finding Cassia was his safest bet. He was risking his life to save hers yet again when leaving her to die would have been easier. Stubborn, noble fool. "I'm not leaving without you."

Derron swallowed, and even that seemed to take effort. For a moment it looked like he was still going to object, but then he nodded. A full body shiver overcame him, running straight through Shara.

Step by agonizing step, they edged away from the fire. Darkness swam at the corner of Shara's vision, but she pushed through the pain to hold Derron's increasing weight. His breathing turned more ragged the longer he held onto the soldiers, until each breath came out in a heaving rasp. The blood was so much now, his cheeks and chin were streaked with it.

Behind them, a shuffle and fatigued grunts alerted them to the Song's weakening hold on the guards. They were starting to fight back, and Derron and Shara were still too close to the camp.

"I-I...can't..."

"Don't give up on me, Argarys."

"I haven't." Derron coughed, and blood spurted out of his mouth. The next moment, he was on his knees, dragging a tired and weak Shara down with him. "But you should give up on me."

Shara curled her fingers around his shirt. "You're not dying now, Argarys. Come on." She hauled herself up with great difficulty and pulled him up. They didn't get far before they hit the ground again, Derron cursing weakly and Shara clutching him like a mussel to a rock. They must have tripped over a tree's exposed roots. The clean smell of wet grass and damp earth was hard to ignore, but it didn't remove the tang of blood and Derron's scent from her nose.

Then she noticed how thick the tree's roots were. Covered by a layer of moss and digging into the forest floor like talons, they were large enough for her to step on without needing to balance. She traced their curling form to the elm's trunk, larger than the others and the only one with a hollow at its heart.

A hollow large enough to step through.

Shara disentangled herself from Derron and stood. Her vision flickered between Tyrra's lush, green forest and one carpeted in white. She could almost feel Deimok's heat by her side. So vivid was the memory that she expected Mykal to approach the tree with that special gleam in his eyes she hadn't thought possible while he was broken by Kael's distance.

"Shara," Derron rasped. "I can't hold on anymore."

"Then let go."

"What are you doing?"

Shara pushed her dagger into the wood and started carving. The Star of Izhan came alive beneath her knife, a cross with three curving lines on each end resembling a gust of wind.

When the marking was done, Shara took a step back.

Counted her breaths.

One, two, three.

A wink of blue light burst from the cross's center.

They'd found the Veins.

"How did you know?" Derron asked, words laced with wonder.

"It's a long story." Shara helped him to his feet. "Come on."

The Veins in Tyrra's underground were similar to those in Daganver, and yet they held a sense of novelty that hadn't belonged to those ancient tunnels. The Ilah's roots spread across the earthen walls, pulsing their silver and sapphire light into the dark. Spots of green moss amassed in the empty patches between roots and surrendered a musky scent to the underground drafts. Skin moist with sweat and limbs trembling, Shara narrowed her focus on the tunnel ahead, the wind's wail and the crunch of their footsteps accompanied by their rasping breath.

Derron pushed out of her hold, letting himself fall against the tunnel's wall. Shara helped him sit straight. "This is my fault," she whispered, her voice cracking. "You knew where to find me. That I was going to do something stupid." She wouldn't cry. Not over Derron Argarys.

She wouldn't.

"I should have told you what I was doing." Derron swallowed, and Shara didn't even want to imagine the amount of blood going down his throat. A dirty hand came around her cheek, his thumb tracing a tremulous circle against her skin. "The Artery..."

"Stop thinking about it."

"The water. You...need..." More coughing, and his eyes widened with a sense of urgency. The veins were so many they almost drowned out the silver. "Whatever happens, I don't want Cassia to get hurt. Promise me that."

Shara's hand came over his against her cheek. "The only Argarys I want is your mother."

Derron's bloody lips curled in a weak smile. "Liar."

Her vision swam with pooling tears as she leaned closer.

How could he tease her at a time like this? How could he even want to, after she'd gotten him into this mess? And yet, despite everything, Shara was glad he was here, that neither of them was alone. "You're a shit enemy, Argarys," she whispered, echoing words she'd said to him once before, and pressed her lips to his. Despite the blood, his mouth was cold as granite against hers, lacking all the warmth of their single night together. He remained unmoving, even after Shara pulled away. A stone dropped in her stomach, and a strangled sound tore from her throat. "Derron?" She brushed the hair off his face. "Please, open your eyes."

Her fingers slid down to his throat, trying to find his pulse.

The sob that had been threatening her finally burst free.

"You don't get to die on me. You don't get to come back and die for me." Any moment, she expected his eyes to open, and for his lips to thin into a fine, irritated line at her outburst. She didn't know when she started begging him to fight her, or when she started calling for the Maiden to help her. Dragon, her chest was caving in. Losing him wasn't supposed to hurt like this. She hated him more now than she ever had when he'd tried to kill her or when he'd betrayed her. Then, he was her enemy. Now, he was the old friend she pestered for a song, and the one who brought her flowers from the Embernest. He was the man who gently tended to her wounds, and who'd made love to her as if there were no blood between them and no uncertain future. Not quite a friend, not quite a lover, but something delicate in between that was ripe with sweet possibility.

Something that would never be.

Shara released his shoulders and cupped his face. "Don't leave me," she whimpered. "I want to see the Embernest again, with you. The real one." The things she would give to see even the one he conjured for her in dreams. If only she'd known how to reach him on the other end of their bond, maybe then she could have convinced him to hold on. She lowered her forehead to his shoulder, hugging him close to her chest as she let the tears flow. "I'm sorry." If only she'd stayed when he tried to explain himself. If only she'd listened. Instead, she'd held onto a sense of righteousness and pushed him away when the truth was that facing the consequences of trusting him, opening up to him, terrified her more than Aerella ever had. She'd run away yet again.

Solana, Deimok, her friends, and now Derron—what did she have to show for her stubbornness? All she'd earned was more loss, more loneliness, more heartbreak.

After what might have been minutes or hours, Shara leaned away from Derron, wiping her dirty hands over her face to dry her tears. Leaving him behind cut through her heart like a knife, but she wasn't strong enough to carry him. He'd be safer here, away from whatever desecration Aerella's soldiers would inflict on him if they found their traitor prince's corpse. Pressing one final kiss to his cold lips, lingering until the new tears pooling in her eyes dripped from her chin, Shara staggered to her feet. The pain lancing through her was blinding, but she forced her feet forward. One step, then another. Somewhere in these caves was a passage that would bring her to Daganver. She might be too far away to find Solana and the others, but she could warn the rebels of Aerella's advance. Prepare them for the battle to come.

A steady sapphire glow bathed the tunnels. The Ilah's roots stopped their pulsing and etched a glowing line to the tunnel's end. The sapphire glow bloomed like a winter rose, tracing an archway.

A portal.

The roots blinked once, as if encouraging her to come closer.

Shara struggled through every step leading her closer to the glowing portal's entrance. At her approach, the glow receded to a barrier like the one that marked the entrance to Ares's home. The veil shimmered and rippled like water, distorting the view of the moonlit riverbank beyond where a hulking tree's glow pulsed like a slow heartbeat.

She stepped through the veil, the momentary vertigo eased

by the gentle breeze stroking her hair. It played between the leaves and cattails growing along the river's edge, creating music to accompany the singing birds and chirping crickets. Fireflies buzzed around her and enhanced the river's natural beauty with their glow. White light emanated from the gargantuan elm tree at the center of the clearing, the same color as the opal leaves adorning its branches. The trunk disappeared into the water, its thick sapphire roots clinging to the shore like a giant's spindly fingers. Up close, she spotted sapphire streaks in the branches and in the leaves. They spread down the trunk like fresh tears, streaming to the roots and the body of water surrounding it, floating over the surface like a pool of starlight.

This was the Ilah.

With a sound halfway between a sob and a laugh, Shara fell to her knees on the water's bank and bowed, drinking in large gulps. The refreshing sensation slid down her throat and spread. Her side burned for all but a moment before the pain subsided to an itch. She drank until her stomach was full to bursting, and even then she threw the water over her face, her arms, her neck. Her strength returned with each drop seeping into her skin.

Asharaya.

Shara's head snapped up, her stomach flipping. Who had called her name? She didn't recognize the voice, and its ancient quality didn't sound like it belonged to a fae. Had she imagined it?

Shara's gaze drifted to the Ilah. If the dragons were the Ilah made flesh, and the Ilah was the root of all magic, could it be that the tree was sentient? Had the voice she heard come from the Ilah?

"Ashari," she whispered. *I am here.*

Twin sapphire roots shot out of the water and wrapped around Shara's wrists, caging them like manacles. With a yelp, Shara pushed to her feet, yanking against the bindings. More roots jumped from the water, wrapping her ankles, her legs, her middle.

The Ilah pulled her down into its depths, the water swallowing her scream.

Drakisa, it whispered. *Dragon Queen. Open your eyes.*

Pronunciation Guide and Glossary

Characters:
Aerella Argarys: Eh-reh-llah Ar-gah-ris
Alavin: Ah-lah-vin
Andren Nahar: An-dren Na-har
Ares: Ah-res
Arkael/Kael: Ar-kell/Kell
Asharaya Myrassar/Shara: Ah-sha-rah-ee-ah
    Mee-rah-ssar/Sha-rah
Baramun: Bah-rah-moon
Cassia Argarys: Cas-see-ah Ar-gah-ris
Darrok Todrak: Da-rrok To-drak
Deimok: Day-mok
Derron Argarys: De-rron Ar-gah-ris
Dougas: Doo-gus
Eileen Todrak: Ayl-een To-drak
Elon Myrassar: Gayl-on Mee-rah-ssar
Elvik: El-vik
Errigen: Ehr-ree-ghen
Imiri Vynatis: Ee-mee-ree Vee-nah-tis
Jaemys Myrassar: Jay-miss Mee-rah-ssar
Jaero: Jeh-roh
Jannas: Jahn-nas
Johan Vynatis: Yo-han Vee-nah-tis
Korban: Kor-ben
Luna Todrak: Loo-nuh To-drak
Mykal Todrak: Mee-kal To-drak
Rami: Rah-mee
Raxan Nahar: Rak-san Na-har
Semal Leneris: Seh-mal Leh-neh-ris

Sera: Seh-rah

Solana Spirre: So-lah-nah Spear

Vaemor Argarys: Veh-mor Ar-gah-ris

Xoro: Ksoh-roh

Places:

Adara: Ah-dah-ruh

Daganver: Dah-gan-ver

Eathelin: Eh-theh-leen

Havanya: Hah-vah-nee-uh

Ilahara: Ee-lah-ha-rah

Lur: Loor

Makkan: Mah-kan

Merania: Mur-ah-nee-uh

Tyrra: Tee-ruh

Other words:

Ashari: Ah-shah-ree (I am here)

Do'strath: Doh-strath (soulbound warrior)

Dragaelan: Drah-gay-lan (friend or beloved)

Drakisa: Drah-kee-sah (Dragon Queen)

Drakasi: Drah-kah-see

Maenar/Maenari: Meh-nar/Meh-nah-ree (scholar)

Vetraze: Veh-trah-zeh (Fire)

Vrahiid: Vrah-heed Acknowledgements:

Acknowledgments

Authors often say second books are hard to write, and though you never doubt it, you also don't really understand it until you have to write a second book of your own. Writing Ilahara started as a passion project that we were then confident enough to share with the world. Ashari instead came with challenges, expectations, and awareness that we didn't have before. There were moments where the discomfort was so great that we wondered, "Is it really worth it?" And the answer was always yes. Yes for our readers, who have given our first book a chance. Yes for our characters, who will always hold a piece of our souls. And yes for those two young women who first thought of a wraith moving through shadows.

So, our first thank you goes to our little book community and the readers who have so graciously picked up Ilahara. We appreciate every review, every post, every message. Your excitement kept us going.

Then we want to thank our brother, Ren, who as always listens to our endless plotting and knows every single draft of this book for the number of times we've had to read them out loud. Your commentary and wicked sass make editing a little less daunting.

To our parents, thank you for trusting us to follow our dreams.

Thank you to our angel queen, Kiche, for being the best writing cave companion. You hold so many of our secrets, know so many of our ideas. You were there when we first started plotting this series, and unfortunately you won't be with us to see its end, but we like to think you're watching us from above. We sure feel you in our hearts.

To our couch princess, Indie pup. Your arrival was miraculous, and though it didn't erase the heartbreak, it did heal us. You heal us every day. Yes, even if you steal the towels and pull the covers and bite the shelves. We might have rescued you, but you saved us.

Thank you to our friend Ve (@ve_xo on Instagram) for all the shoutouts, the chats, the laughs, and for all the times you said, "We should do a read along for Ilahara!" There are time zones, a whole ocean, and who knows how many more miles of land between us, and yet you're always close.

To all our friends, most of whom are also Bookstagrammers:

Aleksandra (@acedimksi),

Giota (@giota_the_reader),

Marina, Jess, Jasmine,

Carmen (@carmen.dmdesign),

Ambrine, Jourdan (@old.enough.for.fairytales,)

and our fellow Book Tour Gals

Thais (@tata.lifepages),

Candice (@canxdancexreads),

Tati (@heartof.tati),

Shelby (@literaryfaery), and

Ve (@ve_xo, again!).

Thank you for always being there, whether to fangirl about books or to vent about life. You are all, each in your own way, an inspiration.

Thank you to our editor, Sharon, for once again putting her expertise in the service of this book. We lucked out when we got you as an editor. We're better writers because of your counsel.

And finally, we thank each other. "Chiara, you're my best friend, and I couldn't write a single word without you (being there to edit me)," Maria says. "Maria, you're my best friend, and there would be a lot more kisses if you weren't there to pace me. So maybe, no thank you," Chiara replies.

About the Authors

C. M. Karys is the pen name of two Italian sisters, Maria Elena and Chiara. As young girls, their love of fantasy was fueled by books and Disney marathons. Now, they've added Game of Thrones to that list—and a whole lot of spicy romance. When they're not hiding away in their writing cave, C. M. Karys can be found discussing books with their online community on Instagram or listening to Måneskin and Taylor Swift until their neighbors know the lyrics, too. C. M. Karys currently lives in Naples with their family and couch princess (dog), Indie.

C. M. Karys can be found online @pagesofmaria on Instagram, @pagesof.maria on Tiktok, and @_mkarys on X (Maria), and @wordsbychiara on Instagram and Tiktok and @_ckarys on X (Chiara), as well as their author Instagram @cmkarys.